DEATH
IN A
WINE
DARK
SEA

LISA KING

DEATH IN A WINE DARK SEA

The Permanent Press
Sag Harbor, NY 11963

For information, address:
  The Permanent Press
  4170 Noyac Road
  Sag Harbor, NY 11963
  www.thepermanentpress.com

Library of Congress Cataloging-in-Publication Data

King, Lisa–
   Death in a wine dark sea / Lisa King.
      p. cm.
   ISBN 978-1-57962-282-4
      1. Women detectives—Fiction. 2. Murder—
   Investigation—Fiction. I. Title.

PS3611.I58335D43 2012
813'.6—dc23   2012013632

Printed in the United States of America.

For Cat Georges and Stephen Bright,
my best and dearest friends

ACKNOWLEDGEMENTS

*T*his book would not exist without the love and support of my children, Lex, Anton, and Irina, and without the input of all my relatives and friends who read and critiqued the manuscript over the years and encouraged me to keep trying no matter how many rejections I collected. I am deeply indebted to my mother, Georgianne King; my siblings and their well-chosen spouses, Margaret King and Joe Guerin, Rob and Kris King, and Phil and Rita King; Mark Lupher; and friends Bill Tracy, Donna Morris, Curt Anderson, Liza Gross, Barry Bergman, Sue Horton, Stephanie Starr, Charli Ornett, Bruce Friedman, Eva Scholtz, Jennifer Blanchard, Kathy Morrisson, and the late Cliff Kaspar. If I've inadvertently left you off the list, put it down to long-term memory loss.

Special thanks to editor extraordinaire Catherine Knepper; my fabulous agent, Sally van Haitsma; and my indulgent publishers, Marty and Judy Shepard. Bon appétit!

CHAPTER 1

*M*artin Wingo stood at the window of his office on a renovated pier just a few feet above San Francisco Bay and contemplated the beauty of his near-fatal heart attack: He was fitter, calmer, and happier than ever before, and he still got to enjoy all the things he'd acquired in his previous life.

He hitched up his raw silk slacks and gave his newly flat stomach a self-satisfied pat. Not bad for fifty. He'd lost weight in the hospital and kept it off by hiring a new chef and putting a gym in his basement. His blond hair was thinning, but that was nothing new. If he took care of himself and stayed calm, he'd have a good twenty years left to enjoy his Italianate mansion in St. Francis Wood, the condo on Maui, his ninety-foot yacht, his red Porsche Carrera, the millions from the sale of Wingo-Johansen Development, and, best of all, Diane.

The Bay Bridge loomed above him, and he knew that by now late afternoon fog would obscure the Golden Gate to the northwest. In a few days he and Diane Shifflett would board his yacht, the *Walrus*, and be married beneath the famous bridge. Thoughts of her brought the familiar tightening in his groin that even his heart medication couldn't diminish.

Jeffrey, the receptionist, knocked lightly and stuck his head into the office. "Mr. Wingo? There's a girl here to see you."

"Have Zeppo handle it."

"Um, you fired him, remember?"

Martin shook off his reverie and faced Jeffrey, a plump young man in a short-sleeved shirt and tie. "I laid him off because his job ended. There's a difference."

"Right. Sorry."

"Who's the girl?"

"Won't give her name. Asked for Zeppo first."

Martin glanced at the boxes of papers and memorabilia on the floor and desk. He'd finished the sorting and packing, and he was curious—anyone asking for Zeppo was bound to be interesting. "All right, I'll talk to her."

In a moment Jeffrey returned with the mysterious caller. The first thing that struck Martin was her exquisite coloring—she had shoulder-length platinum blond hair and cornflower-blue eyes. Judging by her luminous, creamy skin, the hair was natural. Her breasts were small, her hips slim. In heavy makeup, high heels, tight blue miniskirt, and an off-the-shoulder sweater, she looked like a skinny little girl playing dress-up. She was lovely, but Martin had no taste for such underripe flesh. In spite of her obvious youth, her eyes were shrewd and knowing.

"Please have a seat," he said when Jeffrey had gone. "What can I do for you?"

The girl sat down and crossed her bare legs, sullen and seductive. "That boy Zeppo said you pay for information." She had a heavy accent Martin couldn't place.

He smiled. "I'm no longer in the market. I'm retired."

"You want this. It's important."

"What's your name?"

"Oksana."

"Where are you from, Oksana?"

"Kiev."

"How old are you?"

"Nineteen. So you want to buy what I know?"

Martin thought about it. Even if he had no use for it, whatever she knew might be worth hearing. Why not? "I'll pay you $100 now and a bonus if I like what you're selling."

Oksana pouted. "Zeppo said a lot more than that."

"If you tell me something valuable, I'll pay what it's worth."

"OK—$100 now."

He went to the wall safe behind his desk—he'd have to empty that, too, before leaving. He opened it, took out a $100 bill, and handed it to Oksana. A quick search through the boxes turned up the DVD-cam that Zeppo had insisted he buy for this sort of interview. He set up a tripod and attached the camera, focusing on Oksana.

"What are you doing?" she said.

"Recording our conversation."

"Why?"

"Unless you have documentation or photos, I'll need a record of what you say."

She shrugged her slender shoulders. "OK."

He switched on the camera. "Now then. What do you have to sell?"

∽∾

Twenty minutes later Martin looked out a side window and watched Oksana totter out of the Wingo-Johansen building, $5,000 in cash stuffed into her knockoff Prada handbag. A muscular boy with a shaved head and tattoos on his arms waited on the sidewalk. Oksana kissed him, and they hurried away along the Embarcadero hand in hand.

Martin popped the mini-DVD out of the camera and put it into a plastic sleeve. He felt a rush of excitement he hadn't experienced in months. His mind simmered with possibilities. Diane would consider this breaking his word, but she didn't have to know about it. He took a small cream-colored envelope out of the open safe and weighed it against the DVD in his other hand. After all, a man needed a retirement project, and now he had two.

CHAPTER 2

*J*ean Applequist loved having sex on boats but had never managed it on this particular vessel, even though she'd been aboard several times. The moment seemed perfect—she and Peter Brennan lay entwined on a white canvas deck chaise while the *Walrus* cruised in slow circles beneath the Golden Gate Bridge. But Peter was resisting, in spite of the gaudy sunset above them and her fervent efforts to persuade him.

"Let's go find an empty stateroom," she murmured, licking his ear.

"There's no time. They'll be cutting the cake soon."

"We'll make it quick. Don't be such a coward." She kissed him hard and slipped her hands inside his jacket and her knee between his legs.

"Stop it, Jean," he groaned. He pushed her away and sat up. "I swear, you pick the most inappropriate moments sometimes."

Jean gave up and lay back. "It's your own fault. Have I told you how great you look in a tuxedo?"

Peter smiled. "Several times. I'll have to start wearing one to work." He sat at the foot of the chaise out of her reach, smoothing his dark hair and adjusting his clothes. Jean loved the way his big hazel eyes and deep dimples softened his rugged features.

She pulled a mirror from her bag to check the damage and raked fingers through her straight silver hair, short as a boy's on one side and falling just below her chin on the other. She smiled at her reflection; she wasn't a beauty like the bride, but the asymmetrical cut flattered her strong features and the color set off her cobalt eyes. Although her hair had gone gray a decade ago, the rest of her looked her age—a youthful thirty-two.

Peter stood and reached out a hand. "Come on, let's go be sociable. I owe you one, OK?"

Jean led the way along the deck as the sunset faded and dark clouds moved in. She paused at the big window that looked into the salon. Inside, two dozen guests circled and chatted, the lights reflecting on the polished teak surfaces of the elegant room. A huge arrangement of yellow and white flowers adorned a table, surrounded by Champagne flutes and platters of hors d'oeuvres. Just out of sight a jazz trio played Gershwin.

Jean spotted the newlyweds near the buffet table, surrounded by well-wishers. Martin, in black tie and a boutonnière of yellow rosebuds, handed his bride a glass of Champagne. Although Jean had never understood Martin's appeal, it was obvious why he wanted Diane—she was warm and vivacious, a true beauty, and tonight she looked especially lovely. Her pale yellow dress showed off her slender shape and smooth tan skin. Yellow roses adorned her long chestnut hair.

"Now that's a happy couple," Peter said.

Jean snorted. "As far as he's concerned, Diane's just another piece of his estate. He once told her the *Walrus* was his second-favorite possession."

"I'm sure he was kidding." He cocked his head. "You aren't going to make a scene, are you?"

"Of course not. I'll put on a happy face for Diane." She gave him a big false grin.

In the salon, Jean observed how Diane looked up at Martin, her smile incandescent, her green eyes glittering. She recalled the ceremony on the bow of the ship: the way Diane's face had glowed with contentment, the heartfelt "I do's," the impassioned kiss. Jean grudgingly allowed that Martin probably did love her in his own selfish way.

Diane was one of her closest friends, so she'd just have to accept the inevitable as gracefully as she could. Jean resolved to try her damnedest to get along with Martin. That meant no more goading him into losing his temper, no more snide remarks, no more wicked jokes at his expense. It wouldn't be easy—self-control wasn't her strong suit.

The early spring breeze sharpened, the air grew cooler, and Jean felt a smattering of raindrops. Peter held the salon door for her. "Let's get out of the rain," he said.

The room smelled of roses and good food. Jean eyed the buffet, her stomach growling. There were definitely advantages to hanging out with rich people. Her love of the high life and perennial inability to afford it had led her to take a job at a wine magazine instead of a mainstream news publication.

They made their way to where Martin and Diane held court. Peter pulled Martin aside. "The storm's arriving early," Peter told him. "It's starting to rain and blow."

Martin nodded. "Tell Captain Loach to head back a little before we planned. It won't do to have seasick wedding guests."

"No problem." Peter went out the door.

It annoyed Jean when Peter jumped at Martin's commands. Peter had been Martin's personal attorney for years and they were supposedly friends, but Martin still treated him like an errand boy.

Martin extricated Diane from the crowd of guests. "We're heading back a bit early," he told her. "Let's cut the cake soon."

Diane squeezed his arm. "Oh, good," she said. "The sooner we get to the dock, the sooner the honeymoon starts." She bustled off in a scented cloud of Je Reviens to talk to the servers, leaving Jean and Martin alone.

Jean knew he preferred small, dark, delicate women like Diane, but that never stopped him from staring at her as if she were for sale, as he was doing now. She thought she looked great, even if Peter didn't find her irresistible. In flats she was taller than Martin, nearly Peter's height, and the fitted pewter satin suit that she'd copied from a Calvin Klein made the most of her hourglass figure. But that was no excuse for Martin to ogle her so blatantly.

"That was a pretty spectacular sunset," she said. "What did it cost you?"

"The Almighty threw that in for free. I must be living right."

She laughed. "Apparently He's easier to fool than I am. 'Man has heart attack, man changes life'—what a cliché. It's only a matter of time before you revert." Jean realized she wasn't doing a very good job of making nice.

Martin gave her a tolerant smile. "All I can do is prove you wrong."

Jean felt the boat's engines change gear—they'd begun the trip back to the St. Francis Yacht Club.

Martin looked around the room. "I'd better collect the rest of the guests," he said. "Tell Diane I'll be right back."

Jean watched Martin make his way through the crowd. People smiled at him, shook his hand, slapped his back. This was an easy gathering of friends—Martin had no close relatives left, and Diane hadn't spoken to her mother in years. The only person who could be construed as family was Frank Johansen, Martin's former business partner and Diane's foster father.

Near the door, Jean saw Martin waylaid by Jay Zeppetello, a very tall, very skinny young man with curly red hair and an ill-fitting rented tuxedo. He punched Martin's arm. "Congratulations, boss," Jean overheard him say. "Just remember what Shane said: 'You can't break the mold.' Once a gunslinger, always a gunslinger."

"I'm retired, Zeppo," Martin said. "Believe it." A cool gust of wind assailed the guests near the door as he stepped out on deck.

Jean felt a hand on each side of her hips and a gentle kiss on the back of her neck. "Let's get some Champagne," Peter said.

She turned. "You talked me into it."

At the buffet table Jean snagged a glass of bubbly and took a whiff, then a sip. She detected almonds and a pleasant yeastiness on the nose. On the palate it was somewhat closed, with more acidity than fruit. It needed another five years in the bottle.

"As you see, Martin remains in character," she told Peter. "He's not serving the best Champagne, just the most expensive, and he's serving it too young." She grinned. "But I'll shut up—I've sworn not to rag on him anymore. If Diane were any happier she'd self-combust."

"I'm glad you've decided to behave. Hey, I finally got to meet Hugh Rivenbark. I worshipped his books as an undergraduate. Interesting old guy."

"Too bad his books aren't interesting anymore." Jean picked up a plate and worked her way along the buffet table, taking crab canapés, stuffed mushrooms, grilled asparagus, boned quail, huge strawberries with stems. She wasn't big on cake.

"If you've written a masterpiece and won a Pulitzer Prize, I guess you can coast." Peter looked at her plate. "Is that crab?"

She offered him a taste. They stood close together, eating and watching Diane fuss around the elaborate white and yellow cake. When she was satisfied, she came over to them.

"Where did Martin go?" she said. "We're all set."

Jean swallowed a large bite of crab. "He's rounding people up."

Frank Johansen joined them, gazing warmly at Diane. He was a big, heavy man in his late fifties who looked thoroughly uncomfortable in formal wear. He spoke with the same Midwestern twang that Jean had worked hard to lose. She noticed with amusement that he had pale dog hair on the sleeves and pants of his tux—he owned a golden retriever. "Ready to cut the cake, sweetheart?" he asked.

"If we can find the groom," Diane said.

"We'll get him," Peter said. "Jean, you take port and I'll take starboard." They went out their respective doors.

The rain fell harder now, making Jean shiver. She walked toward the bow, thinking Martin might have gone that way, glancing into staterooms as she passed. There were plenty of cozy places where she and Peter could have had some fun.

Jean got to the bridge without meeting a soul, and Captain Loach, a short, sunburned man in a white uniform, told her he hadn't seen Martin since sunset. She went back toward the stern, pausing near the salon to admire the Golden Gate above her and the distant rain-blurred city. The wind died down for a moment, and in the brief quiet she heard an odd scraping noise from the aft deck.

"Martin?" she called. No answer. Jean turned to check it out, and heard a strangled cry and a loud splash. She ran the rest of the way.

The aft deck was empty, but a few yards off the stern Martin's blond head bobbed in the choppy sea.

"Martin!" Jean yelled, leaning over the rail, reaching out as far as she could, knowing she had no chance of saving him—the ship was moving too fast. Soon he'd be out of range of the running lights. Martin looked back at her, struggling to stay afloat in the ship's wake, shock and terror on his face.

Jean looked around frantically—a life preserver hung nearby. She unhooked it and heaved it as far as she could in Martin's direction. He started toward it, swimming stiffly in the cold rough water, his jacket constricting his movements. A black wave and a sharp drumming downpour hid him from view.

"Hang on!" Jean shouted as the *Walrus* motored farther and farther from its owner. "I'll get help!" She caught another glimpse of him in the trough of a wave, still striving to reach the life preserver, and then the darkness swallowed him.

CHAPTER 3

⸺ ✎ ⸺

$\mathcal{J}$ean raced to the salon and threw open the door. "Martin's overboard!" she yelled above the party noise. "Tell the captain!" A stunned silence greeted her announcement, and then she heard an agonized cry that could only be Diane, followed by exclamations and shouted questions.

Jean dashed back to the stern, leaned over the railing, and searched the turbid water for a sign of Martin. Hurried footsteps approached and several guests joined her.

"Can anybody see him?" Jean asked.

"It's too dark and it's raining too hard," Frank said next to her.

Jean caught a whiff of Je Reviens and looked around. Diane stood behind her, unsteady in her yellow satin heels. She leaned on Peter's arm, a stricken look on her face. "What happened?" she demanded.

"I heard him fall off the stern and saw him in the water," Jean said. "I threw him a life preserver but I don't know if he got to it."

The engines died abruptly and Captain Loach joined them. "When did he go in?" he demanded.

"Less than a minute ago." Jean replied.

Loach nodded grimly. "I'm going to bring her around. I'll need you gentlemen to stay on deck and try to reestablish visual contact." He turned to the crewman with him. "Kelly, break out the foul weather gear."

The group—Frank, Peter, Hugh Rivenbark, a few men Jean didn't know—followed Kelly to the equipment locker.

Diane took the captain's hand. "You have to find him," she pleaded. "He's not a strong swimmer."

"We'll do everything we can, Mrs. Wingo," Loach said in a soothing voice. "I hit the man-overboard button and notified the Coast Guard, so every boat in the area will be looking for him. Now go back inside. We'll find him for you." He met Jean's eyes over Diane's head, and Jean took her friend's arm and led her in out of the rain.

Most of the women were still inside. Jean didn't think it was a sexist thing—they all wore skimpy evening dresses and stupid shoes. People gathered around Diane, attempting to calm and reassure her, and Jean explained what had happened.

She needed to catch her breath and think. She left Diane in the care of several friends and moved toward an empty chair across the salon. The musicians, three middle-aged men in dark blue tuxedos, had switched to unobtrusive jazz. The servers sat in a group near the cake, unsure of what to do. One of them jumped up as Jean approached, but she waved him away.

"I'm fine," she said. "Go ahead, have some bubbly. I think the party's over."

Jean sank into the chair, realizing that she was damp and quite cold. The more she thought about it, the more she was certain Martin hadn't fallen. He was an experienced sailor who never drank much, and in the water he hadn't looked like a man having a heart attack. Someone must have pushed him seconds before she got to the aft deck. If she'd looked around the corner at the starboard deck, she would have seen who it was. Surveying the guests, all Martin's good friends, she tried to imagine one of them pushing him into the bay on his wedding night.

Zeppo approached her, holding a snifter of amber liquid. "Hey, gorgeous. I thought you might need a drink."

Cognac was exactly what she wanted. She took the glass gratefully, thanking him. Zeppo did have nice broad shoulders, and big hands and feet were always an encouraging sign, but Jean usually found him obnoxious.

He sat down next to her. "I'm impressed that you threw Martin a life preserver. I bet your first impulse was to let him drown."

"I'm not that much of a bitch. I'd even throw one to you." Jean took a warming sip of Cognac. "Why aren't you out there looking for him?"

He pointed to his thick wire-rimmed glasses. "Can't see very far without these, and they're not much good in the pouring rain."

Jean peered through the big window near her. Out on the bay, raindrops pocked the inky water. "They'll never find him in this weather. It's the proverbial wine dark sea."

"Yeah, but Athena sent those dudes a favorable gale," Zeppo said.

She looked at him in surprise. Had he actually read Homer? "What do you suppose the water temperature is?"

Zeppo thought for a moment. "Fifty degrees?"

"So that means he's only got an hour, hour and a half before hypothermia knocks him unconscious."

"How do you know?"

"I read it in a mystery."

"Who do you think pushed him?" Zeppo said.

"That's just what I've been wondering," she said, surprised again. "But who on this boat would want to kill him?"

"Besides you, you mean?" Zeppo grinned, his braces making him appear even younger than his twenty-three years.

Jean couldn't tell whether he was callous or was covering up stronger feelings. "Doesn't this bother you just a little? The man is your mentor. You owe him everything you have."

"Yeah, I know. I'll be sorry as hell if he's really dead."
He shrugged. "But to me, he's been dead since the heart
attack. I mean, when you lose your edge, they might as
well bury you."

Jean raised an eyebrow. Every time she thought he
might be tolerable, he'd say something that convinced her
otherwise. "I suppose you want to grow up to be just like
the old Martin."

"Nah, not just like him," he said smugly. "Better, because
I don't have his fatal weakness—women."

"Oh come on, Zeppo. With all the money he paid you,
surely even you can get a date."

"Of course I can get dates. But there are a lot more
important things in life than getting laid."

"I don't think very many men your age would agree."

"Maybe I just haven't slept with the right girl." He
leered at her. "I'd love to give you a chance to change
my mind."

"Gee, thanks but no thanks, Zeppo. I don't do charity
work." Jean finished her drink, stood, and walked toward
Diane. "You really shouldn't leer until you get your braces
off," she told him over her shoulder.

Zeppo chuckled; he never seemed to take offense, no
matter what she said to him. She made her way through the
uneasy crowd. Diane, sitting on a built-in loveseat, clutched
a glass of red wine so tightly that her knuckles were white.
Peter hovered nearby, worried and solicitous. Jean hooked
a finger at him and he came over. He said nothing, just put
his arms around her and hugged her tightly.

"You know what I've been thinking?" she whispered.
"That somebody pushed him."

He nodded slowly. "You may be right."

"Peter, did you see anyone on the starboard deck when
you were looking for Martin?"

"No—there was no one on deck so I went down to look
in the galley."

As the search continued, guests took turns watching for Martin and drifted over a few at a time to say words of comfort to Diane. Jean watched her friend as they stroked her hair, hugged her, told her stories about people who'd survived for hours in icy waters, of miraculous escapes from certain death by drowning. Hugh Rivenbark, solid and reassuring, kept Diane's glass filled. He was in his early sixties, looking every inch the famous author with his unruly white hair, full beard, and leonine head. Frank, his face deeply creased with worry, sat with Diane for a long time, doing his best to give her hope. "He's fooled us before," he told her. "He's a survivor."

Frank went back on deck while Jean sat next to Diane, realizing that Martin's hour and a half in the water had ticked away. Diane laid her head on Jean's shoulder. "I don't know how much longer I can be brave," she whispered. "I feel like screaming."

"Go ahead and scream. I'd say you're entitled."

"I'll scream after everyone's gone." Diane stood up, her eyes tearing, arms crossed over her chest, her hands gripping her bare shoulders. "How could this happen? How could he fall? Think how cold and alone he must feel, and how frightened."

Jean thought that if Martin were still alive he was more likely pissed as hell at whoever had pushed him.

"Oh Jean, what if he drowns?" For the first time, Diane started to cry.

"They'll find him," Jean said with conviction, but she didn't believe it. "He's a survivor, remember?"

The *Walrus* had maintained a search pattern for nearly three hours when several guests pressured Captain Loach into heading for port, leaving the search to the better-equipped Coast Guard and Harbor Patrol vessels. Diane protested, but finally agreed that her guests should be allowed to disembark.

At the yacht club, the grim-faced group bid goodbye to Diane and trudged up the dock in their finery to waiting cars and limos. The caterers hauled boxes and bags off the yacht and loaded their truck, and the musicians piled into a blue minivan.

A stunned group—Jean, Peter, Frank, and Zeppo—stayed with Diane in the salon. Someone on the galley staff had made a pot of coffee, and everyone but Diane had a cup. She paced the room, anxious and distraught.

Frank shook his head. "What the hell could have happened? One minute he was here, then he went outside, and then Jean heard him fall in."

"What do you think happened?" Diane said, a note of hysteria in her voice. "He slipped and fell. He'll drown if they don't find him!"

"That's probably right, he fell," Peter said soothingly. "We know he didn't jump."

Diane stopped pacing and looked at Peter. "You think he was pushed, don't you?" She sat down. "Of course, how stupid of me. He would never fall. Pushed. Oh God, this just gets worse and worse." She started to cry again.

Around midnight, Captain Loach came into the salon looking bleak. "Mrs. Wingo, I'm sorry, but there's still no sign of him. They can't use the helicopters until the weather improves. I'm afraid I had to notify the police."

A short while later, two plainclothes inspectors and a uniformed officer came aboard. Captain Loach spoke to them on deck. Jean edged over to the nearest porthole so she could eavesdrop.

The older, heavier inspector was scolding Loach. "Why'd you let them go home before you called us?"

"These are important people," Loach said defensively. "Nobody's going to leave town."

The inspector snorted with irritation. "Well, it's done now. Who's left?"

"His wife and a few friends. But there's one other thing. A crewman found Mr. Wingo's boutonnière on the aft deck under a bench. I have it in my office."

"Baker," Hallock said to the uniformed man. "Go bag it." Hallock moved closer to the porthole and glared in at Jean. "You getting this OK?"

"Sorry," she said, moving back into the salon.

Loach brought the two inspectors into the salon and introduced George Hallock and Oscar Davila. Hallock was a balding man of about fifty-five, stocky and florid, wearing a lumpy brown suit. "We're very sorry we have to question you at a time like this," he said. "Now then. I understand from Captain Loach that you embarked at five P.M. from this slip, cruised for twenty minutes or so to the area under the Golden Gate Bridge, where you circled during the wedding ceremony and reception. Around seven thirty Mr. Wingo noticed it was raining and ordered the ship back to port. What happened after that?"

Jean told her story again as Davila took notes. He was a slim Latino in his mid-thirties with thick, wavy black hair. His light gray suit was stylishly cut. When Jean finished, he looked up. "Do you all agree that it's unlikely he fell?"

"If I might jump in here," Captain Loach said. "We've cruised as far as Hawaii, even gone through the canal to the Caribbean. Mr. Wingo's comfortable on a boat. There's no way he'd fall overboard by accident in this weather."

"He does have a heart condition," Peter said.

"But he has his medication in his pocket," Diane said. "And he knows the symptoms. He'd call for help."

"Then there's the waist-high rail," Zeppo added. "Martin wasn't very tall. It'd take a good strong shove to get him over it. Someone would really have to want him dead." Diane visibly recoiled at his words as if she'd been slapped.

"Watch your mouth," Jean snapped. "And stop talking about him in the past tense."

"Sorry, Diane," Zeppo said. "I'm rooting for him, too, you know."

Officer Baker entered the salon, and handed Hallock an evidence bag containing a small bunch of yellow rosebuds tied with ribbon—Martin's boutonnière.

Davila flipped through his notes. "There's not much more we can do tonight except wait. Captain Loach gave us the guest list, and we'll be talking to everyone on it."

Hallock glanced at the printed list. Jean saw his eyebrows go up as he realized he'd be bothering two judges and three supervisors on a Sunday. He put the list away and took several business cards out of his pocket. "I'll be on call till morning," he said, handing them around. "Give me a call if something comes up." Jean took a card, noticing that Hallock smelled strongly of tobacco smoke.

The two men stood. "Let's hope Mr. Wingo himself can tell us what happened," Davila said. "Mrs. Wingo, we'll call you if we hear anything at all." He had the kind of dark good looks Jean liked, and she saw humor and compassion in his soft brown eyes, qualities definitely lacking in Hallock. She glanced at Davila's hands. A wide gold band circled his left ring finger. Oh well.

CHAPTER 4

Just after two A.M., Jean persuaded Diane to go home. She wrapped her friend in a pale yellow cashmere shawl, and the five of them walked along the dock through a cold drizzle to their cars.

Diane shivered as Jean helped her into the back seat of Peter's Saab. In the next parking space, Zeppo unlocked the door of the 1964 Jaguar XKE coupe that Martin had driven before buying his new Porsche. Jean had been astonished to learn that Martin gave the car to Zeppo as part of his severance package, in addition to stock options and a nice cash settlement.

"Goodnight, Jeannie," Zeppo said, getting into the sleek black car. "Take care of the bride, OK?" Jean heard a trace of New England in his vowels—she'd noticed that before.

"I'll do my best," she said. "We'll call you when they find him."

"Call my cell. I won't be home."

"Where are you going? You're a witness, after all. Maybe even a suspect."

He chuckled nervously. "Not me. After Martin went outside, I talked to that architect guy until you came in yelling. Anyway, I've got to get out of town. This kind of thing bums me out."

"What do you mean, this kind of thing? Does this happen to you often?"

"Often enough," he muttered. He broke into his usual sarcastic grin. "See ya, gorgeous." He shut the car door and zoomed out of the lot.

Jean got in beside her friend, who collapsed against her. "Let's take you home, honey," Jean said. "I'll stay with you tonight."

As they drove across town in light traffic, Diane leaned listlessly against Jean. "The water is so cold," she said faintly. "You can't live long in water that cold." She clutched Jean's hand. "They say drowning is an easy way to die."

"He's not going to drown. He's going to come home to you."

Peter drove to St. Francis Wood, pricy even by San Francisco standards. They passed through the Beaux Arts gate and along curving residential streets, beneath huge cypress and eucalyptus trees, past the white stone upper fountain. The neighborhood was quiet, most of the mansions dark. Diane's was an elegant, two-story Italianate house built in the thirties.

"That's funny," Peter said as he turned into the driveway. "The lights are on in the back of the house. Is anyone supposed to be here?"

Diane sat up. "No. No one."

"Stay here," Peter said. "We'll check it out."

Peter and Frank got out of the car and strode along the stone path that curved around the right side of the house.

"One of the neighbors was burgled last month," Diane said, twisting her hands together. "Maybe it's a robbery."

Before Jean could reply, a dark figure burst from the shrubbery on the left side of the house and ran across the lawn, past the car and down the deserted street. Jean, furious, scooted out of the car and gave chase.

"Jean, don't!" Diane pleaded.

Jean's slick-soled shoes slowed her down on the wet pavement and her tight skirt constricted her legs. She hiked it up, which didn't help much. She heard a ripping sound and felt the skirt loosen—she'd torn a seam.

Her quarry was a big man in bulky black clothes, moving fast. As he ran under a streetlight, Jean saw that he wore a black watch cap pulled low and black gloves.

As the man disappeared around a corner, heading for Portola, Peter ran up beside Jean and grabbed her arm, pulling her to a stop. She didn't resist—the burglar was long gone. "What do you think you're doing?" he demanded.

"Chasing him."

"Were you planning to tackle him?"

"Oh, don't fuss," Jean said. "I didn't catch him, did I?"

"A good thing, too. Frank's calling the police."

"Was he inside?"

"Yeah," Peter said. "He tossed a couple of rooms on the ground floor."

"Jesus Christ. Diane doesn't need this. Did either of you see his face?"

"No. He ran out before we got to the back door. You?"

"He was too far away."

Peter looked her over. "You've torn your skirt."

"I can fix it."

They hurried toward the open front door. Inside, in the living room, Frank sat on a sofa close to Diane, his arm around her shoulders. She stared straight ahead as if in shock. Through the door to the study Jean could see upended furniture, spilled books, and scattered papers. She plopped down next to Diane.

"He's gone, honey," Jean said.

"The police should have responded," Frank said. "Are you sure you set the alarm, Diane?"

"I . . . I thought Martin did. But maybe he forgot. We . . . it was pretty hectic when we left for the wedding." She started to cry again. Frank pulled her close and rocked her gently.

"Look," Jean said, "we can deal with the police. Let's put you to bed."

Diane didn't resist as Jean led her upstairs to her yellow and white bedroom, took off her rain-spattered dress and lacy wedding-night lingerie, and put a flannel nightgown on her.

Jean rummaged through the medicine cabinet and found a vial of sleeping pills. She gave Diane three of them and lay down with her until she fell asleep. From downstairs came the faint sounds of people talking and moving around—the police, no doubt.

Jean shut the door softly and crept down the stairs. The rooms she could see looked unscathed. Diane had decorated the house with sunny wallpaper and cheery blue and yellow fabric. The result was pretty and comfortable, but a little too Mario Buatta for Jean's taste.

Frank and Peter stood in the living room with a uniformed officer. Peter smiled wearily as she approached. "Diane all right?"

"Not exactly. She's asleep, though."

"Officer Norton here says they can wait until tomorrow to get a statement from her, but they'll need one from you now. Officer, this is Jean Applequist."

She shook his hand. His iron-gray crew cut and square jaw made his head resemble a cube. Peter and Frank waited nearby while Jean sat in a corner of the living room with him. All she could tell him was that the man had been big and probably young, based on how easily he ran.

"Do you think this had anything to do with Martin Wingo's disappearance?" she asked when the officer had finished his questions.

"Hard to say. It's probably unrelated. We get a lot of burglaries where someone reads about a wedding or a funeral or sees an ambulance or coroner's wagon at a house, and then goes in when they know everyone's going to be out."

"That's downright inhuman," Frank said.

"You said it. The strange thing here is there's no sign of forced entry. We'll check out the help, anyone who had a key and knew the codes. Have Mrs. Wingo call us when she figures out what's missing."

When the police were gone, Jean, Peter, and Frank sank into overstuffed chairs. Frank rubbed his reddened eyes. "That poor girl," he said. "How do you ever get over a thing like this? I hope they find him soon, for Diane's sake. For all our sakes."

Peter nodded. "Amen to that."

The phone rang, startling them. Frank answered. "Hello? Oh hello, Kay," he said, shaking his head to the question in Jean's and Peter's eyes. "No, they're still looking . . . she's just about as bad off as you'd expect. On top of all that, there was a burglar here when we got home." He listened for several seconds. "All right, I'll tell her." He hung up. "Kay's heard the news. She's in Washington."

Jean had never met Kay, Martin's ex-wife, but knew she and Diane were on civil terms.

"Let me run you to your car, Frank," Peter said, standing up. "I'll be back soon." He leaned over to kiss Jean and she felt the faint sandpaper scratch of his whiskers.

After looking in on Diane, who was in a deep sleep, Jean checked the damage. The intruder had only gotten as far as Martin's office and the den next door. Jean looked the rooms over, appraising them. The destruction seemed more like a search than a burglary. The upholstered furniture was cut up, all the drawers and closets had been ransacked, and books and CDs covered the floors. Jean thought it odd that he hadn't gone upstairs after Diane's jewelry.

Jean saw that only the bottom drawer of a big dresser was pulled out—that meant the intruder was an amateur. He'd started with the top drawer so he had to close each drawer before going to the next one. A professional would have opened the bottom drawer first to save time. Amazing what you could learn from mysteries.

Back in the living room, she noticed a big stack of wedding gifts in a corner. At least he hadn't gotten that far.

Jean's stomach growled, so she went into the spotless blue and white kitchen for a snack. A search of the refrigerator and cupboards turned up nothing substantial—the newlyweds had planned to be gone for two weeks, cruising the coast of Baja. Their new chef had the time off and had clearly let stocks get low. Jean found a phone and dialed Peter's cell.

"Peter, it's me."

"Any news?"

"Not a word. But there's no food here. Can you pick up something to eat? Maybe Chinese. And some breakfast, too. I'm starving."

"Sure, if I can find anything open."

Jean took off her shoes and curled up on the sofa to wait for Peter. As exhausted as she was, she couldn't sleep. Her friend's grief nearly overwhelmed her. Diane had been through a lot with Martin, and to have it end like this was brutally unfair.

Before the heart attack, Diane had often complained to Jean about Martin's cold, callous behavior. Diane finally broke off their affair, only to spend time in his hospital room every day after he got sick. He then divorced Kay and proposed to Diane, who was convinced he'd become a kinder, gentler person. Jean had never believed in his deathbed conversion, but now all she wanted was for him to walk through the door and restore Diane to her earlier state of euphoria.

Jean thought no one deserved happiness more than Diane, whose early life had been a ghastly soap opera. Her mother was a major-league alcoholic and minor-league hooker who'd accidentally produced two children; Diane had never known who her father was. The family lived in a trailer near Fresno, and Diane had worked at after-school jobs since she was twelve.

When Diane was sixteen, her younger brother died at home of rheumatic fever because their mother was too drunk and indifferent to take him to a doctor. At this time, Diane worked as a file clerk at Frank Johansen's construction company. He and his wife had taken an interest in her and fought to keep her out of foster care. She went to live with the Johansens and discovered that comfortable, predictable middle-class life agreed with her. Two years later, at U.C. Berkeley, she was assigned a room with Jean.

Jean was a refugee, too, but not from poverty—from Indiana. She was the youngest of a large, close-knit religious family that she felt was suffocating her. She had persuaded her parents to send her to college near her mother's eccentric but respectable brother in San Francisco. She'd soon found out that her bachelor uncle, who owned a Victorian house in the Castro district, had been living with the same man for several years, but she didn't tell her parents.

The two women had been good friends ever since, and while Jean cut a wide swath through the straight male population of the greater Bay Area, Diane got her heart broken by a series of prosperous older men.

Diane had stayed close to Frank, and met Martin when he and Frank went into business together. Nothing had clicked until last year at Frank's annual Fourth of July barbecue, when Martin arrived alone and spent the evening wooing Diane. Frank, who thought of Diane as a daughter, was furious about their affair, but after Martin's heart attack he relented and gave his blessing to the marriage.

Jean's reverie was interrupted by the phone. She answered on the third ring, bracing herself for bad news. "Hello?"

After a brief pause, a man's voice said, "Is that Jean?"

Jean came fully awake at once, her heart pounding. "Martin!" she shrieked. Then, more tentatively, "Martin?"

"Yes, it's me. Let me talk to Diane."

"Are you OK? Everyone thinks you're dead."

"Not quite. Put Diane on."

"Just a minute." Jean ran upstairs, phone in hand, to Diane's room, calling her name and shaking her by the shoulder. Diane made a faint noise but didn't stir. After a few seconds Jean gave up. "I can't wake her," she told Martin as she walked back downstairs. "She was such a mess when she thought you drowned that I knocked her out."

"Is she all right?"

"No, she's not all right. She started out weepy and then went catatonic. She's shattered."

"Is anyone else there? Frank, or Peter?"

"No, just me and the widow."

"Then you'll have to do. Now listen: I was pushed over-board—"

"By who? I mean whom?"

"You don't need to know."

Jean's eyes narrowed. "I don't need to know? You owe me. You'd be dead now if I hadn't thrown you that life preserver."

"Thank you for saving me. Now shut up, Jean. For once in your life, shut up and listen."

Jean gave a satisfied smile—this was the old Martin talking, imperious and accustomed to command. She shut up.

"I got a lift to the small craft harbor at Marina Green," he said. "I'm calling from a pay phone near there."

"You mean another boat picked you up?"

"Yes, a fellow pirate. He gave me dry clothes and food."

"Where have you been all this time?"

He made a sound somewhere between a chuckle and a giggle. "My rescuer had an appointment he couldn't miss. Since it won't matter to Diane, I'm going to do something first. Call the police and tell them to meet me at the house in two hours."

"Sure, but who—"

"Stop asking questions. I'll tell the police everything."

"What do you have to—"

"Just do as I say."

"Now you listen, Martin," Jean said sharply. "What about hypothermia? Peter can pick you up. You don't want to have another heart attack now that you've risen from the dead."

"No. I warmed up and rested on the boat. Take good care of Diane till I get there."

"But Martin, what . . ." Jean stopped when she realized she was talking into a dead line.

CHAPTER 5

Jean hung up the phone. "Holy shit," she said aloud. What a perfect end to a nightmare—she imagined Diane waking up to find Martin alive in the bed next to her. She phoned Peter.

"Peter, listen: Martin's alive. He just called. He was pushed, all right, but he wouldn't say who did it. Another boat fished him out and took him to Marina Green. He wants the police to meet him here in two hours."

"Wait a minute. Are you sure it was him?"

"Of course I'm sure. He was snarling and giving orders, just like old times."

"Is he all right? Is he hurt?"

"He sounded fine. In fact he giggled."

"Alive. This is incredible. Hold on a minute." Jean could practically hear the gears turning in Peter's head. Finally he spoke: "Why two hours? He could be home in twenty minutes. I should look for him."

"He's probably gone by now. He said he had to do something."

"Do what?"

"He wouldn't tell me."

"How did Diane take the news?"

"She's out cold. So what do I do? Call the cops?"

"Yes, call Hallock and Davila. Tell them what you told me. I'll drive by the marina and see if I can spot him, then come over."

"OK. See you soon." Jean went in search of her purse. She would rather call Davila but only had Hallock's card. She phoned and told him about the call.

Jean wanted a stiff drink and a good night's sleep but forced herself to get up, walk back to the kitchen, and splash cold water on her face. She started a pot of coffee—it was going to be a long night.

Just over an hour later, as Jean poured herself a third cup of coffee, Peter knocked lightly on the kitchen door. He carried a white bag from a Chinese restaurant and a pink bakery box tied with string.

"Oh Peter, you're a saint," she said, wrapping her arms around him.

"I drove over to the marina and looked around but didn't see anyone," he said. "Now tell me again what Martin said."

They sat on tall stools at the counter drinking coffee and eating lukewarm Szechuan food as Jean recounted the phone call.

Peter shook his head. "The man is amazing. This'll make twice he's survived when he should have died. What do you suppose he meant by a fellow pirate?"

Jean shrugged. "Maybe he got picked up by a personal injury lawyer."

"Imagine what it must have been like, swimming in water that cold in the dark, with only a life preserver, all the time knowing someone he considered a friend had tried to kill him."

"I'm sure that's what kept him going," Jean said. "Visions of revenge."

"And visions of Diane waiting for him."

The doorbell rang and Jean admitted Inspector Hallock and Officer Baker. "He here yet?" Hallock demanded.

"No, but we don't expect him until nearly six o'clock," Jean said. "Want some coffee?"

"Thanks." They followed her to the kitchen. "I sent a car over to the marina," Hallock said, "but there was no sign of Wingo."

"I was there about an hour ago and he was already gone," Peter said.

Hallock nodded. "I've got an APB out on him, too—we don't want him confronting whoever it was tried to kill him."

The night crept by, punctuated with Hallock's phone calls to monitor the search. Jean checked on Diane periodically, and once, passing through the living room, she couldn't resist lying down on the sofa for a moment. When she opened her eyes again, sun shone in the windows. She sat up abruptly; the wall clock said seven fifty-two.

In the kitchen, Hallock talked into his cell phone and Peter sat at the table with his head on his arms. He looked up when he heard her come in. "Morning," he said. "No sign of Martin yet."

"Oh, great." Jean still felt exhausted.

"OK, keep me posted," Hallock said into the phone. He closed his phone and turned to Jean. "We've got a problem," he told her. "Wingo's nearly two hours overdue, and there's no sign of him anywhere, no evidence that he ever came ashore."

"What do you mean? I *talked* to him."

"And you're the only one who heard his voice after he went into the bay. The telephone company's tracking system for that area was down during the time in question, so there's nothing to support what you say." Hallock looked at her with his weary cop's eyes. "I've been asking myself, how could a man with a serious heart condition survive in water that cold in a storm?"

"Have you forgotten about the life preserver?" Jean said. "And he didn't have to survive for long—another boat found him."

Hallock yawned. "Are you absolutely certain the phone call wasn't a dream based on wishful thinking? That sort of thing happens after tragedies."

"Just a goddamn minute. I know the difference between a dream and reality. I spoke to Martin."

"How much did you have to drink at the wedding, and after?"

"Not nearly enough."

"She wasn't drunk, Inspector," Peter said.

"Then there's another possibility," Hallock said. "I know you're a good friend of Mrs. Wingo. Maybe you're trying to cheer her up. But if you're putting us on, you're doing her more harm than good."

"You officious ass, how dare you accuse me of making it up! Do you think I'd do a thing like that to Diane?"

"Jean, Jean," Peter said gently, "you have to hold your temper." He turned to Hallock. "Inspector, this line of questioning is premature. There are several other possibilities that could explain his absence. He may have called a cab. Have you checked the taxi companies?"

"We have some people on it."

"What about the boat that picked him up?" Peter continued, all calmness and reason. "I'm sure you can find out who was on the bay at the time. Or suppose that after he called he had another heart attack. He may be in a hospital somewhere as a John Doe."

"We've been looking into all those possibilities," Hallock said. "So far, nothing."

"Did you say he was in a hospital?" Diane said softly from the doorway. She looked frail and bruised in a white quilted robe. "That he's alive?"

"Honey, sit down," Jean said. "This is going to be hard for you to hear."

"Then tell me fast," she said, sinking into a kitchen chair.

Jean sat beside her and put an arm around Diane's shoulder. "Just before four A.M., Martin called here." Diane gasped and closed her eyes, but said nothing. Jean continued. "He wanted to talk to you, but you were out cold. He said he had to do something and then he'd come home. But he's still not here."

"My God," Diane said. "He survived. I can't believe it. I'd given up hope. Did he sound all right? What did he say?"

"He sounded fine. A boat rescued him and brought him ashore. He wouldn't tell me who pushed him."

Diane turned to Hallock. "Where is he? Why can't you find him?"

"Mrs. Wingo, we've been searching for him since about four-thirty, and besides Ms. Applequist's story, there's no evidence that he came ashore."

"So," Diane said slowly, "you're suggesting that Jean made the whole thing up. Well, you can be sure that if she says he called, he called."

Hallock rubbed his chin. "Ma'am, I understand how you feel. But the evidence isn't adding up."

"Inspector, I hope you won't abandon the search for him on land just because you have doubts," Diane said.

"Mrs. Wingo—"

"Because if necessary, I'll call some of Martin's friends and ask if they can help you free up more officers. You've seen their names on the guest list."

Peter and Jean looked at each other in surprise. They had never before heard Diane throw Martin's weight around.

Hallock looked grim. "You can call whoever you like, Mrs. Wingo. We're already doing everything we possibly can."

"I'm sure you are, Inspector. Now excuse me while I get dressed." She stood and walked carefully out of the room.

CHAPTER 6

$\mathcal{I}$nspector Hallock went home, leaving an officer in a patrol car in front of the house. Jean took a shower and put on a pair of Martin's sweat pants and one of his T-shirts.

Diane paced nervously, staring out the front window, jumping at the sound of every car that drove by, every phone call, every knock on the door.

Peter, in tuxedo pants and a rumpled white shirt, sat at the dining room table on phone duty, fielding calls from concerned friends and nosy reporters. Frank arrived soon after Peter called him; he'd cut himself shaving and looked exhausted. Jean let him in the door and gave him a hug.

"Any sign of him?" he asked.

"Not yet. You look as if you've had a rough night."

"I think we all have. Jean, when Martin called, did he say where he was going?"

"No. I couldn't wake Diane, so he said he'd be home in two hours, and that's the last we heard. What could be more important than coming home to Diane, unconscious or not?"

"I can't imagine." Frank rubbed his eyes. "Martin may have tried to call me, too. My cell phone rang around four-fifty A.M., but the connection was bad and I couldn't hear whoever it was. I didn't recognize the number."

"You'd better tell Hallock. Come on, let's get you a sugar and caffeine rush." Jean led the way into the kitchen and gave him coffee and a cheese Danish. She refilled her own cup and they joined Peter in the dining room as he said "no comment" to someone on the phone.

Jean had never seen Peter in crisis mode before, and she liked what she saw. She sometimes found him too cautious and predictable, but that was exactly what Diane needed now. The house was filled with an air of unbearable tension, yet Peter remained calm and solicitous, without ego.

The phone rang again. Peter answered it and held it out to Jean. "It's Zeppo."

She made a face but took the phone. "Hello?"

"Hey, Jeannie, I just saw the news. So he survived. That's awesome. I guess he hasn't lost his edge after all."

"Apparently not. But nobody can find him. Where the hell could he have gone?"

"Beats me. Didn't he say anything to you?"

"No, and he wouldn't tell me who pushed him."

Zeppo guffawed. "That's perfect. The old pirate's really got somebody by the balls now."

"That's what he called the person who rescued him. A fellow pirate. What do you think he meant?"

He ignored her question. "Did they look at the office?"

"I guess so. But the cops don't believe he came ashore. They think I'm lying or crazy."

"If it's any consolation, I believe you. You may be a hard bitch, but you're no liar."

"Thanks for your vote of confidence."

"I'll see you later today. Meanwhile, keep your cork wet."

A few friends visited, most of them wedding guests. Frank took over the phone and the front door, while Jean and Peter cleaned up the mess in the two searched rooms and arranged to have the ruined furniture hauled away and the locks changed. Diane did a cursory survey of the rooms and found nothing missing.

In the late afternoon Inspector Hallock stopped by. "Someone ransacked your husband's office early this morning,

Mrs. Wingo," he said as they sat in the living room. "Not the entire building, just his office. It happened between midnight, when the cleaning crew finished, and about six A.M., when the building manager let one of my officers in. The *Walrus* was tossed as well, probably later in the morning. So now we're assuming this wasn't just a burglary, that the perp was looking for something specific. Do you have any idea what it could be?"

"I wouldn't have any idea," Diane said. "Frank?"

Frank, next to her on the couch, shook his head. "No, I don't."

"The searches were very thorough," Hallock said. "All the stuff at the office was packed in boxes, and the perp emptied them out. He fanned the books, so he was looking for something small. Same as on the boat."

"Do you think it was the man we interrupted last night?" Peter asked.

"It has to be connected," Hallock said. "I'm waiting for the tech crew's report."

"Have you found anything that indicates he came ashore?" Peter asked.

"Not yet," Hallock said, glancing at Jean with annoyance.

They heard a muffled ringing. Hallock pushed himself up from the sofa and fished a cell phone out of his coat pocket. "Excuse me," he said as he retreated to the foyer.

In a few moments Hallock rejoined them, his face stony. "Mrs. Wingo, I'm sorry to inform you that they've found your husband's body. A fisherman hooked him off the Municipal Pier at Aquatic Park."

CHAPTER 7

$\mathcal{D}$iane sank back on the sofa and closed her eyes. "I knew he was gone. He would have found a way to call me if he were alive."

"I'm so sorry, Diane," Frank said, wrapping his arms around her.

Jean met Peter's eyes, and could see he felt as helpless as she did. "Inspector, can I take her upstairs?" she asked.

"Yeah, go ahead."

The two women went up to the bedroom. Jean sat with a sobbing Diane for a long time, murmuring useless words of comfort. She couldn't decide whether she was angrier at Martin for getting himself killed or for surviving the heart attack in the first place.

Finally the sobs subsided and Diane sat up and took a shaky breath. Her yellow silk blouse was crumpled and damp. "I'm OK," she said, blowing her nose.

"You sure?"

"I just need a few minutes alone."

Downstairs, Jean found Peter and Frank in the living room. Hallock had gone. Frank wiped his eyes with a large white handkerchief. "How is she?" he asked.

"Terrible." Jean plopped down next to Peter. "So Martin met someone after he came ashore and he offed him, right?

That means there are two killers—one failed and the other succeeded."

"I suppose so," Peter said. "I can't really get my mind around this thing. Want to hear something wild? Hallock says Martin was wearing his tuxedo."

"No shit," she said. "Maybe I am crazy."

In a little while Diane came downstairs. She looked hollow-eyed and spent, but had combed her hair, washed her face, and pulled herself together. The subdued group said little. Jean's head was full of questions and ideas she wanted to air, but now was not the time. She sat on the blue sofa, holding Diane's hand and holding her tongue.

Peter cleared his throat. "Diane, the police want you to identify the body in the morning. I'd be glad to do it for you."

"Thank you, but no. I'll do it myself. I . . . I want to see him one last time."

Peter got on the phone again, notifying friends and colleagues that Martin was officially dead. Word spread quickly, and before long the house was full of visitors. When Jean's grandmother died, the neighbors in rural Indiana brought tuna casseroles, Jell-O molds, fried chicken; this crowd brought Italian squid salad, boxes of fresh dim sum, and a pan of goat-cheese enchiladas from a trendy Mexican place. Jean set up a buffet on the kitchen table, made endless pots of coffee, and opened bottle after bottle of wine.

Jean heard Keith Yoshiro, an architect Martin had often worked with, telling someone goodbye. She went after him, catching him at the hall closet shrugging into his coat. "Keith," she said, "can I ask you a question?"

"Sure." He was a short, slender, stylishly dressed man in his early fifties with shoulder-length black hair. Jean had spoken to him at parties a few times and liked him.

"It's about last night," she said. "Zeppo told me he talked to you the whole time after Martin went outside. Is that true?"

"Yes, he asked me what I thought of some new 3-D design software he'd read about. Why, do you think he pushed Martin?"

"I'm just wondering if it's possible."

Keith shook his head. "Zeppo would never hurt Martin. You've seen them together—they were like a couple of frat boys, always involved in some ridiculous bet or practical joke. The only time I ever saw Martin laugh out loud was with Zeppo."

"Who do you think pushed him? And killed him? Any ideas?"

"No. The people on that boat were all his good friends. Once he came ashore, though—well, Martin had plenty of enemies." Keith said goodbye, and Jean went in search of someone to talk to before Zeppo cornered her.

The guests departed by ten o'clock. Frank left, too, saying he had to take care of his dog. After Diane went to sleep, Jean and Peter cleaned the kitchen, put away all the food, and took a bottle of Chianti Classico and two glasses into the living room, where they curled up together on the sofa.

"Diane and Martin would have been on their honeymoon now," Peter mused.

"Let's look at the sequence of events," Jean said. "Martin gets pulled out of the water, he sails around awhile for reasons unknown, he calls home from Marina Green, he disappears. And then he puts on his wet tuxedo and someone tosses him into the water at Aquatic Park."

"The big question is, where did he go after he phoned you? Did he deliberately meet the killer or was it chance?"

"His office is right on Pier 3. Maybe the rescuer took him there by boat and he surprised whoever was searching."

"So who was doing the searching and why?" Peter asked.

Jean shook her head. "I wish to God he'd just come straight home." She moved closer to Peter, taking comfort from his solid dependable presence.

He stroked her hair. "I seem to recall that I owe you something."

"You sure do." She put her arms around him and they kissed like teenagers until Jean, fully aroused by his sweet, familiar touch, unbuckled his belt.

"Let's go up to the bedroom," he whispered.

"No, let's do it right here." They undressed and made love on the big sofa, giggling and changing position as the cushions shifted under them. Afterward they went upstairs to the guest bedroom.

"Thank God his will is current," Peter said as they slipped under the fat down comforter. "The day the divorce was final, I rewrote it to make Diane his sole heir. She's now a very rich woman. Her share of the Wingo-Johansen sale alone will be around $13 million."

"That's one good thing to come out of this mess. She's been worried about money all her life. But you know what people will say—that she made a fortune by being married for a few hours."

"Of course they will," Peter said. "She'll have to learn how to manage things, though. Diane would be an easy mark for the wrong kind of man."

They cuddled in the soft bed, and as Jean felt the hair on his chest brush against her breasts she thought about starting something. But she knew that after their romp on the sofa he wouldn't be up for it, so she left him in peace, and soon they both drifted off to sleep.

∽

THE NEXT morning, a Monday, Jean called her editor, Kyle Prentice. He'd heard the news and was hungry for details; he had met Martin under memorable circumstances a few months before. She told him all she could and he gave her the day off.

Jean found Diane at the kitchen table sipping coffee. She looked deeply saddened, but reasonably calm in a simple dark green silk dress.

"Want some breakfast?" Jean asked hopefully.

"I'm not hungry."

"You sure you're up for this?"

"No, but it has to be done. With you and Peter there I'll be OK."

Peter drove them to the monolithic Hall of Justice on Bryant. On the main floor they were shown into a waiting room, where a somber and sympathetic Oscar Davila joined them. After a brief wait he led the way to a viewing room.

Jean knew how the body would probably look. Twelve hours dead was a long time, but the cold water would have slowed putrefaction. With any luck it wouldn't be too ghastly.

Diane stood between Jean and Peter, gripping their hands tightly, her whole body rigid with dread. On the other side of a big window lay a human shape on a gurney, covered with a white sheet. An attendant pulled the sheet back so they could see the face.

Martin's flesh had settled away from his bones and his skin was bloodless and waxy. There were several cuts and bruises on his forehead and along his jawline, but, all in all, Jean didn't think he looked too bad.

It was bad for Diane, though—she uttered a heart-wrenching cry and gripped Jean's hand even harder. "Yes," she said softly. "That's Martin."

CHAPTER 8

*D*iane signed papers without another word, and Davila arranged for Jean and Peter to come back the next morning to give statements.

Peter drove to St. Francis Wood and the three of them walked slowly up the path. Diane, pale and shaky, clung to Peter's arm, and Jean followed. Diane punched in the security code and unlocked the front door. She opened it wide and gasped, staggering backward and colliding with Peter.

"What?" Jean said. She stepped around them and looked inside. The living room was completely trashed—sofas tipped over, cushions ripped open, drawers pulled out, paintings knocked off the walls, books scattered on the floor. "Fuck!" she exclaimed. She charged into the house, enraged that someone would deal Diane another body blow so soon after the last one.

"Jean, come back," Peter called, his arm around Diane. "He might still be here."

"Call the cops," Jean yelled. She passed through the dining room, which had also been searched, to the kitchen, where all the cupboards were open and every container had been emptied onto the floor.

She seized a boning knife from a block on the counter and went from room to room, opening closets and looking under beds, cursing aloud, ready to skin the intruder alive

if she found him. All the dresser drawers were pulled out—
he'd started at the bottom, like a pro. The wedding gifts
were untouched. Every room had been tossed, but no one
was home.

Jean came back to the living room. "He's gone."

"I've called 911," Peter said.

Diane sank into one of the few intact chairs, clenching
her fists. "I can't take any more."

⁂

HALLOCK AND Davila arrived soon after the uniformed officers. Jean and Peter waited in the manicured backyard,
in the shade of a big white umbrella, while Davila took a
statement from Diane in a gazebo at the far end of the yard.
Hallock remained with the tech crew in the house.

When Jean's turn came, she joined Davila in the gazebo.
"Good to see you again, despite the circumstances," he said.

"Good to see you, too." His hand felt warm and strong
in hers. She sat in a white garden chair. "Can you tell me
any more about Martin?"

"Well, he was dressed just as he had been at the wedding, except he'd lost his shoes and necktie. His watch is
missing It's engraved, so we should be able to get a line on it
if it's pawned. Right now we're waiting for the lab reports."

Davila turned a page in his notebook. "You'll be coming
downtown tomorrow to make formal statements regarding
the murder, so we'll just cover the break-in." Jean told him
what little she knew about it.

"You never should have gone through the house like
that," he said.

"I know. Peter already scolded me. How did he get in?"

"Through a rear window. He disabled the alarm. Very
slick job, unlike the first house search and the searches of
the office and yacht."

"What do you mean?" Jean asked.

"Those others were strictly amateur, done by someone with keys."

"So you think two different people were involved?"

"It looks that way."

Jean kept Diane company as Peter took her place in the gazebo. The weather grew markedly cooler as the afternoon fog rolled in, and Diane shivered. "I'll get you a sweater," Jean said.

Rather than go into the house and deal with Hallock, she decided to fetch her sweater from Peter's car. She rounded the house and saw that her evasions were for nothing—Hallock stood in the front yard smoking a cigarette.

He eyed Jean with contempt. "Ms. Applequist, can I ask you a question off the record?"

"Sure."

"It's obvious Wingo never got out of the bay. So I'm curious why you ran me ragged for an entire day and wasted God knows how many man-hours of police work." Anger made his face redder than usual; Jean wondered about his blood pressure.

"Well, Inspector, either I'm totally insane or I really got that call."

"How did you know Wingo, anyway?"

"I'm an old friend of the widow."

"Did you get along with him?"

Jean shrugged. "Diane loved him, so I put up with him."

"Were you a bridesmaid?"

"Of course not."

"Why not?"

"I didn't get along with the groom. Diane thought it was a bad idea."

"Did that bother you?"

Jean looked at him with mounting irritation. "You've got me, Inspector. I confess. I pushed him overboard because I wanted to be a bridesmaid."

"I don't think you pushed him," Hallock said. "But maybe you pulled this stunt about the midnight phone call to punish your friend for marrying someone you hated."

"It wasn't a stunt," Jean said. "And if you can't let go of your idiotic notion that I'm making this all up, you'll never find the killer."

"You're the one who's been impeding the investigation with this bullshit story. Rescind it now, admit it's a total fabrication, and we'll forget about it. Otherwise, I may charge you with filing a false report. Being Mrs. Wingo's friend doesn't put you above the law."

"Don't threaten me, you fat, incompetent—"

"Jean, you don't have to answer any more questions right now," Peter said as he came around the house. "Inspector, this isn't the time or place for such serious accusations. We've arranged with Inspector Davila to make statements tomorrow at the Hall."

"That'll be fine," Hallock said, forcing his anger down. He stomped back into the house.

Peter looked at Jean. "Are you trying to get arrested for assaulting a police officer?"

"I wasn't going to hit him, just excoriate him verbally."

"You have to control your temper, especially with the police," Peter said. "Don't talk to him anymore unless I'm there, OK?"

"OK, I promise."

"Davila says Diane can go now. I called Frank, and she can stay with him for a couple of days. You take her over there, and I'll see about getting a crew in to clean up the house as soon as the police are done."

"That sounds good. I'll be back to help."

The police let Diane pack a bag, and Jean drove Diane's yellow Mercedes coupe to Frank's house. She navigated south to Bernal Heights and pulled into the driveway of a small, narrow Victorian on Winfield Street. The tiny front yard consisted of a patch of grass edged with bright annuals.

Frank, looking haggard and depleted, let them in. Trigger, his elderly golden retriever, greeted them, his tail wagging slowly. Diane usually knelt down to nuzzle him, but today she hugged Frank, excused herself, and went up the open staircase to the guest room.

Jean looked around. After Frank's sons left home and his wife died, he'd moved from a larger house to this small one. The downstairs space was open and appealing, with slightly shabby, comfortable furniture. Sliding glass doors at the back of the house looked out over the undulating San Francisco landscape. Family photos covered one wall: Frank and his late wife, his two sons and their young families, and of course Diane, who looked like a changeling among these large, pale people.

"She shouldn't have had to identify him," Frank said. "I should have done it, or Peter. But I suppose it was some sort of closure for her."

"Closure is when they catch his killer," Jean said.

Frank glanced up the stairs. "Come on, let's talk outside." He led the way out the glass door, Trigger following. The day was cool and breezy, but the fog held off for now.

The back of the property dropped steeply, and Frank had built a big cantilevered deck around the mature trees that grew on the hillside. He and Jean sat in weathered cedar chairs in the shade of a tall pine. Trigger jumped stiffly onto the chair next to Frank and curled up.

"Did Peter tell you what the police said?" Jean asked. "About Martin getting picked up by another boat and being in his tux?"

"Yes, he did. It's all very confusing."

"You knew Martin longer than anyone else," Jean said. "Who do you think killed him?"

Frank gazed out at the view for several seconds, his expression troubled. "I gave Inspector Hallock names of people he antagonized over the years, and it was a long list. But who could kill a man over a business deal?"

"Who was on the list?" Jean asked.

"I can't tell you, Jean. That's police business." He bent over and scratched Trigger's head.

"At least they'll be able to find out who pushed him overboard," she said. "They have a limited number of suspects there. Who do you think it was?"

"I have no idea. I really don't."

"Do you have any guesses about what people are searching for?"

"Look, I've been over this so many times with the police," he said wearily. "I really don't want to talk about it anymore." He pushed himself out of the chair. "I'd better check on Diane."

Jean decided to let it go—he did look worn out. She stood, brushing dog hair off her pants. "I should get moving anyway. I promised Peter I'd help with the cleanup. Call me if Diane needs anything." She gave Frank a wave and left.

THE NEXT day Jean and Peter went down to the Hall of Justice and gave statements. Davila's non-confrontational approach put Jean at ease, but she had nothing to add that could help him figure out what the searches were all about.

When all was said, Davila left the two of them in his office to wait until their statements were ready to sign. After several minutes the inspector returned with Hallock.

"It seems we owe you an apology, Ms. Applequist," Davila said. "I just got the autopsy report, and it says Wingo's last meal was not Champagne and crab, but coffee and a PayDay candy bar, presumably eaten on the boat that picked him up. Also, the phone call Frank Johansen got that night was from the pay phone near Marina Green."

"Well, what do you know?" Jean said with satisfaction, glancing at Hallock.

"What else did the autopsy show?" Peter asked.

"The cause of death was drowning. The killer must have knocked him unconscious and changed his clothes, probably to make it seem as if he'd never come ashore, then thrown him back in the water from the pier. His sleeve caught on a piece of metal in one of the pilings so he didn't wash out to sea, and he finally floated around to where the fisherman hooked him. There are a number of peri-mortem contusions on his head and face."

"What's peri-mortem?" Peter asked.

"Inflicted around the time of death, either just before or just after," Jean said. "I read it in a mystery." She grinned at Hallock. "Inspector, I'll take that apology at your convenience."

"I'll be in my office," Hallock said gruffly. He turned and left.

"What is it with that guy?" Jean said to Davila. "Do I look like his ex-wife?"

"He was sure you'd invented the phone call, and now he feels like a fool. He hates being wrong."

"Did you believe me?"

"I'd decided to wait and see. Also, George is very old-fashioned, and he's got issues with assertive women."

"Assertive women don't scare you?"

He chuckled. "My four-year-old daughter is pretty assertive. I'll have to get used to it."

"Hallock seems like a real throwback," Jean said. "Must be tough being his partner."

"Not at all. He's a good cop, very evenhanded about most things."

They shook hands, and Peter and Jean went out into the warming day. As they got into his car, Jean noticed that he looked upset. "What's the matter, Peter?" she asked. "Aren't you glad for one piece of good news in all the bad?"

"Davila's on your radar, isn't he?"

"Oh, don't start. He's an attractive man, so I noticed him. But he's married."

"What if he weren't married?"

"Stop with the jealousy, Peter." She pulled his head over and kissed him. He resisted at first, but soon gave in and let himself be mollified. Jean reached under his jacket as loud honking startled them. A young man in a new Mazda waited impatiently for their parking space.

"OK, OK, I'm going," Peter said. He started the car and pulled into traffic. "This whole thing has me on edge. It's not you."

"I forgive you," Jean said, patting his knee. "I know how you feel. Me too."

CHAPTER 9

*T*he police released Martin's body a few days later, and Diane turned him over to the Neptune Society for cremation. The morning of the scattering ceremony was cold and overcast; Jean felt suitably funereal in a black wool coat.

When the mourners had gathered on the *Naiad*, the Neptune Society's venerable fifty-five-foot cabin cruiser, the boat backed out of its slip and motored past the noisy sea lions that had taken over a nearby marina.

Out on the bay it was chilly and the wind brisk. Jean and Peter buttoned their coats and joined a few other hardy souls on deck. They edged onto the bow, holding the rail as the boat pitched and heaved in the choppy water. The bay usually looked blue, but today the heavy gray sky gave it an ugly olive-drab color. Jean stared over the railing into its opaque depths. "'The snotgreen sea,'" she quoted.

"'The scrotumtightening sea,'" Peter finished.

A fifty-something man in jeans and a shearling jacket sat on a bench against the cabin. He was familiar, but Jean couldn't place him. He looked over and smiled. "I didn't imagine Martin had any friends besides Hugh who'd read Joyce." The wind whipped his long curly hair.

"We read *Ulysses* together," Jean said. "Peter here owns a sailboat called the *Molly Bloom*."

The man's smile broadened. "Does he? One of my favorite characters in literature."

"Mine, too," Peter said. "This is Jean Applequist, a friend of Diane's, and I'm Peter Brennan. I was Martin's lawyer."

"I'm Edward Bongiorni, Hugh Rivenbark's brother-in-law, and a friend of Diane's as well." He shook hands with them.

"Bongiorni," Jean repeated. "You don't by any chance own a bookstore in Mendocino, do you? Bongiorni's Books?"

"Yes, my wife, Laurel, and I do. Have you been there?"

"Many times." So that's where she'd seen him. "Is your wife Hugh's sister?"

"No, Hugh was married to my sister, Esther. She died years ago, but we're still family."

As they chatted, Hugh Rivenbark joined them. His brown parka hung partly open over a tweed jacket and his white hair was windblown. Peter introduced Jean.

Hugh shook her hand. "Jean, I'm glad to meet you. Lately, every time I get on a boat, you're the most attractive woman there. When I first saw you at the wedding, I thought you were older because of your hair. I was greatly disappointed when I realized you were half my age, not to mention attached to Peter."

Jean grinned. She recognized harmless flirting when she heard it. "Thanks, Hugh. Diane tells me you're going to give the eulogy."

"Yes, and although I'm sorry to be eulogizing Martin so soon, I'm honored to do it." Hugh looked toward the city. "There's a nice symmetry to a scattering ceremony—Martin loved the sea, he perished in the sea, and now he'll be there for all time."

Jean's ears were very cold, so she excused herself and went inside to get out of the wind. Diane, wrapped in a white cashmere coat, sat in the upper salon talking with the Unitarian minister who would perform the service. All the seats were taken, so Jean went down to the less crowded lower salon.

A dark, petite woman standing across the salon smiled at her. She recognized Kay Bennett Wingo, Martin's ex-wife, from TV and newspaper photos. Her brown eyes were large and direct, her other features delicate and telegenic. She was Martin's age, around fifty. This morning she looked concerned but businesslike in a sleek pageboy haircut and beige Chanel suit under a camel's hair coat.

Jean felt her hackles rise as Kay approached. The woman already had two strikes against her. A former state senator, she had founded a group called the Rational Right, which as far as Jean could determine had the same agenda as other right-wing groups but used bigger words. Strike two was that she had married Martin when he was an unapologetic asshole and had stayed with him for more than twenty years. Jean resolved to be polite and restrained for Diane's sake.

"Hello," Kay said, extending a small manicured hand, which Jean shook. "You must be Jean. I'm Kay Wingo." She had a deep, resonant voice and beautiful diction, like a Disney cartoon villainess. "Diane tells me you've been a great help to her."

"We've been friends a long time."

"I wish there were something I could do for her. She's really a charming girl. I've never harbored any ill will toward her—Martin and I would have divorced eventually even without Diane. Our marriage was a casualty of conflicting ambitions. I'm not proud of that failure, but it was inevitable."

"I'm sure Diane realizes you wish her well," Jean said.

"How dreadful for this to happen just when he'd found the kind of wife he needed, someone who'd put marriage and children ahead of a career. I couldn't have children, and I believe childless women tend to overcompensate in other areas, sometimes to their detriment, don't you?"

Jean could think of a number of responses, none of which came under the category of polite and restrained. "Uh . . ."

A young man carrying a tan raincoat materialized at Kay's side. She put a hand on his arm. "I don't think you know my aide, Donald Grimes. Donald, this is Jean Applequist, a dear friend of Diane's."

"Pleased to meet you," he said as they shook hands. Grimes was tall and heavy, with small features for such a large man, and conservatively cut brown hair. The vest of his off-the-rack three-piece suit was too tight across his midsection.

Kay looked past Jean at an elegant older woman coming through the door. "Excuse me," she said. "I must have a word with Judge Morris." She hurried off.

Donald smiled politely at Jean. "Were you Martin's friend, too?"

"Not really. Tell me, what does an aide do?"

He shrugged. "A little of everything. I keep track of her appointments, make travel arrangements, drive her around, whatever needs doing."

"Are you a bodyguard as well?" Jean didn't know what to make of Donald. Men tended to have strong reactions to her, but he didn't seem to be giving off any vibes at all.

"If necessary. She's a powerful leader, after all. There are many anti-Christian forces who wish her harm because she's doing God's work." A hint of the fanatic gleamed in his eyes.

Jean realized what she was dealing with—a born-again Christian, just like the ones in her family. Who else could be so devoted to Kay? "Has anyone ever attacked her?"

"Oh, no. People have heckled her and thrown things, though. I like to think of myself as a deterrent to anything worse."

"Donald," Kay called. "Can I have a word?"

"Nice talking with you." Donald strode to Kay's side.

Jean took a seat, and in a moment saw Zeppo coming toward her. She'd been expecting him to turn up. Whenever they were at the same gathering he'd seek her out, make suggestive remarks, spar verbally with her. At first she'd assumed he was just horny; his insistence that there were more important things in life than getting laid sounded to her like sour grapes. But once she'd caught him looking at her with a longing that went beyond lust, and realized he had a serious crush on her. He was apparently too unsure of himself to do anything about it but joke around, which suited her fine.

"Hey, gorgeous," he said. "You look great in black." He sat down next to her and nodded toward Kay and Donald. "So you met Kay's gorilla?" he said in low tones.

"A nice Christian gorilla. What's his story?"

"Beats me. Martin thought he was a real fool. He used to whistle 'Onward, Christian Soldiers' whenever he saw Donald."

"What did Donald do? Get mad or turn the other cheek?"

"He pretty much ignored Martin. He probably figures the old guy's in Hell, so he got his revenge."

Kay and the judge went into a nearby ladies' room, leaving Donald alone. He came over and shook Zeppo's hand. "Nice to see you again, Zeppo," he said.

"Mutual, I'm sure."

Jean couldn't resist teasing him. "So Donald, do you suppose Martin's soul is burning in Hell right now?"

"I wouldn't make light of eternal damnation if I were you," he said.

"Why not?" she asked, amused. "You think I'm damned, too?"

"You must come to Jesus," he told her, the true believer's look returning to his eyes. "He can save even you. 'For this is the will of God, even your sanctification, that ye should abstain from fornication.'"

Jean recognized the verse from 1 Thessalonians—her father had invoked it many times to her. She'd given up arguing with her family about religion long ago and certainly didn't want to fight with Donald now. "As far as fornication goes," she said lightly, "don't knock it if you haven't tried it."

"I have tried it, and found it empty and degrading. Jesus' way is a better way." He smiled smugly and went up the stairs.

Zeppo grinned. "He just hasn't slept with the right girl."

"Don't look at me. As I said, I don't do charity work. Anyway, how does he know so much about my private life?"

"I guess from Kay, who probably got it from Martin," he said with a shrug. "I heard Martin warn Peter about you a couple of times before I met you."

"Why, that bastard!" Jean exclaimed, making several people look over. She lowered her voice. "What did he say?"

She realized Zeppo was enjoying her anger. "Just that you were a, quote, tramp, unquote, and that Peter shouldn't get too attached to you," he said.

"What a hypocritical asshole! He cheated on his wife all the time." Jean was drawing stares.

"Well, Martin had a double standard," Zeppo said. "One standard for him and another for everybody else. And Jeannie, this is the man's funeral. You should keep it down."

Jean took a deep breath. "Yeah, you're right."

The boat slowed in the water; Jean and Zeppo followed the crowd upstairs. She stood between Peter and Zeppo in the wheelhouse with a few other mourners, looking through an open window into the upper salon, so the less steady members of the group could sit.

The minister welcomed them, glancing at note cards in his hand. "God of grace and tender mercies, bless us who are gathered here to celebrate the life and mourn the death of Martin Newgate Wingo."

The minister introduced Hugh Rivenbark, who stood up, gripping an overhead rail for support. He had no notes. "Martin Wingo was a great and complex individual," he said, his strong voice carrying easily over the engine noise. "As Henry Ward Beecher said of another flawed titan, 'Men

~ 61 ~

without faults are apt to be men without force. A round diamond has no brilliancy.' Martin could be hard and cold, but he glittered with a sharp, piercing intelligence. He was strong-willed and imperious, yet he was capable of deep, warm friendship and great love.

"I'd begun to consider Martin's legacy when he had his heart attack, but he still had the best part of his life ahead of him. His beloved wife, Diane, taught him how to live after he nearly died, and filled his final months with a serenity and contentment he had rarely known before."

Jean noticed Kay making a sour face as Hugh described Martin's happiness with Diane. Zeppo saw it, too, and nudged her with his elbow.

"Diane will, of course, feel his loss the most," Hugh continued. "But he affected all our lives in unforgettable ways." Hugh recited a couple of anecdotes that made the dead man seem clever and just a bit mischievous. Then the minister led them outside.

The boat slowed in the water as the group moved unsteadily onto the bow. As the *Naiad* idled just inside the Golden Gate, at nearly the same spot where the wedding had taken place, the minister spoke again: "We bid farewell to Martin, our cherished friend. In mystery we are born and in mystery we die."

Diane, her expression unbearably sorrowful, opened a jade-colored urn and poured its contents over the side, and the ashes and chunks of bone that had been Martin Wingo fell into the murky water, the dust spun and driven by the stiff, cold wind. Jean felt an unexpected sadness as she thought of him happy and newly married, anticipating a night in Diane's arms, and instead dying alone in cold, dark water.

A crew member brought out an armload of yellow roses, a slash of color in the leaden day, and distributed them to the mourners. They all turned outward and threw flowers into the sea. Jean felt goose bumps as the strains of Aretha

Franklin singing "Amazing Grace" poured from the cabin—
Martin had loved Aretha Franklin. Diane wept quietly, supported by Frank, who wiped away tears of his own. Jean looked at Zeppo; his eyes were dry, but grief showed on his face as he flung his rose after the ashes.

The boat got under way again, and as it headed back to the pier the bright raft of roses drifted and dispersed in the *Naiad's* wake, across the gray-green water and out under the bridge toward the open sea.

CHAPTER 10

On a clear, windy Sunday afternoon two weeks after the funeral, Jean and Diane sat on a bench at Aquatic Park, the walkway along the edge of the bay where Martin's body was found. The long, curving Municipal Pier was crowded with fishermen and pedestrians enjoying the rare fogless day. This evening the two women were also going to dinner and a movie, a first since the wedding.

Diane had circles under her eyes and was too thin, but was starting to resemble her old self. She looked elegant in celadon-colored slacks and matching sweater, and her dark hair hung down her back in a thick braid. She still wore her wedding ring, a big diamond solitaire set in platinum, and she'd put on perfume. Jean recognized Je Reviens.

"How are you doing, honey?" Jean asked.

"Better. I'm trying to keep busy. You'll never guess what I've been reading."

"Romance or chick lit?"

"Neither. Annual reports and financial statements. I'm getting educated—I knew almost nothing about Martin's finances. I was going to turn it all over to Peter, but he's insisting that I make my own decisions. It's taking my mind off things, I'll admit."

"Good for you. You don't want to depend on advisors all your life."

"That's what Peter says. He also thinks I should get an M.B.A." She smiled at Jean. "I suggested that to Martin once and he just laughed."

Jean masterfully refrained from slamming Martin. "Why not? You've got the time, the money, and the brains. What about the Haas Business School at U.C. Berkeley?"

"That's my first choice. Martin taught a few classes there and thought very highly of it."

Jean watched a tall skinny man in jeans, a gray hoodie, and a green Celtics baseball cap work his way down the pier, pausing to talk to each fisherman. Curly red hair peeked from under the cap. "Hey, there's Zeppo," she said.

Diane looked where she pointed. "What can he be doing here?"

Jean stood. "Let's find out." They walked along the water and onto the concrete pier. Zeppo chatted with an elderly Asian man smoking a pipe. The man shook his head no and went back to his fishing, and Zeppo turned away. He broke into a grin when he saw the two women and came over. "Well, if it isn't Jeannie and Diane. How's it going?"

"Getting tips on what bait to use?" Jean asked.

"Not exactly."

"Zeppo, are you asking the fishermen about the night of the wedding?" Diane said.

"No harm in that."

"Have you found anyone who saw anything?" Jean asked.

"Not yet. But since I'm unemployed, I'll keep at it."

They said goodbye and the two women walked back toward the parking area. They got in the car and Diane started the engine. "So Zeppo's investigating on his own," she said.

"Well, isn't that a good thing?" Jean asked. "He may be a weasel, but he's not dumb. Maybe he'll turn up something."

"I suppose so." Diane fell into a distracted silence.

"Hey, no brooding allowed tonight."

"Sorry. Let's change the subject. I've been meaning to ask you how things are going with Peter."

Jean rolled her eyes. "Still trying to get me married off, are you?"

"I think he's just the type of stable, loving man you need. Now answer the question."

"OK. He's great, but a bit conventional for my taste. He wants us to be monogamous. He wants to get married and have kids, and I don't. Other than that, we're doing fine."

"Do you mean he proposed to you?"

"No, that much of a fool he's not. He was speaking theoretically."

"Jean, you're hopeless." Diane sighed. "Martin and I were going to start a family right away. Kay was infertile and wouldn't adopt. After the wedding, I was so hoping I was already pregnant. One of my worst days was when I got my period and realized every part of Martin was gone for good."

Jean squeezed her friend's knee. "It sounds lame right now, but you'll find someone else. You've got years and years left to have kids."

⁓

PARKING IN the Castro was impossible, so Jean pulled into her uncle's driveway. He owned a large gray and blue Queen Anne Victorian a few blocks up from Castro Street. The two women had dinner at a sushi restaurant just off the main street and then walked down to the Castro Theatre, where Jean thought she'd found the perfect movie for tonight. She loved film noir but Diane needed comedy, and a revival of *Dead Men Don't Wear Plaid* fit the bill.

After the movie they drove to St. Francis Wood. Jean planned to stay over; Diane was loneliest at night. As they turned in the driveway, a security guard parked at the curb waved.

"We have to talk," Diane said once they were inside. "Open some wine, will you?"

Jean went through the living room, where order had been restored. Diane had replaced the pieces that were cut up or broken. In the kitchen she pulled a good Barolo out of a wine storage unit and the two women curled up on the new sofa, sipping from Riedel glasses. Jean sniffed the Italian red and rolled it around in her mouth. She caught aromas of plums and violets and vanilla, and the taste was full and velvety with a spicy finish. That was sushi's only drawback—it didn't go with red wine.

"What's up?" Jean asked.

"Well, as you know, there's been very little progress on the investigation, and it's driving me crazy. I can't bear the thought that whoever killed Martin is out there right now having a good meal or listening to music or making love." Her eyes grew moist as she spoke.

"The police just need more time," Jean said. "They'll solve it eventually."

"No, they won't, because they don't know all the facts, and if I can help it they never will."

Jean stared at her friend. "What facts? What are you talking about?"

"Promise you'll keep this to yourself, no matter what happens."

"OK, I promise."

"I really mean it."

"I won't tell, I swear on my tits," Jean said, invoking an oath from their student days. "Now what's this all about?"

"Before his heart attack, Martin did some questionable things."

"No shit."

"These were things you don't know about. One of the reasons I broke up with him was that I couldn't stand the way he did business. He had files on people, of illegal or immoral or stupid things they'd done, and when he needed something he would threaten them."

"He was a blackmailer?" Jean asked in amazement.

"I know it was wrong, but I also know he changed. Before the wedding he sent all the files back to the people they were about. He put a note on each one that said there were no copies, he was through, that his victims were free of him. We burned his 'blue box,' the old blue storage box where he kept the files."

"You mean it was just a bunch of paper files? Wasn't the information on a hard drive somewhere?"

"You know what a Luddite Martin was," Diane said, affection in her voice. "He could barely work a cell phone. He was terrified that someone would hack into his computer and steal the secrets. So he only kept hard copies—papers, disks, photos, DVDs, things like that."

"If he sent it all back, why are people searching every-where, assuming that's what they're looking for?"

"That I don't know. Maybe someone thinks Martin had copies."

"Duh. He had to have copies."

"He gave me his word there were none."

"And you believed him?"

"Yes, I did. I had no reason to doubt him."

"Uh huh. How'd you find out about the blue box, anyway? Did he show you the stuff?"

"No, of course not," Diane said. "I saw him pulling people's strings, but I didn't know how he was doing it. Then something happened—do you remember the night he served Le Pin?"

"You bet. They still talk about it at the magazine." Jean recalled the evening vividly. A couple of months into their affair, Martin had thrown a small dinner party for Diane's birthday at her apartment. The only guest besides Jean was Peter Brennan, whom Jean hadn't met before. Martin had paid nearly $2,000 for a bottle of 1998 Le Pin, a great vintage of a rare cult Bordeaux. Jean had been positively sweet to Martin that night—she had tried the '98 only once before and was eager to repeat the experience.

A chef hired from a local restaurant for the evening prepared the meal, and after an appetizer of oysters in Champagne *beurre blanc* served with a lovely *grand cru* Chablis, they moved on to rack of lamb with braised leeks and fingerling potatoes. The rented wine steward had done a beautiful job of opening, decanting, and pouring the precious wine. The color had been good, ruby with just a hint of garnet at the rim. Everyone sipped the wine and made appreciative noises. They all waited for Jean, the expert, to weigh in.

Jean inhaled the fragrance deeply—and stopped dead. When she tasted the wine, her suspicions were confirmed. "Martin," she announced, "you've been had. This wine is not as advertised."

"I think it's delicious," Diane said.

"Oh, it's a very nice wine. But it's not what you paid for."

"And just how do you know that?" Martin asked, irritated.

"I tried it about a year ago. I'm not a star, but I do have a decent taste memory. This is probably a Pomerol, but it's not a '98 Le Pin."

Peter examined the bottle. "How could it not be? Look at the label." He passed it to Jean. Sure enough, the simple off-white label looked authentic.

"The bottle and label look good, but let me see the cork." Jean examined the long cork. "These guys are good, but not perfect. This is a bogus cork—the chateau's name isn't on it."

Martin examined the cork with growing rage. "I want to taste a real bottle. Where can I get one?"

"At auction or through one of the better wine merchants. My editor has a couple of bottles he bought as futures, but he's saving them for his fortieth birthday."

"What's his phone number?"

"Now wait a minute, Martin. You can't go around—"

"I'll call him now. We'll taste the other bottle tonight."

"Be serious. Those bottles are worth—"

"I'll buy one from him. Diane, please bring me the phone."

Diane, responding to Martin's steely, inexorable tone, went on her errand without a word.

Jean was warming to the idea. "OK, if you're determined, let's pour the rest of this wine back into the decanter so it doesn't change too much."

Martin had the wine steward return the ersatz Le Pin to the decanter and serve the other bottles he'd brought, a good but less exalted Pomerol, Vieux-Château-Certan. Jean recited Kyle Prentice's cell number. Martin dialed, and after a brief wait spoke to Kyle. "Mr. Prentice, this is Martin Wingo, a friend of Jean Applequist. I'm very sorry to bother you so late, but we have a situation here that I think you can help us with." Martin used his most charming and persuasive tone.

Jean knew that Kyle, who was something of a social climber, would eat this up. Martin was just the kind of mover and shaker he longed to rub elbows with. Kyle was a good friend in spite of this shortcoming; he and Jean had worked together on a now-defunct regional lifestyle magazine, and he'd hired her when he became editor in chief of *Wine Digest*. She'd loved wine before, but working for the *Digest* had made her into a real wine geek.

Martin explained about the bottle of Le Pin. "So we'd like to taste a bottle of the real thing. I'd be happy to buy one of your bottles for fair market value plus a twenty-five percent fee for your inconvenience." He listened for a while. "Here, tonight. I can send a messenger for it . . . oh, that would be even better. Thank you." Martin gave Diane's address and hung up. "He's bringing it over himself," Martin said with satisfaction. "He'll taste it with us."

Kyle arrived, bottle in hand, visibly pleased to be socializing with Martin. He was a slim man in his late thirties with short dark hair and long sideburns. He wore black jeans and a maroon 1950s vintage shirt with flap pockets. He was good-looking and simpatico, but Jean had never slept with him, for the most basic of reasons: She didn't like his scent. It wasn't that he smelled bad, he just didn't smell right. In any case, his taste ran to gamine brunettes.

After the dinner plates were cleared away, the sommelier set up clean glasses and they tasted the two wines side by side. Martin got angry again when he tasted the real Le Pin, which was as spectacularly rich, complex, and silky as it should have been. Jean sniffed the wine and rolled it on her tongue. It showed aromas of chocolate and tobacco, with raspberries and currants on the palate, velvety tannins, and just enough oak, everything in perfect balance. She knew it would be even better in another ten years.

Peter swirled his wine. "Now that I taste this, I wonder how anyone gets away with selling the phony stuff."

"If Jean hadn't been here, we wouldn't have known the difference," Diane said. "We all thought it was fine because none of us had ever tasted the real thing."

"That's right," Kyle said. "These fake wines get sold to people with money who aren't wine experts. They just want a great bottle for a special occasion. Usually their guests are too polite to complain if they recognize a problem."

"Fortunately, Jean is not constrained by common courtesy," Martin said. "For once I'm grateful for your big mouth, Jean. Thank you."

"You're welcome." Jean winked at Diane.

Kyle tasted the fake wine again. "Whoever blended this knows his stuff. Where'd you get it, Martin? Jean can do a piece on it."

Martin smiled and shook his head. "No. I'll deal with it myself."

Kyle shrugged. "If you say so." He held out his other glass. "How about another hit of the genuine article?"

Sitting in Diane's living room all these months later, Jean remembered the taste of the real Le Pin with an almost physical longing as she poured herself another glass of Barolo. "Now *that* was a memorable dinner party," she said. "But what's the connection?"

"He was in one of his silent rages all the next morning," Diane said. "That afternoon he went to Treadway's, the fancy wine shop near Union Square."

"Sure, I know it. They cater to rich ignoramuses."

"When he got home he told me we'd be getting a case a year of the current vintage of Le Pin free of charge. He told Treadway he'd expose the counterfeiting operation if he didn't make it up to him. So I asked him if that was how he'd gotten some other things done, by putting pressure on people. He admitted it. I accused him of blackmail, but he just laughed and said, 'That's not blackmail, that's business.'"

"Treadway's is dirty? That'll make a great story. Kyle will love it."

"You can't tell Kyle or anyone else," Diane said. "If it gets around that Martin was blackmailing Treadway, people might figure out the rest of it, as I did."

Jean shrugged. "OK, if you insist. So you think someone from the blue box killed him. But why would they, if he sent everything back?"

"I've thought about that, too. What if you knew there was evidence of something bad you'd done, and then you get the evidence back. You destroy it, but there's a problem—Martin still knows. Before, you couldn't kill him because someone might find the evidence against you. But now you can safely eliminate him."

Jean nodded thoughtfully. "That could be. But there's a simpler explanation. Look at what's happened: Someone searched your house, Martin's office, and the *Walrus*.

That sure as hell makes me think he kept something important."

"Jean, I know he didn't. He gave me his word."

"Then what's this guy looking for?"

Diane sighed. "I don't know. I only know we can't tell the police about the blue box."

"You really should let Hallock and Davila in on this. Your efforts to protect Martin's reputation are going to screw up the investigation into his murder."

"This isn't all about Martin's reputation," Diane said. "Obviously that's a factor, but mostly I'm trying to keep all the secrets that were in the blue box from ending up in the news."

"But one of those people probably killed him."

"I know, but the rest of them didn't, and they deserve to have their secrets kept."

Jean poured them both more wine. "But what if the secrets were really nasty? What if someone's a pedophile or a serial killer?"

"Martin would have gone to the police with anything like that. I'm sure the blue box was full of people who embezzled or cheated on their spouses or took bribes. I don't want anyone's life ruined because of a stupid mistake."

"OK," Jean said. "I see why you won't tell the police, but why not hire a detective?"

"I don't dare. If I hired an ethical one, he'd report anything criminal he uncovered to the authorities. I could pay a crooked detective enough to keep quiet, but what's to stop him from blackmailing the people in the blue box himself?"

"Well, what's left?" Jean said in exasperation. "You can't stand the killer being free, but you won't do anything to catch him."

Diane clasped her hands in her lap. "I've been thinking about this ever since we ran into Zeppo. I want you to do me a big favor."

"I'd do anything for you, honey, except stop drinking."

"Jean, this is serious."

"OK, sorry."

"You know how no one could ever figure out what Zeppo did all the time or why Martin paid him so much, gave him the Jaguar and stock options and so forth? His job title was 'special projects.' He must have been doing research for the blue box."

"I believe that," Jean said. "Martin wouldn't have wasted time digging up dirt on people when he could pay the weasel to do it. Plus Zeppo knows all about computers."

Diane nodded. "And now he's looking into Martin's death on his own."

"Well, sure. Martin was really important to him. But how do I fit in?"

"I want you to find out if Zeppo knows about the blue box. If so, I want you to offer to help him so you can keep an eye on him and protect the people who were being blackmailed."

"Say what? You want me to work with Zeppo?"

"Yes, as a favor to me. Please." Diane's voice shook slightly. "If the murderer is in the blue box, how else can we prove it? I only suspect a few names, and Zeppo must know all of them. He's the best chance I have of finding Martin's killer without revealing all the others. He obviously has a crush on you, so I'm sure he'll agree to let you help. Besides, you're smart, pushy, and incredibly nosy, and you've read a thousand mysteries. You're perfect for the job."

Jean thought about it. Diane was right—she *was* incredibly nosy. It was part of what made her a good reporter. She always examined other people's medicine cabinets, read their mail if they left it lying around, listened in on conversations. She was intensely curious about the blue box. She found it incomprehensible that Diane had never looked through it. Also, she loved mysteries, and the prospect of being involved in a real one was exciting. On the downside, she wasn't thrilled about spending time with Zeppo. Diane watched her, waiting for an answer.

"OK, I'll talk to him. But I'm not promising anything." Jean made a face. "Of course, this means I'll have to go to his apartment."

"I know, sorry. Maybe you should take a whip and a chair."

"Nah, he's harmless. I'm going over to Roman's for dinner tomorrow. I can see the weasel after that."

"Thank you, Jean."

"No problem." She yawned. "Now I think it's past our bedtime." They recorked the wine, went upstairs to the master bedroom, and climbed into bed.

CHAPTER 11

*A*t five o'clock the next day, Jean saved the file with her article on California sparkling wine, took the bus to Castro and Market, and walked toward her uncle Beau Reed's house. Beau, a retired professor of Russian history, was in St. Petersburg for a month doing research for a book. She bypassed his door and unlocked the side gate—she'd come to see Roman Villalobos, Beau's tenant and good friend, and her close friend, too.

Jean went through Beau's garden, a small, perfect oasis in the city, with a tall fence on either side and Roman's old carriage house at the back. A big shade tree with a bench around it dominated the yard, and a cedar table and chairs sat nearby. The mature perennial garden of deep blue and purple flowers was starting to bloom, and Jean could smell hyacinth.

She knocked on the door of the little gray house. "Roman?" she called, opening the door. She inhaled the earthy aroma of garlic and mushrooms.

"In here," he said from the kitchen. She walked through the house, which was done in pleasing shades of blue and gray, with Stickley and Mission-style furniture. The wallpaper and rugs bore William Morris designs. A Bach partita played on the stereo.

As she went down the hall, she turned away from the one disturbing element in this elegant home—a wall of framed portraits and snapshots of Roman's friends, more than fifty of them, mostly men and a handful of women, all young and smiling, all dead now of AIDS. She caught a glimpse of the latest addition, a man with curly brown hair and a wide, engaging smile—Chris, Roman's lover who'd died last fall. Jean sighed. At least Roman wasn't adding photos at the rate he used to.

Roman sat at the kitchen table slicing tomatoes and laying them on a plate. Jean came in behind him and kissed the top of his bald head, next to a long white scar that ran across his skull just above his fringe of short black hair. He turned and smiled at her. "Good to see you, Jean," he said in his deep, soft voice. He had high cheekbones, full lips surrounded by a neat goatee, a straight nose, and eyes so dark they looked black. A single gold earring made him look like a Spanish gypsy. He was the handsomest man Jean knew.

Roman stood and took a container of fresh mozzarella off the counter. Jean smiled with appreciation as she looked him up and down. He was tall and muscular, with dense black hair on his arms and the backs of his hands. He wore jeans and an old Hawaiian shirt with orange and yellow pineapples on it that Jean had made for him. Black chest hair peeked out the collar.

"Good to see you, too," she said. "What's for dinner?"

"This *caprese* salad, and pasta with a wild mushroom sauce. I found some chanterelles at the market today."

"Can we have Bordeaux? Diane and I were talking about Le Pin last night."

"Certainly. I'm out of Le Pin at the moment, but there should be something drinkable. How is Diane?" He interleaved basil leaves and slices of fresh mozzarella with the tomatoes.

"She's pulling herself together."

Roman poured boiling water and pasta through a colander in the sink, and put the drained pasta into a skillet full of mushroom sauce. "Pick out the wine, will you?"

Jean rooted in Roman's pantry and chose a dependable Bordeaux, which she opened and carried into his elegant dining room, setting it on the round pedestal table. She sat in one of the dining chairs, upholstered in a William Morris vine print. As they ate mushroom pasta and drank claret, Jean explained the blue box and Diane's concerns. She hadn't forgotten her promise not to tell anyone, but to her, "anyone" didn't include Roman. Besides, she wanted him to know all about the investigation in case she needed his help.

"Fascinating," Roman said when she had finished. "Although it doesn't surprise me—from all I've heard, Martin was a world-class bastard."

"He was that." She helped herself to tomato salad. "But finding his killer is important to Diane. One of his former employees is looking into his death, and she wants me to help."

"Really?" Roman said, arching a black eyebrow. "Has she lost her mind?"

Jean made a face at him. "I imagine she'll end up turning the whole works over to the police. This is just a way for her to feel that she's done everything she can to protect the people in the blue box."

"You two need to be careful," Roman said as he poured more wine. "Even if Diane doesn't know what the searchers are looking for, someone may think she does."

"We thought of that. She's hired some security guards to keep the bad guys out of the house and the press out of the azaleas." Jean ate a bite of mozzarella. "What about you? Keeping busy?"

"Very. I'm translating an opus on global warming into English."

"What language is it written in?"

"English, ostensibly. You'd never know it was the man's native tongue."

"You know," Jean said, "before Beau left he asked me to keep an eye on you."

"Whatever for?"

"He's worried about you. He says you sit home at night, brooding and drinking too much."

"Beau should mind his own business."

"How are you doing, Roman?"

"I have tolerable days, but they're still mostly bad."

"Are you seeing anyone yet?"

"No. I don't seem to be interested anymore."

She reached across the table and touched his hand. "I wish I could do something for you."

"I know how you'd handle it—you'd fuck me into sweet oblivion. I do appreciate the sentiment."

"Hey, why not give me a tumble?" she teased. "I might convert you."

He smiled at her. "You're cute in an extreme sort of way, but not really my type. Too much over-the-top muliebrity."

"Are you going to make me look that up?"

"It's the female equivalent of virility."

"Oh. Good word." She folded her napkin and laid it on the table. "Now I'm going across town to see the guy who's doing the investigating."

"What's he like?"

"A tall, skinny, obnoxious redheaded kid. He's hot for me."

"Not an unfamiliar situation for you."

"It's all that muliebrity. The guys can't leave it alone."

"Some of us can," he said, smiling. "Good luck detecting."

Jean knew she should stay and keep Roman out of the Bourbon, but she was too anxious to find out what Zeppo knew. After helping clean up, she said goodbye and caught a taxi to Cow Hollow.

CHAPTER 12

Zeppo's apartment was on a side street a couple of blocks from Union in an unremarkable two-story stucco building with a garage. Jean went up a short flight of steps and rang his bell.

Zeppo opened the door wearing sweat pants and a green Celtics T-shirt. "Jean!" he exclaimed. "I knew you'd change your mind. Let me take a shower and we'll get right to it."

"Cut the shit, Zeppo. I need to talk to you."

"All right—talk first, sex later. Come in."

He led her into his apartment, his big bare feet slapping like flippers on the hardwood floor. There were no rugs. "You want some wine?" he asked, going into the kitchen.

"Sure." She looked around with interest. His sparsely furnished studio was even smaller than hers. A navy comforter covered the single bed in the corner. A dinette table and two spindly chairs sat near the kitchen door. He'd tacked a poster of Van Gogh's self-portrait with a bandaged ear above the computer. Against one wall, shelving held a modest sound system, a small TV, CDs, and books. Jean had expected college-dorm clutter, but everything was neat and orderly.

Zeppo brought out two wine glasses and a nearly full bottle of an inexpensive Côtes du Rhône. He poured her some and she sipped it appraisingly. OK, but not great.

Zeppo turned the computer chair around so it faced the room and sat down. Next to the computer, a big glass paperweight with a plastic lobster inside held down a stack of papers. Jean, glass in hand, perused his books, a large and eclectic mix with a good selection of classic literature, including Homer's *Odyssey* and *Iliad*. She counted three of Hugh Rivenbark's novels. Zeppo's musical taste was also unexpected: He had a huge collection of CDs, mostly old blues. She saw no photos of the tall, redheaded, dysfunctional family she'd always imagined for him. In fact, there were no personal mementos visible at all.

"Have you read all these books?" she asked.

"Yeah, I've read them."

"Your apartment is even smaller than mine. Didn't Martin pay you enough for a nicer place?"

"I'm saving for a rainy day. You're a nosy broad, you know that?"

"So I've been told."

Zeppo took a sip of wine. "OK, if you didn't come here to seduce me, what brings you to my lair?"

Jean sank into the one overstuffed chair, which was covered in soft brown corduroy and very comfortable. She couldn't resist slipping off her shoes and pulling her feet up. "Diane has asked me a favor," she said. "Obviously you're looking into Martin's death. She wants me to find out if you know about the blue box."

"The blue box, huh? So the old fool showed it to her."

"Nope. She just noticed things that didn't seem right and confronted Martin about it."

"You're telling me the widow figured it out all by herself?"

"Yep. Diane's smart."

"You'd never know it. She works that helpless female thing to death."

"Stop insulting her. She happens to be one of my best friends."

"Don't get me wrong—I like her. And I know she had a rough childhood. But she's way too needy for my taste."

"That shouldn't bother anybody. I don't think you're in the running to replace Martin."

Zeppo laughed. "God forbid. She's too small, anyway. I prefer something I can get my teeth into, like you."

"Zeppo, could we please have one conversation that doesn't come back to sex?"

"OK, but just this once."

"She thinks your special project was the blue box. Is she right?"

Zeppo hesitated for a moment. "Yeah," he said. "I was in charge of research and verification for Martin's pet project."

"Why haven't you told the police about it?"

"I promised Martin I'd keep it quiet no matter what happened."

"Did all the material really get sent back to the victims?" Jean asked.

"All of it. I FedExed it myself. So Diane thinks the killer's one of them, right?"

"What do you think?"

"I think it's probable, since the police eliminated the suspects on the boat."

"How did you know that?" Jean asked in surprise. "The police told Diane, but I haven't heard it on the news."

He made a dismissive gesture. "Bribed a public servant. They're all underpaid. The woman I bribed said there were only seven people, including you and Peter, unaccounted for when Martin was pushed. The police checked those people's whereabouts for the time he was actually killed. They're in the clear, apparently. Which means someone pushed him off the boat and someone else killed him."

"And the second murderer could be anybody in San Francisco."

"Right. The woman also told me that Martin had THC in his system, and I've never known him to smoke dope. He barely even drank."

"That explains why he giggled on the phone—his rescuer must have gotten him stoned," Jean said. "Why do you suppose no one's claimed credit for saving him?"

"They don't want the hassle, or they've been at sea and don't realize what's happened. Or they were up to something illegal." He sat up straight. "Hey, I just had a brainstorm. Diane should offer a reward. Whoever pulled Martin out of the bay may have taken him to meet his killer. Let's give him an incentive to tell us."

"That's a great idea," Jean said. "How much should she offer?"

"Make it a lot of money. Say ten grand. If that doesn't work, she can up it."

"But she'll have every wacko in the Bay Area calling in."

"She can hire somebody to screen the calls."

"I'll phone her in the morning." Jean took a swallow of wine. Here came the distasteful part. "Diane asked me to help you investigate."

"You?" Zeppo chuckled. "What, she thinks you're Kinsey Millhone?"

"Nah, I have a much better haircut than Kinsey."

"And I bet you get laid more often."

"Zeppo, you promised."

"Sorry. So you want to be partners in detection, like Nick and Nora?"

"Not exactly."

"And I'm supposed to tell you everything Martin ever dug up on anyone, just like that, so you can broadcast it all over town. Give me a break."

"Listen, you weasel, Diane asked me to do this because she doesn't want any of the dirt getting into the media. After finding Martin's killer, her main concern is protecting the people you two were blackmailing."

Zeppo sighed. "Weasel. Most people would find that insulting. But I'll think of it as a term of endearment, coming from you."

"Could you focus on this, please?"

"You know, the more I think about it, the more I can see where you'd be useful to my investigation," Zeppo said. "For one thing, Diane can use her influence to get people to talk to you. I don't think she likes me. You're not dumb, and if you dress up right, we can get any information we want from the average straight male."

"I see. I'm going to wag my ass at the suspects until one of them confesses."

Zeppo grinned, showing his braces. "Exactly."

"You're a funny guy. What did you have on these people, anyway? What was so heavy that one of them would kill Martin even though he'd retired and sent all the proof back?"

"That's the big question, isn't it?" Zeppo leaned forward, his elbows resting on his knees. "Before we go into that, let's get a few things straight. You may have Diane's blessings, but I'm the one with all the dirt. Although there's a lot less of it than there used to be—Martin wasn't exactly keeping things current. Anyway, I've got good reasons to want the killer caught, too."

"Like what?"

"Like Martin did a lot for me. Other than money, I mean. I'll always owe him. Getting some justice for him is the least I can do."

"The people in the blue box probably think justice has already been done."

"Hey, we couldn't have blackmailed anybody if they hadn't screwed up first."

"Are you certain you never put the squeeze on an innocent person?"

"I'm absolutely certain," he said sharply. "I took verification seriously. Accuracy is very important to me."

"I'll take your word for it. For now."

"Just remember: All that's left of the blue box is right here," he said, tapping his temple with a long freckled finger. "Martin asked me not to make copies and I kept my promise. So if you want to know what was in it, you have to agree to do this my way."

"All right."

"I'm breaking a promise to Martin by telling you any of this, so we'll take it one suspect at a time. As soon as we eliminate someone, I'll tell you the next name on the list."

Jean frowned. "Come on, you're breaking the promise to find his killer. Don't you think he'd approve?"

"Maybe, but I have to live with myself."

"OK," Jean said, regarding him with a little more interest.

"You're hating this, aren't you?" Zeppo said. "You're only doing it for Diane. Come on, it'll be great—you get to see how a master operates."

"What's second prize? A month with you on a desert island?"

Zeppo sat up straight and raised his right hand. "How's this: I solemnly swear to cease all references to your awesome endowments or to the possibility of intimate relations between us for the duration of the investigation. When and if we bring the killer to justice, I reserve the right to resume harassing you." He put his hand down. "Happy?"

"Ecstatic." Jean thought of what Diane would owe her when this was over. Possibly her first-born child. Jean decided she'd rather have Martin's Porsche. "So can I get in on this?"

"Yeah, sure. It's probably a good idea not to do it alone. Let's drink to it." Zeppo poured them more wine and they clinked glasses. "You want to start now, partner? This won't take long. I've eliminated a lot of people."

"How?"

"Well, several of them have good alibis, like they were out of the country or recovering from surgery."

"What if someone hired it done?" Jean asked.

"We can think about that if the obvious suspects don't pan out."

"Who else you got?"

"In a lot of cases there's no longer an issue. We had one guy on the hook because he was cheating on his wife, but now they're divorced. There are a few more like that." Zeppo's nose was reddening and he was making gestures with his wine glass. He poured the last of the wine into their glasses.

Jean took a sip. "So how did you fill the blue box in the first place? How did you find all these sinners?"

"You really want the whole ugly story?"

"Yeah, I really do."

"Well, that calls for another bottle." He jumped up and went into the kitchen.

Jean recognized the trajectory of the inexperienced drinker. She'd leave when his speech started to slur—she didn't want to deal with any sexual advances from him. *In vino veritas* was a sound principle, but only up to a point. As far as tomorrow was concerned, it wouldn't be the first time she'd gone to work with a hangover.

Zeppo came back with another bottle of Côtes du Rhône and a plate of supermarket cheese and crackers. "Not exactly elegant, but I'm hungry," he said. He poured wine into her glass. "OK, here's the story. For years, Martin had a private detective working on the blue box, but he retired in 2007 and moved back to the Philippines. I got hired in 2008."

"What were you doing before that?"

"I was a bike messenger."

"Really? How'd you get from there to being Martin's assistant?"

"Let's not go off topic. Basically it worked like this: Martin would need something for a project, and we'd look at all the people who could give him what he wanted. I'd do research, pick up gossip from neighbors or servants or former spouses or employees. We usually found something we could use. Word was out that Martin would pay for information, and every now and then someone approached him with something to sell. He'd buy all reliable dirt just in case he'd need it later."

"How much did Frank know about this?"

"They had a very clear division of labor. Frank handled the day-to-day stuff like construction materials, labor, logistics. Martin was the idea man. Frank must have known Martin got things done outside conventional channels, but he never complained. It was sort of a 'don't ask, don't tell' kind of thing. Martin made him rich, after all."

"What did he think your job was?"

"Research. Everyone thought I did background research for Martin's long-range plans. Martin was vague about a lot of things, so no one thought it was weird."

"What about Kay? Seems he would have been quite a political liability."

"She must have realized that his business practices weren't strictly kosher, but I don't think she knew what was actually going on. Anyway, I bet she would have dumped him if he hadn't dumped her first."

Jean ate some cheese and crackers. "So who are you looking at seriously?"

"I'm nearly done with the first group of suspects, all the able-bodied men. You've seen the pier where they found Martin. It'd be hard to get an uncooperative or unconscious man out there and over the rail unless you were big and strong. And even though the pier is pretty deserted at night, especially in bad weather, you'd have to move fast so no one would see you."

"You could do it at gunpoint and hit him once you got there. There were bruises all over his head."

"Yeah, but it's not easy to hit someone hard enough to knock them out. That's another argument for muscles. The women in the box are either on the small side or too old to do it."

"Unless a small woman had help," Jean said.

"That's possible. We can look into that later. One of the last things Martin worked on was Armand Setrakian. He's the guy I like best for it."

"What did Martin want from a sculptor?"

"Land. Martin wanted to enlarge a housing development he was planning near Sonoma. In fact, that's the only project he was still involved in when he died. We needed something on one of the neighbors because none of them would sell, so Martin sent me after Setrakian, who owned a big chunk of land right next to the project. I'd heard of him, of course. I even like his work. I went up there and spent a couple of days talking to the locals, saying I was doing a profile on him for the U.C. Davis campus newspaper. I even interviewed the great artist. He was a pompous asshole, but I figured, so what? Picasso was an asshole, too.

"A few people made offhand remarks about him chasing women, but he's not married. Then this bartender got pissed as hell when I mentioned his name. She told me to go see her friend in Sausalito if I wanted to know what he was really like. Setrakian spends a lot of time in Sausalito because he shows in some galleries there. The friend worked at one of those waterfront restaurants. She was young and pretty—not in your league, but cute.

"I bought her a cup of coffee, and she told me that he was a regular at her restaurant and they got friendly. He asked her if she'd model for him and she said sure, figuring he's a nice guy, he's famous, what could happen? So she went to his studio and he came on really strong—she thought he was going to rape her. She got out of there in one piece, but it was close. She didn't do anything about it because it was her word against his and nothing actually happened, just groping and wrestling."

"What a prick!"

"You said it. Once I knew what I was looking for it was easy. I bribed a clerk at the county sheriff's office and hit the jackpot. Setrakian's had four complaints of attempted rape filed against him over the past five years, but in each case the charges were dropped. Since it never made the news, I assume he paid the women off."

"I guess if you're not bruised and bloody and full of semen, it's hard to get people interested," Jean said. "Too bad those women didn't go after him together."

"Even so, it would have been tough to convict him. Anyway, he recently got a million-dollar commission for a dozen statues from Elan, the women's clothing company. But Elan would cancel the commission in a heartbeat if they found out he was molesting potential customers—they sell to teens and young women and they've got a squeaky clean image. So Martin had a talk with lover boy and bought the acreage he needed."

"Served him right, the piece of shit."

"Yeah, I really enjoyed that one. I hate that kind of arrogant bully."

"So if he killed Martin, not only would he eliminate someone who could screw up his life, he might even stop the development right next to him," Jean said. "He sounds promising."

"After we talk to him, we'll start with the second group: women and men who could have killed him with help."

"Tell me something: Did Martin ever lose?"

"Oh sure. A lot of times the people I investigated were clean, so he had to give up on what he wanted or go through regular channels. A few people decided to 'fess up rather than do what he asked. And one guy got even."

"How?"

"Martin wanted to buy a building from a dude named Simon Emory who owned a few nightclubs, but he wouldn't sell. The building was in a neighborhood where Martin planned to build a mixed-use development. I found out that Emory employed a lot of illegals. But he told Martin to go fuck himself, that when *La Migra* came around all they'd find would be documented workers. The development had to be scaled back, which really pissed Martin off."

"It's good to know he didn't have it all his way," Jean said.

"It gets better. At the time, Martin was also building a business park in Modesto. The roofing contractor employed a bunch of illegals, and about a week after Martin talked to Emory, a guy from Immigration showed up at the Modesto site and arrested everybody. Martin paid a big fine. Emory must have done some research of his own and then called the *federales*."

"I'll bet Martin went ballistic."

"You should have seen him—it's amazing he didn't have his heart attack then. He wanted me to find more dirt on Emory, but I talked him out of it. I had a lot of other projects going and I told him we couldn't afford to waste our time on revenge."

"Is Emory on your list of suspects?"

"He's on the 'improbable' list—the clerk I bribed told me he has an alibi. But we still have to check him out. I'm not sure why the cops questioned him."

"Frank gave the police a list of people Martin had problems with. Emory must have been on it." Jean excused herself and went into the bathroom, which was as neat and clean as the rest of the apartment. A small framed print of a smiling, voluptuous Modigliani nude hung on the wall. The contents of the medicine cabinet were disappointingly ordinary. The only prescription drug was a bottle of sleeping pills. So his worst medical problem was insomnia.

She sat back down in the corduroy chair. "Is that all I get tonight?"

"There is one other thing. It's probably not important, but it's weird. Martin had something of Hugh Rivenbark's."

"Something he gave him? I thought they were buddies."

"Oh yeah, for years, but this wasn't in the blue box and Martin had me send it back right before I left the job. It was a handwritten manuscript of *Home to Greenwood*, the book that won the Pulitzer Prize in 1977. I read some interviews with Rivenbark, and he's got this thing about the creative process—it belongs solely to the writer and shouldn't be scrutinized by talentless academics. He shreds all earlier versions of his books once they're published. And he writes every draft longhand because he believes a writer's physical connection to the written word is essential, or some such horseshit." Zeppo emptied his glass. "So it didn't really seem like blackmail material—more of an annoyance."

"How did Martin get hold of it?" Jean asked.

"Rivenbark was married years ago, but his wife died soon after he got his Pulitzer. Her brother lives up in Mendocino, runs a bookstore, and he and Rivenbark are pals."

"Oh sure, Edward Bongiorni. I met him at the funeral."

"Rivenbark's got this big modern house called The Eyrie. Once when Martin was visiting he found the manuscript in a drawer and kept it, but I don't know why. Maybe just out of habit."

"That doesn't sound like much of a motive. Was there anything strange about it?"

"Not that I could see. I compared it to the published book, which wasn't easy—he's got big, sloppy handwriting all over the page. There were editing suggestions in different writing, and some of them were in the book and some weren't." He shrugged. "Like you said, not much of a motive. He *was* in the city that night—he has an apartment on Telegraph Hill, and he stayed there with the Bongiornis after the wedding."

"We can ask them about it," Jean said. "But unless we find out something new, I guess we should put Hugh on the 'improbable' list." They sat in silence for a few moments. "Tell me this," she asked. "If you sent everything back, why is someone searching everywhere?"

"All I can figure is that the old pirate had a game on the side I knew nothing about."

"You know what?" Jean said. "I think I may have another suspect."

"Oh yeah? Who?"

She told him about the counterfeit Le Pin from Treadway's wine shop.

Zeppo looked skeptical. "So you think this guy Treadway killed Martin over a bottle of wine?"

"Not just one. If he has a big counterfeiting operation going, we could be talking hundreds of bottles worth thousands of dollars. What if Martin threatened to shut him down?"

"He's worth a look. Why don't you make an appointment for us to see him? Tell him you're a famous wine writer."

"I *am* a famous wine writer."

"If you say so." Zeppo leaned back in his chair. "I never heard of Treadway before now. Sounds like Martin really did have stuff going on I didn't know about."

"I'm surprised he didn't get murdered a long time ago." Jean looked at Zeppo as if seeing him for the first time. "You're pretty good at this, aren't you?"

"That's what I've been telling you."

"I'll bet people underestimate you all the time."

"Yeah. Martin counted on it."

"So why hasn't the killer come after you? You know everything Martin knew."

"Right, but nobody's aware of that. They either didn't know I existed or thought I was just a gofer."

"But if we go around asking questions, they'll realize what you know. And what I know."

"We just have to be careful. We'll make it very clear that there are no copies and that we aren't interested in blackmailing anyone—we just want to know where they were on the night of the wedding. Of course, everyone will come up with some kind of alibi. Our job is to figure out who's lying."

"This is starting to sound dangerous."

Zeppo looked at her over his glasses. "You want out?"

"No way. Now that I know all this fascinating dirt, I have to see how it ends. I'm just worrying out loud." Jean wanted another cracker, but Zeppo had finished the entire plate of food. She looked at her watch. "Oh shit. It's late. I have to go home." She stood up.

He swayed a little as he stood. "You don't have to leave just because you got me drunk. I promise not to attack you unless you insist."

"I'm not afraid of you. I have to get some sleep."

"I'll call a cab."

"So what's our next move?" Jean asked after he'd ordered the taxi.

"Any chance you can take some days off?"

"I'll try to use my vacation days, but I'll have to go to work for a day or two to set things up."

"OK, when your vacation starts we'll talk to Treadway. Then later we'll go up north to see Setrakian."

In a few minutes, the cab honked in front of Zeppo's building.

"That was very enlightening, Zeppo," Jean said. "This is the first time I've seen you without your clown suit."

"Say the word and I'll take everything off."

Jean rolled her eyes. "Good night, Zeppo." She trotted down the steps to the waiting cab.

CHAPTER 13

$\mathcal{T}$he next day Jean, wearing a gray pencil skirt and white sweater with a wide black belt, went to work with only a slight hangover. The main office was an open room filled with a dozen cubicles. Four private offices lined the back wall, and a corridor led to the production department and conference room. Jean phoned Diane from her cube. "You were right about Zeppo and the blue box," she told her friend. "And you've got yourself a crack team of investigators."

"Thank you so much, Jean. I feel better just knowing that."

"But if we don't make any progress by the end of my vacation, you'll have to turn the whole thing over to the police. Agreed?"

"Agreed. Why don't I pay you for your time? I know you never have enough money."

"No thanks," Jean said. "But I might need some if I have to travel. And you can give me a few bottles of Le Pin."

"I'd be happy to."

"Zeppo came up with a suggestion last night." She told Diane about offering a reward.

"That's a good idea. I'll get right on it. Oh, and you'll need a car. I thought of letting you use the Porsche, but I don't want your death on my conscience. So I arranged for you to borrow one of the company cars. How's that sound?"

"Just because a person totals a car doesn't mean she can't drive."

"What does it mean when she rolls a car in broad daylight on an empty highway?"

"I'm a good driver," Jean insisted. "The Escort's engineering wasn't up to the demands I was making. The Porsche wouldn't have rolled."

"Nonetheless, I think a Corolla is a better idea. You'll have to go to the office and get it. Ask for Jeffrey, the receptionist. And drive carefully, for God's sake."

"Hey," Jean said, "you set it up already. How'd you know I'd go for it?"

"Because I know you. You're a born snoop and can't resist a challenge. You couldn't say no to a thing like this, even if it meant spending time with Zeppo."

"I hate being such an open book. Talk to you later."

Jean poked her head into her editor's office. Kyle, in a vintage camp shirt with a royal flush in hearts embroidered on the chest pocket, was on the phone, but motioned for her to sit down. "You know we love your work," Kyle said into the phone. "But it's all about digital now. You don't want to be stuck in the Stone Age when everyone else is riding the wave of the future."

He must be talking to their Central Coast photographer, a retired newsman who had no email and would only submit slides. "You're mixing your metaphors," Jean told him when he'd hung up.

Kyle rolled his eyes. "Everybody's an editor."

"Any luck with him?"

"Not so far. If his images weren't so good, I'd hire some kid with a digital camera."

"But they are really good, and he'll work for the pittance we pay," Jean said. "Hey, listen, I need a favor. Is it OK if I take my vacation now? Diane Wingo wants me to help her with some things relating to Martin's death." Jean thought mentioning the name "Wingo" might influence Kyle in the right direction.

"Let's take a look." Kyle typed on his laptop. "OK, I've got your Central Coast piece, the Merryvale profile, the California bubbly story, the two restaurant reviews, and five shorts for the news page. How's the Port story coming?"

"I'll finish it today."

"When that's done you can take your vacation. Put a note on your blog that says you'll be out. And you have to come in early next week when we get the slides from Mr. Stone Age and ID the Central Coast people. I don't know half those bozos."

"I thought you knew everyone in the wine world," Jean said.

"Everyone important. These are a bunch of geographically challenged wannabes."

"Didn't you read my article, you snob? They're making some pretty fabulous wines."

"So come in and ID the poor slobs."

"All right. Call me when you get the slides."

"You got a cell yet or you still living in the Stone Age, too?"

"Still hate them," Jean said. "Call my home phone."

Back in her cube, Jean did some research on Treadway's Fine Wines and Spirits and made an appointment with the owner for six o'clock. She then pulled out her handwritten notes and focused on writing up a tasting of two dozen vintage Ports she'd attended recently. Contrary to what most of her friends thought, her job wasn't all fun and games. She'd sat through more tastings of bad wines than she cared to remember, and writing up a big tasting like this one was a real challenge—she had to convey in words exactly how each wine looked, smelled, and tasted without being repetitive.

Zeppo called in the afternoon and arranged to meet her at the Wingo-Johansen office after work to pick up the Corolla. He'd decided to leave the Jag home.

At five o'clock Jean turned in the Port story and was officially on vacation. She took the bus to Martin's former office, a low modern structure built right on Pier 3. In the spacious reception area, light reflected from the water danced across the room's surfaces. A dozen architectural models were displayed on Lucite pillars near the big windows.

Jean went up to the reception counter, where a plump, clean-cut young man answered phones. A plaque on his desk said "Jeffrey Weiss."

"Hi, I'm Jean Applequist. You have a car for me."

"Oh, sure. Here you go." He handed her a set of keys. "The cars are in the lot across the street. And Zeppo just called—he's going to be late on account of his bus broke down."

Jean thanked him and wandered over to look at the models. In a nearby alcove she saw one she hadn't noticed before. The building was off-white cardboard and foam core with tiny fake trees like the rest of the models, but it was a bizarre conglomeration of Greek columns, flying buttresses, Islamic arches, and Russian onion domes. Several little gray gargoyles stared down from a section of pagoda roof. A plaque on its base said "The Martin Wingo Building."

In the corridor to her right she spotted Keith Yoshiro carrying an armload of rolled-up blueprints. "Keith," she called, gesturing at the patchwork model. "What in the world is this?"

Keith came over, chuckling. "Martin's forty-eighth birthday present. It was Zeppo's idea. I drew it for him and the production department built it. That was the kind of thing he did for Martin. I hope you've stopped suspecting him."

"Yeah, he's in the clear."

Keith glanced at his watch. "Sorry, Jean, I have to run. Good seeing you."

He headed down the hall and Jean went back to the receptionist's desk. She had an idea. "Jeffrey, is there anybody on the staff who was friendly with Zeppo?"

"He used to hang around the production department."
Jeffrey grinned. "That's where most of the young single
women work. Gwen Lansing is still here. He went out to
lunch with her sometimes."

"Could I talk to her?"

"Sure. Go down the hall and turn right. She's the one
who looks like Morticia Addams."

The production department reminded Jean of the one
at her magazine—a large desk and two smaller ones, each
with a large-screened Macintosh computer on it, with a
light box on an old drawing table off to the side.

Jean spotted Gwen right away, a slim young woman with
long black hair, a black leotard, raggedy black velvet skirt,
and black cowboy boots. Her nail polish, lipstick, and heavy
eye makeup were also black. She sat at one of the Macs
using Photoshop to sort through images of buildings.

"Excuse me, are you Gwen?"

"Yeah." She looked up.

"Hi, I'm Jean Applequist, a friend of Diane Wingo's.
Could I have a minute?"

"Sure. I've heard of you—you're dating Peter Brennan,
right? I think he's a real hunk."

"I agree," Jean said. "So Gwen, didn't Martin harass
you about your look? Even my haircut bothered him."

"Oh sure. He complained to the production manager
a couple of times, but she told him to butt out. Anyway, I
tone it down for the office."

Jean tried to imagine Gwen on her day off. "Well, the
reason I'm here is I'd like to ask some questions about Jay
Zeppetello. I'm going to be working on a research project
with him, and I don't want to end up doing everything
myself or getting groped if we're working late."

Gwen gave her a skeptical look. "A research project,
huh? You work at a wine magazine. Zeppo doesn't know
dick about wine except that he likes it if it's red."

Jean had a white lie ready. "It's research for an article on land use in wine country."

"OK, ask away," Gwen said. "There's not a lot I can tell you, though. He's a pretty reserved guy."

"Did he ever talk about his job here?"

"Not really. He did research for Martin is all I know. He was out of the office a lot." Gwen swiveled her chair to face Jean. "Martin was a real asshole, but he had a soft spot for Zeppo."

"I guess Zeppo's sort of a junior asshole, huh?"

"Nah, he's a sweetie. We miss him. He was always buying stuff for us—the gals back here in production. Like See's candy or fresh croissants from that bakery in the Ferry Building."

"You know much about him? Like where he's from?"

"He never talks about himself. And if you ask him about his family, he tells a different tall tale every time. They were eaten by lions on safari, they drowned when their yacht sank, they committed suicide as part of a doomsday cult. I figure he's got a nice religious family in the Midwest somewhere and doesn't want to admit it. You know, lots of normal siblings, Dad coaches football, Mom makes quilts."

Jean blinked. That was a pretty good description of her own family.

"He seems sort of goofy, but he's really smart," Gwen said. "You don't need to worry about being groped, either. He's always coming on to you, but in a silly way. It was strange. He obviously loved hanging out back here, but he never really got to be good friends with anyone."

"Have you gone out with him?"

"Nah. I like him, but I'm not his type. That boy's got a type, for sure. My friend Polly dated him, and so did one of the girls in word processing. They're tall and curvy, like you. They both told the same story: They went out a few times, fucked a few times, but pretty soon he stopped calling and wouldn't return their calls. They say he's fun and nice to be with, but kind of distant, you know?" Gwen grinned. "And also that he goes all night."

"No kidding," Jean said.

"Yeah, they both said so. Polly thought he was too much. Sometimes when I get an itch I think about calling him. Haven't done it yet. But every now and then a girl's in the mood for some serious fun with no strings attached, you know what I mean?"

Jean grinned back. "Yeah," she said. "I know what you mean."

CHAPTER 14

Jean got back to the lobby just as Zeppo pushed open
the big glass door. He looked almost like a grown-up in
a yellow button-down shirt, black slacks, and gray tweed
jacket.

"Sorry I'm late," he said. "I had to walk from Stockton
Street."

"No problem. I've been keeping busy."

"Hey, Zeppo," Jeffrey called. "What's happening, dude?"

"Not much," Zeppo said, walking over to the reception
counter.

"Too bad you got laid off when you did. There was a hot
girl in here looking for you."

"Oh yeah? Who was she?"

"Beats me. She ended up talking to Martin. Skinny little
blue-eyed blonde with great skin and an accent. Maybe
Russian. I've got a thing for natural platinum blondes."

Zeppo glanced at Jean. She saw a flicker of something
in his eyes and moved over to the counter. "Not my type,"
he said. "When was this, exactly?"

"The last day Martin was here cleaning out his office.
He talked to her for twenty minutes or so. Set up the camera
and everything."

"What else did you notice about her?"

Jeffrey made a face. "She had a boyfriend waiting for
her. I thought of hitting on her until I saw him. Really buff,

shaved head, spider-web tattoos all over his arms, one of those guys."

"That's tough. Hey, if you think of anything else about her, give me a call, OK?"

"I'll do that. Later, dude."

Jean followed Zeppo toward the door. They passed the models on the way out and she gestured at the Martin Wingo Building. "Martin's building is hilarious."

"He liked it a lot, too. Said he was going to take it home with him. I guess he never got around to it."

They dashed across the Embarcadero. "Why were you asking about that girl?" Jean said.

"Remember Simon Emory, the guy who hires illegals? A lot of them are Eastern European. She asked for me first and Martin used the DVD-cam. That means she was selling information. What if she works for Emory?"

"We should check it out," Jean said.

"He's usually here in town at the nightclub Martin tried to buy. Sputnik."

"I've heard of it. Supposed to be full of club kids from the Peninsula."

"I wouldn't know. I tried to get in a couple of times but couldn't."

"Why not?"

"Too geeky. They've got these fierce bouncers who only let you in if you look cool enough. That's where you come in, partner—you can get us inside. We'll go tonight. OK with you?"

In the lot across the Embarcadero, the parking attendant pointed out a beige Corolla. Jean unlocked the doors and Zeppo folded himself awkwardly into the passenger seat. As his shoulder brushed hers, she thought of what Gwen had said about his sex drive. At least nature had given him something to compensate for his unlovely appearance.

"What'd you dig up on Treadway?" Zeppo asked as Jean pulled out of the lot.

"Nathan Treadway moved here from London and opened his shop in the mid-1960s, selling fancy wine," she told him, navigating through rush-hour traffic toward Union Square. "This was before anybody but the most effete snobs could tell Chablis from Shinola. Nathan knew his wine, and he developed quite a following. He supports good causes, like feeding the homeless."

"I guess you can't complain too much about his high prices. Sounds like he's robbing the rich to give to the poor."

"That's why his running a phony wine scam sounded so unlikely," Jean said. "But Nathan retired in 2001 and turned the business over to his son Travis, a former dot-com executive whose company had just imploded."

"I get it: High-end wine meets dot-com ethics. What was he selling?"

"Online dry cleaning, if you can believe it." Jean zipped across an intersection at the tail end of a yellow light, narrowly missing a city bus. "I told Travis I'm doing a story on fine wine shops in San Francisco."

"We can have dinner after we talk to him and then go to Sputnik," Zeppo said.

"What about Setrakian?"

"I don't want him to know it's me until we get there. You email him and say you're an art lover who wants to see the great man at work. We'll include a photo, so he'll go for it."

"If you say so." Jean cut off a limousine as she darted around a car turning left.

Zeppo seemed unfazed by all the honking. "Let me do the talking with him, OK?"

"What, you think I'm an idiot?"

"No, I think you might lose your temper. You may be the girl of my dreams, but you have lousy self-control."

"And I suppose you have great self-control."

"Yeah," he said. "That's one thing I've got. I've had a lot of practice."

She looked at him quizzically—he didn't seem to be joking. "OK, but I'm not going to sit there like a lump," she said. "I get to ask questions, too."

"As long as you stay calm. In fact, you take the lead with Treadway—you're the famous wine writer."

Treadway's was right off Union Square next to a very expensive florist. Behind its glass front it looked like the inside of a wine cave, with arched ceilings and rustic wooden beams. The shop was cool and smelled faintly of good wine. At a small tasting bar off to one side, a tall, athletic-looking guy poured white wine for a pair of under-dressed tourists.

A man of about forty with slightly protruding teeth greeted Jean and Zeppo. He had wavy brown hair cut in a stylish mop and wore a green Tommy Bahama shirt and dark slacks.

"You're Jean Applequist," he said warmly. "I've seen you at a couple of tastings. I'm Travis Treadway."

Jean shook his hand. "This is Jay Zeppetello."

"Good to meet you. Are you the photographer?"

"He's a student intern," Jean said. "He wants to be a wine writer just like me when he grows up." Zeppo smiled faintly.

"He looks pretty well grown to me," Travis said, winking at Jean. His glasses were trendy narrow rectangles.

"How about a tour of your shop?" She pulled a note-book out of her purse and pretended to take notes.

"Well, sure. We're famous for our extensive offerings of top-notch tequilas. We now have the largest selection of tequila in Northern California. We're reaching out to a younger clientele, and tequila's *the* happening spirit right now."

"I'm here from *Wine Digest*," Jean said, stressing the word "wine." Zeppo poked her in the ribs and she forced a smile.

"Of course," Travis said. "Step over here."

He led them to a long display case of premium California wines. All the top names were there, even older vintages of wines available only through mailing lists. The prices were so high they made Jean blink. She looked closely at the foils on the necks of the bottles but could see no evidence of tampering. "You've got all the cult Cabs, I see. Seven Stones Winery, Screaming Eagle, Harlan Estate, Harrison Vineyards, PlumpJack . . . oh, and here's a twenty-year-old Stony Hill Chardonnay. How'd you get your hands on these?"

"A lot of it is from auctions and the rest from private sources. I just bought an awesome cellar from a guy in Atherton who had to quit drinking on doctor's orders."

Jean picked up a Carneros Pinot Noir she especially liked. "I saw this for ten dollars less at a wine shop in Noe Valley. Your markups are pretty high, aren't they?"

Travis shrugged. "I have to pay the rent on Union Square, not in Noe Valley. I provide free delivery and free consulting. At the end of the day, my customers are willing to pay a little more for a lot more service."

"Customers like Martin Wingo?"

Travis hesitated. "He came in here a few times. Terrible what happened to him."

"Wasn't it, though?" Jean said mildly. "Don't you have a good selection of Bordeaux?"

"Right over here." Travis led them to a locked glass-front cabinet that held several top Bordeaux from good vintages—Margaux, Ausone, Lafite, Haut-Brion, Pétrus, and a single bottle of 1998 Le Pin.

"Martin was particularly fond of '98 Le Pin, wasn't he?" Jean asked.

Travis's toothy smile faded a little. "That's right. Like many of my clients, he wanted only the best and could afford to pay for it."

The tourists bought a bottle of wine and left, and the tall man went into the back room. The store was empty. "Look,

Travis," Jean said. "I do work for *Wine Digest*, but that's not why we're here. I'm the one who spotted the fake Le Pin last fall. I know all about your arrangement with Martin."

His geniality disappeared and he looked around nervously. "Let's talk in my office." He led them back to a small storeroom packed with boxes. "Felix," he said to the clerk, who was shifting cases around, "take over for a few minutes, will you?"

"Roger that," Felix said.

They went into a tiny office in the corner of the storeroom. Inside, Jean and Zeppo squeezed into two uncomfortable wooden chairs facing an old metal desk. On the wall was a framed studio portrait of a pretty dark-haired woman and two equally pretty adolescent girls in braces—they'd probably inherited Dad's toothy grin.

Travis sat behind the desk and glared at Jean. "So you're the wine expert he threatened me with," he said. "What's your angle? His widow doesn't want the case of Le Pin anymore. Should I send it to you?"

"We don't want your wine either," Jean said. "We're looking into Martin Wingo's death. All you have to do is tell us where you were when he died."

"Why should I talk to you at all?"

"If you don't cooperate, I'll write about your little hobby in my magazine."

"You're looking at a libel suit if you print a single word that implicates me in any way. I'll even charge you with extortion. Felix will back me up a hundred percent."

"So he's in on the scam, too, huh?" Zeppo said. "Don't worry, we won't print it in the mag—too much legal hassle. We'll tell your father."

Travis's eyes widened. "Hey, don't do that," he said, his threatening tone gone. "It would really upset him. It might kill him—his health isn't good."

"I bet your wife is clueless, too," Zeppo said. "She probably thinks you're just a great businessman."

Jean saw fear and defeat in Travis's eyes. "No. You can't tell her. If she finds out, I'm finished." He ran a hand through his mop of hair. "You don't understand how it is. When everything crashed I had a huge mortgage and two girls in private school. This place barely generated half what I was earning at the dot-com. What was I supposed to do? Move my family to a trailer in Pacifica?"

"Your father lived on the income from this shop and gave money to charity," Jean said.

Travis made a dismissive gesture. "Yeah, and he's got a house he bought for nothing in the sixties and three kids who went to public schools. I'm living on a different planet. Look, I'm not putting Night Train into those bottles. I've worked in this shop since high school, so I know as much about wine as my old man. I always give them something that tastes like what they paid for. Ninety-nine point nine percent of the people who come in here don't know the difference. If someone complains, I tell them it must have been a bad bottle and give them one of the real thing or something equivalent. It's only happened a few times." He pushed his glasses up and rubbed his eyes. "Once with Wingo."

"Here's the deal," Zeppo said. "We won't bother you again if you tell us where you were that night, and if your story checks out."

Travis looked hard at Zeppo, then at Jean. "OK. I was over at Felix's place in the Richmond working on a batch of counterfeit bottles. My wife thought I was at a tasting in St. Helena. We worked until around one A.M., then had a few drinks at a bar down the street from his house, the Cock and Bull. Afterward we went back to his place and I slept on the sofa."

"What's Felix's full name?" Zeppo asked.

"Felix Ursini."

"He looks more like a boxer than a wine geek," Zeppo said.

"He was in the fight game for a while, but he got smart and got out."

"What were you making at his place?" Jean asked.

"Whipping up a batch of Marcassin Chardonnay, the 2003 Sonoma Coast Marcassin Vineyard. I can sell it for $400 a bottle. I've got my own special blend. The result might fool even you."

"Not a chance," Jean said. "That's one of my favorite wines."

Travis leaned forward, elbows on the desk. "Now, I hope we're all on the same page here. I've told you what you want to know, so I expect you to leave me in peace."

"If your story checks out, no problem," Zeppo said. "Let's talk to Felix."

They went back to the store and waited while a well-dressed older man bought a bottle of Bollinger Champagne. Jean observed Felix as he worked. His white polo shirt was snug across a muscular chest, his khaki slacks tight around his thighs. He had strong Mediterranean features, close-cropped dark curly hair, and a scar through his right eyebrow.

As soon as the customer left, Travis went behind the counter and clapped Felix on the shoulder. "Felix," he said, "tell these lovely people where I was the night Wingo died."

Felix narrowed his muddy brown eyes. "At a tasting up valley, with me."

"Now tell them where I really was. I'll explain later."

Felix looked them over for a moment. "At my house and the local bar, all night." He grinned. "We were working on my stamp collection."

Travis spread his hands and smiled at Jean and Zeppo. "I rest my case."

"Thanks for your time, Travis," Zeppo said. "I hope you won't hear from us again."

They left the shop and walked toward the parking garage. "How many of those pricy bottles do you think were fakes?" Zeppo asked.

"Impossible to say without opening them," Jean said.

"What's Marcassin? I never heard of it."

"It means 'wild pig.' The owner-winemaker makes really kick-ass Chardonnay and Pinot Noir. Hell, everything she makes is kick-ass. And he's right—it sells for hundreds of dollars."

Zeppo shook his head. "I can't believe a bottle of wine could be worth that much."

"You would if you tasted it," Jean said. "What did you think of Travis?"

Zeppo leaned toward her, frowning solemnly. "Reaching out and going forward, I hope we'll all be on the same page at the end of the day."

Jean laughed. "Besides that."

"I think he's a sleaze, but that guy Felix is another story. He looks dangerous."

"Travis may be a sleaze, but I can't see him committing murder. Why would he? Martin wasn't threatening to shut down his operation—he was just costing him money. And the man's a wimp. You saw how fast he folded when you mentioned his wife."

"Felix could have done it on his own," Zeppo said. "We'll look into it. Although I'd hate to fuck things up for Travis's wife and kids. They'll figure out Dad's a dick soon enough."

They passed the Fault Line, a new California grill Jean hadn't been to, and Zeppo paused to read a menu posted in the front window. "Hey, this looks good. You want to eat here?"

"Sure." Jean looked the menu over as well. "But it's expensive."

"I'll buy you dinner in honor of our partnership."

Jean thought about it. Three businessmen exited the restaurant and she caught the seductive aroma of grilling meat. "Let's do it," she said.

The big, hushed restaurant was a sea of beige—walls, carpets, tablecloths, and upholstery were all the same neutral shade. The waiters even wore beige aprons. The lighting was subdued, the classical music soft. "This place looks like a sensory deprivation chamber," Jean said.

"It sure doesn't smell like one," Zeppo said.

The maître d' seated them in a booth, and Jean read the impressive wine list with professional interest. The list of wines by the glass was extensive; she looked behind the bar and saw a large Cruvinet, a machine that could keep dozens of open bottles fresh using nitrogen. *Wine Digest's* readers should know about this place; she made a mental note to pitch a profile to Kyle.

Zeppo told her to order for him, and she asked for two glasses of New Zealand Sauvignon Blanc. Jean loved its clean, crisp, grassy flavors.

"Hey, this is great," Zeppo said as he sipped his. "I usually only drink red."

"I'm broadening your horizons. We'll have red with dinner."

Zeppo ordered filet mignon with scalloped potatoes and porcini mushrooms. Jean wanted something that would suit a fine Cab, so she ordered lamb with polenta and beets. She chose a Napa Cabernet and soon was in ecstasy, eating perfectly cooked lamb loin and drinking fine red wine.

Zeppo seemed to be enjoying his meal as much as she was. He held his glass up. "I love this wine, Jeannie. You'll have to get me more like this to try."

"Sure. Full-bodied reds are my favorite, too."

They spent a pleasant hour and a half talking about wine, Zeppo asking questions and Jean holding forth on the differences between California Cab and Bordeaux. As they walked to the car Jean had to loosen her belt a notch. Hanging out with Zeppo would make her fat if she weren't careful.

"What now?" Jean asked. "It's too early to go to the nightclub."

"Let's go to your place. We can send the email to Setrakian and you can change clothes. You've got red wine on your sweater, by the way."

Jean looked. "Shit. That always happens. It's not easy having a shelf right there."

Zeppo started to say something, but stopped himself. "No comment."

CHAPTER 15

Jean's building was on a steep hill above the 24th Street business district. Miraculously, they found a parking place half a block away. She retrieved her mail and led Zeppo up two flights of stairs to her studio apartment.

Like many San Franciscans, Jean had sacrificed space for a good view, and she could see a sliver of the bay in the distance out the front window. The apartment itself was less than scenic. Clean laundry filled the window seat. Against one wall stood a table where a sewing machine was barely visible beneath a pile of fabric, patterns, and notions. A dressmaker's form stood nearby. Books and magazines were stacked here and there. The bed wasn't made and a large heap of shoes blocked the open closet door. Dust covered the few exposed surfaces.

Zeppo glanced around the room. "Why, Jeannie. You're a slob."

"There are worse flaws." She flipped through the mail.

"Oh sure. It's just interesting."

"If you want to sit down, move something."

"I'm fine." He examined her sewing area. "You make your own clothes?"

"Most of them. I'm hard to fit."

"I can imagine." He ran his hands over the dressmaker's form. "Ah, perfection," he said with a sigh.

"Enjoy yourself. That's as close as you'll ever get."

Chuckling, he wandered over to the bulletin board above her desk and looked at her collection of photos. "You travel a lot, huh?"

"Whenever I can afford it, which isn't often enough. I get to travel for my job sometimes. A few months ago I went to Bordeaux."

"Does Peter go with you? He's not in any of these pictures."

"I prefer going alone. You meet more interesting people that way."

Zeppo pulled down a large photo. "Is this the whole Applequist clan?"

She glanced over his shoulder. "Yeah. Dad's seventieth birthday."

"That's quite a crowd."

"I have five older siblings, all married, with a total of fourteen kids."

"Jeez. What are they, Mormons or Catholics or something?"

"Baptists. Similar principle."

"Do all the sisters have bodies like yours?"

"They did until they started having babies."

"You look out of place with all these happy breeders."

"I feel out of place. I'm the official black sheep."

"Me too."

Jean cleared magazines off the desk chair, sat down, and booted up her computer. She pressed the message button on her phone and Peter's voice asked her to call him at work. "What's Setrakian's email address?" she asked Zeppo.

"I emailed it to you earlier today."

"Here it is. OK, what do I say?"

"Tell him you'd like to come up sometime this week."

"What about a photo? I don't have anything scanned in."

"Open the attachment on my email."

"If it's Pamela Anderson, he'll know we're lying." Jean opened the image—a photo of her in the salon of the *Walrus* with a wine glass in her hand, wearing shorts and a red parka.

Jean looked up at him. "How do you happen to have a photo of me?"

"I won't tell," he said. "You'd get too conceited."

Jean typed what she hoped was a gushing, starstruck note explaining that she was a tourist from Indiana who planned to drive up to Sonoma this week and wanted to stop by Setrakian's studio. Zeppo read it over and she sent it.

"You know what?" Zeppo said. "We'll be halfway there, so why don't we go up to Mendocino and see Hugh Rivenbark? I don't consider him a suspect, but maybe he'll have some ideas. He knew Martin pretty well."

"That's a good idea. Let's do it."

"We might have to stay overnight—that's a three-hour drive. We can take my car."

"Great. I love your car." Jean thought about eating in restaurants for two days—she'd need some exercise. "Can the Jag take a bike rack? We might have time for a ride."

"Oh sure. I had a rack made for it. That would be fun, Jeannie. I've never been there, but I hear it's great cycling."

"My friend Roman and I go up there a lot to ride." She stood up.

"Shouldn't you call Peter?"

"Oh yeah." She sat back down and dialed his number. "Hi, Peter. What's up?"

"Diane told me about the blue box," he said, clearly upset. "It's unbelievable."

"Believe it. Martin was even worse than I thought."

"I only handled his personal affairs, so I didn't know much about the business. It really blows me away."

"I hope you understand why she wants to keep things quiet," she said.

"I understand, but I don't agree. I think she should tell the police everything."

"You're not going to spill the beans, are you?"

Peter sighed. "No, I'll respect her wishes. Why don't you come over? I'll make dinner and we can talk about this mess. I'll rent a film noir."

"I already ate. Anyway, I can't come right now. We're going to see a suspect."

"Who?" he demanded. "Are you sure it's safe?"

"It's a nightclub owner and it's perfectly safe. We'll be in a public place."

"How about coming over after that?"

"OK, but it may be late. I'll call you."

"This is crazy, Jean. Some of those people on Martin's list might be desperate, and the killer certainly is."

"Peter, I don't want to argue. See you later." Jean hung up and turned to Zeppo. "Diane told him about the blue box and he's all hot and bothered, but says he won't go to the cops."

"Will he keep his word?"

"Of course. But he's worried we'll bumble around until someone kills us, too."

"He's got no reason to have confidence in me, but he must know you're not helpless." Zeppo gestured at the bulletin board. "I mean, some of these places you've been look pretty rugged. This one with the giraffe has to be Africa."

"Kenya."

"And where's this one with the far-out mosques or whatever they are?"

"That's Registan Square in Samarkand."

"Wow. Did you ever get into trouble, going alone?"

"A couple of times, but nothing serious." That wasn't strictly true. Once she'd hidden for two hours in a Mayan tomb while a couple of drunk Australians she'd brushed off in a bar searched for her; she'd been saved from rape or worse by the timely arrival of a Japanese tour group. In Medan, on Sumatra, she'd been chased by a stone-throwing mob of Muslim fundamentalists because of her immodest shorts and T-shirt. That time an Agence France-Presse reporter in a rented car had rescued her. But usually she got out of scrapes by herself. The thrill of a little danger was one of the things that made traveling alone so much fun.

"Then Peter ought to trust you not to screw up," Zeppo said.

"He's just overprotective."

"Well, I'll do my best to make sure that neither of us gets hurt." Zeppo glanced at his watch. "OK, go ahead and get changed. I assume you've got something skimpy and black."

"Everyone else will be wearing black." Jean looked through her closet with a critical eye. It had to be sexy enough to charm puffed-up, self-important bouncers and cool enough to get Zeppo in, too. She pulled out a designer dress she'd bought for next to nothing because it had a broken zipper, which she'd repaired easily. The short, slinky dress had a deep V-neck, and best of all it was red, her favorite color. As an afterthought, Jean dug in her jumble of shoes for a pair of black peep-toe sling-backs with three-inch heels she'd bought on sale and never worn. She changed in the bathroom, adding a pair of silver hoop earrings and a squirt of Opium perfume.

"Wow," Zeppo said when she emerged. "That should get us inside. I've never seen you in heels before."

"You may never see it again. These are fucking uncomfortable."

"They look great. You'll just have to suffer. Got any makeup?"

"I'll do mascara, but no lipstick. I hate the way it sticks to wine glasses."

When Jean was dolled up to his satisfaction, she put on a short black jacket and they drove to Zeppo's apartment. Jean pawed through his neat drawers and closet, coming up with black jeans, a lightweight crewneck sweater, also black, and dark loafers.

Jean looked him over when he came out of the bathroom. His hair was cut too short and the braces were a disaster, but he would do. "Push the sleeves up," she told him. "That's better."

They decided to avoid crowded Union Street and take side streets back toward Van Ness. Jean drove through the residential neighborhood and noticed Zeppo turning to look behind them every few seconds. "What's up?" she asked.

"I think someone's following us."

"For real?" She glanced in the rearview mirror. "Which car?"

"That dark green one three cars back. He's been with us at least since my house. Let's make sure." Jean made a few turns at random.

"He's still there," Zeppo said. "It's too dark to see his face."

They passed through a bright streetlight, the green car just a few yards behind them now. "Wait a minute," Zeppo said as their tail drove through the pool of light. "Shit. It's Felix."

"Now what?"

"We could lose him. I've seen it done in movies."

Jean wasn't sure what they should do, but she knew who to ask. "Look, Zeppo, I'm going to drive out to the main drag and park. Let's talk this over."

She drove across Van Ness and pulled into a bus stop off Union. Felix cruised by once. When she didn't see him again, she assumed he'd found a nearby spot to watch from.

"I think we need professional advice," Jean said. "I'm going to call my friend Roman. But before I do, you should know something. I told him about the blue box."

Zeppo frowned. "How come, Jeannie?"

"He's one of my best friends, he's really smart, and he can keep a secret. I want his advice on all this."

"The whole point is to keep this thing quiet," he said. "Too many people already know about it."

"But he can help us. And I swear I won't tell another soul."

Zeppo thought about it. "What does he do for a living?"

"He's a freelance book editor."

He gave her a look. "So when you're in a jam, you call an editor?"

"Roman's also one of the founders of Bash Back."

"Self-defense for gays and lesbians, right? They're supposed to be tough."

"They are tough. Roman teaches martial arts. I've taken several of his classes."

"OK, give him a call," Zeppo said.

Jean took the offered phone and dialed. "Hey, Roman," she said when he answered. "We just talked to one of the suspects, a man named Travis who runs a high-dollar counterfeit wine scam, and now his partner is following us. A big guy named Felix who used to be a boxer. I'm afraid if we lose him he'll just pick us up later. What should we do?"

"Do Felix and Travis have alibis?"

"Supposedly they were across town together at the time. We have to check it out."

"Sounds as if a warning is in order," Roman said. "Where are you?"

"Near Van Ness and Union."

"OK, stay put. I'll call you when we're in position. What's the phone number?"

She told him. "Who's 'we'?"

"Trust me." He hung up.

In about twenty minutes Roman called back. Zeppo's phone played the opening bars of *The Ride of the Valkyries*.

"All right, Jean," Roman said, "remember that small clearing in the Presidio where we sometimes have lunch? Can you find it in the dark?"

"Of course."

"Let Felix follow you there. Get out of the car and go through the clearing to the path that leads into the woods. Walk for fifty yards or so and wait until I tell you to come back."

"What are you going to do?"

"Nothing very illegal. Now get moving."

Jean explained their orders as they drove to the decommissioned army base that encompassed several hundred acres of wooded open space at the northern tip of San Francisco. She drove deep into the Presidio, past houses and former military buildings to a wild, heavily forested area. Traffic was light once they got off the main road, and occasionally she caught a glimpse of Felix's car behind them.

Finally they turned down a narrow gravel road that ended at a small grassy clearing surrounded by pine trees. When Jean shut off the engine and headlights, the only illumination came from the gibbous moon overhead. Traffic sounds filtered through the brush that completely hid the road. Roman had to be somewhere nearby, but she could see no sign of him.

"How do you know this place?" Zeppo asked.

"Roman and I eat lunch here sometimes when we cycle through the Presidio. It's really pretty in the daytime." She heard a car door shut nearby. "That must be Felix."

"OK, let's go," he said.

They followed a narrow path that led through the clearing and into a grove of trees where the moonlight barely penetrated. Jean cursed her heels, which sank into the soft ground. When they'd gone only a few feet, she grabbed Zeppo's arm and pulled him into the woods and back toward the clearing, stumbling on tree roots in the dark.

"We're supposed to keep going on the path," he whispered.

"I don't want to miss the show." Jean found a spot behind a dense bush where they could see the clearing yet remain hidden. "Isn't this exciting?"

"Sure, if you like being scared shitless."

"Shh!" Jean heard someone walking along the gravel road. In a few moments Felix appeared at the mouth of the clearing, moving cautiously, staying close to the trees. As he stepped onto the grass, two men in black clothes slipped out of the darkness, one in front of Felix and the other behind him.

Roman, facing Felix, held a revolver. "Clasp your hands behind your head," he ordered. The man did as he was told. Roman's companion, a wiry man with a ginger handlebar mustache and shaved head, patted Felix down, reaching into his pants pocket to withdraw a large folding knife. He handed it to Roman, who put it into his own pocket. Jean recognized the man from Bash Back events—Nick Rigatos.

Nick nudged the back of Felix's knees with his foot. "Kneel down."

Jean pushed through the brush into the clearing, Zeppo following. "Nice work, fellas," she said. "Thanks."

Roman nodded. "Felix, I hope this will teach you not to underestimate how devious Jean can be."

Felix looked angry and unhappy. "What do you want, asshole?"

Roman flicked the man's ear with the revolver. "I simply want your attention."

"You've got it."

Jean took a few steps toward him. "Why were you following us?"

"Eat me, bitch."

"Mind your manners, Felix," Roman said. "If you don't answer my friend's questions, I'll be forced to resort to violence."

Zeppo came up beside Jean. "What were you going to do to us?"

"I thought you were having an outdoor screw." He gave an ugly grin. "I wanted to throw a little scare into you."

"Did Travis put you up to this?" Jean said.

Felix made a disgusted noise. "That pussy-whipped wimp? Nah. You've got him scared good."

"Listen carefully, Felix," Roman said. "If you follow them again or harass them in any way, Jean will contact the media regarding your counterfeit wine operation. If you harm either of them, you and Travis will have the police and my entire organization on your backs."

"Oh yeah? What organization might that be?"

"Bash Back. Have you heard of us?"

"Sure. You're that bunch of hard-ass pansies."

"That's correct, Felix," Roman said softly, putting the muzzle of the gun against the man's neck. "So do we have an understanding?"

"Yeah, I'll leave them alone."

Roman took a step back. "Good. Now on your way."

Felix unclasped his hands and stood up. There were dark stains on the knees of his pants. "What about my knife?"

"I'll find a more suitable home for it," Roman said.

Felix turned and stomped out of the clearing.

"I think he'll stay away," Roman said to Jean and Zeppo. "But keep your eyes open."

"We will," Jean said. "By the way, I've neglected to make introductions. This is Jay Zeppetello. Zeppo, meet Roman Villalobos and Nick Rigatos."

"Named after the dumb, handsome Marx brother, are you?" Roman said as they shook.

Zeppo grinned. "Yeah, but I'm neither."

"What's on the agenda for the rest of the evening?" Roman asked.

"We're going to Sputnik, a nightclub south of Market, then Zeppo's dropping me at Peter's and going straight home," Jean said.

"I'll follow you as far as the nightclub," Roman said.

"OK. I'll phone you tomorrow, Roman," she said, hugging him. "And thanks again."

Jean and Zeppo walked out to the Jag and got in. "Wow," he said. "That was intense. I guess calling an editor was a good idea after all."

"Roman has all sorts of useful skills."

"What's Nick's day job?"

"He's a nurse."

"I bet that comes in handy. OK, partner, it's party time. Let's go to Sputnik."

Jean drove out of the Presidio, Roman following, and turned south toward Sputnik.

CHAPTER 16

The nightclub occupied a converted warehouse in the trendy part of the South of Market neighborhood, not too far from the Museum of Modern Art. The club's theme was kitschy science fiction, and a plump silver spaceship with a tail of orange cartoon fire surmounted the lime-green neon "Sputnik" sign over the door. Jean took off her jacket and a leering bouncer let them both in after carding Zeppo.

The cavernous interior, equal parts Flash Gordon and early Star Trek, was hung with rockets and satellites, and the huge dance floor was painted with a swirling silver and black pattern. The young, straight, overwhelmingly white patrons and indifferent club music weren't Jean's idea of a good time, but she had to admit this was an attractive, well-dressed crowd; the bouncer had done his job.

"We'll split up," Zeppo said as they looked the place over. "I'll work my way over by the dance floor and you go that way, near the bar. You know what to do?"

"Sure. Find out if anyone like that little blonde ever worked here. Look for a guy with spider-web tattoos. Talk to Simon Emory."

"Got any money?"

"Not much."

"I'll give you some. Tip heavily. And try to keep a low profile." Zeppo took out his wallet and looked through it.

"I've only got twenties. Let's buy a couple of drinks and get change."

They made their way toward the long curving bar, where patrons on futuristic stools and waitresses carrying shiny silver trays kept several bartenders busy.

Men turned to watch and made appreciative noises as Jean passed. She glanced back and saw Zeppo looking pleased with himself—she was doing a little inadvertent ego-building. She didn't mind; he could certainly use it.

At the bar Zeppo ordered a draft beer and Jean a mojito. There were several wines by the glass listed on a board, but here the bottles might have been open for days. Zeppo gave her an assortment of bills and headed for the dance area. Jean sat on a stool next to the service station, hoping to strike up a conversation with a waitress or bartender.

In a few minutes a waitress with spiky dark hair and a short silver-and-black Jetson-style uniform came up to the station near Jean. "Hey, Rudy," she called to a bartender. "I need a pitcher of cosmos." Jean picked up an Eastern European accent.

Jean smiled at the waitress. "You worked here long?"

The woman smiled back. "A few months."

"I'm looking for a waitress job," Jean said. "What's the boss like?"

"Pretty cool, and the tips are good." She set four glasses on her tray. "But I don't think he's looking for anyone right now."

Rudy put a pitcher of icy pink liquid on her tray and she was gone. Jean looked him over—young and dark-skinned, with short brown dreadlocks and a lean face. His long-sleeved silver-and-black T-shirt hung loose on his bony frame.

"Can I have another mojito?" she asked him.

"Sure thing." He mixed the tall drink and set it in front of her.

She took a sip. "Mmm, that's good. You're an artist, Rudy."

"Thanks," he said, grinning.

"So Rudy, how about you? Worked here long?"

"Almost a year."

"You like it?" she asked.

"It's pretty OK. At my last job I had to wear roller skates."

"That must have been a challenge. Where was that?"

"Retro place in Hollywood."

"Where else?" Jean took another sip. "Hey, last time I was here I had a great talk with one of the waitresses," she said. "We were going to have lunch sometime, but I lost her number and I can't remember her name."

"What'd she look like?"

"Petite and slender, with light blond hair and blue eyes. Russian, I think."

Rudy lost his grin. "Don't know her," he said. He walked down the bar and began washing glasses.

At the end of the bar a man wearing what looked like a good Italian suit flipped through a stack of receipts. A tall black bartender hurried past Jean and gave the man a paper. "Here you go, Simon," the bartender said. This must be Simon Emory, the owner. Time to make something happen.

As the bartender hurried back, Jean made her move. She grabbed her drink and deliberately slipped off the stool into his path, colliding with him. She planted her left foot but somehow fell off the heel and went down, spilling the mojito all over her dress. Shit. All she'd wanted was to bump into the guy to get Emory's attention, not end up soaked and embarrassed on the barroom floor.

"Whoa," the bartender said in alarm. "Hey, I'm really sorry." He took Jean's hand and pulled her up, grabbing a stack of napkins off the bar to wipe at her dress.

"I'm fine, really," Jean said, taking the napkins from him. "It's my own fault."

The man at the end of the bar approached her. "Are you all right, Miss?" he asked. He had an intelligent, conventionally handsome face and looked to be around forty.

"Just a little damp," Jean said.

"That'll do, Jack," he said to the bartender. "Get back to work." The bartender left and the man turned back to Jean. "I'm Simon Emory. This is my club."

"I'm Jean Applequist."

"Delighted," he said, taking her hand and kissing it. "I apologize for Jack's clumsiness." He smelled good, like expensive cologne. His eyes were an unusual shade of light brown, his well-cut hair darker brown. She would have found him attractive, but his jewelry was a tad too flashy and his unbuttoned shirt showed a little too much chest hair. On the other hand, he'd beaten Martin Wingo at his own game.

"No problem," she said. "I wasn't watching where I was going."

Simon was looking her over, too. "May I buy you a drink?"

"Sure."

He led her to the bar and she spotted Zeppo nearby. He gave her a thumbs-up and faded into the crowd.

At the bar Jean ordered another mojito and swabbed ineffectually at her dress with cocktail napkins. The bartender brought Simon a cup of espresso without being asked.

"I haven't seen you here before," Simon said. "How do you like it?"

"It's a fun place," Jean said. "The décor's very imaginative. You own some other clubs, don't you?"

"Yes, three on the Peninsula and one in Oakland."

"Do they all have the same outer-space theme?"

"All but the one in Palo Alto. It's got live cabaret music and a French wine list."

"I'll have to check that one out." Jean looked more closely at his hair—pale roots were just starting to show.

"Are you interested in wine?" he asked.

"Very. I write for *Wine Digest*."

"Really? I often read it. I'll have to watch for your byline."

A hostess interrupted them. "Sorry, boss. The cashier needs some twenties."

Simon sighed with annoyance. "Duty calls," he said to Jean. "It's my own fault—I don't believe in delegating anything important. Perhaps we can continue this fascinating conversation some other time."

"I'd like that."

He took a business card from his wallet and gave it to her. "I look forward to hearing from you, Jean." He kissed her hand again and followed the maître d' through the crowd.

As soon as Simon was out of sight Zeppo slipped onto the stool next to her. "You OK?" he asked.

"I'm fine. I wouldn't have fallen if I'd been wearing different shoes. But at least I met Simon Emory. Pretty smooth guy. I didn't have time to ask him about the blond woman, but he wants me to call him. Did you come up with anything?"

"Yeah," Zeppo said. "She worked here as a waitress. Name's Oksana something. She quit a few weeks ago, must be right after talking to Martin. No one's seen her since. Dated a bartender named Spider. He quit around the same time."

"Looks as if they took Martin's money and ran," Jean said. "Hey, did you see the bartender I was talking to? He clammed up when I described Oksana."

"Oh yeah? Let's find him."

She got up and adjusted her stiffening dress. Simon stood near the door looking through the reservation book. Jean and Zeppo threaded their way through the crowd toward him.

"Excuse me, Simon," Jean said. "Where's Rudy? I owe him a tip."

"He stepped out to make a phone call. Should be right back."

"Well, thanks. I'll call you." Jean said. She and Zeppo walked back into the crowd. "My dress is all sticky."

"We'll come back another night," Zeppo said. "Where does that guy get off, kissing hands like that?"

"Probably trying to pass himself off as a gentleman." Jean got her jacket from the coat check and they went out into the cool night; the line to get in was much longer now. Jean glanced around warily but didn't see Felix lurking anywhere.

They'd parked nearby, just off Howard. As Zeppo unlocked Jean's door, a young man stepped out of the darkness. The short dark stubble on his head showed a seriously receding hairline. A black bar pierced his eyebrow and he wore a black T-shirt with "Rhino Fitness" written on it in yellow. Underneath, his exaggerated build was the kind that came from hours at the gym. Jean thought of a description of the young Arnold Schwarzenegger she'd read somewhere: that he looked like a condom full of walnuts. Most interesting of all, spider-web tattoos covered his forearms.

"Why were you asking my friend about Oksana?" he demanded.

"It's what I said. I couldn't remember her name," Jean said in what she hoped was a placating tone.

"Bullshit." He took a step toward them, his hands in fists at his sides. "Your buddy here was asking about her, too. If you know where she is, you better tell me."

"Hey, just a minute," Zeppo said. "Why would we be asking about her if we knew where she was?"

The man looked less sure of himself now. "So why do you want to find her?"

"I'll level with you," Zeppo said. "We're looking into Martin Wingo's death. We know Oksana saw him right before he died. You were there, too. We want to know what they talked about."

"Why? Are you a detective?"

"No, I used to work for Wingo. Oksana came to see me but I wasn't there. I'm Zeppo."

Recognition flickered in his eyes. "Yeah?"

"What's your name?" Zeppo asked.

"Spider Brandt."

"Why don't you tell us why she went to see Martin? Maybe we can help each other."

Jean could see both pain and indecision on Spider's face. "No way," he finally answered. He turned and ran. The back of his shirt bore a big yellow rhinoceros logo.

Jean looked at Zeppo. "So Oksana's missing."

"Or maybe she took all the money for herself. Either way, we have to find her. Rudy must have called Spider and told him about us."

They got into the car and Zeppo headed toward Peter's apartment in Pacific Heights.

"Maybe you should talk to Rudy," Jean said. "I couldn't get anything out of him."

"Right. We should also check out Rhino Fitness. It's in the Mission. Meanwhile, you set something up with Slick."

"Who?"

"Emory. See what you can charm out of him."

In a few minutes they pulled up in front of Peter's apartment building, a big white 1920s pile on Pacific.

"Today went really well," Zeppo said. "We got a lot of useful information. We're a good team, huh, Jeannie?"

"Maybe, but don't get any ideas," she said.

"Too late. I've already got ideas."

She saw a hint of longing in his eyes as she got out of the car.

CHAPTER 17

*T*he next morning Jean checked her email when she got home; Setrakian had answered. She read the note and called Zeppo.

"Setrakian's hot to trot," she told him. "He wants me to come by his studio around two o'clock today."

"Good work, partner. I'll give Rivenbark a call."

"Pick me up around noon, OK? I have to stop at Roman's and get my bike."

"See you then," Zeppo said.

Jean phoned Peter to say goodbye. Last night they'd quarreled—Peter had tried to convince her to stop investigating, which had only made her more determined. But she'd ended up having a fine time once he calmed down and she got him out of his clothes and into his king-sized bed.

Her next call was to Roman. "Hi, it's me. Thanks again for saving my ass."

"*De nada*," he said. "Yours is an ass that frequently needs saving."

"I need to get my bike around noon. OK with you?"

"Sure, I'll be here. Where are you going to ride?"

"Zeppo and I have to talk to a couple of people about Martin, in Sonoma and Mendocino. We were hoping to get a ride in. It turns out Diane was right—Zeppo was in charge of the blue box. He did all Martin's detective work."

"He must be a bright guy."

"He is. But it's strange—he never talks about his family or where he's from. And he doesn't seem to have any friends." She thought she could hear Roman pulling on a cigarette. He'd quit several years ago but had occasional lapses.

"You know, Jean," he said, "if he wants to get your attention, the best thing he can do is pretend to have a mysterious past. You're a sucker for a secret."

"But he was doing this act long before he met me."

"What are you up to, anyway?" he asked. "Solving Martin's murder or doing a background check on Zeppo?"

"A little of both, I guess."

"Why hasn't he told the police about the blue box?" She heard the puffing sound again.

"He promised Martin he wouldn't. Seems he has a sense of honor. Roman, are you smoking?"

"Just having a little eye-opener."

"Dope or a cigarette?"

"An unfiltered Camel, you nosy bitch."

"You keep that up and I'll have to find a new cycling partner," Jean said. "It's bad enough that you're nearly fifty."

He chuckled. "If you ever beat me to the top of Twin Peaks, I'll let you complain."

"It's a deal. See you later, Roman."

Jean pulled out her overnight bag and packed, a slow process because almost nothing was put away in the right place. Zeppo arrived on time, and she threw her toiletry kit into her bag and zipped it up. "OK, that's everything. Let's saddle up."

"Wait a minute. Is that what you're going to wear when we talk to Setrakian?"

She looked down at her ripped black jeans, old polo shirt, and sandals. "Yeah. Why not? You're not dressed up either." He wore jeans, a dark blue T-shirt, and Adidas.

"Put on a dress, OK? Something sexy. We know what he likes, so I want you to show some tits and ass."

"Forget it," she said. "I don't do that kind of prick-teasing bullshit unless I intend to follow through."

"What about at the nightclub?"

"That was impersonal. Everyone was dressed that way."

"Look, Jeannie, we've got to use all the weapons we have, and that includes your distraction factor. It'll be a lot easier to open him up if he's thinking about getting into your pants. Nothing will happen—I'll be there to defend your honor. Come on, it's for the cause."

Jean didn't like it, but she saw his logic. "OK, I'll compromise. I'll change my shirt." She went into the bathroom and put on a snug red T-shirt with a low scoop neck that showed plenty of cleavage.

"Wow," Zeppo said when she emerged. "That's better. He'll never know what hit him."

Jean locked up her apartment and they walked to his car. His bike, locked to a metal rack on the back of the Jag, looked new and expensive.

She snuggled into the car's old leather seats and inhaled deeply—delicious. This was going to be a great car for a road trip.

Zeppo pulled smoothly into traffic and headed over the hill to the Castro. "I couldn't sleep last night so I downloaded a picture of Travis from the Net and drove over to the Cock and Bull."

"Without me?" Jean said indignantly.

"You were busy."

"What did you find out?"

"It's a neighborhood dive with old-fashioned dart boards and ten kinds of British beer on tap. The bartender knows Felix and he recognized Travis, but couldn't say if they'd been in that particular night. So that's a dead end."

Jean directed him through the narrow streets off Castro toward Roman's house. "Did you talk to Hugh Rivenbark?" she asked.

"Yeah. He said we should come by around eight o'clock. He made us reservations in town."

"Great. OK, it's the big blue and gray house on the right. Park in the driveway."

✧

JEAN EMBRACED Roman as he let them in the gate. Luxuriant body hair poked out of his shorts and Bash Back T-shirt.

"Hey, thanks for helping us out last night," Zeppo said, shaking Roman's hand.

"I had no choice," Roman said. "Jean owes me money. Would you like some coffee?"

"Thanks," Jean said. "Black for Zeppo, too. And you'd better bring him something to eat. He requires about 10,000 calories a day."

Jean and Zeppo sat at the table under the big tree. The yard was still cool and shady; the sun wouldn't reach it until midafternoon. Roman brought out a tray that held three mugs and a plate of almond biscotti and green grapes. As they sipped coffee, Jean told Roman about their visit to Sputnik and the people they'd spoken to. Zeppo added occasional asides and made steady progress through the biscotti.

"A lot of people are going to be very irritated with the two of you," Roman remarked.

"Maybe," Zeppo said, "but the only one who seems dangerous is Felix, and I think you took care of him."

"What about Emory?" Roman said. "If he's harboring illegals from Eastern Europe, he might be mixed up with organized crime, and no one's rougher than the Russian or Ukrainian mafiya."

"I thought about that when I was investigating him, but couldn't find any connection at all," Zeppo said. "Just that he hires a lot of illegals and is pretty good to them. He seems to be an independent operator. Of course, I didn't go back very far—just enough for Martin's purposes. But he's definitely still on our list."

Roman drank his coffee. "I think you should look harder at the people closest to Martin. Kay Wingo, for instance. She is the ex-wife, after all. And wherever you find that kind of high-level money and power and ambition, you'll find people with a lot at stake and a lot to lose."

Jean looked at Roman. "You wouldn't be sending us after Kay just because the Rational Right thinks you're a sorry degenerate who needs aversion therapy and chemical castration, would you?"

"Of course not," Roman said. "I'm much more high-minded than that. Did Martin have anything on Kay, Zeppo?"

"Nothing that I know about."

"But if she wanted to kill him, why not do it before the divorce so she'd end up with all the money instead of just half?" Jean said.

"Good point." Roman dipped a biscotti into his coffee and took a bite. "What about Martin's partner, Frank Johansen? Maybe the reason he never challenged Martin about how he did business was that Martin had something on him."

Jean shook her head. "Even if he had it in for Martin, Frank would never kill Diane's husband on her wedding day. He treats her like his own child."

"People have done worse to their children," Zeppo said, taking another biscotti.

"I was just going to say the same thing," Roman said.

Jean knew what Roman was talking about—his father had barred him from the house when he came out in high school, and most of his conservative Catholic family hadn't spoken to him since. Zeppo was obviously alienated from his family, and that remark made it sound as if he, too, was the injured party. She added it to her list of clues about him.

Roman drained his cup. "Jean, didn't you tell me that Diane never knew her father? What if it's Frank Johansen?"

"Wow," Jean said. "I never thought of that. But Frank is coarse-featured, big-boned, and pale-skinned—there's nothing of him in Diane. Even if it's true, where's the motive for him to kill Martin? His wife died years ago, and who else would care?"

"It's just a thought," Roman said.

"You're absolutely right," Zeppo said. "We should talk to Frank and Kay when we get back from Mendocino." He grabbed a handful of grapes and the last of the biscotti. "OK, let's get going."

They thanked Roman and got Jean's bike from his garage. As Zeppo loaded his rack, Jean gazed longingly at the sleek black car. "Zeppo, can I drive?"

"Correct me if I'm wrong, but didn't you roll your last car near Devil's Slide?"

"Everyone blames me for that. The Escort simply wasn't a good enough machine for what I was trying to do."

"Which was what? Set a new land speed record?"

"I was just having some fun. But I'll be like a saint today. I've driven you around—haven't I been good? All I've been driving lately is that crummy little Toyota, and Diane won't let me near the Porsche. Please?"

"On one condition. We play my music."

"I'd listen to country-western if you let me drive." Jean felt a rush of excitement that was almost sexual as she slid into the driver's seat.

CHAPTER 18

⎯⎯⎯⎯ ✑ ⎯⎯⎯⎯

Jean took Highway 101 north out of San Francisco across the Golden Gate Bridge, the weather warming as they headed inland. She drove conservatively at first, but Zeppo seemed relaxed, so she pushed it. She sped up, testing his tolerance. He looked calmly out the window and listened to Bluesville on XM radio. By the time they hit Sonoma County she wasn't pulling her punches. On an empty straightaway she floored it and watched the needle edge over a hundred before she had to slow for traffic. Zeppo didn't bat an eye.

"Whee!" Jean exclaimed. "This is the kind of car I need."

"Now that you know how fast it'll go, can we slow down?"

"Oh sure. Just testing." She slowed to seventy-five.

"Exciting, isn't it?" Zeppo said. "I hope I can afford to keep it."

"This is turning into a fun trip, Zeppo. Fast car, good music, and I've even got a big nasty redhead by my side, just like the Randy Newman song."

Zeppo laughed. "And the best part is, we're not in L.A."

"Or Indiana either." They passed a spectacular vista of low rolling hills covered with vineyards and dotted with live oak trees. "Why would anybody live in the Midwest when they could live in Northern California? Of course, I'm glad most of them stay there."

"Yeah, I know what you mean," Zeppo said. "It blew me away the first time I took a walk across the Golden Gate Bridge. It was like living on a movie set."

Jean couldn't restrain her curiosity. "Where are you from, Zeppo? Where's your family?"

"Aw, come on. You don't really want to know all that boring stuff, do you?"

"Sure I do. I'm nosy."

He looked out the window in silence for half a mile. Finally he said, "Jeannie, I don't want to bullshit you, so can we please not talk about my family?"

"OK," she said. "How about after that? Where'd you go to college?"

"Never did."

"You went to high school, didn't you?"

"Not really, not a regular one. But enough about me. You're from Indiana, right? East Jesus or somewhere."

"West Chilton. OK, I give up. No more about your distant past. Can I ask how you ended up working for Martin?"

"Sure. It's kind of funny, actually. When I first moved to San Francisco I worked as a bike messenger, like I told you, and one of the guys, Sparky, was in this green group that fought development in San Francisco. They asked me to hack into Wingo-Johansen's system and find out about a project that would involve relocating some businesses South of Market. It was a piece of cake and I got what Sparky and his pals wanted. I poked around some more and found some other interesting stuff."

"Where'd you learn so much about computers?"

"I'm self-taught. Anyway, they used the material I got to stir up controversy and delay the project's approval, which cost Wingo-Johansen a lot of money. So Martin did what he did best—he found out Sparky was dealing Ecstasy, and instead of turning him in he did a trade. He'd forget about it if Sparky told him how he got the info, so Sparky told him.

"Martin came to my apartment. It blew my mind, this big honcho tracking me down like that. He wanted to do a deal. He wouldn't press charges if I agreed to hack into some of his competitors' systems. I made him a counter-offer. See, when I was fooling around in his system, I got into the personal files of his employees. One guy was double-billing for construction materials, charging for loads that were never delivered, logging in more workers than actually showed up, and pocketing the change. The moron left all his bogus bills on the company computer—I guess he thought he'd hidden them well. I told Martin if he wanted the name of someone who was cheating him, he had to leave me alone.

"He agreed, and after we talked for a while, he asked if I'd work for him. He said he'd been looking for someone like me to help out with a special project. I said sure. I worked on minor stuff, and when he decided he could trust me, I got to see the blue box."

"I'll bet he was glad to find you. It can't be easy, filling a job like that."

"That's what Martin said. And he didn't fire the guy who was skimming, either. He let him quit, gave him great recommendations, and when he got hired somewhere else, Martin had another informant."

"The man was amazing."

"That he was."

Jean punched it on a brief straightaway, barely passing a lumbering RV before the road curved sharply. "Diane says there are no copies of the dirt. Is that really true?"

"Yeah, it's true. There were copies of some of the stuff on Martin's computer at home, but when he saw how easily I hacked into his system and his competitors' systems, he had me scrub the hard drive. I explained that I could make it pretty much impossible to hack into, but he said, 'You're smart, but there's always somebody smarter out there.' I couldn't argue with that. I tried to talk him into having some sort of backup copies. I mean, what if his house burned down? But he insisted one copy was enough. Did I mention that he was a control freak?"

"I figured that out myself. "

On the outskirts of Sonoma, Zeppo had her turn east, and they wound through the countryside past a big empty field studded with survey markers.

"That's Martin's development," he told her. "Work has stopped for now, of course."

Just beyond the field Jean pulled the Jag into a circular gravel drive in front of an old blue and white three-story clapboard house, complete with a broad porch and a bench swing. A classic red barn sat to the left of the house and a garage to the right. A well-kept lawn surrounded the buildings and mature trees provided shade. It reminded Jean of an Indiana farmhouse, except for the ancient vineyard beyond the lawn. Bud break had been early this year, and Jean could see tiny green leaves emerging from the gnarly black vines, which stood out starkly against the bright yellow mustard that grew between the rows.

A big brown mutt ran up to the car, barking. Jean hesitated, her door half open, but Zeppo got out, knelt on the gravel, and talked softly to the animal. The dog stopped barking and went up to him. She sniffed his hand, then licked it, tail wagging. Zeppo ruffled the dog's neck, calling her a good girl.

A trim man about six feet tall in faded jeans and a light blue peasant shirt came out of the barn. He was in his late thirties, very tan, with a handsome, clean-shaven face, and he wore his dark brown hair in a ponytail. He smiled when he saw her. "Are you Jean Applequist?" he asked, extending a hand. "I'm Armand Setrakian." They shook; he had a big silver and turquoise bracelet on his right wrist. He squeezed hard, holding on just a bit too long.

His welcoming smile changed to an expression of surprise and suspicion, and Jean realized that Zeppo, initially out of sight on the other side of the car, had stood up.

"I know you," Setrakian said. He took a few steps toward Zeppo. "You're that reporter who came up here asking questions. That was right before Martin Wingo paid me a visit. You worked for him, didn't you?"

"Uh . . . yeah," Zeppo said.

"I ought to kick your ass for what you cost me. Get off my property now."

Zeppo put his hands out. "Now be cool, Armand. We just want to ask you one question and then we're gone."

The dog hopped around Zeppo's legs, trying to get his attention. Setrakian snapped his fingers. "Kali! Beat it!" he ordered. The dog flinched and slunk away behind the barn. "What's this all about?" Setrakian demanded.

"Sorry to come out here under false pretenses, Armand," Jean said. "This is about Martin's death."

"Someone cut off the head, but the body's still twitching," Armand said. "That's the way it is with snakes."

"We're not here to put anything on you," Zeppo said. "We just want to know where you were the night he died."

"Or you'll tell the world about those bitches who've been hounding me. Well, I don't care what you do—I'm not talking to you, you fucking toady."

"We're not here to threaten you," Zeppo said reasonably. "And if you don't like me, you can talk to Jean."

Armand eyed Jean. He gestured at the barn. "OK, come in here out of the sun."

Jean followed him cautiously around the side of the barn, where the big doors were wide open. Zeppo walked out into the yard.

The barn had been converted into a studio—benches were strewn with sculpting tools, rags, and sketch pads, and bags of clay leaned against one wall. Skylights lit the interior. A work in progress, a metal armature partly covered in clay, stood in the center of the work area. Jean had seen Setrakian's sculptures before; usually he did mature, life-size female nudes. This was an adolescent girl in tennis clothes. The statue was stylized and graceful, and had a quality of weightlessness and movement about it. "Will you cast this in bronze?" she asked.

"Yeah. I make a negative cast in plaster, then a positive in bronze. What's an incredibly sexy woman like you doing with a piece of trash like him?" He stood a little too close.

Jean took a step back. "Just what we said—investigating Martin's death."

Armand looked at Zeppo, who stood in the shade of a tree watching them through the open barn door. He turned back to her. "I'll be happy to answer your questions, but we don't need him here. Tell him to come get you in two hours. We'll talk, and I'll show you how I work."

Jean felt the hair on the back of her neck stand up. He wasn't doing anything threatening, but he set off all her alarms. She had a sense about men with the potential for sexual violence, and so far it had never steered her wrong. It wasn't what she knew about Setrakian—the man himself gave off all the wrong vibes.

"I'd love to do your body in bronze," he said. "Tell the kid to leave—I'll do some sketches of you."

"Not in this lifetime, Armand." She glanced out at Zeppo. Kali had come back and he was throwing a stick for her to fetch. "This must be a statue for Elan. It'd be a shame if they had to cancel that commission."

"I thought you weren't going to threaten me."

"I changed my mind. I've decided I don't want to stay here a minute longer than I have to. Answer the question: Where were you when Martin drowned?"

"I was with a woman."

"You were assaulting her?"

He leaned toward her and said softly, "No, I was fucking her."

"Do you happen to remember her name?"

"Blythe Newman. She works at a real estate office in Sonoma. Fletcher-Newman Properties. We were at it all night. Ask her."

She took another step back. Now she was up against the railing that delineated the old stables.

Armand held up his big muscular hands, gesturing at the statues. "See what these hands can do to a lump of clay? Don't you wonder what they could do for you?"

Jean laughed. "Not for an instant, asshole. I've never been into hate sex."

He was inches from her now. He'd moved between her and the door, blocking Zeppo's line of sight. "Your body is one in a million. Why not let an artist appreciate it?" He put a hand on her left breast and squeezed. "Oh yeah. These are real. I knew it."

Jean jabbed him hard at the base of his throat with two stiffened fingers. He released her and stumbled back, clutching his neck, coughing and choking. She thought about kicking him in the testicles—she had a clear shot and he was in no condition to fight back—but decided against it. After all, she'd promised Zeppo to stay calm.

Zeppo ran toward her, Kali chasing him. "What happened?"

"The son of a bitch checked me for implants."

Armand sat down hard on a workbench, bent over, his cough subsiding, his face red. Jean stood over him, hands on her hips. "You know what, Armand? You just fucked yourself. We were going to leave you alone if you didn't kill Martin. Well, not anymore. Now I'll ruin you—not for land, not for money, but because you're a predatory shit and everyone should know it."

Zeppo took her arm. "Come on, Jeannie," he said, leading her down to the car. He opened the passenger door and helped her in. They sped out of the driveway as Jean glanced back at the barn. Armand watched them from the door, rubbing his throat, a look of pure malice on his face. Kali lay on the lawn chewing her stick.

"I'm sorry," Zeppo said. "That's not exactly what I had in mind."

"Isn't it?" she snapped. "You're the one who made me put on this shirt."

He looked at her, a hurt frown on his face. "You don't really think I wanted that to happen, do you?"

Jean took a deep breath. "No, Zeppo, of course not. Sorry. I'm just mad. God, I hope he's the killer."

"Yeah, that would be sweet. What did you do to him, anyway?"

"A little something Roman taught me. I know I lost my temper, but I did refrain from kicking him in the balls."

"You should have kicked him, Jeannie. Let's turn him in, like you threatened. We'll write a letter to Elan and one to the press. I mean, I was just a few feet away, we were there on serious business, and you were pretty hostile, and he went after you anyway. He'll keep doing that to women if we don't stop him. Not everyone can fight back like you did—sooner or later he's going to rape somebody. If he hasn't already."

"Great. I was going to insist on exposing him." She looked out the window, letting the scenery calm her. "He did give me the name of his alibi. Says he was with a woman, and apparently it wasn't against her will. She works at a real estate office in Sonoma."

"Let's go over there now." They headed into town.

Jean felt bad about snapping at Zeppo. "You were good with Kali."

"Yeah, I love dogs. I wish I could have one, but it's impossible in a studio apartment. I used to have—" He stopped.

"It's OK, Zeppo. I won't ask you about anything else. What kind of dog did you have?"

"Two chocolate Labs. Did you have a dog in Indiana?"

"Oh sure. We always had a couple of mutts when I was growing up. I prefer cats."

As they drove toward Sonoma, Zeppo handed Jean his cell phone. She called the real estate office and got

Blythe Newman's cell phone number. A husky female voice answered.

"Ms. Newman? My name is Jean Applequist. I wonder if we could meet. I'd like to talk to you about Armand Setrakian."

"Armand? What about him?"

"He might be in legal trouble. I'd rather not elaborate on a cell phone. It won't take long."

Blythe paused. "OK, go to the northeast corner of the plaza. I'll meet you at the bear flag statue in half an hour."

"Great, thanks. I'm tall with silver hair and a red T-shirt. I'll be with a redheaded guy." She hung up. "At least we're easy to spot."

"For better or worse." Zeppo drove into Sonoma and parked near the plaza, a big park in the center of town that held the city hall, a duck pond, playgrounds, and several historic markers. They went into a deli and bought sandwiches and juice, then found the statue, a rugged pioneer raising the bear flag. They sat at the base of the statue while they ate and people-watched.

About forty minutes later, a woman in a light green long-sleeved gauze dress came up to them. She was medium height, small-boned, and curvy, with shoulder-length auburn hair and very pale skin. "Are you Jean Applequist?" she asked.

Jean introduced Zeppo, and Blythe Newman sat down on the bench.

"What's this all about? Armand and I are *so* over." She removed big sunglasses to reveal heavy-lidded blue-gray eyes, then took a pack of cigarettes out of her purse and lit one. She seemed about Jean's age.

"We're trying to find out where he was on a certain night a few weeks ago, the night Martin Wingo drowned," Jean said.

"Who are you, anyway? You don't look like the police." She took a drag on her cigarette. Several narrow silver bracelets on each of her slim wrists jingled as she moved.

"We're looking into Martin's death for his widow," Jean said. "She's a friend of mine. Armand says he was with you that night."

"He does, does he? Well, I don't have to tell you anything."

"Of course you don't," Zeppo said soothingly. "This is very informal. We've just come from his house, by the way, and Jean nearly crushed his trachea when he groped her."

Blythe looked at Jean, appraising her. "Good for you." She had another puff. "What night was that again?"

"March 6th, a Saturday. Martin died around five A.M. Sunday."

"Is Armand a suspect?"

"Not officially," Zeppo said. "We're just trying to find out if he could have done it. He and Martin had some business dealings that went bad."

"So if I give him an alibi, that'll eliminate him as a suspect, right?"

"Pretty much."

"No, he wasn't with me," she said with a satisfied smile. "I was home alone the whole night. I have no idea where he was."

"Uh . . . you're sure about that?" Zeppo asked. "Don't you need to check?"

"No, I have a very good memory. Whoever asks me, that's what I'll say, and you can tell him that." She pushed her bracelets back and looked at her watch. "I've got to show a house." She dropped her cigarette onto the grass and crushed it with a slender booted foot. "I hope they execute him." She walked out of the park.

Jean watched her retreating back. "Well, do we have an alibi or not?"

"Nothing that'll hold up in court, given her attitude, but yeah, I think she was with him."

"I can't imagine actually dating Armand. I'm sure he's a real brute in the sack. But maybe that's what she likes."

"Didn't you notice her wrists?"

"What was wrong with them?"

"She had bruises all the way around on both of them. Like she'd been tied up. That's why she was wearing long sleeves on a warm day, and all those bracelets."

"Jesus. I guess she and Armand were made for each other." She looked at him speculatively. "How come you noticed and I didn't?"

"Sometimes when you see long sleeves in warm weather it's to hide cutting or suicide attempts. I was looking for scars." Zeppo shook his head. "I can't figure women out. Even if they're not full-on masochists like her, lots of them go for mean guys."

Jean wondered where in the world he had encountered people with scars on their wrists, but didn't ask. "When we get home, we'll get even with this particular bastard," she told him. "Come on, let's hit the road. Can I still drive?"

CHAPTER 19

Jean cut over toward the coast, through Boonville and along the Navarro River. On Highway 1 south of Mendocino they drove along sheer, rocky cliffs that rose right out of the ocean, with another breathtaking view of sea, sky, and rough green landscape around every bend. Finally they came over a rise to the town of Mendocino, low wooden buildings scattered on a bluff above a small harbor.

"It looks kind of like a New England whaling town," Zeppo said.

"It's passed for one on TV, in *Murder, She Wrote*."

Zeppo pulled out his cell and had a brief chat with Hugh Rivenbark. "He put us at the Elkhorn Inn," he told Jean.

"I know right where it is." Jean drove to the bed and breakfast inn, an old three-story house painted gray with white trim. A young woman at the front desk gave them keys, and after locking their bikes to a rack behind the inn they started for the stairs.

Their rooms were next to each other on the second floor. Jean dropped her bag on the bed and went to look at Zeppo's room. Like hers, his was decorated in shades of dark pink and rose.

"What a romantic place," Jean said. "I'll have to bring Peter here sometime."

"I don't understand what you see in that guy," Zeppo said. "I mean, just because he's handsome, charming, smart, has a good job . . ."

She laughed. "Let's go outside." They walked out into the late afternoon sun, the ocean breeze cool and fragrant. A few blocks from the inn Zeppo stopped in front of a small seafood restaurant. A sign in the window announced "Live Maine Lobster—Special This Week."

"Look," he said, excited. "I haven't had lobster in a long time. Let's eat here tonight."

"I'd love to, but it's pricy."

"Buying your dinner is the least I can do after making you put on that shirt for Setrakian."

"He probably would have groped me even if I'd been wearing a muumuu. But I'll let you buy me a lobster anyway."

They walked around the small town, browsing in shops and galleries. At one end of the main street was a large bookstore with a hand-carved wooden sign that read "Bongiorni's Books"—Edward's store.

The shop was a rarity, a successful independent bookstore. A prominent display near the door was dedicated to Hugh Rivenbark, "the bard of Mendocino," offering his twelve novels, with special play given to his latest, *Redwood Diary*. Half a dozen patrons browsed the shelves. Edward Bongiorni sat behind the counter reading a paperback, his curly dark hair tied back with a rawhide strip.

"Hello, Edward," Jean said. "Remember me? We met at Martin Wingo's funeral."

Edward put his book down and smiled warmly. "Of course, Jean and Zeppo. What brings you to Mendocino?"

"We're going out to The Eyrie this evening, but wanted to stop in and say hi," Jean said.

"I just made a pot of coffee," Edward said. "Want a cup?" He told a young man to watch the register and led them back to his office, a small room with a wooden desk in one corner surrounded by bookshelves and cartons of books. Jean and Zeppo sat in folding chairs.

"So you're visiting Hugh?" he asked as he poured them coffee.

"Yeah," Jean said. "Diane asked us to look into Martin's death. The police are getting nowhere and she needs to believe that something's being done."

"How well did you know Martin?" Zeppo asked.

"Not well, although we saw him occasionally at Hugh's," Edward said. "We were much closer to Diane. I always thought of Martin as another member of Hugh's menagerie. He collects colorful characters to use in his books. At The Eyrie we've met everyone from Sacramento gangbangers to minor British royalty."

"I never thought of Martin that way, but I guess he was a colorful character." Jean noticed several framed photos on top of a bookshelf and got up to look at them. "Your kids?" She held up a shot of two skinny, smiling teenagers, a boy and a girl.

"Yes, a few years ago. They're both in college now," he said.

Jean picked up another picture, a portrait of a lovely woman sitting on a low tree branch. She was slender and long-necked, with masses of dark curly hair and dangling earrings, dressed in a multicolored caftan. Her slender face and intelligent blue eyes reminded Jean of Edward. "Is this your sister Esther?"

"Yes."

"Who was older?"

"She was, but only by a few minutes. We were twins. I took that picture on our twenty-eighth birthday. Three months later she died."

"I'm so sorry. I know it happened a long time ago, but losing a twin must be awful, even worse than losing a regular sister."

"It was pretty bad for both Hugh and me. He never really has gotten over it."

Jean found a photo of a young, slim, dark-haired Hugh with his arm around Esther, both of them smiling, in front of the bookstore. A sign in the window announced that his

Pulitzer Prize-winning book was in stock. "How did they meet?" Jean asked.

"Esther and I were born here, and Hugh moved up in the mid-1970s. He met Esther when I had a book signing for him. He wasn't well known yet, but we were promoting local writers. It was so funny—Hugh was supposed to talk to people and sign their books, but all he did was follow Esther around. She was a frustrated writer herself, of short stories."

"It's unusual for a bookstore like yours to last this long, isn't it?" Zeppo asked.

"We're always struggling. But Hugh helps us out a lot— he bought in as part-owner when we went through a really bad spell a few years back. He also does readings here every couple of months and signings for each new book. People come from all over the world to see him."

"You stayed with him in the city the night of the wedding, didn't you?" Zeppo's tone was studiously casual.

Edward smiled. "Do you suspect one of us?"

"Nah. Just covering all the bases."

"Laurel's my alibi," Edward said, still amused. "We slept in the spare room. Hugh came home after the wedding and told us what had happened. We finally went to bed and I could hear him snoring like a chainsaw." Edward glanced at his watch. "Excuse me, but I've got to set up chairs. We're having a reading this afternoon."

"Who's the author?" Zeppo asked.

Edward mentioned a popular mystery writer Jean didn't like. Her books featured an aerobics instructor who solved crimes with the help of her pet ferret.

"Thanks for the coffee, Edward," Jean said, and she and Zeppo went back out into the breezy day.

⨎

THE PAIR strolled down to the cliff at the ocean's edge and explored the tidal pools. As the sun got lower in the sky, they walked back to the inn and changed clothes. Jean put on a white button-up shirt and narrow black pants, silver earrings, and black flats. The pants had a touch of spandex, so she hoped she wouldn't have to unbutton them if she ate too much. Zeppo wore his usual tweed jacket, slacks, and button-down shirt, this one blue.

The small, cozy restaurant was half full when they arrived; a hostess led them to a table. The walls were decorated with interesting pieces of marine hardware. A young man with a buzz cut and a white half-apron introduced himself as their waiter.

"We're going to have lobster," Zeppo announced. "Can we pick our own?"

"Of course."

"Come on, Jeannie. I'll show you about lobsters." A large tank of live ones burbled near their table. Zeppo pushed his sleeve back, reached in, and pulled out a flailing lobster, turning it over. "See, these are the swimmerets," he said, pointing to the appendages just behind the legs. "You look at the top pair. The males' are hard and bony, like this, and the females' are soft and feathery. The females have sweeter meat." He picked up several of the struggling creatures in turn, hefting and examining them. "You want one that hasn't shed recently. These are in pretty good shape, but they're never the same after a few days out of the ocean. They're really incredible right off the boat."

Their waiter came over. "Looks like you know what you're doing," he told Zeppo.

Zeppo nodded. "These are all males, right?"

"Yeah. The company we buy from protects the females so they can live a long life and make lots of new lobsters."

"OK then. We'll take this one." He handed the waiter a lobster and checked a few more. "And this one. Split and broiled, please."

The waiter carried the crustaceans into the kitchen, and Jean and Zeppo returned to their table. "Why not boiled?" Jean asked.

"Trust me, this is the best way to eat them."

Jean ordered a local Chardonnay, crisp and intense to go with lobster. "So tell me, how did Martin meet Hugh Rivenbark?" she asked. "He wasn't the kind of guy I'd imagine hanging out with a famous author, colorful character or not."

"Martin came up to Mendocino sometimes, and once he was driving around and spotted Hugh's house," Zeppo said. "Apparently it's pretty spectacular, on a high cliff above the sea. Martin really liked it, so he went right up to the door and made Hugh an offer. Hugh said no thanks, but he invited him in and they got to be friends."

"I guess since they were buddies, Martin decided not to use the *Home to Greenwood* manuscript to make Hugh sell him the house," Jean said.

"It wouldn't have worked anyway. Hugh loves the house, and like we said before, he'd just be annoyed if the manuscript went public. It wouldn't really cause him any trouble."

The waiter delivered their lobsters, split lengthwise, the exposed surface delicately browned, accompanied by salad and sourdough bread. "Mmm, you're right," Jean said as they dug in. "This is delicious, better than boiled." She dipped a chunk of meat into melted butter. "I love eating with my hands."

"Me too," Zeppo said as he skillfully extracted the meat from a leg.

"Zeppo, how did Esther die? I didn't want to ask Edward."

"Martin said he and Hugh talked about it. And I did some research after I got the manuscript. See, Hugh had wooden steps built into the cliff below his house so he could get down to the water. She fell off them one day at low tide and smashed her head on a rock."

"Where was he when she fell?"

"Up at the house, writing at his desk. The investigation cleared him. They got along great, he didn't have a girlfriend, she didn't have a boyfriend. He had no motive to kill her. Like Edward said, he was really broken up. He never remarried."

"He must have had girlfriends. That was thirty years ago."

"Martin said there've been women, but they never last. Have you read any of his books?"

"Of course. I was an English major." Jean washed down a bite of lobster with Chardonnay, enjoying the combination.

"What do you think of them?" Zeppo asked.

"I love his descriptions of the Mendocino coast. His plots are heavy on male posturing and father-son angst, neither of which fascinates me, and most of his female characters are too wimpy, but he knows how to write. You've read him, too, haven't you?"

"Yeah. I like *Home to Greenwood* best, like everybody else."

Jean ate her last bite of lobster. "That was wonderful. I could almost eat another one."

"Well, why don't we? I can afford it. Plus we have time."

Jean laughed. "That's pretty decadent, even for me."

"Hey, I once ate five of them at one sitting."

"Did you? OK, let's go for it."

"Good. I admire a woman with healthy appetites." He called the waiter, and before they were through Jean was glad she'd worn stretchy pants.

CHAPTER 20

*A*fter dinner Zeppo drove south along Highway 1 for a few miles, turning west on a side road. It was dark, but they could hear and smell the ocean ahead of them. They rounded a bend and saw, on the edge of a nearby bluff, a large well-lit house built of weathered wood and glass, all dramatic angles and sweeping lines. Zeppo turned into the driveway, drove through a grove of trees, and came out into a clearing next to the house. Floodlights illuminated a gravel area where a silver Nissan sedan and an old Chevy pickup were parked. Zeppo pulled the Jag in next to them.

Hugh, in jeans and a cable-knit sweater, opened the massive front door and shook their hands. "Welcome," he said warmly. "You're providing a much-needed diversion."

He led them into the house. The interior was as dramatic and grandly scaled as the exterior—big open rooms, high ceilings with exposed beams, oversized chairs and couches, rough-hewn wooden tables. A bound manuscript with a pen clipped to it lay open on one of the tables next to a pair of reading glasses.

Jean and Zeppo settled into chairs near a wall-sized window that looked out over the cliff and the dark ocean. Hugh brought a bottle of wine from the kitchen. "I'm making final corrections on my latest novel," he said. "It's always disheartening to realize it isn't as good as I thought it was when I wrote it." He poured them wine, a Mendocino

Petite Sirah Jean wasn't familiar with, and sat down in one of the big chairs. "Zeppo says you're looking into Martin's death."

"We thought you might have some ideas about it," Jean said. She sipped her dark purple wine, tasting black cherries and smoke, with traces of buttery oak and vanilla on the finish. Delicious—she made a mental note to research the winery.

"Martin was a fascinating man," Hugh said, leaning back in his chair. "He was entirely in the tradition of the Borgias in fifteenth-century Italy or the nineteenth-century American robber barons. Unlike our current crop of corporate scoundrels, he actually produced something useful. Do you know why he called his yacht the *Walrus?*"

"Sure," Zeppo said. "That's the name of Flint's pirate ship in *Treasure Island.*"

"Exactly. As you two know full well, he was completely unscrupulous in business. What I found refreshing was that he didn't pretend to be anything else. And he was a good friend to me." Hugh chuckled. "Although I must admit I was taken aback when I got my old *Home to Greenwood* manuscript in the mail. I thought it had been burned years ago. Thank God it didn't fall into the hands of a desperate graduate student."

"Have you really written all your books longhand?" Jean asked. "I could never be a writer without a computer."

"In fact I have. I pride myself on it. The act of putting words on paper clarifies my ideas and physically embodies my thoughts. Martin was a creature of habit—he had no use for the manuscript, yet for some reason he kept it with all his other incriminating material. He told me about the blue box, Zeppo. I know what you did for him and how highly he valued you."

"You knew about that?" Zeppo said, surprised.

"Oh yes. I may even use the idea in a book I'm planning. I didn't know the details, of course, but I knew what it was and how he used it. That's why Diane asked you to investigate, isn't it? Knowing her, I imagine she doesn't want the police to make all the secrets public."

"That's why Jean's involved," Zeppo said. "I'm doing it for the old pirate himself. We're operating on the assumption that someone from the blue box killed him."

"We're also taking a look at Kay," Jean said. "What can you tell us about her?"

"Kay. That woman terrifies me. She has absolutely no convictions, but she's very intelligent and a natural politician. I'd even call her Machiavellian. And with her Rational Right movement, she's becoming a major player."

"Do you think she could have killed Martin?" Jean asked.

"She wouldn't have any moral qualms about homicide. As far as that goes, I don't think she'd have any moral qualms about genocide. But there would have to be a very strong reason for her to risk everything. I've been thinking a lot about who could have killed him, of course, and I haven't come up with any sort of motive that would work for Kay. Their divorce was amicable—the grounds were the usual irreconcilable differences. I think you're probably right that the motive is in the blue box."

They sipped their wine in silence for a few moments. "We talked to Edward today," Jean said. "He showed us Esther's picture. She was lovely."

"Yes, she was beautiful. Edward and I are a couple of sorry old men when it comes to Esther. We have a tendency to drink too much and reminisce. But at least he has Laurel and his children. Before long he'll have grandchildren, too. Esther was all I had."

He got up and went to the window, looking out at the breakers below him. "This is going to sound bathetic, but I know I haven't written anything worthwhile in decades. Something went out of me when she died." He turned back to them with a self-deprecating smile. "But enough of this morbid self-absorption. How's Diane doing these days?"

They talked about other things as they finished the Petite Sirah. Jean and Zeppo thanked Hugh and left around ten, Jean driving.

"What do you think of Hugh?" Zeppo asked.

"I like him. Although I wonder about people who're still hung up on a lover who's been dead for decades. There's always an ulterior motive. Hugh's using it as an excuse for the decline in his writing."

"But if he really loved her, maybe he was never the same after she died."

"Oh come on. He couldn't get over it in thirty years? He couldn't meet anyone else in all that time?"

Zeppo smiled at her. "Not everybody's as tough as you are."

"Too bad he couldn't tell us anything useful about Kay," Jean said. "Roman would be so happy if we could tie her to Martin's death." Jean pulled into a parking space near the inn and they went inside.

"That was a good day, Jeannie, except for your run-in with Setrakian," Zeppo said. "It doesn't seem to bother you too much, though."

"If you let that kind of thing get to you, you're giving the assholes power over you. Getting mad helps."

"And hitting back helps, too, I bet."

"Yeah, that helps a lot." They said good night on the landing and went into their pink rooms.

⌘

THE NEXT morning Jean and Zeppo donned helmets and tight-fitting cycling clothes and headed south on Highway 1, Jean in the lead, past The Eyrie to the tiny town of Elk. They turned inland there and climbed through the green wooded hills that rose above the coastal plain, passing vineyards, apple orchards, and herds of sheep and cattle grazing on the steeper slopes. Traffic was light on the back roads. A couple of times they had to ride on the shoulder when fully loaded logging trucks passed too close.

Jean felt relaxed and elated, and slowed to enjoy the view as they rode in the outside lane, winding along a steep green slope.

"Jean!" Zeppo yelled. "Get off the road!"

With his shout, she became aware of an engine coming up behind them. There was no shoulder. Thinking they were about to be crushed by a logging truck, she turned her bike sharply and rode down a grassy bank onto a flat area a few feet below. Zeppo landed next to her. An old white Jeep Cherokee nearly slid down after them—the driver cut his wheels back just in time, spraying them with gravel.

CHAPTER 21

"*T*hat car tried to run us down," Zeppo panted. "Let's get away from the road."

The downward slope continued for several yards. They rode to the bottom and along its base, on a bumpy cattle track that followed the road to their left. Another steep hill rose on the right. Jean could hear the Jeep's engine revving.

Zeppo looked back. "He's coming after us."

Jean glanced over her shoulder—the Jeep had found an easier way down and was behind them on the cattle track, gaining fast. The driver was unrecognizable in a ski mask, sunglasses, and a bulky jacket.

"Fuck!" she exclaimed. "Let's go over the hill." She turned off the track and sprinted up the slope, standing on her pedals, pumping as hard as she could. Zeppo hung back long enough for her to get ahead and pulled in behind her. "What are you doing?" she yelled.

"Shut up and ride, Jeannie."

As they ascended a steep grassy pasture scattered with oaks, they kept the trees between them and the Jeep, which came up after them. Jean pushed up the hill, her lungs straining and legs quivering with effort, fear and adrenaline fueling her. Finally she flew over the crest, both tires leaving the ground, Zeppo right on her tail.

The landing jarred her bones, and it took all her strength and concentration to navigate the sheer, rocky downhill slope as they skidded and slid to the bottom of the hill. There were fewer trees on this side, but the Jeep would roll if it tried to follow them.

As the ground leveled out, the forest got thicker and they rode quickly into a stand of trees. Jean looked back at Zeppo. Suddenly her front wheel struck something and she went down, sprawling on the rocky ground. Soon Zeppo knelt beside her. "Are you OK?"

Jean was stunned for a moment. Her right arm and leg were skinned, but everything seemed intact. "Just scraped up, I think." She listened briefly. "I don't hear the Jeep anymore, but we should get out of here anyway."

Zeppo helped her up and they pushed their bikes deeper through the trees to a dense grove of pines. Jean laid her bike down and fell exhausted onto a thick carpet of pine needles. She struggled to catch her breath.

Zeppo was breathing hard, too. "What a rush!" he exclaimed. "I've never ridden like that before in my whole fucking life. Of course, I've never been that scared before. Let's have a look at your leg." She extended it for him. There was a four-inch cut just below her knee, bleeding profusely. "Oh shit." His face, flushed from the ride, grew pale, and he closed his eyes.

"Hey Zeppo, don't faint on me," she said.

"Man, I hate the sight of blood." He took a breath and then examined the cut. "It's not deep. I don't think you'll need stitches." He raised her leg and gently rotated the ankle and flexed the knee. "How does that feel?"

"Fine. Nothing's broken."

"Can you ride?" he asked.

"Sure. I've had worse falls. Did you see the driver? Ski mask and all?"

"Yeah. It could have been anybody."

Zeppo rinsed her cut with water from his bottle and patched it with bandages from his first-aid kit. When he was done, he patted her knee. "That's the best I can do for now."

"It's fine, thanks." Jean carefully stretched her cut leg and touched her side. She'd have some bruises there as well. "He must have followed us all the way from the inn," she said. "I guess we're doing something right, partner. We sure as hell pushed somebody's buttons."

"I'd say Setrakian—he hates me and you threatened him. But we didn't exactly sneak out of town, and we're not what I'd call inconspicuous. I mean, consider: a six-foot-five redheaded geek and a silver-haired Amazon driving a Jaguar that's older than we are."

Jean laughed. "Incognito. That's us. By the way, thanks for getting between me and the car, you idiot."

"I'm here to serve and protect, Ma'am. Let's go take a look."

Zeppo helped Jean up. The cut stung, but she was able to move around fine. They pushed their bikes back through the woods to the base of the hill.

"You wait here," Zeppo told her. He climbed the rocky slope and went over the top. Soon he reappeared and gave her a thumbs-up as he slid back down. "The Jeep's still there, stuck. Has two flat tires. I don't see the driver anywhere. I got the license number."

"Did you bring your cell?" she asked. "We could check on people's whereabouts."

"Nah, I don't usually take it riding." Zeppo sat beside her. "Jeannie," he said, "I'd rather not get the police involved, because if they are, we'll have to explain why someone would want to run us down. We'll have to name all the people we've talked to and explain about the blue box. If we report it as a hit and run and the car turns out to belong to one of our suspects, same result. The whole thing will end up in the news. I'd like to keep going without reporting this. But I'll understand if you want to tell the police."

"I'm with you. Let's keep it quiet. And it's my own fault I fell. I wasn't watching where I was going."

"I was hoping you'd say that. I'm determined to find out who killed Martin, and I'd love your help. But if you want to bail—"

"I'll stay in. I haven't had an adrenaline rush like that in years. This is really exciting."

"It's also dangerous."

"We still have to narrow down our list of suspects," Jean said. "We haven't really eliminated anyone but Setrakian, and I don't want to ruin Emory or Treadway if they're innocent."

They walked their bikes around the hill; it was longer than going over, but Jean didn't think she could climb it now. They got back on their bikes, and she felt her bruises and exhausted leg muscles protesting as they worked their way back down to the main road. Zeppo had to slow for her several times. He rode ahead so she could slipstream him, which she really appreciated once they got onto Highway 1 and had to fight a headwind.

In Mendocino they bought gauze bandages, tape, and antibiotic ointment. In her hotel room Jean took a long shower. The hot water stung but made her feel better. Bruises were coming up all along her right side and leg, and she knew she'd be stiff and sore by the time they got home.

Jean dried herself carefully, trying not to bleed on the pink towels, and bandaged her leg sitting naked on the rose-colored bed. She struggled for a few minutes with her skinned arm, but soon gave up and phoned Zeppo's room.

"Zeppo, it's me. Can you bandage my arm? I don't want to leak on my clothes."

"I'll be right there."

She put on her red silk robe with a dragon embroidered on the back and opened the door for him. He was barefoot, still in his riding shorts and shirt.

"Now Zeppo," she said, "I'm not trying to be a tease, but I can't put my clothes on until this thing is covered up. Is it going to bother you?"

"No way," he said. "I've always wanted to play doctor with you."

She pulled the robe off her right arm and tucked it across her breasts. They sat on the bed near the pile of bandages. "Leave it to me, sweetheart," Zeppo said. "I'm descended from a long line of big-time physicians." He was still warm from the ride and smelled not unpleasantly of perspiration. He put ointment on the scrape and wound the gauze around her arm, taping it up neatly. "There you go." He patted her shoulder. "See? Didn't I tell you I have great self-control? I'll go take a cold shower and then we'll hit the road."

Jean smiled. "Meet you downstairs in an hour, OK?"

They were on the road well before noon. "I made some calls," Zeppo told her. "Emory's at Sputnik. Treadway's at the shop but Felix isn't. Setrakian's not home. I called Blythe Newman, and she says he owns an old Mercedes station wagon and a new Corvette."

"Which could mean he borrowed a car or stole one. Did you call Rivenbark?"

"No. I guess I should have."

"Don't worry about it," Jean said. "He'd have had plenty of time to get home before we got back to the hotel, even without a car. This is one of the few places on the planet where people still pick up hitchhikers. Anyway, we don't have a motive for him."

They tossed ideas around and listened to the blues, and before Jean knew it they were inching across the Golden Gate Bridge in heavy afternoon traffic.

CHAPTER 22

*A*fter dropping Jean's bike at Roman's, the two drove to Zeppo's apartment.

"Let's write those letters about Setrakian," he said as he booted up his computer. "We'll send one to Elan's head of PR and one to the reporter of your choice."

"How about Helen Tang?" Jean offered. "She wrote that great series on sexual harassment in the workplace for the *Examiner*. She'd love to screw Armand. Metaphorically, of course."

They composed brief anonymous letters detailing the complaints filed against Setrakian. Zeppo printed out the letters, and they dropped them in a mailbox on the way to Jean's apartment.

"Jeannie," he said as they drove toward Noe Valley, "we have to be careful now. Don't open your door unless you know who it is. Don't go out alone after dark. Stay in crowded areas. And we should keep track of each other. We can't forget that we're in danger."

"Definitely. What are you going to do tomorrow?"

"Get on the Net and do research on Kay and Frank, like Roman suggested, and see what I can find out about Spider and Rhino Fitness. What about you?"

"I'm supposed to see Peter tonight, and later I'll tell Diane what's going on. Otherwise I'll stay close to home."

They stopped at Whole Foods Market on 24th Street for groceries, then Zeppo dropped Jean at her apartment. She thought about Peter as she unpacked her purchases. She should see him, but didn't really want to. Her cuts and bruises hurt, for one thing. The unedited version of the trip to Mendocino would make him angry and he'd scold her. Even if she didn't tell him, she'd have to give Diane the whole story, and Diane would tell Peter, and then he'd be angry with her for holding things back. She decided to postpone the whole problem.

Jean called him at work. "Hi. I'm home. Armand Setrakian is a dick and Hugh Rivenbark is really interesting."

"Have you cracked the case yet?" he asked sarcastically.

"Come on, Peter, lighten up."

He sighed. "Sorry. I'm leaving work soon—I'll pick you up."

"Listen, I'm going to cancel. I fell off my bike and I'm all bruised and skinned up."

"Are you OK?" His pique was gone now; she heard only concern in his voice. "Do you need to see a doctor?"

"No, I just want to rest for a day. We'll do something tomorrow."

"That's no good. I have to go to Seattle and take a deposition. I won't be home until midday Saturday."

"Then we'll go out Saturday night. I'll be ready to dance by then."

"It's a date. But call me if you start to feel worse, OK? Call Diane if I'm gone."

"I promise. Have a good trip, Peter."

Jean slept late the next day and woke to pain and stiffness all along her right side, so she decided to stay in bed as long as possible. She lazed around listening to music and reading her current mystery, the latest installment of John Burdett's Bangkok saga. By the time Diane called her in the late afternoon, she was craving Thai food in the worst way. Diane invited her to dinner—no Thai food tonight.

Zeppo phoned after she'd hung up with Diane. "Hey, Jeannie," he said. "How are you feeling?"

"Not too bad. I'll live."

"I'm glad to hear it. I called Rhino Fitness. Spider used to work there as a personal trainer, but he quit a few weeks ago to take a job in San Jose."

"You have any theories?" she asked.

"Not enough information yet. I need to talk to that bartender, Rudy. Why don't I come over tomorrow and we'll see what we know?"

"OK. I'll call you then." They hung up.

In the evening, Jean slipped into a loose red knit dress that didn't constrict any of her wounds and drove to St. Francis Wood.

"What in the world happened to you?" Diane said as Jean limped into the house.

"I fell off my bike."

"I wish you'd be more careful, Jean." In the living room, the coffee table held a motley grouping of high-end objets d'art and expensive knickknacks. Empty gift boxes were piled on the floor and a nearby trash can held ribbons and wrapping paper.

"Finally opening those wedding presents, I see," Jean said.

"Yes. I debated for a long time whether to keep them. But sending them back seemed even less appropriate. I'm writing to thank everyone for the gifts and for their help and support."

"I'll give you my gift in a month or so. I'm making you a quilt."

"I can't wait. I'd love to have something you made."

Jean usually dreaded Diane's cooking, but was looking forward to dinner tonight—Martin's chef, Celia, had stayed on. She'd left them a lovely meal of quiche Lorraine, green salad with caramelized pecans, and a bottle of Oregon Pinot Noir.

"Tell me all about what you've been up to," Diane said as they ate.

"Let me ask you a question first," Jean said. "Back in high school, how did you get the job with Frank?" She loved the wine, which smelled and tasted of plums and roses.

"I answered an ad in the paper. Why?"

"Indulge me. Do you have a copy of your birth certificate?"

"Of course."

"What does it say for 'father'?"

"Unknown." Diane smiled. "You think Frank is my father, right?"

"It occurred to me."

"I thought of that, too, when he and Connie invited me to move in with them. I couldn't understand why they'd be so nice to me otherwise. I had self-esteem issues back then. When I asked Frank, he explained that he loved me like a father but wasn't mine. I wanted proof, so he had his family doctor test our blood since that was easy, if not necessarily conclusive, but in this case it was—he couldn't have fathered me. So I think you can cross him off your list."

"OK." But not until she ran it by Zeppo.

As Jean finished a second slice of quiche, she told Diane about Treadway's, Felix, the visit to Sputnik, the interview with Setrakian, the Bongiornis, and the evening at Hugh's. The story of the perilous bike ride horrified her friend.

"Jean, we have to go to the police," Diane said. "Peter's right—he's angry at me for putting you in harm's way. You have to stop now."

"Not yet. Zeppo and I want to keep going for a little while longer, at least until we can narrow our list of suspects. Anyway, Zeppo will keep investigating no matter what, and I don't want him to do it alone. That really *would* be dangerous. We're being careful, and besides, it's very exciting. Please don't tell Peter about the Jeep, OK?"

"You can't keep him in the dark forever, Jean. He cares about you."

"I know, but it's safety first with him. That's never been my philosophy." Jean told Diane about the letters they'd sent detailing Setrakian's peccadilloes.

"How could you do that?" Diane demanded angrily. "You know I don't want to expose anyone in the blue box. That's the whole reason I asked you to help."

"Yeah, but we agreed that didn't apply to anyone whose crimes were serious. I consider serial sexual assault serious."

"Setrakian's going to be furious. You've made things even more dangerous for yourself."

"What can he do?" Jean said. "He'll get a lot of bad publicity, and then other women he's attacked will come forward. He may even be prosecuted. We'll be the least of his problems. Look, I'm sorry. If something like it comes up again, I'll talk it over with you first, OK?"

They cleared the table and went back to the living room. Jean noticed a beautiful bentwood glider-style rocker with curling, elegant lines where the pile of wedding gifts had been. She sat down and rocked. "What's this great chair?" she asked.

"That's from Hugh. Isn't it beautiful? It's been here since a month before the wedding, but presents got piled on it. He sent a rocking chair as a joke about Martin's retirement, but what a rocking chair."

"Here's a card, taped to the back." Jean handed it to Diane.

"Isn't that pretty. He writes, 'When a man steps back from his life, he can judge it and know its true worth, like a painter stepping back from his easel.'"

"That's from *Home to Greenwood*," Jean said. "The father is explaining why he's retiring early even though it'll screw up the family logging business. Let's see it." The front featured a stunning black and white photo of a Mendocino landscape, windblown trees jutting out of steep, rocky cliffs. Jean opened it. The few lines were neatly written in a bold, clear, upright hand, with Hugh's signature at the bottom. She stared at the card, immobile.

"What's wrong, Jean?"

"Eureka," she said softly.

"What is it?"

"I have to show this to Zeppo. Right now."

"Why?"

"I can't say. I don't want to upset you for nothing."

"Jean, come on. What is it? You can't just leave me like this."

"Please, let me do this my way. That's what you hired me for."

"But why go over there? Use the fax in Martin's office."

"I want to do this in person."

"Oh, all right." Diane frowned as Jean dialed the phone.

"Zeppo, it's me. I have to come over right away, and don't say anything crude."

"*Moi?* I don't know the meaning of the word."

"See you in twenty minutes." She hung up and turned to Diane. "I'll have him look at this and then I'll call you, OK?"

"OK, but call soon, will you? I want to know what this is about."

Jean drove to Cow Hollow and parked at a fire hydrant a block from Zeppo's apartment. She ran up the steps as he opened the door.

"What's so urgent, Jeannie?"

"You have to see this." Inside his apartment she handed him the card.

He looked at the picture and opened it. "Very nice. Sounds familiar. OK, signed by Big Hugh." He stared at it for a couple of beats. "And congratulations, you win a month with me on a desert island. This is a completely different handwriting from the manuscript."

"Ha! I knew this wasn't the big sloppy writing you described."

"You're absolutely right. This has a different shape, different slant, different everything. Remember I told you there were editing notes? That's what this writing is like." He looked at her. "What if he didn't even *write* the fucking book?"

"That's exactly what I thought. There's no other reason it would be in someone else's handwriting."

"I bet Esther wrote it. She was a writer, too, and who else would let him take credit?"

"He could say he dictated it to her, but then there are all those interviews where he ranted on about the physical connection between him and his work. All we have to do is get a sample of her writing from Edward. And you know what else—now I'm wondering about her death."

Zeppo nodded. "Yeah, what if he had writer's block and persuaded her to write it for him? And what if she had second thoughts after the book won the Pulitzer? Hugh couldn't face the humiliation, so he pushed her off the steps. That sure would explain why Martin kept the manuscript all these years. Now that's a damn good motive for both their murders."

"Hugh must have thought the manuscript was long gone. He panicked when he realized someone else had seen it. If Martin hadn't had you send it back, he never would have ended up in the bay. But why did Hugh wait until the wedding to do anything about it?"

"He was on a book tour until the day before," Zeppo said. "He must not have seen the thing until he got back. Man, if this is true, what a show he put on for us at his house. All broken up over his long-lost wife. He was 'taken aback' when he got the manuscript. He must have practically had a stroke. And don't forget the touching eulogy he delivered. It's a cinch he tried to run us down. I'm the only one who saw it, but he must figure you know too much about it, too." Zeppo thought for a moment. "You know, Hugh could be the actual murderer. He's really tight with the Bongiornis. If Edward didn't know Hugh killed his sister, they might lie for him."

"They sure might," Jean said. "Why do you suppose Martin wouldn't say who pushed him when he called me?"

"He must have had something special planned for his old pal. Maybe he was going to force Hugh to sell him The Eyrie. Or give it to him outright."

"But Martin would have had to tell the police who pushed him as soon as he came home. I wonder what he was up to." She gripped his arm. "Hey, even though we don't know who killed him, we actually figured out part of it. We'll go to the police in the morning. You can tell the whole story. This means we won't have to mention the blue box at all—you can say Martin gave you the manuscript to send back, period."

Zeppo pulled away and handed the card back to her. "I can't do that, Jeannie." He was strangely subdued.

"Why not? I'll go with you."

"No, I can't go to the police. I . . . uh . . . I have a record."

"A police record?"

"Yeah."

"You're not a fugitive, are you?"

"No, it's over. I just can't deal with the police. I can't take any more publicity."

"When did it happen? If you were a juvenile, the records would be sealed."

"Just drop it. I can't do it."

"Why won't you tell me what it's about?"

"Because . . . because . . ." He began to pace. "Trust me. I can't."

"But we haven't found any other evidence against him. He probably tried to kill us, remember? He might try again."

"Jeannie, please. I don't want to fight with you."

"Goddammit, what did you think would happen when we got evidence on someone?"

"I thought you could tell the police, that I wouldn't have to be involved."

"You're more involved than anyone! What about before I joined up, when you were working by yourself? What were you going to do if you found the killer?"

"I figured I'd tell Peter and he'd tell the police. Look, you can go to Davila. He likes you. Say you saw the manuscript."

"But I didn't see it. I can't answer any questions about it. Only you can."

"No."

"Don't shut down on me, Zeppo. Tell me what you did. Do you think I'll be shocked? I know you, and I know it can't be that bad."

"It might be worse than you think."

"Oh for God's sake, stop playing games and tell me what it is!"

"You'd better go," he said.

"What am I supposed to say to Diane?"

"Please, Jean. I never thought I'd ask you to leave, but I'm doing it now."

Jean stopped herself before she lost her temper and insulted him. He seemed in genuine pain. She took a deep breath. "OK," she said, "I'll go. But you haven't heard the end of this." She slammed out of his apartment and drove to Noe Valley.

After a long search for a parking space and a long walk home, Jean felt less furious. She tacked Hugh's card to her bulletin board and sat at the kitchen table with a glass of Cognac. When she felt calmer, she called Diane.

"Well?" her friend demanded.

"I wasn't able to resolve anything. Can I get back to you in a day or so?"

"Jean, you're giving me a headache. Is it about Hugh?"

"Could be. Please don't mention it to Peter or anyone, OK?"

"OK, but I think you're way off base. Hugh was one of Martin's oldest friends. He's my friend, too, you know."

"That's why I want to check it out thoroughly. I'll call you as soon as I can." Jean went to bed early, the Cognac putting her into a troubled sleep.

CHAPTER 23

*A*s Jean drank her coffee and ate a croissant the next morning, she thought about why Zeppo felt so threatened by official attention that he would let Rivenbark go. Zeppo wasn't a coward and didn't care much about what people thought of him, so whatever happened must have been serious. Well, if he wouldn't tell her, she'd find out by herself. He feared more publicity, which meant he'd been in the newspapers. She was going to do some digging.

A web search using his name turned up nothing relevant, and she had no other name or date or keywords to use. She'd have to do it the old-fashioned way. Based on things he'd said and done, she had a good idea where to start.

Jean's arm felt better, and anyway, there was no one to help her. So she slapped on a couple of adhesive bandages, dressed in jeans and a purple sweatshirt, put a notebook in her shoulder bag, and walked to the Toyota. The trip to the Civic Center was quick on Saturday, and she arrived just as the public library opened.

For the next few hours Jean sat in front of the microfiche machine, getting a headache from the bad light as she read endless old headlines and looked at blurry black and white photos. At noon she went outside, where she bought a falafel from a stand and washed down two Motrins with more coffee. Then she got back to work.

Just after five o'clock she found it. It wasn't arson or burglary or drug dealing or anything else she'd been expecting—it was murder.

Jean read the accounts with growing horror, but couldn't reconcile the man she knew with the boy in the newspaper stories. She studied the photos of the beautiful victim, the crime scene, Zeppo's stone-faced family, and of course Zeppo himself: sullen in a school portrait, scared but defiant in handcuffs, grim and alone in the back of a police car, and painfully young. After reading all the articles, she sat stunned for several minutes. She slowly rewound the film, shut off the machine, and left the library. Halfway to the Muni station she remembered she'd driven down. She walked back to the car, turning things over in her head.

Should she believe the newspapers or trust her own judgment? Her instincts about men had always been very reliable—she knew no subject better. Zeppo might be obnoxious and oversexed, but then a lot of people thought *she* was obnoxious and oversexed. The better she got to know him, the more good qualities she found and the more she liked him.

She remembered what Gwen had told her—how he never got close, even to the women he dated. He clearly loved women and craved their company, and now she understood why he always kept his distance.

Jean knew innocent people were sometimes incarcerated and even executed. Zeppo had been acquitted, but on technicalities, and the newspaper articles strongly implied that he'd gotten away with murder. To her, though, only one explanation made sense—he really was innocent.

What did she have to lose by confronting him? If she was wrong, was she in any danger? No. Jean recalled the way he'd gotten behind her when Rivenbark was trying to run them down, his gentle touch when she was hurt, his reaction to Setrakian. She'd been alone with him in his apartment when he was drunk and no dark side had emerged. He'd never touched her except as a friend. Yesterday, when she yelled at him, he hadn't fought back at all. She didn't think he was capable of violence. And if she couldn't tell whether a man she knew had committed that type of murder, she might as well hang up her spurs.

Deep in thought, Jean missed the turn onto her street and had to drive around the block. She went up to her apartment and sat for a long time staring out the window at the fog pouring in from the bay. The message light on her phone blinked, but she didn't feel like hearing from anyone. She thought through the evidence on both sides, and her resolve remained unshaken.

Dark was falling. She was hungry, so she heated some leftover pasta. When she was done eating, she took a half-full bottle of Cognac out of her cupboard, put it in her purse, and drove across town to Cow Hollow.

CHAPTER 24

Zeppo's light was on, and when he answered the door, wearing jeans and an old black *Mask of Zorro* T-shirt emblazoned with a big red "Z," he was as troubled and subdued as he'd been the night before.

"Hi, Jeannie," he said hesitantly. "Are we still friends?"

"Of course. Can I come in?"

"Please do." He stepped back and she walked past him into the apartment. "But I don't want to fight anymore, OK?"

She faced him. "Zeppo, I know why you won't go after Rivenbark."

"You do, huh?"

"Listen: I spent all day finding out. I know what happened eight years ago in Cheswick."

Zeppo sagged visibly and turned away from her. "Ah, hell," he said, his voice low and defeated. He leaned on the windowsill, looking down at the street.

"Now I know why you live like a transient, lie about your family, never date the same girl for long. All your quirks make sense."

"So your curiosity is satisfied. Weren't you afraid to come over here alone?"

Jean touched his arm. "No, I wasn't, and I'll tell you why. I've been with a lot of men in my life, taken a lot of chances, and nothing has ever gone really wrong. That's because I learned early to spot men with the potential for that kind of violence. There's a brittle, hollow quality, something I can't put into words, and when I sense it I run like hell. Setrakian has it in spades. But you don't have it. You love women. The bottom line is, I don't think you killed her."

Zeppo put his hand over hers and squeezed. "Thank you for that, Jeannie."

"I understand what you're afraid of—if we go to the police and they run your fingerprints, you're finished as a credible witness. And then the media will be all over you. I can see the headlines now: 'Murder Suspect Worked for Murdered Developer.' "

"They already have my fingerprints. For elimination purposes so they could check the prints in Martin's office after somebody searched it. I couldn't refuse without looking suspicious. For all I know they've already run them." Zeppo rubbed his face. "Have you told anyone else?"

"Of course not."

"God, it's so hard for me to talk about this. The only person I've ever discussed it with is my shrink. Martin knew about it, of course."

"He didn't!"

"Sure did. He never missed an angle. One day he noticed something weird in my personnel file. I'd written down two different birth dates by mistake. So we made a bet. If he could figure it out, I'd work a week for free. I didn't think he'd bother, but he dug around in his spare time, and it shook him. I never saw him so surprised, before or since. I had him call Hannah, my shrink, and she convinced him I didn't do it, so he never mentioned it again. He just told me, 'Too bad I don't want anything from you—I've got a hell of a handle.' "

"Are you still in touch with Hannah?"

"Yeah. In fact she's my alibi. After the wedding I took a long drive down the coast and called her. We talked for a couple of hours. I was on the phone with her when Martin died."

"Well, now you need to talk to me."

"It's not that easy, Jean. I'd feel . . . exposed."

"But I'm not going to hurt you, Zeppo. I like you. I want to understand how things could have gone so wrong for you."

"I'm still working on that one myself."

Zeppo, pale and dejected, flopped into the brown corduroy chair. Jean got two wine glasses from the kitchen and poured them each a generous ration of Cognac. "Here. Cognac's always good in a crisis."

"Thanks." He took a big swallow.

Jean pulled the computer chair next to him. "All right, here's what I know: Your real name is Michael Van Vleck. You're the youngest of three brothers from a rich family in Cheswick, a suburb of Boston. Dad's a prominent surgeon, Mom's a big noise in society.

"It's late December 2002. Your oldest brother and his wife are home for the holidays. On Christmas morning just before dawn, your family runs downstairs when they hear you yelling. They find you kneeling next to your sister-in-law's body. There's a bloody knife lying on the floor. You both have her blood all over you."

Zeppo stared into space. He took another sip. "You OK?" she asked. He nodded.

"So the police arrest you, the misfit brother who's been in and out of trouble for years. You're fifteen but they try you as an adult, mostly because you won't make any kind of deal. Throughout the trial you insist that you're innocent. Then you get lucky—key evidence is thrown out because of police errors. You walk, but everyone assumes you're guilty, just like O.J."

"That's about it."

"What happened after that?"

Zeppo didn't speak for several seconds. His eyes looked different now, sad and tired and old. "After that my family had me committed to a private psychiatric hospital for disturbed adolescents outside Boston. One of my dad's psychiatrist friends signed the papers. I spent two years there, until I was eighteen. See, my family thought I was guilty, too. All but one of them."

"The one who did it. Do you know who it was?"

He shook his head slowly. "I'm not sure, but I think it was my dad."

"Oh Zeppo, what a hell of a thing." She reached out and touched his arm.

"You really want the whole ugly story?"

"Yes, I really do."

"OK, then." He drank more Cognac. "I was a mistake from the beginning—they wanted a girl, and I could never do anything right. My two brothers were basketball stars, honor students, president of everything. To them, and to my father, I was a clumsy, worthless, embarrassing loser. So of course that's what I turned into. I cut class, smoked dope, sniffed glue, vandalized the school, stole a car, stuff like that."

He spoke faster, staring straight ahead. "Eric, my oldest brother, followed in my dad's footsteps and went to Harvard. He married Sarah after his junior year. She was a real beauty—long blond hair, big green eyes—and I had a huge crush on her. See, my brothers and father treated me like shit and my mother always acted disappointed, but Sarah was nice to me and defended me.

"That Christmas she was visiting over vacation. Eric had to stay and finish up a lab project, and he got back on Christmas Eve. Andy, my other brother, was still living at home. There must have been incredible tension in the house, something building up, but I didn't see it. I was just glad she was there." He took a deep breath.

"I couldn't sleep, and then I heard a noise from downstairs. So I went to look. The living room was dark. Sarah was lying on the floor, and at first I couldn't figure out what was wrong with her. I knelt down and saw the knife, and I pulled it out. I tried to find a pulse on her wrist and neck. She had blood all over her. I realized she was dead, and I hugged her. Then I was covered with blood, too. She was still warm. I called for help, and people came running. Eric attacked me when he saw her. Andy pulled him off. My father tried to resuscitate her, but it was too late. She'd been stabbed five times. My father said, 'Michael, what have you done?'"

"Oh Zeppo . . ."

"It had to be someone in the house. All the doors and windows were locked and there was fresh snow on the ground but no footprints, and the dogs never barked. They got me a good lawyer—I was their son, after all. He showed that the chain of custody on the knife and some other evidence was so bad a lot of it was disallowed. Some cops got fired because of it, but my family still thought I did it.

"They found semen in her. Eric said it wasn't his. There was no evidence of rape."

"Wait a minute," Jean said. "What about DNA testing?"

"The sample got contaminated in the lab. Some techie fucked up. They disallowed that, too."

"That's a whole lot of screw-ups for one case. You know, if I wrote an article about all this and sold it to a national mag, we could get people interested in taking another look."

"Hannah suggested something like that. I know that's what I should do, but not yet."

"Tell me about the hospital."

"That was bad. At first I was in shock, feeling betrayed, hating that Sarah was dead and no one was going to pay for it. No one but me, that is. I wouldn't cooperate with the therapists since I figured they were all on my dad's side. Whenever my parents visited me, my dad would tell me how much it cost to keep me there, how I was using up my college fund and my inheritance, and that I'd have to stay until I admitted I killed her and got help."

"Good God."

"They couldn't keep me after I turned eighteen, so all I had to do was tough it out. But the last few months I was there they assigned me a new therapist, Hannah Greenwald. She got me to talk, and pretty soon I really *was* in therapy. She read the police reports and trial transcripts and decided I was innocent. I can't tell you how that made me feel, like maybe there was hope. She wanted to talk to my family, but I said no. I'm finished with them.

"Hannah brought me all those books you saw, which helped. I realized there was a whole big world out there beyond my family and the nut house, and that I wasn't the first person who ever got fucked over. I got less angry about everything and tried to be more philosophical.

"When I turned eighteen, Hannah gave me enough money to move out here. I'd worked up a new identity. You know the drill—find someone born around the same time as you who died young, get a birth certificate through the mail, and the rest is easy. I got the bike messenger job and started to have a life. Sort of."

"What a way to grow up. I don't know how you survived."

"Sometimes I didn't think I would."

Jean poured more Cognac. "Is the hospital where you learned about computers?"

"Uh huh. The only good thing about the loony bin was I got to spend a lot of time on them. I became a pretty good hacker. When I moved out here I built myself a decent system and kept up with things."

"And then Martin found you."

"Yeah. I loved working for him. He thought I was funny and smart. For the first time since I moved here I had enough money. We dealt with really interesting stuff that not even Frank knew about, so I finally had some power and some control over my life. Plus I got along great with the people in the office. It was a perfect setup. Well, you know the rest.

After Martin recovered from the heart attack he decided to be good, and I got laid off. It made me mad, because I didn't believe he'd really changed, and I lost whatever social life I had."

"Gwen misses you."

"How do you know her?"

"I was snooping around the office," Jean said. "Trying to figure you out."

"Were you really? I miss her, too."

"You should call her."

"Maybe. Then I met you when Peter brought you to the office Christmas party last year. You wore a strapless red velvet dress. You were tormenting Martin and he was trying hard not to blow a gasket. It was hilarious."

"I remember. I spilled Champagne on my shelf and you offered to lick it off."

"Sorry I was such a jerk."

"It's OK. What'll you do now, Zeppo?"

"Martin gave me enough money to live on for a while, and this fall I'm going to college. I've had a shitty education, but I did pretty well on the SATs and created some very nice high school records, so I got into U.C. Davis. There's a good computer science program there."

"That's a great idea. I'm glad you're doing that."

Zeppo drank the last of his Cognac. "So there it is. You still want to be partners?"

"Of course. Did you think I'd run out screaming?"

"I guess I knew you wouldn't." He sank back into his chair. "This is such a relief, Jeannie. It's so hard to have friends when you can't tell the truth about anything important. When you asked about my family on the way to Mendocino, I tried not to lie, and I ended up sounding totally lame. And last night, I hated not being able to explain. I hated making you angry, just when you were starting to like me." He took off his glasses and laid his head on the back of the chair, eyes closed. "I feel like I just ran a marathon."

Jean regarded him fondly. Not only did she like him, she'd come to admire him. He had survived worse things than she could imagine, and although the ordeal had scarred him, it had made him strong and self-reliant. Ten years ago she might have been more shocked by his family's reaction, before she had seen—in the lives of some of her lesbian and gay friends—how quickly a family could reject a nonconforming member. Someday she'd ask him what the police had bungled, why he thought his father had done it, and a thousand other questions, but not tonight. Tonight she was going to take him to bed.

Jean smiled to herself, feeling a warm surge of anticipation. This could be a lot of fun. She thought briefly about how upset Peter would be, but put it out of her mind. He'd get over it; he always did. She knew Zeppo was half in love with her, but didn't think he'd assume anything afterward or make demands.

Jean went over to his chair and knelt in front of him, putting a hand on each of his knees. "Zeppo," she said. "Do you have any condoms?"

He raised his head, startled. "Do I . . . yeah, in the bathroom."

"Go get them."

He gaped at her. "Are you serious?"

"You should see the look on your face. Of course I'm serious." She leaned over and kissed him softly on the lips.

He put on his glasses and lurched to the bathroom. Jean heard water running and drawers slamming. The overhead light was too bright, so she turned it off and switched on the small bedside lamp. To give him the full effect, she quickly took off her clothes, pulled back the covers on the bed, and lay down. The sheets were light blue and smelled clean. The bandages on her arm and leg detracted, but she didn't think he'd mind. He came into the room carrying a small green box and froze when he saw her. "Jesus fucking Christ, am I dreaming?"

"Come over here and I'll pinch you."

He sat down next to her and kissed her hungrily. His braces were hardly noticeable. She could tell he was nervous—he was awkward, tentative, and his hands trembled as he touched her. "Relax," she said, pulling off his Zorro T-shirt. "I know you've done this before."

"This is different." He stood and shed his pants and boxers, then lay down, moaning aloud at the feel of her body against his.

Jean ran her hands along his lean contours, liking the way he smelled, the way he felt, his newness and strangeness. She combed her fingers through the thatch of curly red hair on his chest. His pale rangy shape was so different from Peter's dark bulkiness, and she was surprised by the strength of her response to him. This seemed more and more like a really great idea. "Zeppo," she whispered, "you feel so good."

"So do you, Jeannie."

Jean knew he was excited enough to have a hair trigger, so she didn't waste any time. She unrolled a condom over his erection, and then he was inside her. They began to move together and, as she expected, he came almost at once.

"Oh shit, I'm sorry," he said as he lay next to her, dropping the condom into a bedside trash can.

"It's OK. We have all night."

"I've been fantasizing about this for so long I got ahead of myself. I'm sorry."

"Stop apologizing," she said gently. "Relax."

He rolled on his side so he could stroke her. "You're absolutely beautiful. This is unbelievable. Do you know how long I've been jacking off thinking about you?"

"I have some idea."

His big hand moved over her, his touch not too rough, not too gentle. "I never thought this would happen. I figured I'd have to be content with just spending all this time together."

Jean sighed as he fondled her in all the right places, as if he were working from a really good map. "Don't be so amazed," she said. "I just had to get to know you. Besides, after Gwen told me how oversexed you are, I had to see for myself."

"Gwen! What does she know about it?"

"Her friend who dated you complained. Polly. You were too much for her." Jean felt dizzy with desire, but didn't want to rush him.

"Yeah, she thought I was a sex fiend. But I'm not so bad. Just healthy."

"I'll bet most women like you fine." As his hand moved to her breasts, she wondered if she could have an orgasm without being touched below the waist. She'd only done that once.

He looked sheepish. "Well, I haven't actually had very many lovers, and none for very long. I always worry that if I tell them stuff, it'll be *adios*, psycho."

"That's no way to live." She couldn't believe what he was doing to her.

"It feels great not having any secrets. I've never been with a woman who knew the whole truth. I'm glad it was you who found out." He leaned over and gave her a gentle kiss.

She pulled him down and kissed him fiercely. She needn't have worried; as she caressed him, he stiffened against her immediately, finally realizing how aroused she was. "Hang on, Jeannie," he said as he took a condom out of the box and put it on.

She moved under him, guiding him in, losing herself completely, and this time it was Jean who came almost at once.

CHAPTER 25

*A*s they lay close together in the narrow bed, Jean stretched happily, her whole body still throbbing with pleasure. After his initial case of nerves subsided, Zeppo was a revelation. His awkwardness fell away in bed. He was passionate, playful, intensely considerate, and in a perpetual state of high arousal. His healthy, uncomplicated sexuality made her doubly certain of his innocence. *In coitus veritas,* she thought with a smile.

The digital clock on the nightstand said two twenty-four. It didn't matter—today was Sunday. Zeppo lay on his stomach, his face turned away from her, as still as a dead man. She hated to disturb him, but there was so much she wanted to know.

"Zeppo, are you awake?"

"Barely. What's left of me."

"Who was Jay Zeppetello?"

He turned his face toward her. "He was born ten days after me in Manhattan. That's how Martin got on to me—I screwed up and wrote June 5th on one form and June 15th on another. The kid died in a car wreck when he was eight months old. I liked the name, and it was more fun being Italian than Dutch. The bike messengers called me Zeppo, and I liked that, too."

"Do you want me to call you Michael?"

"God, no. Only Hannah calls me that. It makes me think of my family and the nut house, which I don't want to do."

Jean stroked his back with her fingertips. She had turned off the bedside lamp, and in the faint light that filtered through the curtains her hand looked dark against his skin. She traced the cycling muscles in his ass and thighs, laughing.

"What's funny?" he said.

"I was thinking about how hard I tried to discourage you."

"You couldn't do it, could you?"

"No, and I'm glad. Were you too shy to say anything to me? Anything serious, I mean."

"Nah, I knew you'd shoot me down. You made that pretty clear. So I figured I'd skip the rejection. Besides, you were with Peter. Even if you did go out with me, there'd be the same old problem—you'd want to know about me and I couldn't tell you anything."

"Sorry I was so hard on you, Zeppo."

"That's OK. You're doing a good job of making up for it."

"*Now* will you tell me the rest of the names in the blue box?"

He looked at her with alarm. "You know I can't. Ask me anything but that."

Jean laughed and whacked his ass. "Relax, I'm kidding."

Zeppo rolled over toward her. "Tell me something, Jeannie. Did you come over here planning to do this?"

"I didn't have a plan. I simply wanted to tell you I found out what happened, and that I knew you didn't kill her."

"That's the thing I can't get over—you're the only one who ever assumed I was innocent. Hannah and Martin had to be convinced. Even my lawyer thought I was guilty. But not you. I'll never forget that." Zeppo pulled her closer and she felt the heat rise, as if he'd thrown a switch.

"Where did you learn to touch a woman like this?" she asked, melting under his hands.

"I don't know. I just always imagined touching you this way. I guess it works, huh?"

"Yes, it works." She closed her eyes, and soon she was lost again.

✧

L~ATER~ ~THEY~ lay with his long frame curved against her back, his hand on one of her breasts. "How'd you figure it out, anyway?" he asked. "It only took you a day. Very impressive."

"Well, it had to be in the papers—you said you didn't want any more publicity. I can hear a New England accent sometimes when you talk, you know all about lobsters, and you're a Celtics fan. I didn't have enough information for a web search, so I went to the library and spent all day looking at the *Boston Globe* on microfiche."

He pushed himself up on his elbow. "Hey, you're turning into a real detective. How'd you know when?"

"You said you didn't go to a regular high school, so I figured it probably happened around age fourteen. I started in 2000, looking for something like 'Teen Burns Down Prep School' or 'Local Boy Sodomizes Sheep' buried on a back page. But there you were, on the front page above the fold, the day after Christmas 2002."

"Did you remember the story? It had everything—beautiful young female stabbed to death on Christmas day by deranged teen from wealthy family. It was in the national news the whole time."

"No, I was knocking around South America back then. I spent that Christmas in a youth hostel in Buenos Aires."

"I'm glad you missed it. Some asshole reporter called me the Cheswick Ripper."

"Yeah, I read that. I followed the story until you were acquitted, and then I thought things over, and then I came here."

"And the rest is history." Zeppo rolled onto his stomach and put his arm over her. She'd almost dozed off when he spoke again. "Hey, Jeannie? Remember when I told you there were more important things in life than getting laid?"

"I remember."

"Well, you've changed my mind." He was asleep before she could answer.

⌒∽⌒

JEAN WOKE before Zeppo and studied him in the midmorning light. He slept on his stomach, and his face was turned toward her. He would never be handsome—he had too much nose and not quite enough chin—but his red-blond lashes were thick and long.

He woke and smiled at her. His eyes were pretty, a light greenish-blue with a dark blue border around the iris. If he wore contact lenses, grew his hair out, got his braces off, and bought some stylish clothes, who knew? She'd have to work on it.

"Good morning, Zeppo."

"Good morning, gorgeous." He yawned and stretched, his legs hanging over the edge of the bed, and gave her a kiss. "I haven't slept this well in as long as I can remember. Just a minute." He hopped out of bed and went into the bathroom, where she heard him moving around. Time passed, and finally he exclaimed, "Goddammit!"

"What's the matter?"

"I can't piss with this hard-on."

She laughed. "Men are so poorly designed. Think about Dick Cheney in a thong."

After a few seconds she heard him urinating.

"That worked," he said as he got back into bed. "Of course, I may never get it up again."

"Somehow I can't see impotence ever being a problem for you. Hey, I did more detecting yesterday. I asked Diane

~ 190 ~

if Frank could be her father." Jean told him about the blood tests.

"So if Frank is searching for Diane's real birth certificate with his name on it, we still have to explain the incompatible blood types," Zeppo said. "I did some detecting, too. I ran the license plate from the Jeep. Someone from Ukiah reported it stolen in Mendocino early that morning. Also, I made an appointment to see Frank at his office on Tuesday."

They lay close together in companionable silence. "Jeannie," Zeppo said after a while, "I know you won't like it if I get all sentimental, but I want to thank you. This is one of the few times in my whole fucked-up life I got something I really wanted."

"You don't have to thank me, Zeppo. Can't you tell I'm having as much fun as you are?"

"Oh yeah, I can tell. It's hard to miss, all the noise you make."

"A girl has a right to express herself. Anyway, I can't help it."

"I think it's great, a real turn-on." He kissed her neck, giving her goose bumps. "Everything about you is a turn-on." They made love again, Jean straddling him, and soon Zeppo had fallen back to sleep.

Jean slipped out of bed and took a shower. Her arm was healing rapidly, so rather than wake him, she decided to go without bandages. As she tiptoed toward the door, Zeppo called her name. She came back and sat on the bed.

"You leaving?" he said.

"Yeah. Peter will be going nuts by now. He hates it when he can't find me."

"OK, if you've gotta. So what's the deal? This isn't just a one-time thing, is it? I'm not trying to push you, but I'd love to do it again."

"You big dope, of course it's not a one-time thing. Let me recover for a couple of days and then you can come to my place. I've got a bigger bed."

"A couple of days? How about tonight?"

"Have mercy—I'm only human. And I still have to deal with Peter."

"Why tell him?"

"He'll know anyway. He always notices when I've been having great sex with someone besides him."

He reached up and brushed the long side of her hair off her face. "Did you have great sex last night?"

"How did it feel to you?"

"Are you kidding? This is the best time I ever had in my whole life."

"Oh Zeppo. Yes, I had great sex. You surprised me all night. It turns out we're highly compatible, sexually speaking."

"I knew we were compatible the first time I met you, but you wouldn't listen." He pulled her close and put his hands under her sweatshirt.

"Oh no, I'm too sore," she protested.

"Then we'll do something else." He took off her sweatshirt.

"I have to go home."

"Stay awhile." Her jeans were tight and he had trouble getting them down.

Jean stood and took them off. "Polly's right," she said as he pulled her back onto the bed. "You are a sex fiend."

CHAPTER 26

*I*n a moment of weakness, Jean promised Zeppo they'd get together the next day. They agreed that before then Zeppo would talk to Rudy and she would arrange to see Simon Emory. He bandaged her arm and she drove home.

Walking to her apartment, singing under her breath, Jean noticed Peter's Saab parked just down the street. She stopped singing. He'd come over to wait for her—this was going to be worse than she'd thought. She paused at the downstairs door to consider her options. There was nothing to do but get it over with. She went up the stairs.

The apartment smelled of coffee and she could hear Peter in the kitchen. At her desk she saw several phone messages waiting.

He came in behind her. "Don't bother with those. They're all from me."

"Hello, Peter," she said without turning around. "What a nice surprise."

"Where have you been?" he demanded, an ominous chill in his voice. "I was really worried about you. We were supposed to have dinner together, remember?"

"I'm sorry. I forgot."

"Tell me where you were."

She turned around. "I was out."

"I knew it. Look at your face. You've been with a man, haven't you?"

"Peter—"

"Who was it this time?" he said, his voice rising in anger. "An old boyfriend or someone you just picked up?"

She sighed with resignation, knowing she was a terrible liar and knowing he'd find out anyway. "It's Zeppo."

"Zeppo! You can't be serious. You slept with . . . what do you call him? The weasel?" He was angrier than she'd ever seen him.

"That was before I got to know him. He's really an interesting man."

"And that's a reason to fuck him?"

"The reasons were complex."

"Oh Jean, I know you've cheated on me before, but this is too much!"

"Don't accuse me of cheating. I've never promised you anything."

"But you know I hate it and you don't care. I don't even exist if I'm not in the same room with you. All that matters is whatever new man is trying to get at that body of yours!"

"Try to remember that it's *my* body and *I'll* decide who gets at it."

"You can't go through life like this, Jean. People just can't jump into bed with whoever they want, regardless of the consequences."

"There wouldn't *be* any consequences if you weren't so jealous and possessive!"

"You think I'm possessive? How many times have I sucked it up when you cheated? How many times have I tried to ignore my own feelings?" He shook his head. "I can't imagine how you keep us all straight. How many times have you called out the wrong name?"

"I've *never* called out the wrong name! I may have other lovers, but when I'm with you I'm all there, Peter, a hundred percent."

"So I get your full attention only when I'm fucking you, is that it?" He stepped close to her, his voice choked with emotion. "Jean, I can't stand this. I give you everything, but it's not enough. You go after some horny kid just to feed your ego."

"It had nothing to do with my ego!"

"What else is this about?" He gripped her upper arms too tightly, hurting her scrape. "You want to see how many men you can string along, how much shit you can make me eat!" He was so angry she thought he'd strike her.

"Don't you dare," she said in a low voice.

He let go and turned away. "I'm not going to hit you," he said wearily.

Jean took a breath. "Despite what you think, I never intended to cause you pain. I've been as faithful to you as I can be. Monogamy isn't in my nature, and you've always known that."

Peter looked at her sadly. "You're thirty-two years old. What's going to happen when you're forty-two? Or fifty-two? Do you think you can live this way when you're middle-aged?"

"Ask me then."

"Why am I arguing?" he said. "You'll never change, and I should have seen that long ago. But I was in love with you, and I thought that would make a difference."

"Oh Peter—"

"Here are your keys. I've taken my things out of your closet and there's a bag of your clothes by the door. Goodbye, Jean. I won't be back." He walked out and shut the door behind him.

CHAPTER 27

*J*ean wanted to go after him, but didn't. If she called him back it would just happen again, and she hadn't the heart to hurt him anymore. She stared at the Brooks Brothers shopping bag near the door. So he had come here knowing she was with someone else, intending to end it. She was sorry she'd hurt him, sorry he'd spent a bad night waiting for her, sorry she'd made this calm, controlled man so angry he'd nearly hit her.

She erased the phone messages without listening to them. Would she still have slept with Zeppo if she'd known what it would cost her? She knew it was the wrong answer, but she wouldn't have missed last night for the world.

Jean felt dazed and disoriented from finding Zeppo and losing Peter in the space of a few hours. She needed to talk to Roman, and she was also anxious to tell him what had happened in Mendocino. Although he'd be concerned, he wouldn't nag about going to the police—he distrusted them even more than most gay men did. The scar on his head was from a police baton.

She picked up the phone and dialed. "Roman," she said when he answered. "Are you busy? I need to see you."

"Is this another rescue operation?"

"More like a counseling session. Can you come over? I'll buy you dim sum."

Roman agreed, and in half an hour she let him in.

He held her at arm's length. "Well, don't you look radiant," he said. "Lips slightly bruised, eyes sleepy, body languid and relaxed. And there's a little whisker burn on your chin, right here. That can only mean one thing. Who's the new stud?"

"You'll never guess."

"I wouldn't know where to begin."

"It's Zeppo."

"Very interesting. Did you use . . ."

". . . a condom? Yes, Dad, don't worry. Several, in fact."

"So he's a young satyr?"

"He was unexpectedly great. He has a lot of pent-up sexual energy and he's been hot for me for months."

"How nice for you. But won't he follow you around now like a whipped puppy?"

"There's a lot more to him than that. You met him—he's no doormat."

"He didn't seem to be, but that was before he had the total Jean Applequist experience. When did all this happen? In Mendocino?"

"No, just last night."

"Did you screw his secret out of him?"

"I figured it out before I went over to his place, and it's a mind-blower. If it's OK with Zeppo, I'll tell you the whole story sometime."

"I look forward to it." Roman sat on the red sofa. "You know, Jean, it's time to let Peter go. He's a good man, for a lawyer, but he's not for you. You can't keep doing this to him."

"That's the bad news. He dumped me just now."

"Because of Zeppo?"

"Because of everything. Zeppo was the last straw."

"I'm sorry. Or should I be?"

"I'll miss Peter, but in a way it's a relief. He put a lot of pressure on me. He needs someone whose biological clock is ticking as loudly as his. I was born without one."

"So you say. I'll check again in five years." He stood. "Shall we go? I'm hungry."

Jean's injuries ached and she took it easy going down the stairs. Roman, behind her, frowned with concern. "You're hurt," he said. "I'm assuming Zeppo's not responsible."

"Oh please. I fell off my bike in Mendocino. Zeppo took good care of me." At the Chinese restaurant on 24th Street they took a window table. As they sipped green tea and ate assorted dumplings, Jean told Roman all about the visit to Sputnik, the trip up north, and Hugh Rivenbark's manuscript and Esther.

"Fascinating about the great writer," he said when she was done. "Won't feminist critics love it? Well, I'm not going to lecture you about the danger you're in because I know it won't do any good. Just be careful." He smiled at her. "I'm proud of you for punching Setrakian and getting away from the Jeep."

"I couldn't have done either of those things without you, Roman. Thanks."

"I'm happy to have helped. If you persist in this investigation, it may be time to teach you some more serious forms of self-defense."

"I hope I won't need them," she said. "Our problem now is that the manuscript is long gone and there are no copies. Zeppo won't go to the police, and he's the only one who saw it."

"Zeppo's secret sounds very intriguing."

"Stay away from it, Roman. I'll tell you about it when I can."

"Whatever you say."

Jean paid for their meal and they walked slowly up the hill toward her apartment. As she always did after a night like last night, Jean felt the sun, the cool breeze, and the working of her muscles with exquisite clarity, as if all her nerve endings had become more sensitive. She gave a deep, satisfied sigh.

"You're a simple creature, Jean," Roman said. "A good night with a new man and you're positively blissful."

"It was more than a good night. It was one of those times where you let your body take over and neither of you can make a wrong move. And there's no end to the desire, you know?"

"Yes, I know. That's how it was with Chris. We just couldn't get along the rest of the time."

Jean took his arm. "The best way to get over Chris is to find someone else."

"I don't want to find someone else. It's the same problem I've told you about before—sex and death have become inseparable to me."

Jean stopped walking and put her arms around him. He hugged her back, and they stood on the sidewalk in a tight embrace for several seconds. Jean thought they must look like a pair of happy lovers to passersby.

Finally they pulled apart and resumed their walk. "How do you two get along when you're not rutting like minks?" Roman asked.

"Just fine. I really like him."

"Don't tell me you're falling for a boy who still wears braces."

Jean's grin widened. "Too early to say, but I wouldn't rule it out."

CHAPTER 28

$\mathcal{A}$fter Roman left, Jean oiled her sewing machine and pulled out the quilt top she was making for Diane, a double wedding ring pattern in yellow and white calico. Jean's mother had tried to make her into good wife material by teaching her to cook, sew, iron, clean, and garden. Sewing was the only thing that stuck—not only did she find it relaxing, but it allowed her to dress much better than she could afford and wear clothes that fit her exaggerated figure.

While she worked, Jean thought about Peter. As far as her "infidelities" were concerned, she thought he was being unreasonable. They were together six months, and there had only been three other men in all that time. Well, four if you counted René, the château owner on the trip to Bordeaux for her magazine, but Peter hadn't found out about him. Since then she'd been like a saint—until last night.

Jean finished the section she was working on and decided to do something useful for the investigation. She had a glass of red wine to put herself into flirtatious mode and called Simon Emory at Sputnik.

"Hi, Simon," she said when he came on the line. "It's Jean Applequist."

"Jean, good of you to call. I've been thinking about you."

"Have you?"

"As you know, I usually work nights. Are you free for lunch tomorrow?"

"Sure," Jean said. He was moving fast. "That would be nice."

"I'll be out in the Avenues on business," he said. "Do you like Greek food?"

"Love it."

"Let's meet at Aphrodite's on Clement at one o'clock."

"I know it well. See you there." She hung up. A love of good food was important to her in a man, and Simon was sounding better and better. She wondered briefly what he looked like naked, but pulled herself back to reality. Now was not the time to be juggling two new lovers.

Jean got into bed early and thrashed around, her bruises bothering her. She almost phoned Zeppo, knowing he'd come over in a minute, but decided she should have the decency to mourn Peter for at least twenty-four hours. Besides, she really was sore in places that had nothing to do with her fall. That was the one drawback to oversexed men.

Jean knew Zeppo was starved for emotional as well as physical intimacy, and that was the source of a lot of their fireworks. She realized how much she'd mean to him after all that had happened, but didn't think he'd cramp her style as Peter had. Once he had a little more self-confidence, she hoped he'd be too busy having erotic adventures of his own to resent hers.

JEAN ATE a forkful of cold octopus in lemon and olive oil and washed it down with a crisp Pinot Grigio, taking care not to drip on her red cashmere sweater and black jeans. She'd put on a couple of pounds lately and had resolved to eat light. She smiled at Simon across the table. Today he wore gray slacks and a silk shirt; his only jewelry was a slim gold watch. He offered her a stuffed grape leaf, which she traded for a hunk of octopus. Even if he didn't know a thing, this lunch was worth the trip. The tiny blue and white restaurant smelled of oregano and garlic.

So far the conversation had been playful and light-hearted, and Jean realized he was very interested in her. She was used to that—all she had to do was sort out the men who were merely horny from those who had something to offer. In spite of what everyone thought, she did have standards. She found herself liking Simon—besides being physically attractive, he was intelligent and well traveled, with a dry sense of humor. On the downside, he was wound a little tight and was also vain—he had touched up his roots since she'd met him at Sputnik.

He poured her more wine. "So Jean, are you seeing anyone?"

"My situation's in flux," she said. "I just broke up with my boyfriend. What about you?"

"Right now there's no one."

"But you work with a lot of good-looking women."

"I do, but most of them are very young and uneducated. I prefer someone I can talk to in the morning. I meet very few women like that in my line of work." He gave Jean an inviting look; she decided his eyes were beige.

The waiter delivered Simon's roast lamb, and Jean cut to the chase. "I know someone who works for you," she said. "Oksana."

"Oh?" he said, concentrating on his lunch. "How do you know her?"

"She goes to my gym. Is she on vacation or something? I haven't seen her in a few weeks." Jean had decided to keep the lie simple.

"That would be Spider's gym."

"Yeah. Rhino Fitness. Spider works for you, too, right?"

"He used to. They both quit around the same time. Caused some staffing problems."

"I'd like to get hold of her. Do you know where she is?"

He sighed and set his utensils down. "Yes, I know. I'm going to break one of my rules and tell you something. Many of my employees are illegals, mostly from Eastern Europe. They're brought in by scumbag traffickers to work the lowliest jobs—in sweatshops, as laborers, even as prostitutes—to pay off their travel costs. You wouldn't believe how brutal some of these traffickers are, especially to women. They use threats, intimidation, beatings, rape, whatever keeps the girls in line."

"Yes, I've read about them."

"I help these kids get a start by paying off their debts to the traffickers on the condition that they work in one of my nightclubs, in a safe environment, until they've paid me back and saved a bit above that. Then they're free to go wherever."

"How do you keep them from running away before they've paid you off?"

"A little psychological manipulation. I tell them I have a file on each of them, and if they run off, I'll make an anonymous call to Immigration. There really are no files and they could easily disappear if they wanted to, but most of them are so terrified of being deported that they believe it. Besides, I offer them a good situation, so they don't leave me in the lurch very often."

"You're a philanthropist."

He smiled. "Not at all. I get an energetic, reliable workforce and make money on the deal. They pay a reasonable interest rate on their debts."

"What about Oksana?"

"As I'm sure you know, Oksana is a very beautiful, very intelligent girl. You may not know that she was lured here from Kiev with the promise of a modeling job, but was forced into prostitution. Another girl I'd helped sent her to me. Most of the time it takes more than a year to work off the debt, but Oksana is ambitious. She waitressed at

Sputnik for only a few months. She came to me a few weeks ago and paid off her balance. I haven't seen her since."

"How'd she get the cash so quickly?"

"Apparently she found a boyfriend with money."

"Spider?"

"Someone else. She didn't say who."

"Where did she go?"

"Hollywood. Where else? Maybe we'll see her in the movies someday." Simon took a sip of wine. "Poor Spider came looking for her and I told him what I've told you. He was very upset."

They chatted about other things as they finished their meals. Finally Simon glanced at his watch. "I'm sorry to say I have an appointment. I'm checking out an antique mahogany bar at a bankrupt restaurant near here."

"Don't you have managers to do that sort of thing for you?"

"I don't believe in delegating the important stuff." He smiled at her. "Can I call you?"

Jean gave Simon her number, and he kissed her cheek as they parted on the sidewalk. There was that nice cologne again. She didn't believe in faking a show of interest in a man for ulterior motives, but in this case she thought her interest might be genuine. She shook off another image of Simon naked.

⁓

JEAN VISITED Diane around four o'clock. A different security guard patrolled the front yard, an older man who looked like an ex-cop.

Although Diane's clothes were still loose on her, she looked calm and healthy. In the living room a silver teapot and a plate of little sandwiches and cookies were arrayed on the coffee table.

"What's all this?" Jean asked.

"I'm having tea. It's Celia's idea. She thinks if she throws in an extra meal every day at four o'clock, I'll eat more." She sat and patted the sofa next to her. "Come and join me."

Jean sat down and took a cup of tea. It smelled lovely— Earl Grey.

Diane gave her a serious look. "Peter was here this morning. He told me you broke up. I'm so sorry. What happened?"

"Didn't he tell you?"

"He said I'd have to ask you."

"Take a wild guess."

"Oh Jean, not again. Did one of your old lovers show up?"

"No, it's Zeppo."

Diane looked at her uncertainly. "Are you joking?"

"Nope."

"Well, that's one I never thought I'd hear. No wonder Peter was furious."

"I think Zeppo's really great. I've gotten to know him working on this thing."

"Martin liked him, too," she said. "I guess you two did have something in common after all. I've never seen his appeal. He must have hidden talents."

"You have no idea," Jean said with a salacious grin.

Diane shook her head. "After all these years I still don't understand you, Jean. I know you love sex above all things, but it seems so stupid to lose Peter just for a one-night stand."

"It's more complicated than that. I can't explain it now. But you know Peter and you know me. It never could have lasted."

"That's such a pity—I had high hopes for the two of you. Zeppo must think he's died and gone to heaven. You should see the way he stares at you when you're not looking. Martin used to tease him about being sweet on you."

"Zeppo really misses Martin."

"So do I." Diane sipped her tea. "Well, moving on, what did you find out about Hugh?"

"He had a really strong motive to kill Martin, but we can't go to the police with it yet."

"What motive?"

Jean explained about the handwriting on the manuscript and the card, and their suspicions about Esther's death.

Diane looked more and more uncomfortable as Jean spoke. "So you're basing all this on what Zeppo told you about the manuscript? What if he's wrong, or lying?"

"He's too smart to make a mistake like that, and why would he lie? He wants to find Martin's killer as much as you do."

"I've always wondered if he made copies of the material from the blue box. You only have his word that he didn't."

"Oh come on, Diane. He wouldn't do a thing like that. He's very honorable." Jean was starting to worry about the direction of the conversation.

"Jean, I love and trust you, but I also know you. I've seen you blinded by good sex before. If Zeppo is giving you multiple orgasms, I don't think you can be a reliable judge of his character."

"Goddammit, I've only spent one night with him. He told me about the manuscript days ago."

"But he's been after you for months. Don't you think this could all be a way to manipulate you into bed?"

Jean put her teacup down sharply. "Look, working with him was your idea. I can't help it if you don't like the results I'm getting. I just followed where things led."

"Where Zeppo led, you mean. I know Martin wouldn't have been interested in evidence about one of his friends. The blue box was only for business."

"In case you haven't figured it out yet, Martin would have kept dirt about his own grandmother if he thought he might need it someday."

"How dare you attack Martin," Diane said indignantly. "He wasn't like that at all. You're being very irresponsible.

First you expose Setrakian without consulting me, and now you accuse my good friend of attempted murder."

Jean was trying hard to keep her temper. "There is one other minor point. Your friend Hugh not only tried to kill Martin, he tried to kill Zeppo and me, too."

"I think that must have been Armand Setrakian. He sounds like a terrible man. Or maybe that nightclub owner is hiding something."

"OK, forget about that. Why is this so difficult for you to grasp? Hugh was the only one on the boat with a motive to hurt Martin. Can't you even consider that he could have done it?"

"No, I can't, because he's a good person. I've spent time with him, been a guest in his house. He never treated us with anything but kindness and friendship."

"Aren't you listening? That's because he didn't know until right before the wedding that Martin had the fucking manuscript."

"You're asking me to believe that one of my husband's closest friends tried to kill him and probably killed his own wife based on the word of some marginal character who happens to be making you happy in bed."

"Marginal character? This is someone Martin liked and trusted."

"His judgment wasn't infallible. And that was before the heart attack, when he had a use for an unprincipled slacker like Zeppo."

"Stop running him down!" Jean yelled. "He's a better man than Martin ever was, and Martin was good enough for you!"

Diane looked at her coldly. "At your worst you remind me of my mother, all urges and appetites with no sense or restraint." She stood up. "This investigation is over. You'd better go. There's no dealing with you once you've lost your temper."

Stung by Diane's words, Jean stomped out of the house feeling wounded and enraged and drove home.

CHAPTER 29

$\mathcal{J}$ean hadn't fought with Diane since they were room-
mates, and never about anything so serious. It really hurt
that Diane would compare her to her despised mother.

This was turning into a hell of a week. She'd infuri-
ated and alienated her lover and her good friend, solved
an attempted drowning and maybe a thirty-year-old murder,
been groped by a prominent artist and nearly run down by
a prize-winning author, found out a terrible secret, and had
glorious sex, all because of Zeppo.

Jean decided she needed some uncritical lust, so she
called him, but his cell was off. He was due at her place at
seven o'clock, a couple of hours away. She looked around
her apartment and, since she already felt like shit, decided
to clean house.

She put some Dandy Warhols on the stereo and got to
work. She felt sympathy for Diane in spite of what she'd said
about Zeppo. Diane was a very loyal person, and without
convincing evidence Jean couldn't expect her to believe that
an old friend had tried to kill Martin.

Jean pulled off the bedclothes and searched her closet
for a set of red cotton sheets she'd bought in Milan. Just
the thing for tonight. She remade the bed and smoothed
down the brightly colored handmade quilt she'd gotten last
Christmas. It was her mother's idea of a joke; her teetotaler
parents didn't approve of her job at a wine magazine, and

the quilt's curving, meandering pattern was called "drunkard's path."

Zeppo arrived right on time carrying an overnight bag and a large bunch of flowers—proteas, red anthuriums, and a few other tropical blossoms she didn't recognize. "Here, Jeannie," he said. "These seemed like your kind of flowers."

"They're beautiful. I love them." Jean went into the kitchen and put them into a red glass vase. She set the vase on her desk and stood back to admire them.

Zeppo moved up behind her and put a hand on each of her breasts. He kissed the back of her neck, inhaling her scent. She turned around and kissed him, biting his lip, pressing her body into his. As he ran his hands over her, she let desire obliterate the anger, hurt, and uncertainty she'd felt since leaving Diane's. She pulled off his glasses and dropped them on a table as he tossed his jacket to the floor. They fell onto the bed and made rough, frenzied love with their clothes half on, pausing only to find a condom in the chaos of the bedside drawer. Soon they lay side by side on the quilt, panting and disheveled.

"I missed you," Zeppo said.

"So I see. I missed you, too. I almost called you last night."

"Weren't you with Peter? What happened?"

"We had a fight and he left. For good."

"Jeez, I'm sorry. I didn't mean to cause anything like that."

"You didn't cause it. It's been coming for a long time."

"He's going to be pissed at me."

"No, he won't. He knows whose fault it was."

"You don't deserve all the blame. You sure didn't have to ask me twice." Zeppo put on his glasses and lay back down on the bed. "After you left yesterday, I slept past noon. I've never done that before."

"You had a pretty intense evening. True confessions, emotional and physical catharsis, the works."

"Yeah, well, among other things, you cured my insomnia. Hey," he said, looking around, "you cleaned the place up. It looks great."

"Thanks. You know, I had lunch with Emory today. He has good taste in restaurants and he wants to see me again."

"I can't blame him," Zeppo said. "By the way, I've decided you don't have to sleep with him to get information."

"Gee, thanks."

"He's pretty good-looking," he said with studied nonchalance. "You as interested in him as he is in you?"

Jean was usually annoyed by jealousy but decided to go easy on Zeppo. "Nah," she said. "He's a little too slick for me." She told him Simon's story about Oksana and Spider.

He nodded thoughtfully. "That sounds plausible— Spider didn't seem too bright. So maybe she had another boyfriend and maybe she took Martin's money and just ditched Spider."

"She may have made up the other boyfriend to discourage Spider from coming after her," Jean said. "Did you talk to that bartender? Rudy?"

"Yeah. I went over to Sputnik and caught him as he was going to work. I bribed him to ask Spider if he'd meet us. He says he'll get back to me."

Jean rolled toward him. "Let's go out," she said. "I'm starving—all I had for lunch was a salad."

"OK by me. I'm hungry, too."

Jean declined Zeppo's invitation to join him in the shower, knowing she wouldn't eat for another two hours if she did. She looked through her closet and chose black silk slacks and a low-cut wrap blouse the color of her eyes.

Zeppo came out of the bathroom with a towel around his waist. She dodged his hands as she went in to take a shower, then dressed in the bathroom, examining herself in the mirror as she combed her hair. Sexy but not slutty. A pair of lapis earrings and a squirt of Opium and she was ready to create a stir.

"Jean, you look fantastic," Zeppo said when she came out. "Did you make that outfit?"

"Yep."

"Put on those heels, OK? I promise not to let you get knocked over tonight."

"All right, I'll do it for you. But I'm not wearing them to bed."

They walked to Zeppo's car. He'd parked in a bus stop close to her apartment and now had a very expensive ticket on his windshield. "Where am I going?" he asked as they slid into the leather seats.

"Let's try that new Peruvian place in the Mission— they've got a great wine list and the food's supposed to be good." Jean took off her heels. "These shoes are killing me, but it's great being six-foot-one, just like Carlotta Carlyle."

"Too bad you can't play blues guitar like her."

"You read a lot of mysteries, too, don't you?"

"Yeah. I like the way justice is done at the end, unlike real life."

Jean sensed he didn't want to delve into his past, so they talked about mysteries until they got to the restaurant.

"We'll use the valet parking," Zeppo said. "One reason I love going out in this car is that they always put it right in front with the Bentleys and Ferraris."

At this early hour the place wasn't too crowded. The host led them through the room and a few men turned to watch Jean. She was glad she managed it without falling off her heels.

Once they were seated in a booth, Zeppo squeezed her hand. "Hannah will love you—you're great for my self-esteem."

"I'd like to meet her someday."

"That's another selling point for me. Other guys take their girlfriends home to meet Mom and Dad. I get to take mine to meet my therapist."

"Look at the family you put together for yourself," Jean said. "Martin as Dad and Hannah as Mom."

"Now there's a picture. I called her last night, by the way, to tell her what happened."

"What did she say?"

"It blew her away that you figured it all out and came right over and jumped me. Also, she knows I was hung up on you before, and now she's worried I'll really lose it. Become your sex slave or something."

"Now that sounds like fun. Although I don't know what I could make you do for me that you're not already doing."

"If you think of anything, let me know," he said softly. He put his hand on hers and squeezed, leaning toward her. Their eyes locked for a moment, and Jean suddenly felt warm all over.

"Whew," she said, pulling back. "We'd better talk about something else."

"Right." Zeppo cleared his throat. "OK. What are we going to do about Rivenbark?"

The waiter interrupted Jean's answer. "Well, there's been a slight setback," she said after he'd delivered a bottle of Albarino, a white from Spain, and taken their orders. "I told Diane about the manuscript and Esther."

"What did she think?"

Jean hesitated, sipping wine. It tasted of almonds and peaches, and showed the varietal's characteristic bracing acidity. "She doesn't buy it," she said. "She thinks you're making it all up for obscure motives of your own and I'm too blinded by lust to think critically. We had a fight, and she says the investigation is over."

"Hell. First Peter and now Diane. I'm really screwing up your life."

"No, you're not. It was my own fault—I got angry and said some unkind things. So did she." Jean drank more wine. "I have to work on my temper. It's my major character flaw."

"I don't think so."

"Oh Zeppo—"

"No, I mean it. I'm not in sex-slave mode now. I know what I'm talking about. My family was totally repressed. I never knew what anybody really thought or how they really felt, and look what happened. That's one of the things I like about you—you don't repress anything. I always know exactly what's going on, whether you're throwing a fit or getting off."

She kissed his cheek. "You're sweet. But this time I really screwed up. I don't want to quit any more than you do. As it is, Diane won't believe that her old pal Hugh could have done it. Lots of people are going to feel the same way. I was wrong to think we could waltz into Hallock's office with Hugh's wedding card and he'd arrest a famous author on your say-so."

"And while we're sitting here planning what to do about Hugh, he's planning what to do about us."

"Last time he waited until we were in the middle of nowhere before he tried anything," Jean said. "He's less likely to go after us in the city with people all around."

"I hope you're right. The good news is, he probably doesn't realize we know what it's all about, so he thinks there's no hurry." The waiter brought two orders of scallop ceviche.

"Hey," Zeppo said as they ate, "how about this: I'll say I scanned the manuscript so I could try and figure out why Martin kept it. I'll tell the truth—we just saw the wedding card and realized why it was such a big deal."

"Good. You can say that if anything happens to us, it's public. That should hold him off for a while." They finished their ceviche and the waiter delivered roasted red snapper with coconut rice. Jean tried a succulent bite. She should never diet at lunch—it just meant she ate more at dinner. "Then there's our next project: Who killed Martin?"

Jean heard the faint opening bars of *Valkyries*, and Zeppo pulled his phone out. "Hello?" he said. "Hey, Spider. Thanks for calling. We'd like to talk to you. No pressure. Can I buy you a drink?" He listened for a while. "Sure, that'll be fine. Give us forty-five minutes or so." He hung up, grinning at Jean. "Spider wants to meet us at that sports bar off 24th Street. I must have convinced Rudy we're harmless. Or maybe it was the fifty bucks I slipped him."

CHAPTER 30

$\mathcal{T}$he bar was in Jean's neighborhood, so Zeppo parked legally a few blocks from her apartment—they didn't want the Jag to get more tickets or be towed during the night.

Even though the place was close to home, Jean had been there only once. It had a shitty wine selection and an obnoxious, largely male clientele. The cavernous, low-ceilinged bar was as grungy and unpretentious as Sputnik was sleek and plastic. A large group of young working-class men and a few women watched a basketball game on the many TVs over the bar. The walls were decorated with sports memorabilia and signed photos of famous athletes. Jean and Zeppo were definitely overdressed.

Spider sat alone at a table in the back, away from the TVs, a glass of half-melted ice in front of him. His freshly shaved head gleamed in the overhead lights. Jean and Zeppo made their way past the cheering crowd.

"Thanks for coming, Spider," Zeppo said. "What'll you have?"

He looked up, a little bleary-eyed. Probably already drunk. "Red Bull and vodka," he said.

Zeppo went for drinks and Jean pulled up a chair. Spider wore jeans, a white T-shirt, and an orange and white high school jacket with leather sleeves and a big capital "II" on the front.

"What did you letter in?" Jean asked.

"Wrestling and shot put. You work for Wingo, too?" Spider eyed her suspiciously.

"No, I'm a friend of his widow. Name's Jean Applequist."

"Spider Brandt." His handshake was surprisingly gentle.

Zeppo came back with Spider's drink and two draft beers. "I think we can help each other, Spider," he said. "We're all looking for Oksana. We want to ask her why she visited Wingo."

Spider stared sullenly into his drink. "Who says she did?"

"Someone at Wingo's office saw her, and you, too," Zeppo said patiently. "Come on, we don't want to get the police involved in this."

Spider took a big drink. He seemed to be very drunk, and the caffeine wasn't helping. "Why do you want to know?"

"Wingo paid for information. Maybe she told him something about someone and that person got pissed and killed Wingo. Do you know why she went to see him?"

Spider said nothing, just stared into his drink, rubbing a hand over his shaved head. The people at the bar groaned and someone cursed the referee.

"I know you just moved to San Jose," Zeppo said. "Moving's expensive. Money must be tight." He produced a folded $100 bill, which he slid across the table to Spider. "We can help you out there, too."

Spider eyed the bill but made no move to take it.

"Simon Emory says Oksana went to L.A. to be an actress," Jean said, losing her patience. "He says she went with another man."

Spider looked up. "Bullshit! Emory lies! She's going to live in San Jose with me. We love each other."

"What's in San Jose?" Zeppo asked.

"I'm managing a gym there. I come back here to look for her when I'm not working."

Jean sipped her beer. Now that she'd shaken things loose, Zeppo could take over.

"Is that why she went to see Wingo?" Zeppo said. "To get money to pay off Emory so she could leave with you?"

"Yeah."

"What did she sell to Wingo?"

Spider shrugged his muscular shoulders. "She said it was safer if I didn't know."

"Was it something about Emory?"

"She wouldn't tell me."

"When was the last time you saw her?"

"She was going to pay Emory off after work and then come to my apartment. We were supposed to leave that night. But she never showed up. I went to her place and all her stuff was gone. I asked Emory where she was and he told me that bullshit story."

"If she didn't go to L.A. and she's not here, where is she?"

"I think something bad happened to her."

"Like what?"

"Like maybe the person she told Wingo about went after her." His eyes began to tear up. "If I find out someone hurt her, I'll tear them apart." He wiped at his eyes with the back of his hand. "Look, I gotta go."

"We should keep in touch," Zeppo said, laying a business card on the folded bill. "Here's my number. Call if you find out anything. How can we reach you?"

"I'll call you." Spider grabbed the card and the cash and dashed out the door.

Jean and Zeppo looked at each other. "We still don't know if someone offed her or if she ditched Spider," Jean said.

"I can see it happening either way," Zeppo said.

"Yeah, me too. Why would a smart woman like Oksana hook up with such a dope?"

"From what Emory told you, she's had a really rough time. Maybe because Spider loved her and was good to her."

They left their beers on the table and went outside, holding hands as they walked uphill into the residential neighborhood above 24th Street. Crossing an empty street, Jean stumbled in a pothole and came halfway out of one shoe. As she bent over to fix it, Zeppo pulled her back toward the curb, nearly yanking her arm out of its socket. An old black Taurus with no lights bore down on them. Jean lost her balance and fell on top of him as the car sped past so closely she could have reached out and touched it. She heard tires squeal as it took a sharp right a block down.

Zeppo sat on the sidewalk with Jean sprawled in his lap. "Are you OK, Jeannie?"

"I'm fine," she said. "You?"

"Just a sore butt." He scrambled to his feet and helped her stand. "Heads up—he's coming back."

The black car drove slowly down the street. Zeppo pushed Jean into a darkened doorway. They could see the driver turning his head from side to side, looking for them. Jean recognized the same ski mask and bulky jacket worn by the first attacker. A noisy group of young men and women spilled out of an apartment building across the street, whooping and laughing, and a city bus pulled up to a stop on the corner. The black car sped up and disappeared down a side street.

"Saved by the cavalry," Zeppo said.

"Jesus. I didn't even see him coming. Did you get the license number?"

Zeppo shook his head. "Nah, I was too busy falling on my ass."

"Probably stolen anyway."

"Looks as if Rivenbark has followed us to the city. Let's go before he tries again."

Jean took off her other shoe and they hurried to her apartment, cautious and watchful this time. She let them in and looked at the shoes in her hand. "Goddamned heels almost killed me!" She threw them across the room. After locking the door and windows she plopped on the sofa, feeling giddy from another close call. "Well, it's not a total loss. I'll give the shoes to a drag queen I know. Those boys love my size elevens. Zeppo, remember telling me if you lose your edge they might as well bury you? I think we're losing our edge."

Zeppo sat beside her. "We have to go to the police," he said. "This is getting too scary."

"We can't. You know what'll happen. They won't believe us, and Hallock will run your fingerprints because you're annoying him."

He put his arms around her. "I don't want anything to happen to you. It's not worth it."

"I don't want anything to happen to you either, including having your life ruined again."

"But it would ruin my life if you got killed. I never had so much to lose before." He kissed her gently. "Let's not go out anymore. We'll just stay here in bed and have food delivered. We'll have to wash the sheets now and then, but we won't need any clothes."

"A nice idea, but not practical. I know—we'll go to my Uncle Beau's. He won't be back for nearly a month. He's a security nut. He has bars on the downstairs windows, an alarm, all that stuff. But the main reason to go there is Roman. As you saw, he's pretty good protection."

"That sounds OK."

"We'll go tomorrow." She pulled him toward her. "Now where were we?"

Jean felt emotionally and physically battered from her fights with Peter and Diane and the car attack, and their lovemaking that night was as slow and tender as this afternoon's had been hurried and rough. She was pleased at how well Zeppo could read her, and after only a day.

✍

THE NEXT morning Jean put on jeans and a black T-shirt, packed some clothes, and poured the water out of the red vase so she could take her flowers along. When she opened the door a cardboard box fell into the room.

"What's that?" Zeppo asked.

"Looks like a bottle of wine. We get a lot of them at work, of course, but every now and then someone sends one here. I'm in the phone book." She put her flowers down, picked up the box, and read the return address. "Whoa. It's from Treadway's." She took it into the kitchen and cut through the tape with a paring knife. Inside the Styrofoam casing was a bottle of 2003 Marcassin Vineyard Sonoma Coast Chardonnay. The label looked authentic—a black on white illustration of the sorceress Circe turning one of Odysseus's men into a pig.

Jean pulled a piece of paper out of the box: "It says, 'You're the expert: Am I real?'"

"Or am I poisoned?" Zeppo said.

"Would he send me a bottle of poisoned wine with his name on it? He may be a wimp, but I don't think he's an idiot."

"Would he send you evidence of his scam? Or a bottle worth $400?"

"It might be a bribe."

"Even so, I don't think we should drink it."

Jean looked at it wistfully. "If it's real, it's incredibly delicious."

"Hey, I know a bike messenger whose brother works at a lab. Let's have him test it to see if it's safe to drink. And maybe he could tell whether it's real."

"How much would it cost?"

"Beats me. Your magazine could pay."

"What a great idea. Let's bring it along." She grabbed her flowers and locked up.

They only needed one car, so they dropped the Toyota at Wingo-Johansen's office, then headed across town to

Zeppo's apartment, where Jean set the bottle of Chardonnay on the dinette table in the main room. He could deal with it later.

Zeppo pulled out a suitcase and tossed in a few books and CDs with his clothes.

Jean looked at his Van Gogh poster. "Now I know why you like these old blues singers and that other misunderstood redheaded Dutchman. Their problems were as bad as yours."

"Something like that. They keep me from feeling sorry for myself."

They went down to his garage, and Jean gazed at his bike while he put his things in the back of the Jag. "I suppose we shouldn't go cycling anymore."

"Not till this thing is over."

"I'll gain weight if I can't ride," she warned.

"Yeah, you'll get so fat no other man will look at you, and then you'll be all mine."

Jean smiled, and he let her drive to Beau's.

CHAPTER 31

"Uncle's bedroom is ready for you," Roman said as he let them in Beau's front door. "When you get settled we'll have lunch in the garden."

Jean taught Zeppo how to work the alarm system and led him through the house, a beautifully restored period piece with fanciful moldings and high ceilings. Most of the furniture and art was Russian, and the upholstery and rugs were in shades of deep red and gray. Nearly every room was lined with overflowing bookshelves.

They hauled their bags up the stairs to a bedroom at the back of the house. A big bed with a carved wooden headboard dominated the room. A collection of malachite eggs and Russian lacquer boxes sat on the dresser. Jean filled the red vase with water, added the flowers, and set it next to the eggs.

"I better tell Hannah where I am," Zeppo said. He took out his cell phone and punched buttons. "Hi, it's me. I wanted to let you know I'll be staying at Jean's uncle's house for a while, with her." He smiled, and she heard the affection in his voice. "Oh sure. I'm retaining my identity and free will, but just barely." He winked at Jean, then laughed at something Hannah said. "Don't worry so much. I'm having a great time." He said goodbye.

"So you don't tell her everything," Jean said.

"She worries enough as it is. I'll tell her all about it once it's over."

The leather-topped end table beside the bed held a phone and a small wrapped box with a bow on it. "This must be from Roman," Jean said, picking it up and tearing off the paper. "Condoms. Definitely from Roman."

Zeppo looked over. "Doesn't he think we're being good?"

"He wants to make sure. He's a real crusader for safe sex. Half the people he knows have died of AIDS."

"Is he HIV positive?"

"No, thank God, and in a way that's part of his problem. He did everything his friends did back in the day—went to the baths, had lots of different partners—but now so many of them are sick or dead and he's not. Logically, he should be dead, too, or at least positive, and he can't figure out why he isn't. He's suffering from survivor's guilt, like some Holocaust victims who walked out of the camps and went on with life."

"Jeez, I never thought about that."

"Back in 2006 he lost Perry, a man he really loved. Then last year he took care of Chris, one of his old lovers, who died here at his house. Roman's so down about all of it that he's been celibate for months. It's good for him to have us here, to get his mind on other things. Come on, let's go see him."

The table in the garden was set for three. Roman came out of his house carrying a tray of sandwich materials. The sun overhead made the garden warm and fragrant despite the cool breeze.

"Thanks for letting us come over," Jean said as they constructed sandwiches. On the phone that morning she'd told him about their narrow escape.

Roman poured himself mineral water. "So now Rivenbark's trying to kill you in the city. Why don't I go have a word with him?"

"No, Roman, stay away from him," Jean said. "He's not just some random goon like Felix—he's a famous writer.

~ 223 ~

You'll get into trouble and they'll connect you with Zeppo, and then you'll be in jail and he'll be on the front page."

Zeppo looked at her with alarm. "Jeannie!" he exclaimed.

"Don't worry," Roman said. "She hasn't told me a thing, only that you can't go to the police because of your deep, dark secret."

"Oh. OK." Zeppo settled down.

"Here's a piece of advice, if it's not too late. If you want to hold her interest, don't tell her all about it right away. Ration it out, like Scheherazade. She loves a good mystery."

"Zeppo's keeping me very interested," Jean said. "There are things I love even more than a good mystery."

"Tell me, Zeppo," Roman said. "How are you holding up against the demands of Jean's insatiable lust?"

Zeppo sighed. "OK, I guess, but it's not easy. She treats me like a piece of meat."

"Get used to it, my friend," Roman said. "That's all a man can ever be to her."

"Well, Roman, how would you treat a man who gets a hard-on if you wink at him?"

"Like the rare and wonderful creature he is." He had a bite of his sandwich. "OK, back to business. I took another look at *Home to Greenwood* after you told me about Rivenbark's wife. If Esther did indeed write it, she did a remarkable job of mimicking his style, but in a richer, more fully realized story. It's a shame she never published anything in her own style."

"We've got a plan to discourage him from coming after us again," Zeppo said. "I'm going to tell him I scanned the manuscript, and if either of us gets hurt it's public."

Roman nodded. "That sounds reasonable, but you'd better do it soon."

"I want to see a sample of Esther's handwriting first," Zeppo said. "Meanwhile, we talk to Frank Johansen today at three o'clock at his office."

"I'll drive you down so I can watch your backs," Roman said.

"Thanks," Jean said. "I was going to ask if you would. And Zeppo, don't mention Rivenbark to Frank—he'll believe whatever Diane tells him anyway."

There was a knock at the gate and Zeppo got up to answer it. "Who is it?"

"Just little old me," said a familiar voice of indeterminate gender. "I'm here to see the hairiest queer in captivity."

Roman and Jean smiled at each other. "It's OK, Zeppo," Roman said. "Let him in."

Zeppo opened the gate to admit a slender man with shoulder-length platinum blond hair. His lime-green T-shirt and black capris were tight, and he wore zebra-print mules. He'd plucked his eyebrows into thin arching lines, and his lipstick and nails were red. In spite of his clothes, his form was unmistakably male.

"Hello, big boy," he said, looking up at Zeppo. "Who do you belong to?"

"I . . . uh . . ."

Jean got up and came to Zeppo's rescue, taking his arm.

"Well, if it isn't Jean 'The Body' Applequist. How are you, sweetheart?" The man gave her a kiss.

"Hi, Lou," Jean said. "This is my friend Zeppo. Zeppo, Lou Kasden."

"Pleased to meet you." They shook hands.

"Would you like a sandwich?" Roman asked.

"No thanks." He took a seat under the big tree. "I've got to watch my slim girlish figure." Lou watched Zeppo sit back down at the table and pick up his sandwich. "Zeppo, honey, I'll bet you can eat anything you want."

"Pretty much," Zeppo said.

"Lucky boy." Lou glanced at Zeppo's Adidas. "What size shoe do you wear?"

Zeppo grinned. "Thirteen and a half, same as Larry Bird."

"Mother of God. Tell me, Jean, does the old rule of thumb apply here?"

"That all his extremities are proportionate? Yep."

"And red body hair, too. You're sure he's straight?"

"Pretty sure," she said. Zeppo blushed, but she could tell he was amused.

"If he's making Jean happy, you don't have a chance, Lou," Roman said.

"You can't blame a girl for trying."

"Lou, should he grow his hair out?" Jean asked.

"Definitely. Lose the glasses, get a Kenny G 'do. I assume the braces aren't permanent."

"God, I hope not," Zeppo said.

"Well then, he should be quite presentable by the time he reaches the age of consent."

"Let's see the new pamphlet, Lou," Roman said, chuckling.

Lou reached into his lime-green patent leather purse and brought out a glossy black pamphlet with a purple Bash Back logo on it.

Jean took it and unfolded it. Inside were listings for Bash Back self-defense classes and numbers to call for people who'd been assaulted or needed legal help. She handed it to Zeppo.

"It looks good," he said. "What's it for?"

"Those of us who are too dainty to patrol are going to hand them out at the Gay Freedom Day parade in June," Lou said. "We always get a lot of interest after big events like that."

"What kind of patrol?" Zeppo said.

"On Halloween, New Year's Eve, and other occasions when rednecks come to the city to beat up queers, Bash Back patrols the Castro and Polk Street areas," Lou said. "Lord help anybody they catch in the act."

"So you don't have to be a tough guy like Roman to join?" Zeppo said.

"Not at all. I joined because I'm a satisfied customer. After the parade four years ago, three *cholos* cornered me in an alley. I was terrified. I thought I'd never play the skin flute again. But then two bruisers in black and purple T-shirts came into the alley and the big furry one said something very rude in Spanish—that was Roman. The next thing I knew Roman and his friend were stomping the *cholos*." He grinned. "I'm sure those boys never told anyone who did it. Now I always have one of the bruisers walk me home."

"We're a full-service organization," Roman said.

"Lou," Jean said, "before I forget, I have a pair of shoes for you." She went into the house and got the high heels out of her suitcase.

Lou took them from her. "Oh, how nice," he said. "Fuck-me pumps. And nearly new. Why would you give these away?"

"I fall down when I wear them. I can't walk in high heels."

"She's more of a round-heeled kind of gal," Roman said. Jean stuck her tongue out at him.

Lou slipped off a mule and put on one of the heels. "A perfect fit. Thanks, Jean." He put the shoes into his big purse. "Well, I've got to run. I'm designing a website for my friend who owns the fetish boutique. She's going to try online sales with some of her exclusive items. Victoria's Secret just doesn't meet everyone's needs."

"What a good idea," Roman said. "Now the people in North Dakota can have rubber merry widows in men's sizes."

"See you all later." Lou headed out the gate.

When everyone had finished eating, Roman took the pamphlet into his office, while Jean and Zeppo carried the lunch things back to Roman's kitchen and worked on the dishes.

"I'm glad you get along with those two," Jean said. "Lou makes a lot of straight men nervous. And if Roman detects any ambivalence in the way you feel about him, he gets nasty."

"Don't worry—one thing the loony bin did was make me a lot more tolerant of harmless deviants. Although Roman's not exactly harmless, is he?"

"Not exactly."

When they'd finished cleaning up, Zeppo phoned the bookstore in Mendocino and Jean listened on the extension.

"Hi, this is Zeppo," he said when Edward answered. "I have a weird request."

"What can I do for you?"

"I need to see what Esther's handwriting looked like. I can't say why, but I promise I'll tell you in a couple of days. Could you please fax me a sample?"

Edward hesitated. "What does this have to do with Martin's death?"

"We don't know for sure, but it may help answer some questions."

After a moment, he said, "OK, I guess I can do that. Good luck reading it—Esther's handwriting was awful."

Zeppo gave him Roman's fax number, and in about ten minutes they heard Roman's fax come to life and start printing.

Jean looked over Zeppo's shoulder as he examined the sheet with Esther's writing. It was part of a letter to Edward, about visiting a friend and going for a hike. The writing was large, loopy, and very hard to read.

"Bingo," Zeppo said. "This is exactly like the writing from the manuscript. OK, let's call Big Hugh." Back in the living room, Zeppo dialed as Jean picked up the extension just as Hugh answered.

"Hello, Hugh. This is Zeppo."

"Zeppo! Good to hear from you."

"I'm glad you think so. I wanted to run something by you."

"Oh? What's that?"

"When Martin gave me your manuscript to send back, I was intrigued, because I couldn't figure out why he kept it. Well, I just figured it out."

"What are you saying?" Hugh's voice had lost its warmth.

"I saw your handwriting on the wedding card you sent to Martin, and I have a sample of Esther's handwriting. I know who wrote *Home to Greenwood.*"

Hugh chuckled. "Very well, I confess: I dictated it to her."

"I don't think so. Martin would never have bothered with something that was just embarrassing. He only saved really prime dirt. And you're always saying that you wrote every book by hand. You want to spend the rest of your life explaining this?"

"I have nothing to explain because you don't have the manuscript."

"True, but as it happens I took the precaution of scanning it onto a thumb drive before I sent it to you."

There was a long silence. "What do you want?"

"I know you pushed Martin off that boat, but I'll never be able to prove it. Just stay away from us."

"First you accuse me of attempted murder and then you insult my intelligence. This is nothing more than a prelude to blackmail. You're obviously taking up where Martin left off."

"I give you my word I'm not," Zeppo said.

"Then you're a blundering moron," Hugh said angrily. "Threatening me is the biggest mistake you've ever made."

"Now wait a minute—"

Hugh hung up.

CHAPTER 32

Zeppo hung up, too, and looked at Jean. "Not exactly the response we wanted."

"What do you think he meant?" she asked.

"No idea. But I can't believe a famous guy like him would be dumb enough to keep after us now that he thinks we have the manuscript. Unless he thinks he can steal it from us."

Roman came out of his office. "How did it go with Hugh?"

"Not great," Zeppo said. "I don't know if we scared him, but we sure pissed him off."

"Maybe when he cools down he'll realize it's in his best interest to leave us alone," Jean said. "That's what we're hoping."

"Yet desperate people don't always act in their own best interests, do they?" Roman said.

When it was time to see Frank, they piled into Roman's white Prius and he navigated to Pier 3 in heavy traffic. Jean and Zeppo left Roman waiting in a no-parking zone and found Frank in his office.

He looked drawn and had lost some weight, but his ample midsection still bulged in his blue golf shirt. His arms and shoulders showed traces of the construction worker he'd been as a young man. Trigger lay on the floor in a patch of sun. He raised his head and wagged his tail in greeting as Zeppo knelt down to pet him.

Frank motioned them to a couple of chairs and sat on the edge of his desk. "Diane tells me you two are looking into Martin's death. I think it's a bad idea, but I'll help if I can."

"We appreciate that," Zeppo said. "Let me ask you something, Frank. How much did you know about Martin's methods and what I did for him?"

"I knew he manipulated people, but I didn't want to know how, and after talking to Diane I realize it was much worse than I thought. I'm as anxious as she is to keep things quiet. If it all comes out, I'll be tarred with the same brush. I should have put a stop to it long ago, but Martin was impossible to derail once he found something that worked. I should have gone back to working alone, but business was too good." He sighed. "I should have done a lot of things differently."

"Can you think of anyone who would have been angry enough to kill him?" Zeppo asked.

"You'd know that better than I would."

"What about that list of people you gave to the cops?" Jean said.

"The police told me not to talk about that."

"Was Simon Emory on it?" Zeppo asked.

Frank hesitated. "Yes, he was. Martin blamed him for a problem with illegals on a job."

"What about Armand Setrakian?"

Frank looked blank for a second. "Oh, the sculptor who sold us that land in Sonoma. No, he wasn't on it. Don't tell me Martin was blackmailing him, too."

"Yeah," Zeppo said. "But don't lose any sleep over it. I found out that Setrakian—"

Frank put a hand up. "I really don't want to hear it."

"OK, if you say so."

"How'd you become partners in the first place?" Jean asked.

"Years ago he hired my construction company on a housing development. We were having trouble with one of the unions, and Martin came on the site and threatened the union rep. Well, the rep took a swing at Martin. I stopped him and talked everybody down. Martin was grateful. We worked together on a few more projects and finally formed a partnership. I came between him and a black eye more than once over the years."

There wasn't anything more to ask, so Jean and Zeppo thanked him and left.

"Frank couldn't add much," Zeppo said to Roman as they got in his car. "He says Simon Emory was on the list he gave to the cops, but not Setrakian. Did Jean tell you about Emory?"

Roman turned south on the Embarcadero. "Yes, and about his explanation of Oksana's disappearance. Do you think it sounds plausible?"

"That she ran off with Martin's money, with or without a boyfriend?" Zeppo said. "Sure, but there's another explanation that makes just as much sense. We still don't know what Oksana sold Martin. There's a good chance it was information about Emory. What if he found out when she came to pay him off? He might have scared her into running away or even hurt her. That would also explain why someone's searching all of the places Martin spent time."

"Could be," Jean allowed. "I like Simon, but he's hard to read. He seems to be doing some good for his illegals. He dyes his hair."

"How do you know?" Roman asked as they inched along Howard toward the Castro.

"His pale roots showed the first time I met him. He's probably prematurely gray, like me."

"What color was your hair before, Jeannie?" Zeppo asked.

"A very boring shade of light brown. Silver is far superior. It was rough at first, though—I got my first gray hair at eighteen."

Roman ran a hand over his bald head. "I started losing my hair at about the same age."

"At least you don't have any gray yet, Roman" Jean said. "If all your hair turns my color, you'll look like a yeti."

"Another possibility is that Martin had something on Kay and she's looking for it," Roman said. "But I can't believe Kay would do the searching herself. She must have had help."

"She's got this big guy who drives her around," Zeppo said. "Donald Grimes."

"What do you know about him?" Roman asked.

"Nothing," Jean said, "except that he's a self-righteous Christian."

"It's obvious why Martin would have kept something on Kay—she's moving up politically," Roman said.

"But her enemies would dig up any dirt from her past," Zeppo said. "She's pissed off a lot of people with the Rational Right movement."

"That she has," Roman said. "Zeppo, what were Martin's politics?"

"I guess you'd say he was a libertarian. He believed in personal freedom, like he supported abortion rights and gay rights and that kind of thing. But he also thought just about every aspect of business should be deregulated. Kay was a narrow-minded fanatic as far as he was concerned. Hey, maybe she's screwing Donald."

Jean shook her head. "No way. No fornicating for him. He probably doesn't even masturbate. Besides, if she were screwing him she'd dress him better."

"You've got a point."

"So we can assume there are at least two pieces of evidence still out there," Roman said. "Any ideas where else Martin might have hidden something?"

"I've thought a lot about that, and I can't come up with anyplace new," Zeppo said. "I searched the Jag myself. Nothing."

Back at his house, Roman let them in. "Come with me, children," he said. "We have to be ready in case of enemy assault, so let's distribute the hardware."

Zeppo looked questioningly at Jean. "He means guns," she said. They followed Roman to his office. Even though Roman had taught Jean to shoot years ago, she'd never enjoyed going to the practice range and guns still made her very nervous.

Roman unlocked his gun safe. "Zeppo, have you ever fired a gun?" he asked.

"No."

"Well, don't be shy. Guns are as American as Applequist." He took out a revolver. "This is a thirty-eight caliber double-action Colt Agent Special. It's a nice little gun. They don't make them anymore. You get six shots with this one." Roman emptied the chamber and checked the barrel, handling the gun with easy familiarity. He held it out to Zeppo, who took it reluctantly. "Now it's empty," Roman said. "Hold it like this. Squeeze gently, don't jerk. Try it."

Zeppo pulled the trigger twice. "I thought it would be heavier."

"Most of them are. This one has an alloy frame. Now remember, since you're probably not much of a shot, aim for the torso. That's where you have the best chance of hitting something important."

"I don't think I could actually shoot anybody," Zeppo said, handing the gun back.

"You'd be amazed what you can do if you're cornered." Roman took two blue steel automatics out of the safe. "These are nine-millimeter Berettas. Very reliable. Here's the safety—it has to be off to shoot. Chamber a round like this." He unloaded one of them and let Zeppo pull the trigger.

"That's all the training you get right now. I'll take you to the firing range later." Roman reloaded the guns. "Let's put these where they'll do some good."

Roman placed one of the Berettas in the drawer of an end table in his living room. They all walked over to Beau's, and he put the second Beretta in a desk drawer in Beau's office and the Colt upstairs in the leather-topped nightstand.

"If anyone breaks in, which would be very difficult, get out of the house and go to a neighbor's or down to the main street," Roman said. "But if you're trapped, use one of these. There's a bullet already chambered in the Berettas. If the intruder is armed and you're in immediate danger, don't hesitate to shoot. If not, have him lie face down on the floor with his hands behind his head while you call the cops. The guns are all legal, registered to me, so there shouldn't be a problem."

Zeppo put his arm around Jean's shoulders. "This isn't exactly how I imagined the investigation ending up, with us hiding out in a house full of guns."

"Let's hope it doesn't last long," Roman said. "Things will get tricky when you have to go back to work, Jean, or if Beau comes home before it's settled. Now that we're all set up for safety, how about dinner?"

They spent a convivial evening making and devouring lasagna and green salad, washed down with bottles of good Italian wine.

❧

THE NEXT morning, Jean and Zeppo were eating leftover lasagna for breakfast when Roman knocked on the kitchen door. He carried a small gun case.

"I'm at a stopping point now, so why don't we go to the firing range?" he said.

"Good idea," Zeppo said. "I really should try it a few times so I don't shoot off my dick if I have to do it for real."

"You're right to be concerned," Roman said. "Jean would discard you in an instant if that happened."

Jean made a face. "I hate the firing range. It always gives me a headache. Do I have to go?"

Roman shrugged. "I suppose you've practiced recently enough. You can stay here with the doors locked. While we're out, we'll stop at the market. Any requests?"

"Will you make Mexican food tonight?" Jean said. "I'll help."

"Certainly," Roman said. "I'd like that."

He and Zeppo went down the back steps while Jean locked up and set the alarm.

Jean, in sweat pants and an old T-shirt, curled up on the sofa and read the morning newspaper. As she had for the past couple of days, she searched for a mention of Armand Setrakian. Nothing so far. She finished her Bangkok mystery—Thailand was now at the top of her travel wish list. Feeling restless, she moved the coffee table so she could do some sit-ups and a little yoga, being careful of her healing bruises. Halfway through her second sun salutation, the doorbell rang.

Jean looked through the peephole. A man she'd never seen before stood on the threshold. She could make out a round head, completely bald on top, surrounded by frizzy gray curls that blended into a shaggy beard. Wire-rimmed glasses rested on a small nose. She thought of ignoring him, but for all she knew he was one of Beau's neighbors wanting to borrow an egg. "Yes?" she called.

"You Jean Applequist?" His voice was deep and rumbling. How in hell did he know she was here? "Who's asking?"

"I'm the guy pulled Martin Wingo out of the bay."

CHAPTER 33

*J*ean gripped the doorknob. "How do I know you're telling the truth?"

He held something up to the peephole. "I've got the man's watch."

Jean could make out a black and white watch, but not much else. If it really was Martin's, this guy was important. She looked at her own watch—Roman and Zeppo should be home soon. "Look, can you come back in an hour? I'm alone, and I don't feel comfortable letting you in."

"Sorry, I can't wait around."

"How about if I call the detectives on the case? You can talk to them."

"No way—no cops. That's why I'm here and not down at the Hall."

Jean was at a loss. She couldn't let him get away, yet knew how dangerous it might be to open the door.

"You got a gun in there?" he said.

"Yeah."

"Then we don't have a problem. You can hold the gun while we talk about my ten grand."

Jean had to know if he was telling the truth, and she was confident enough in her nerve and her shooting skills to chance it. "OK, just a minute." She hurried to Beau's study and got the Beretta from the desk drawer. She flicked off the safety and held it in her right hand, unfastening the locks with her left. As she opened the door, she stepped back and raised the gun.

The man on the stoop was about Jean's height but must have weighed eighty pounds more, a lot of it muscle. His massive shoulders strained against an old brown plaid flannel shirt, which hung loose over his gut. A Grateful Dead patch, a gaping rose-crowned skull, adorned his breast pocket. His sleeves were rolled up, and Jean could see a faded tattoo on a muscular forearm, the letters "U.S.M.C." His camouflage trousers were tucked into combat boots that had come partly unlaced over his huge calves. When he grinned, his small brown eyes nearly disappeared behind his cheeks. Jean put his age at around sixty.

"That's better," he said. "Now be cool, because I don't want to get shot by accident."

"Who are you?"

"Name's Ivan. Can I come in?"

In spite of his size, his vibe was nonthreatening. "I guess so." Jean moved out of the way. "Two of my friends will be here any minute, though," she warned.

"OK with me, as long as they're not cops." He stepped into the foyer. "Now, you don't want to pat me down, because if I'm any good I'll disarm you. So I'll just show you that I'm clean." He pulled his shirt up over his barrel chest, showing weathered, hairy skin as he turned in a circle. Generous love handles spilled over his belt. He emptied his pants pockets and pulled them inside out. "OK?" he said. He returned wallet and keys to his pockets.

"OK." Jean gestured with the automatic. "Go into the living room and sit on the straight-back chair." She sat across the room, training the gun on him. "Let's see that watch."

Ivan took the watch from his breast pocket and tossed it to her. She examined it, one eye on Ivan. It was a top-of-the-line Patek Philippe, platinum with a white face and a black alligator band. The band showed a little water damage, but the watch still ran. The monogram on the bezel read "MNW."

"It's his watch, all right," Jean said. "How'd you get it?"

"I warmed him up, fed him, gave him dry clothes, and took him where he wanted to go. He was grateful. Can I have it back now?"

She threw him the watch. "Where'd you take him?"

Ivan shook his head. "Money first."

"That's not up to me," Jean said. "His wife's offering the reward."

"Yeah, but there are pigs and reporters crawling all over her. I saw you going in and out of her house, so I figure you're a friend. You can broker the exchange."

"Let me see if I understand. You want the reward but don't want to talk to the cops."

"On TV they said she'd pay ten grand to find out who picked him up and where they dropped him off. What you do with the info's up to you." He shifted on the chair, which was too small for him. "Anyway, you and that redheaded kid have been going all around town talking to people. A couple of junior detectives. I tell you where he went, you figure out the rest."

"You've been following us?"

"Sure." He grinned again. "I like following good-looking women."

Someone unlocked the back door, and Jean heard Zeppo and Roman come into the kitchen, talking and laughing.

"Guys," she called. "Come here. I want you to meet someone."

The two men stopped abruptly when they saw Ivan and the gun in Jean's hand. "What's going on?" Roman demanded.

"These are my friends Roman and Zeppo. Guys, this is Ivan. He rescued Martin. The gun is just insurance. Can I put it away now?"

"I'll take it," Roman said. She handed it to him, glad to be rid of it. He frowned down at her. "You'll hear from me later about the foolishness of letting him in."

Ivan gave a rumbling chuckle. "Don't be too hard on her—she did OK. Had the safety off from the get-go and kept her distance."

Zeppo sat next to Jean and Roman took a chair near Ivan, putting the automatic on an end table. Jean summarized the negotiations so far.

"Ivan, will you please expound on the events of that evening up until you dropped Martin off?" Roman said.

"Sure. That afternoon I motored down from up north and came into the bay after dark. I heard the man-overboard on the radio. About half an hour later I fished Wingo out with a boat hook. He slept for a while. Later on I took him to Marina Green, where he made some calls from a pay phone, and then he got back on board and I dropped him somewhere else. I'll tell you where when I get the ten grand."

"What type of boat do you have?" Roman asked.

"A forty-foot fishing trawler."

"What took you so long to get him back on shore?" Zeppo asked.

Ivan grinned. "I had a business commitment. They were late."

"At that hour?" Jean said. "What sort of work do you do?"

"I'm in the agricultural sector."

"Ah," Roman said. "That would explain why Martin was stoned when he died and why he called you a pirate."

"A pirate, huh? Nah, I'm not into pillaging and looting. I'm a farmer."

Roman smiled. "Don't worry, we're not interested in your dope business. But I can see why you won't go to the police."

"You got it," Ivan said, nodding. "They'll want to check my boat, and I've been hauling herb in it for so many years it'll never get clean. So if anyone tells the cops about me, I'm gone. If they track me down, I'll have witnesses who'll say I never left Humboldt County. Either way, you'll never find out what happened to Wingo."

"We'll try to work around that," Roman said. "Shall we call Diane and ask her to come over?"

"I'm not going near her," Ivan said. "I want you to find out if she'll play it my way. If she will, Jean can bring me the money and I'll tell her where I put Wingo ashore."

Zeppo leaned forward. "How do we know you didn't put him ashore at Marina Green and then leave? You could be making up the second drop to get the reward."

"Lying creates too much stress in my life. I do most of my business on a handshake. Anyway, I don't need the money bad enough to piss you off, make you tell the cops about me."

"Even if it's true, the police have to be able to make a case that'll hold up in court," Zeppo said. "You can't expect Diane to pay the whole amount for information she may not be able to use."

"A few grand isn't worth my time and aggravation," Ivan said with a shrug. "I might as well sail back up north right now."

"How about $5,000 for the location and another five for the watch?" Zeppo said.

Ivan gave it some thought. "Yeah, OK. I know it's worth a lot more than that, but I can't fence the thing and I never wear one."

"We'll have to run it by Diane," Zeppo said. "What's your cell?"

"I don't own one. Those things stress me out. Give me a number."

Jean recited Beau's number, and Ivan took a pen from his breast pocket and wrote it on his forearm near the faded tattoo.

Roman gestured at Ivan's tattoo. "I see you were a Marine. You're the right age for Vietnam. Were you there?"

"I was there, all right. Did three tours of duty." He smiled wistfully. "Those were some good times."

Roman raised an eyebrow. "Are you staying nearby?"

"I'm anchored over in Sausalito." He stood. "Well, I should hit the road."

"We'll talk to Diane today," Jean promised.

"Later, then," Ivan said. "Peace." He went out the front door.

"This could be a major break," Jean said. "Once we know where Martin went, we can work on how he met his killer."

"Zeppo may be right about Ivan's story being a fabrication," Roman said. "Wait and see what the money buys." He looked at Zeppo with amusement. "How clever of you to get Martin's watch thrown into the bargain. I see you've had some experience with this sort of transaction."

"Yeah. I graduated from the University of Martin Wingo."

"Now I'd better call Diane," she said, dialing her mobile number.

"Thank God, Jean," Diane said. "I wish you'd get a cell. Where are you?" She sounded upset, and Jean could hear traffic noise in the background.

"Beau's."

"Can I come over? I have to see you right away."

"Sure," Jean said. "Is something wrong?"

"Can't talk. See you soon." She hung up.

"Diane's on her way over," Jean told the two men. "Something's up. Hey, how was the firing range?"

"It gave me a headache, too," Zeppo said. "I didn't really like shooting a gun."

"Yet he's not a bad shot for a man who's probably legally blind without his glasses," Roman said.

"Check this out." Zeppo handed her the newspaper he'd brought with him, pointing to a headline on page three: "Sculptor Accused of Sex Crimes." The subhead said "Armand Setrakian Will Lose Lucrative Elan Commission." They'd run a photo of Armand looking handsome and harmless. The byline was Helen Tang.

"All right!" Jean exclaimed. "The shit has hit the fan." She read the article. Helen Tang had tracked down the women Zeppo knew about, and three of the four had admitted being paid to drop the charges. A spokesman for Elan had announced they were withdrawing the commission, saying that "an investigation into recent allegations indicates that Mr. Setrakian does not embody the spirit of Elan." Through his attorney, Armand had denied everything.

"This is perfect," Jean said. "Now we wait for other women in his life to come forward."

"Meanwhile, we'd better unpack the groceries so we can eat," Roman said.

The three of them worked in the kitchen until the doorbell rang. Jean let Diane in—she hadn't looked this bad since right after the wedding. She was shaky and pale, her white jeans had a spot on the leg, her white and gold Hermès sweatshirt was rumpled, and she wore no makeup. Any residual anger Jean felt vanished. "Honey, what's the matter?"

"Oh Jean, the most terrible thing has happened," Diane said. "They've arrested Peter for Martin's murder."

CHAPTER 34

"**W**hat!" Jean exclaimed.

"It's true. He came over yesterday with papers for me to sign, and he was so upset about breaking up with you that I persuaded him to take the rest of the day off and go sailing. After that we went to his apartment and he made dinner. We had some wine and talked until really late, and . . . I don't know how to tell you this, but I ended up spending the night."

Jean sat down, stunned. "Why didn't I think of that? It's perfect!" Zeppo and Roman had come into the living room.

"Jean, please. Then Hallock and Davila pulled him out of bed at six A.M. to arrest him."

"How awful."

"I should never have let it happen. But we were both feeling sorry for ourselves, complaining about your temper and your . . . bad habits, and I'm very fond of him, and I've been so lonely, and he was so sweet."

"Peter must be in shock."

"He is. We had no idea he was even a suspect. The police think he planned to kill Martin after I married him to get me and the money. They believe that whatever his plan was, he took advantage of the situation and pushed Martin overboard when he found him alone on the aft deck. Hallock was obviously trying to trick me when he told me they'd eliminated all the suspects on the boat.

"The worst thing is, Peter's fingerprints are on Martin's boutonnière, on the satin ribbon and the backing. There are other prints, too, of course. Peter says he straightened it early in the evening, but the police think he grabbed it when he and Martin were struggling. And then Peter drove by Marina Green after Jean called to see if Martin was still there. He was the only one who was definitely in both places. They say he forced Martin into the car and killed him by hitting him on the head and throwing him off the pier at Aquatic Park. They think he changed Martin's clothes so it would look as if he never got to shore, that Jean was making it all up."

"Why that's . . . that's outrageous," Jean sputtered. "I was with Peter on deck. No, wait, we separated several times. Oh shit. When I gave my statement, Davila asked me about that. They must have suspected Peter for a long time."

"He thinks they've been following him at least since the autopsy," Diane said. "He's spent so much time with me, and they think we've been having an affair for months and just got sloppy last night. I can tell Hallock thinks I'm involved. At least I was able to get Rex Pfeiffer to represent Peter."

"Smart move," Jean said. Pfeiffer was a high-priced, high-profile criminal lawyer who had a reputation for manipulating juries with courtroom theatrics. He was also known for winning. "So I guess you don't want us to stop investigating after all."

"You're right—I want you to keep going."

"We have some news that might help Peter." Jean told Diane about Ivan. "But it's up to you—are you willing to pay him off without involving the police?"

"Yes, of course," Diane said at once, "if that's the only way he'll tell what he knows. And I'll be glad to get the watch back." Diane ran a hand through her tangled hair. "I must look awful. What with tracking down Pfeiffer and being questioned and waiting around to see Peter, I haven't been home yet."

"What did Pfeiffer say about bail?" Zeppo asked.

Jean knew he'd been denied bail for Sarah's killing and had spent the entire trial in custody.

"He thinks it depends on the judge," Diane said. "There's a bail hearing tomorrow morning."

"If *you* post bail it'll confirm suspicions that you two are co-conspirators," Roman said.

"I know," she said, "but no one else can afford it, and I can't bear to let him spend any more time in jail for a murder he didn't commit."

Jean reached over and squeezed Zeppo's hand. She saw Roman watching her with his sharp black eyes.

"Diane," Jean said, "are you going to tell the police about the blue box?"

"They let me see Peter for a few minutes at the jail, and we decided to wait until we find out how strong the case against him is. I'll get into a lot of trouble for not telling them about it sooner. You and Zeppo will be in trouble, too, Jean. Of course if things look bad for Peter, we'll have to tell them about both Ivan and the blue box."

"Let's hope it doesn't come to that," Zeppo said.

Diane's cell rang and she carried it into the library, emerging a few moments later.

"That was my chef, Celia," she said. "Hallock and Davila are on their way here, and my house is under siege by the press."

"You can stay here," Jean said. "There's plenty of room."

"Thanks, I will. Can I take a shower? I feel awful."

"Come on upstairs." Jean led Diane to the small bedroom down the hall from Beau's. "Zeppo and I are in Beau's room, so you can have the guest room."

"Why are you two staying here?"

"Because your pal Hugh tried to run us down again last night, here in the city."

"I still think you're wrong, Jean. I saw the paper today about Setrakian. He knew you were going to do that. It couldn't be Hugh."

"So you think Peter pushed Martin off the boat."

"Of course not." Diane sat on the bed, her head in her hands. Jean noticed that she no longer wore her wedding ring. "I don't know who pushed him—I just know it wasn't Peter or Hugh. I'm sorry about what I said. Please, I can't stand to fight with you anymore."

"I'm sorry, too. Let's agree to disagree about Hugh until I can prove it. Right now we have to concentrate on clearing Peter." Jean got her a clean shirt and left her alone.

Downstairs Jean could hear Roman rattling around in the kitchen. The smell of roasting chiles drifted out to the living room, where Zeppo paced, nervous and uneasy. She knew he dreaded talking to the cops again.

"Hey," Jean said, "it'll be fine. Just be cool or they'll think you're guilty of something."

Zeppo took a deep breath. "Yeah, you're right. I haven't felt this stressed since Martin went into the bay." He put his arms around her waist. "Normally I'd phone Hannah. But I like your brand of therapy better."

The doorbell rang within the hour and Jean admitted Hallock and Davila. "Hello, fellas," she said. "Inspector Hallock, have you come to apologize?"

"We need to ask you a few questions," Hallock said, irritated.

"If you're polite, I may answer them."

"Is Mrs. Wingo here?" Davila asked. "We won't bother her any more than we have to."

"Yeah, she's here." Jean showed them into the living room, where Diane waited, her damp hair braided and Jean's T-shirt much too big over her white pants.

"Mrs. Wingo," Hallock said, "we have a few more questions for you."

"Very well, Inspector." Diane was giving them her icy grande dame attitude.

Roman leaned against the doorframe, arms crossed. Jean was amazed at how a man could put so much hostility into the way he stood.

Hallock eyed Roman. "You're that guy from Bash Back, aren't you? Villalobos."

"That's right, Inspector." Roman managed to be soft-spoken and insolent at the same time.

"You live here?"

"No, in the small house behind this one."

"We've been talking about you down at the Hall," Hallock said. "A friend of mine from General Works is looking for whoever beat up a couple of sailors last Wednesday in North Beach. One of them has a ruptured spleen. It wasn't a robbery. Looks like they were hassling some queer and got more than they bargained for. You know anything about it?"

"It wasn't I. When it comes to sailors I'm a lover, not a fighter."

Davila looked at Roman with disgust. "*Maricón*," he said under his breath.

The harsh, ugly word startled Jean. Any attraction she'd felt for Davila evaporated in an instant. Roman gave the inspector a wicked smile and said something softly in Spanish. Davila's face flushed and he took a step toward Roman, his hands clenched into fists.

"Easy, Oscar," Hallock said, grabbing his partner's arm. "Don't let the asshole rile you. Mrs. Wingo, why don't you go in that room with Inspector Davila? I'll stay here with Ms. Applequist." Davila pulled himself back and accompanied Diane into Beau's library, closing the door. Hallock turned to Roman and Zeppo. "If you gentlemen will excuse us? And Mr. Zeppetello, stay close by. We'll want a word with you, too." Jean could hear Roman chuckling as the two men retreated to the back of the house.

Hallock asked Jean about Peter and Diane's alleged affair, coming at it from different angles, but finally gave up.

After questioning Zeppo briefly, he and Davila left, looking frustrated and annoyed.

When the police had gone, Diane got on the phone with Rex Pfeiffer and the other three gathered in the kitchen to make dinner. Jean poured a rich, berry-scented Paso Robles Zinfandel for Zeppo and herself, and Roman sipped Bourbon, grinning broadly as he stuffed cheese into roasted chiles.

"You look pleased with yourself, Roman," Jean said. She handed Zeppo the rice cooker. "I guess it cheers you up to get the police all hot and bothered."

"Always. It's not usually so easy to do."

"What did they want from you, Zeppo?" Jean asked.

"It was all about Diane and Peter and whether they were cheating on Martin. I told them I thought it was bogus. It wasn't so bad—Roman talked me down beforehand."

Jean looked at Roman. "You're teaching him the correct attitude toward cops, huh?"

"That's right. In Zeppo I recognize a kindred spirit—another outlaw who has serious problems with authority figures."

"You know, I was really surprised by Davila's attitude toward you, Roman," Jean said as she cut up a cucumber. "He seemed so reasonable before."

"Nobody's more homophobic than Latin males," he said, "unless it's Latin male cops."

"What did you say that got him so upset?"

Roman grinned. "Just boy talk."

Diane came into the kitchen. "Can I help?"

"Don't let her near the food," Jean warned. "How about setting the table?"

They dined on *chiles rellenos,* salad, rice, and homemade venison tamales from Roman's freezer. Diane, exhausted, excused herself and went to bed early.

"Diane and Peter," Jean said when her friend had gone upstairs. "It's perfect. They'll have a baby within two years or I'm Sarah Palin."

Roman smiled. "You're quite a matchmaker, driving them into each other's arms like that."

"Nice work, huh? I couldn't have done a better job if I'd planned it."

"There's nothing like a little adversity to make the sparks fly," Roman said. "Look at the two of you."

"Let's have the sparks without the baby, OK?" Zeppo said as he helped himself to another tamale.

"That's my plan, too," Jean said. The phone rang and she answered it.

"Hey, sweetheart, this is Ivan. You talk to the widow yet?" She could barely hear him over rock music and bar noise in the background.

"Yes, and she says she'll go along. How do you want to work it?"

"Let's meet in Sausalito tomorrow afternoon. Somewhere public."

"How about Spindrift Restaurant?" Jean said. "It's right on the main drag."

"I know it. Be there around six. If there's a problem, leave a message at the bar. Peace." He hung up.

"It happens at six," Jean said.

"Good," Zeppo said. "That'll give Diane plenty of time to get to the bank."

"What sort of place is Spindrift?" Roman asked.

"It's a touristy restaurant and bar on the water," Jean told him. "Has a big singles' scene."

Roman poured himself another Bourbon. "While you're meeting Ivan, why don't I borrow Nick Rigatos' sailboat and take a look at the boats anchored in the harbor there?" he said. "If I can spot Ivan's, you'll be able to find him later."

"Perfect," Jean said. "We may need him if things get ugly for Peter. But meanwhile we'll work on getting the charges dropped before it even goes to trial."

"Let's not forget the Castro Street Irregulars are on the job," Roman said. "Regarding Peter, perhaps we should consider the possibility that the police are right."

Jean gave him a look. "That Peter pushed Martin off the boat? That he's been screwing Diane for months? It's preposterous. Neither of them would ever betray anyone. Even if I wouldn't consider it betrayal, Martin sure as hell would have."

"It's ridiculous," Zeppo said. "The guy has a heavy-weight job and he was sleeping with Jean. Where's he going to find the time and energy for Diane? Besides, Martin and Diane were really hot for each other. They were so cutesy sometimes it made me gag."

"Maybe Peter and Diane weren't lovers," Roman said in his soft, reasonable voice. "What if Peter planned to kill Martin and then pursue Diane as soon as he'd dumped you, Jean? He knew he wouldn't have to wait long for you to give him a reason. Diane needn't have known a thing about it."

Jean shook her head. "Peter may be a lawyer, but he's not slimy. How could he count on Diane falling for him? What if she weren't interested? He'd have killed Martin for nothing."

"They spent a lot of time together. Maybe he could tell she was attracted to him, but wouldn't do anything about it because of Martin and you. Did you see Peter straighten Martin's boutonnière?"

"No, but we weren't together the whole time." Jean frowned. "I hope you're playing devil's advocate, Roman."

"I merely think the possibility can't be dismissed out of hand."

Later, upstairs in Beau's room, Jean lay in bed and stared into space, replaying her confrontation with Peter—his pain and rage, the marks he'd made on her arms, the way he'd nearly hit her. But he hadn't; he'd controlled himself. Killing Martin wouldn't have been an act of passion anyway. It would have been cold and calculated, done for money. Unless there really was something between Peter and Diane. She shook her head, dismissing the idea.

Zeppo got in beside her. "What's the matter, Jeannie?" he asked.

"I'm thinking about what Roman said. That I should consider whether the police might be right, that Peter killed Martin. How can I? I'd trust Peter with my life. Could my judgment really be so fundamentally flawed?"

Zeppo pushed himself up on an elbow. "Hey, don't ever doubt your judgment. You could tell I was innocent after hanging out with me for less than a week, and you know Peter a lot better than you know me."

"I suppose you're right. Roman does have a tendency to be suspicious of people. He likes you, by the way."

"I like him, too. He's a cool dude. But this time he's wrong."

Jean kissed him. "Thanks. You've talked me down." Their lovemaking pushed her doubts even further from her mind over the course of another long night.

CHAPTER 35

$\mathcal{J}$ean woke up first the next morning. She put on her red dragon robe and crept down the hall to see Diane, who was making the bed.

"Good morning," Jean said. "How was your night?"

Diane looked at her with mock disapproval. "I forgot what it was like trying to sleep nearby when you have a lover. I'm surprised the neighbors don't complain."

Jean sat on the bed. "Diane, you don't have any doubts about Peter, do you? You don't wonder if he could have planned this whole thing?"

"Of course not," Diane said. "I'd never sleep with someone I didn't trust completely."

"Why not? According to you, I'm screwing a lying, conniving loser."

"I'm sorry for what I said about Zeppo. Anyway, you have to admit your standards are . . . more relaxed than mine when it comes to men."

"Let's just say our tastes are different, except for Peter."

Diane smiled. "You know, you're right. This is the first time we've ever been attracted to the same man."

"So you agree with me that he's completely reliable and that he never killed anyone."

"I definitely agree. Now all I have to do is convince Martin's friends that he's innocent, and that I'm innocent, too. A lot of them are going to wonder. If he gets out on bail, can he stay here, too?"

"Of course. We'll be one big happy family, unless Peter's still pissed at me."

"How could he be, after all that's happened?"

"You didn't see how mad he was," Jean said. "Anyway, it's great that you two hooked up. He's just right for you."

"You know, I feel bad about sleeping with him because of what happened the next morning," Diane said. "But I know Martin wouldn't mind, even though he's been gone less than a month. He liked and trusted Peter. Once he told me that if he had another heart attack and died, he wanted me to find someone else, someone who didn't care about the money."

"Someone like Peter." Jean had always thought Diane was a bit on the shallow side emotionally, but now she found herself wishing that Roman could get over Chris the way Diane was getting over Martin—by jumping right back into the game.

Jean remembered an important piece of news. "Hey, Ivan called last night. He wants us to drive to Sausalito late this afternoon and do the deal. We'll need the cash by five-thirty."

"That's fine," Diane said. "I'll get it after the hearing."

After breakfast Roman drove Jean and Diane to the bail hearing, escorting them past crowds of reporters and onlookers. It hurt Jean to see how bad Peter looked, but at least his expensive lawyer, Rex Pfeiffer, successfully argued for bail—$2 million.

Pfeiffer's machinations and Diane's money got Peter out within a few hours. When the paperwork was done, Peter joined them, red-eyed and rumpled, his chin covered with brown stubble.

Diane gathered them together just inside the main entrance. "You and Roman take Peter home," she said to

Jean. "One of Pfeiffer's clerks will drive me to the bank and then to Beau's."

"Will do," Jean said. Peter was too shell-shocked to resist as she took one arm and Roman took the other, and they walked him through the crowd to the car, ignoring the cameras and shouted questions. Peter collapsed into the front seat, leaning his head back and closing his eyes. He smelled strongly of nervous perspiration.

"Are you all right?" Jean asked from the back seat.

"Just exhausted and filthy. God, what a nightmare. I'm glad I didn't go into criminal law. I'd hate to spend my time with the kind of people I had to deal with in there."

Jean leaned forward as Roman pulled into traffic. "We got a response to Zeppo's ad. The man who pulled Martin out of the bay came to Beau's house." She told him the Ivan saga.

"That's great, if it's true," Peter said.

"Peter, how much trouble are you really in?" Jean asked. "What have they got besides the fingerprints on the boutonnière and the theory about you and Diane?"

"I'm not sure. They have my credit card records, they impounded my boat, my car's in the police lab, and they searched my apartment. I feel as if I'm being dissected under a microscope. Pfeiffer's worried, which really scares me."

Roman waited in a bus stop half a block from Peter's Pacific Heights apartment building while Peter ran up and got a bag. Back at Beau's, Jean showed him to the guest room, where he sank exhausted into a gray overstuffed chair.

"I want you to know how happy I am about you and Diane hooking up," Jean said, patting his shoulder.

"We were both in a lot of pain, thanks to you. Not the best way to start a relationship."

"I suppose it's all my fault you needed to salve your wounded male pride."

He shook his head. "I don't know what I was thinking. She's only been a widow for three weeks. I like and admire her very much, and yet I took advantage of her loneliness and vulnerability. And look where it got me."

"If it'll make you happy, I'll take the blame," Jean said gently. "*Mea culpa,* OK? But you have to get over it and concentrate on the bigger problem."

He gazed at Jean. "You know this is insane, right?"

"Of course. If you were a killer, you'd have strangled me long ago. And Peter, I'm sorry I caused you so much pain. Please believe that I never meant to. But you know we never could have made it."

"I suppose you're right."

"Now take a shower," Jean said. "You stink."

She changed into capris and a T-shirt while Peter got cleaned up. Downstairs they found Zeppo in the kitchen.

"They granted bail," Jean told him. "It's two million bucks, so let's not lose track of him."

Zeppo eyed the other man warily. "Great, Peter. I'm glad they let you out."

"Don't worry, Zeppo, I'm not angry," Peter said. "I know how hard she is to resist. In any case, jealousy is the least of my problems now."

Zeppo made a pot of coffee and gave Peter a cup. As they sat at the kitchen table, Jean brought Peter up to date on their theories about Hugh Rivenbark and their two close calls.

"My God," Peter said. "I was right to be pissed at you. This really is dangerous."

"Shall we stop now?" Jean said sharply. "We're the only ones who know all about Martin. Do you want to be tried for his murder?"

"No, of course not. I just don't want you to get hurt. But I can't very well rely on the police to find the real killer. I just hope I don't have to tell Pfeiffer about the blue box."

"We're with you there," Zeppo said. "Let's keep the lid on it."

The doorbell rang and Jean let Diane in. "Where is he?" she demanded, rushing past Jean. She dropped her purse and a manila envelope on the dark red sofa.

"In the kitchen." Jean followed her friend, and saw that Peter and Diane were embracing. "You two are going to have beautiful children," she said.

Zeppo, leaning against the counter, asked if anyone was hungry.

"I'm starving," Peter said. "It's been hours since I've had any food worthy of the name."

Soon they were all seated around the kitchen table, feasting on leftover Mexican food while they told Zeppo the details of the bail hearing.

"I'll do dinner," Diane announced when they'd finished eating.

Jean looked at her aghast. "You're not going to cook, are you?"

"Of course not. I'll call up Jardinière and have them send something over. We'll plan dinner for eight o'clock— the three of you should be back by then."

The phone rang and Jean picked up.

"I know you did this to me, you fucking cunt," a man said harshly.

It took Jean a few seconds to place the voice. "Armand? How did you get this number?"

"I touch your goddamned tit and you ruin my life. You must think a lot of yourself."

"Hey, you're finally getting what you deserve for all those times you did a lot more than touch someone's tit."

"You'll get what you deserve, too, bitch. Wait and see. I know exactly where you are." He hung up.

Chapter 36

Zeppo looked at her with concern. "Setrakian?"

"Yeah, and he's really pissed." She sat on Zeppo's lap. He put his arms around her tightly. "What did he say?"

"That he's going to get even. He says he knows where I am."

"How in the world did he find you?" Diane asked.

"Probably bought the information from one of San Francisco's finest," Roman said.

"You don't think much of the police, do you, Roman?" Peter remarked.

"They start out no worse than anyone else, but it's a dehumanizing job. Eventually they develop what Garcia Lorca called 'el alma de charol,' patent leather souls."

Peter yawned hugely and rubbed his eyes. "I've got to lie down. Roman, thanks for letting us stay here. I realize it's an imposition, and it'll only get worse if the press finds us."

"No problem," Roman said. "I'm sure Beau won't mind our turning his house into Refugees R Us."

"We'll be leaving soon, so let me show you how to work the alarm system," Zeppo said. Diane and Peter followed him to the front door.

"Jean, you never know what the police are cooking up," Roman said, serious now. "If things start to look bad, I can get Peter out of the country. Let him know that's an option."

"OK, although I can't believe it'll come to that."

A few minutes later Roman left for the marina where Nick kept his boat. Zeppo divided the cash, all in hundreds, between two smaller envelopes and put them in Jean's purse. As they went out the door, he placed his hand gently on her back. "I'll drive, Jeannie. I don't think you've got the right temperament for rush-hour traffic."

"OK, but I get to drive home. Promise?"

"It's a deal."

Zeppo navigated through town and got on the bridge approach, which was jammed. Sausalito was the first town on the Marin side of the bridge, a quaint mix of nautical-themed waterfront restaurants, expensive condos, and pricy tourist shops.

Spindrift Restaurant was a blocky structure of gray weathered wood with a blue and white Hokusai wave on its sign. The parking lot was a third full. Inside, the dining room was nearly empty, but the bar did a lively business. Most of the clientele were B-list singles in their thirties and forties drinking blended Margaritas made with bar mix.

Jean spotted Ivan at a booth near the bar, well away from the other diners, most of whom sat at window tables overlooking the bay. He wore the same plaid shirt over jeans, and was working his way through a half-eaten cheeseburger and a mountain of fries. He waved and they sat down across from him.

"Sorry I started without you," he said. "You want something?" He gestured for the waiter.

Zeppo ordered fried calamari and a draft beer, Ivan had another beer, and Jean ordered a familiar if unexciting Chardonnay.

"This is an OK place," Ivan said. "I usually go to one of the dives nearer the harbor. There's no Dead on the jukebox, but there's some real talent here." His head swiveled as two curvy blonds walked by. He looked back at

Jean and winked. "Come to think of it, there's some real talent at this table."

Zeppo cleared his throat. "Here's my proposal. You give us the watch and tell us where you took Martin, and we give you $5,000 for the watch and whatever portion of the other $5,000 we deem appropriate once we've heard your information."

Ivan grinned. "You trying to jew with me again, kid? I may look mellow, but don't let that fool you. You don't want to stress me out. And Roman isn't here to back you up this time. So let's keep it simple: Hand over the ten grand and I'll give you the merchandise."

The waiter delivered their drinks and food. "Be reasonable," Zeppo said. "You can't expect us to hand over the money before we've heard your story. And I don't think you're going to make a scene in public. So how about we give you five and you give us the watch. Then you tell us the location and we give you the other five."

Ivan shrugged. "Sure. I've wasted enough time on this thing."

Jean handed him one of the envelopes. "Thanks," he said. "You're awfully young for gray hair. I bet they call you the Silver Fox."

Jean rolled her eyes. "Don't you want to count your money?"

"I'm getting to that." He emptied it onto the seat next to him and counted it quickly, then pulled the watch out of his breast pocket and gave it to her. She stuck it in her purse.

Ivan leaned on his elbows. "OK, here's the rest of it. After I finished my delivery, I took your man to Marina Green because I knew of a pay phone there. I waited on the pier to make sure he got a lift. He made a few calls—had to borrow change—and then asked if I'd take him to the South Beach Marina. He said he was going to see some woman."

Jean's leg was pressed against Zeppo's, and she felt him shift and tense up. "Oh yeah?" he said casually. "Who?"

"He didn't say. So I motored down there and dropped him off. He thanked me and said, 'I'll forget about meeting you if you forget about meeting me.' That's when he gave me the watch. Last I saw he was walking up the guest pier. I went straight back to Humboldt, and by the time I saw a newspaper they'd found his body. I was sorry to hear it. While I was waiting for my buyer, we smoked a spliff and talked awhile. He was an interesting dude, for a straight."

Zeppo nodded thoughtfully. "That sounds OK. I think we have a deal."

"Good. I was hoping I wouldn't have to get mean. You have any idea who did him?"

"Not yet," Zeppo said, "but this information may help."

Jean handed Ivan the second envelope, which he counted as well. He grinned hugely at Jean, his round cheeks nearly obscuring his eyes. "A pleasure doing business with you. Tell me one thing —does the collar match the cuffs?"

Jean laughed. "You'll just have to wonder, fat boy."

Zeppo, who'd taken out his wallet, put it away again. "For that," he said, "you can pay the tab."

Jean heard Ivan's rumbling chuckle as she and Zeppo slid out of the booth and headed for the door. "Peace," he called after them.

Out in the parking lot, Zeppo shook his head. "What an asshole."

She gripped his arm. "You know something. What?"

"I know where Martin went," he said. "And I know who the woman is."

CHAPTER 37

They got in the car. "All the years I worked for him, Martin always had a girlfriend," Zeppo said. "One of his long-term ones was a Brazilian woman named Flavia Soares. You remember those waterfront condos he built? He gave her one. They're right next to the South Beach Marina."

"That's quite a gift. They must be worth millions. Was he still screwing her?"

"I didn't think so. I thought he was stuck on Diane. But now I'm not sure."

"Did you ever meet Flavia?" Jean asked.

"Oh yeah, lots of times. She and Martin were really tight for a while."

"What's she like?"

"Small and dark, of course. Beautiful, but really plastic. She was always getting her nails done and her hair straightened and her crotch waxed. Martin bought her a nose job, a boob job, botox treatments, you name it. She's one of those women you wouldn't recognize after a month on a desert island."

"What does she do for a living?"

"Nothing much. She's sort of a professional mistress."

"How come you never mentioned her before?"

"I figured Martin's old girlfriends were history. Come on, let's get moving."

They got back on the freeway, Jean driving. "Why would Martin go there?" she asked.

"Beats me. Tomorrow we'll ask Flavia."

They'd expected a quick trip into the city, but near the bridge traffic slowed, and by the time they were on the span they were creeping along. Jean's legs, still sore from the bike ride, got tired working the brake and the stiff clutch. "God, I hate the traffic in this town," she said.

"I don't mind being stuck with you for company," Zeppo said. They inched along for several minutes. The incoming fog obscured part of the skyline and the orange art deco bridge towers loomed above them. In spite of the beautiful setting, Jean felt herself getting cross as the traffic slowed even more.

"Jeannie," Zeppo said thoughtfully, "I know what's going to happen after we're not hiding out anymore. I probably won't see you that often. I just want you to know how great this has been, being with you all the time."

"Why won't you see me that often?"

"Because you have a regular life. Friends, boyfriends . . ."

"Don't be so goddamn dumb," she snapped. "I thought you were over this loser mentality." She honked as the car in front of them nearly rolled back into the Jag.

"I'm just being realistic."

Traffic was at a dead stop, so Jean turned in her seat. "What kind of a shallow slut do you think I am? Do you really believe I could spend a week like this with a man and then forget all about him?"

"I don't want to expect too much."

"Don't be so pathetic!" she yelled. "I suppose you think this is the world's longest sympathy fuck." Two women in the car next to them looked over.

"Jeannie, I'm sorry. I—"

"Stop apologizing! I hate your gutless wimp act!"

He grinned at her fondly. "You're sure cute when you're angry."

Jean glared at him, ready to explode, then burst out laughing.

"I'm sorry," she said. "The traffic is making me cranky. When this is all over we'll see as much of each other as we can, and when you go to Davis we'll work something out. I've grown very attached to you. And where will I find another sex fiend like you?"

She put the Jag in neutral and set the hand brake, and they made out feverishly until the car behind them honked. Jean managed to pull away and eased the car up a few feet. "OK," she said, "I'll drive, and you think about Dick Cheney in a thong."

The women in the next car smiled at them. The Jag inched along, Zeppo's hand on her thigh. "It's not working, Jeannie," he said. "All I can think about is wanting you."

"If we ever get off this fucking bridge, I'll pull over."

Up ahead on Park Presidio they could see flashing lights and impenetrable traffic, so Jean took Lombard Street, poking along but at least moving. She turned right on Divisadero and pulled into the first space she found, about three blocks up.

She killed the engine, grabbed Zeppo by his curly hair, and kissed him long and deeply. He put his hands around her torso and brushed his thumbs against her nipples, filling her with a sharp, aching desire. "Zeppo," she whispered, "I want you right now."

He seemed as desperate as she was. "Oh Jeannie . . . ouch!" He hit his knee on the gearshift knob. His hand under her skirt made her thrash against the car door. As they grappled, Zeppo banged his elbow on the dashboard and she bumped her knee on the steering wheel, making them both laugh and bringing them partway to their senses.

"Too bad there's no back seat," Zeppo said.

She pulled her skirt down. "It's just as well there isn't. We'd get arrested."

"If we go to Roman's, we'll have to sit around and be sociable until after dinner."

"I can't wait until after dinner," she said.

He put his hands on her again. "Neither can I."

"It's not safe to go to our apartments," Jean said.

"We could check into a motel. Wait a minute—you have anything against an outdoor screw?"

"Brilliant idea." Jean restarted the engine and drove into the Presidio, to the clearing where they'd confronted Felix.

The air was cool and damp, and moonlight filtered through the incoming fog. Zeppo took a heavy blue cotton blanket from behind the seats and spread it on the thick grass near the car before pulling Jean into a hungry embrace. Off came their clothes, which they dropped on the damp ground. They lay down on the soft blanket, the scent of earth and greenery strong. Jean, greedy and impatient, pulled him close, but Zeppo wouldn't be hurried. He teased her endlessly, doing all the things she liked best but denying her any release, until she could bear it no longer.

"Zeppo, I can't stand it," she moaned.

"What's the magic word?"

"Please," she said. "Please."

He put on a condom, laced his fingers over the top of her head, and shoved into her all at once, making them both groan with relief. She closed her eyes and let go of everything but him, rocking her hips with his as he moved at just the right angle, just the right speed, until she climaxed again and again, clawing him and crying out. Only then did he let go, too, and he came with a long, rolling shudder, calling her name.

Jean lay utterly spent, Zeppo still inside her, his weight welcome on her. "Oh Zeppo," she breathed, "you fuck like an angel." She heard a rustling noise nearby and opened her eyes. Hugh Rivenbark stepped from the bushes holding a black automatic.

CHAPTER 38

*J*ean gasped, and she and Zeppo disentangled and sat up.

"That was quite a performance," Hugh said. "There's nothing else like the mindless, athletic couplings of youth." He gave a nasty chuckle. "Martin was right about you, Jean. You'll fuck anything, won't you?"

"*Almost* anything, old man." She pulled the blanket around herself, her feelings of outrage and violation making her more furious than afraid. She was sick to death of hearing Zeppo belittled by everyone she encountered, even the rapists and murderers. "Weren't you paying attention? I can't believe you've ever done that much for a woman in your whole miserable life."

"Come now, the least you can do is thank me for letting you finish."

"Isn't that the whole point with impotent perverts like you? Now that you've had your jollies, what do you want?" Hugh wore surgical gloves, and Jean realized with horror that his gun had a silencer on it. Probably got it from one of his colorful characters. "How'd you find us, anyway?"

"Diane was thoughtful enough to call and tell me where she's staying, and happened to mention you'd gone to Sausalito and would return for dinner. I merely had to wait for your rather ostentatious car to come back across the bridge. Now put your clothes on. We're going to your apartment, Zeppo. I don't wish to continue our discussion in public."

Jean glanced at Zeppo, who looked pale and frightened. They gathered their damp clothes and put them on.

"How'll we get there?" Zeppo asked, tying his shoes. "We won't all fit in my car."

"We'll use mine." Hugh went to the Jag and opened the front door, never taking his eyes from Jean and Zeppo. He set Jean's purse on the passenger seat and rooted through it with one hand. "Nothing dangerous. Here, take it." He grabbed the garage door opener clipped to the sun visor and dropped it in his pocket, then stood behind Zeppo and frisked him. He turned off and pocketed Zeppo's cell phone. "Now walk back out to the road. And remember, if either of you escapes, I'll shoot the other one."

Hugh's silver Nissan sedan was parked on the shoulder about fifty yards from the mouth of the gravel road. He gave the keys to Zeppo and sat in the back seat with Jean. She knew they should try to escape while they were still in public, but the silenced gun prodding her ribs terrified her into compliance.

Zeppo drove to his building without a word and pulled into the garage. In a few moments they were in his apartment. Hugh ordered Jean to sit on the bed and put Zeppo in the computer chair.

He stood in the middle of the small room, gun in hand. "Good," he said. "I prefer to conduct our business in private. I'll take that thumb drive now, Zeppo."

"It's not here."

"Where is it?"

Zeppo shook his head. "No way I'm telling you. You'll kill us if I hand it over."

Hugh pointed the gun at Jean. "If you don't, I'll shoot Jean in a non-vital area. I'll keep shooting her until I have the thumb drive."

Zeppo looked at Jean. "OK, I lied. There is no thumb drive."

Hugh smiled. "Just as I thought. You wanted to try a little blackmail, in the manner of our departed friend Martin, but with nothing for collateral. You're both fools."

"You going to kill us for being fools?" Jean said. "Is that why you tried to kill Martin?"

"That was impulsive, an act of rage. I confronted him on the aft deck and he told me he found the manuscript years ago. I demanded to know what he wanted from me. He said he didn't want anything. All those years he knew I didn't write it. He laughed at my anger."

"I suppose trying to run us down was impulsive, too," Jean said.

Hugh looked at her in confusion. "What are you talking about?"

Jean met Zeppo's eyes. She knew what he was thinking— that it must have been Setrakian in the Jeep and the Taurus, and that Hugh was threatening them now only because Zeppo had called and given him a reason. Shit.

"Never mind," Zeppo said. "Wrong psycho."

Jean returned her attention to Hugh. His admission that he'd pushed Martin overboard scared her as much as the silencer. The only reason he'd be so frank is that he really was going to kill them. She'd have to keep him talking until they could find a way out of this—not a difficult task, given his love for the sound of his own voice.

"What about Esther?" she taunted. "Was that impulse or cold blood? Did you push her or rig the stairs? You killed your own wife, after what she did for you, to save your precious ego." She noticed Zeppo rolling the chair back ever so slightly toward the computer table.

Hugh's smug expression turned ugly. "Don't you speak her name, you meddling whore. I chose between love for a woman and self-love. I've lived with my decision for thirty years." Jean saw real pain in his eyes. "I'd give anything to make that choice again. But I can't, and if the truth gets out now, she'll have died for nothing."

Hugh took a breath and collected himself. "Peter Brennan is free on bail. I think this is the perfect time for him to kill you both in a jealous rage. Take off your clothes. We'll make it look as if he caught you *in flagrante delicto.*"

"That'll never work," Jean said contemptuously. "Why would he be jealous enough to kill us if he's hot for Diane?"

"Diane's about money—you're about sex. There are different impulses involved. Peter can service his rich widow and still hate losing you to a younger man. I'll say you confided in me that Peter threatened you."

"This isn't one of your piss-poor novels. What if he's got an alibi?"

"Diane is his alibi, which means he has none at all. They're being very secretive, so no one else knows where they are."

"The police know," Jean countered.

"The police won't watch him twenty-four hours a day, and by the time they find your bodies they won't be able to tell exactly when you died."

"You underestimate Diane," Jean said. "She has a lot of powerful friends."

"Those are all Martin's friends. They'll drop her fast if she's connected to his murder, or if her lover is. In the end, she's just a delectable bit of trailer trash who got lucky." He motioned with the gun. "Now get undressed," he said sharply. Zeppo took off his shirt and dropped it on the floor, but remained seated.

Jean was really frightened now and felt the beginnings of panic. Hugh had no reason to let them live. She had to do something fast. Time to use her distraction factor.

Jean stood, slipped off her shoes, and slowly unbuttoned her blouse. "There are still plenty of things wrong with your scenario," she said. She took off the blouse, unzipped her skirt, and slid it down. "What if the police *are* watching Peter 24/7? What if they already know he doesn't have your gun?" She unhooked her bra and shrugged it off, then stepped out of her panties, watching Hugh closely. In spite of the situation, Jean could tell she was getting to him.

She walked over to the dresser, searching for a weapon. Everything was neatly put away. She thought of her own apartment, and wished Zeppo left scissors and kitchen knives and blunt instruments lying around the way she did. "Face it, Hugh—there are too many ways your plan could go wrong." The bottle of Marcassin Chardonnay stood on the dinette table near the bathroom door.

Hugh followed her with his eyes. "Very impressive—a pornographer's dream. Now go sit on the bed."

"In a minute. I have to pee. You don't want me to get a bladder infection, do you?" She walked toward the bathroom.

"Do it now," Hugh commanded. "Sit on the bed."

"You want to shoot me there? It's better theater, right? Well, I'll be damned if I'll make this easy for you." She moved past him toward the bottle.

"Do as I say or I'll kill you where you stand." Hugh turned away from Zeppo and raised the gun. Zeppo seized the glass lobster paperweight from the desk and threw it, striking Hugh on the temple hard enough to make him stagger. Jean lunged for the bottle. Zeppo dove toward him as Hugh fired at him, and Jean brought the bottle down on the back of Hugh's head. He sank to his hands and knees, still gripping the gun. She stood over him and hit him again and he fell insensible to the floor. She kicked the gun away with her bare foot.

Jean put the bottle on the floor and ran to Zeppo's side. He lay near the corduroy chair, conscious but dazed. He was hit high in the left shoulder and blood was oozing out, too much blood. Jean grabbed the sheet off the bed and pressed it to the wound.

"Oh Zeppo, come on. Come on, talk to me."

He looked at her. "Jeannie. Tell me that's not your blood."

She glanced down and saw blood on her hands, her arms, her breasts. "No, it's all yours." She put his right hand on the sheet and told him to hold it tightly. "I have to call 911."

She stumbled to the phone and brought it back with her. His eyes were closed and the sheet had fallen off his wound. "Zeppo!"

He opened his eyes. "Did you hit him with the wine bottle?"

"Yeah. I hope I killed him."

"I saw you were going for it. We're still a good team, huh?" His eyes closed again as he fell unconscious.

The 911 operator answered on the fifth ring. "A man's been shot," Jean said, her voice unsteady. "I need an ambulance right away." She gave Zeppo's address.

"Where's the shooter?" asked the calm woman at the other end.

"He's unconscious." She looked over at Hugh and saw blood seeping through his white hair. "You'd better send an ambulance for him, too."

The operator instructed Jean to keep Zeppo warm and apply pressure directly to the wound. Jean covered him with his comforter and did her best to staunch the bleeding. After what seemed like an eternity but was only three minutes by the bedside clock, she heard sirens.

Jean stood, realizing she was still naked. She looked around and spotted Zeppo's cell phone, which had fallen out of Hugh's pocket. She might need it later. She dropped it into her purse, where Martin's watch nestled next to her wallet. Shit. How would she explain that? She grabbed a thick book from the nearest shelf and laid the watch inside. She dressed hurriedly, her bloody hands leaving streaks on her clothes. As she slipped on her shoes, the buzzer rang.

Jean opened the door. The stoop was crowded with blue uniforms, and outside she saw an ambulance, fire engine, and squad car, lights rotating.

"There." Jean pointed to where Zeppo lay. Two young men knelt next to him, uncovering him and talking in low tones as they worked. Jean was aware of movement all around her, but could only focus on Zeppo.

A policeman with dark hair and a mustache touched her arm as she leaned over to see better. "Miss, step back and let them work," he said. "Are you injured?" His name-tag said "Gary Blumberg."

"No, I'm OK." Jean backed up and stood close to the wall, trying to stay out of everyone's way.

Two fire department paramedics worked on Hugh. "What happened to him?" one of them asked.

"I hit him with a wine bottle, twice. That one." Jean pointed to the Chardonnay, which stood near the brown corduroy chair. She anxiously watched the men near Zeppo.

"You hit him?" Officer Blumberg asked.

"Yes. He'd just shot my friend and I didn't want him to shoot me. Can I get my purse? I'm going with him." Her voice sounded shaky, so she took a deep breath.

"Hey, Kim," Blumberg called. "Give me a hand here. She wants to go to the hospital."

Another officer, a bony young woman with short blond hair, came out of the kitchen and turned to her partner. "There's a garage next door. I can question her there."

"I'll check it." Blumberg went out the door.

She approached Jean. Her tag said "Kimberly Snyder." "What's your name, miss?" Her voice was soft and soothing.

"Jean Applequist."

"Well, Jean, we have to wait until the crime scene technicians get here. We'll take you to the hospital as soon as we can. Meanwhile you can tell me what happened."

Jean realized Officer Snyder was trying to calm her down, that the police thought she was getting hysterical. Maybe she was. She watched the paramedics put an IV in Zeppo's hand, a big bandage on his shoulder, and an oxygen mask over his face. They lifted him onto a gurney and rolled him out the door. Soon the other paramedics wheeled Hugh out, his neck in a brace, an oxygen mask over his face as well. Jean was disappointed that he was still breathing.

She turned her attention back to Officer Snyder. "Now Jean," the woman said as if to a child, "we're going to bag your hands until the technicians get here, OK? So we can test for gunshot residue and eliminate you as the shooter."

Snyder put plastic bags over her bloody hands, securing them at the wrists. Jean took another deep breath and tried to loosen the knot of fear in her stomach. She realized the whole process was out of her control, and that if she wanted to be taken to Zeppo she'd have to calm down and cooperate. What should she say? Her story had to be consistent with the facts, but not too revealing.

Blumberg stuck his head into the apartment. "I'll ride along in the ambulance," he told Snyder. "See you there." He went out the door.

Snyder took Jean into Zeppo's garage and had her sit on a cardboard box next to Hugh's car, shutting the door behind them. Snyder took notes, leaning on the car. Jean gave her name and address and the names of the two injured men. "This is Zeppetello's apartment," Jean said. "Rivenbark forced us to come here. That's his car. He was going to kill us."

"Why?"

Jean sighed. "It's a long story." Her hands felt sticky and itchy in the baggies.

"Just tell me what happened tonight."

Without mentioning the manuscript, Jean recounted how Rivenbark had followed them from the bridge, and gave Snyder directions to the clearing where they'd left Zeppo's car.

"What's your relationship with Rivenbark?" Snyder asked.

"It's all about Martin Wingo. Zeppetello used to work for him and Rivenbark was Wingo's friend."

Snyder raised her eyebrows. "In that case we'll hold off any more questioning. I'll get in touch with the investigating officers on the Wingo case. They'll want to talk to you." Snyder turned a page in her notebook. "Who's Zeppetello's next of kin?"

"He has no immediate family. He's an orphan."

"What about Rivenbark?"

"He's a widower. His brother-in-law lives in Mendocino." Jean thought about how hard it would be on Edward to learn the truth.

The evidence technician finally arrived and swabbed Jean's hands, and she was allowed to rinse off in the utility sink in the garage. Clutching her purse, which the police had searched, she rode in the back of Snyder's squad car to the hospital.

CHAPTER 39

$\mathcal{A}$t San Francisco General, which housed the main trauma unit for the city, Officer Snyder took Jean through the emergency entrance into the waiting room, where they found Blumberg.

"They're operating on Zeppetello now," he told Jean. "You'll be notified as soon as they're finished. The dispatcher is trying to reach Hallock and Davila."

"Is there anyone you can call to be with you?" Snyder asked.

"Yes, my friends."

Jean pulled out Zeppo's cell and called Beau's. Roman answered on the first ring. "Where the hell are you?" he demanded. "I've been calling Zeppo's cell for over an hour."

"I'm at S.F. General. Zeppo's been shot."

He was silent for a moment. "Is he alive?"

"So far."

"Are you hurt?"

"I'm fine."

"We'll be right there."

She flipped the phone closed. "My friends are on the way," she told the officers.

"We've got another call," Snyder said. "I spoke with Inspector Davila, and he says it's OK to leave you here. He and Hallock will contact you as soon as they can."

Snyder turned and followed Blumberg out the door. "Good luck, Jean."

"Thanks," Jean said to her retreating back. She sat down in the vast waiting room, her stomach in a knot so tight she thought she might vomit. The night was busy, and the less urgent cases would wait a long time—a young Latina holding a crying baby, an obese old woman in a wheel-chair, a middle-aged man holding a handkerchief over his eye. In a corner, two uniformed cops questioned a sullen gangbanger with cuts on his face and what looked like a broken nose. Ambulances arrived and their passengers were whisked past, medical personnel running alongside like bobsled teams.

Jean knew Zeppo's wound was her fault. If she'd driven back to Roman's, none of this would have happened. If Roman had gone with them, if they hadn't been stuck so long on the bridge, if she hadn't pulled over, if she hadn't insisted they make love right away, if she'd been faster with the wine bottle, if she weren't a selfish, sex-crazed imbecile . . . her self-recriminations made her head ache. She'd never before had such a memorable sexual experience that she regretted so deeply.

Jean knew Zeppo's body almost as well as her own, and it was agonizing to think of him pierced by a bullet, cut with scalpels, stuck with needles, invaded by tubes. She was lost in nightmare imaginings of blood clots, infections, and incompetent doctors when she looked up to see Roman hurrying toward her, Peter and Diane right behind him. She stood and let Roman enfold her in his arms, leaning into him, grateful for his strength. Peter and Diane stood close by.

"What happened?" Roman said into her hair.

"Hugh Rivenbark forced us to go to Zeppo's apartment at gunpoint. We kept him talking and Zeppo threw something at him. Before I could stop him, he shot Zeppo in the shoulder."

"Will he be OK?"

"I don't know. They're working on him now. Someone's supposed to come out and talk to me."

"Are you hurt?" Peter asked anxiously. "There's blood on your clothes."

"It's all Zeppo's."

Diane's eyes were wide with shock. She gripped Jean's arm. "Hugh did this?"

"Not only that, he admitted he pushed Martin off the boat and killed his wife. We both heard him. Convinced now, Diane?" Jean regretted her sharp tone immediately.

Diane sat down hard on a plastic chair. Peter took her hand. "What happened to Hugh?" he asked.

"He's here, too. I hit him with a wine bottle. I hope I fractured his fucking skull."

"How did Hugh find you?" Roman asked. "You were supposed to come straight home."

Jean sighed. Here came the part where she sounded really stupid. "We . . . we got the urge to make love and went to that clearing in the Presidio. Hugh followed us and watched the whole show." She didn't want to make Diane feel worse by telling her how Hugh had known where they'd be.

"Good God, Jean," Peter said. "Zeppo's shot because you couldn't control yourself?"

"I know, I know. I screwed up big time. Go ahead and say I told you so." Again it came out sharper than she'd intended

"Jean, shh," Roman said, pulling her close, rubbing her back. "You didn't shoot him. You're guilty of nothing more than poor impulse control and an overactive libido."

"I'm sorry," Peter said. "I didn't mean to blame you. After all, Hugh's the one who's been trying to kill you."

"No, that wasn't him in the cars," Jean said. "He knew nothing about it."

Roman digested this piece of news. "So Zeppo's phone call about the thumb drive set him off."

"What phone call?" Diane asked. "What thumb drive?"

Jean explained the mythical scanned copy. As she talked, she realized people were looking at them and whispering—Peter and Diane had been all over the news lately. "Hey," she said. "You two are notorious. You'd better leave before someone alerts the media."

Roman looked around. "She's right. Take the car and go back to Beau's. We'll get a cab later." He handed Peter his keys.

Diane, teary-eyed, put her arms around Jean. "I'm so sorry. I might have prevented this if I'd believed you."

Jean hugged her back. "It's OK, Diane. I can't blame you for being loyal." She kissed Peter goodbye and watched the two of them leave the hospital.

Jean and Roman sat close together and waited. She knew how much he hated hospitals, especially this one, where he'd been on so many deathwatches over the years. Jean had been here too often herself, visiting friends now dead. She put her hand on his knee. "I'm sorry to bring you here again."

He laid his arm across her shoulders. "It's OK. This time no one's going to die. While we're waiting I want to hear a blow-by-blow account of your encounter with Hugh."

Jean told him, and when she was done he smiled at her. "You did fine. Once you were in that situation, with him holding a gun on you, there weren't many options. It's because of you that no one got killed."

"It's because of me that we were there in the first place."

"Wait until Zeppo's back in the saddle and Rivenbark's in prison. You'll forgive yourself then. Now tell me what Ivan had to say."

"He dropped Martin at the South Beach Marina. Zeppo says one of Martin's old girlfriends lives there. Will you go with me to talk to her?"

"Of course."

"How'd your sailing excursion go?"

"Ivan's boat was easy to find," Roman said. "It's named the *Sugar Magnolia*, predictably, and I got the CF number." Roman looked across the room and stood, pulling her up. A nurse was calling out Zeppo's name.

They followed her into another room and were soon joined by Dr. Boles, a weary-looking young man in green scrubs. He gazed at Jean and Roman doubtfully. "Are you his family?"

"He has no family. I'm his girlfriend and this is another friend."

The doctor shrugged. People in San Francisco were used to unorthodox social relationships. "The EMTs did a good job and he was lucky," he said. "The bullet fractured his left clavicle, grazed a rib, and exited just below his scapula. He has a non-union of the clavicle ends, which may close up by itself. There's soft tissue damage but the lung is unaffected. We still have to watch for infection, but he's young and very fit, so he should recover completely."

Jean felt giddy with relief. "Can I see him?"

"Not tonight. He's in the recovery room now, and later we'll move him to the ICU. Tomorrow you can see him briefly. He lost a lot of blood, so he'll be weak for a while."

When the doctor left, Jean turned to Roman. "You might as well go home," she said. "I'll wait until they move him to the ICU and then follow you."

Roman raised an eyebrow. "The last time I left you alone, there were casualties."

"I'm not going to screw up twice in one night. I'll stay where it's crowded and come straight home. No fooling around this time."

He thought about it. "Very well. I'm concerned about Setrakian coming to Beau's. He can't know you're here, but stay on your guard."

"See you later, Roman, and thanks."

He went out the front entrance to catch a cab.

Jean paced around for an hour or so until Zeppo got settled in the ICU. He was still out cold, but a sympathetic nurse let her look at him through the glass wall of his room. His pale skin seemed translucent and the bones in his face were even more prominent than usual, reminding Jean eerily of Martin's corpse. An oxygen tube ran out of his nose, a bandage covered his left shoulder, an IV line was taped to the back of his right hand, and a catheter snaked out from under the covers. Jean wanted to touch him, but the nurse said she couldn't go in until morning.

It was nearly midnight; Jean sat for a few minutes in the ICU waiting room pulling herself together. A slender male shape at the edge of her vision made her glance up. "Edward," she said in surprise. He looked at her, dazed and anxious. "How's Hugh?" she asked.

"There's no fracture," he said. "He has a severe concussion, though, and they're worried about a subdural hematoma, bleeding inside the skull. And Zeppo?"

"He's stable. They say he'll be fine." Jean wondered how she could have hit Hugh so hard and not cracked his skull.

"I can't believe what the police are saying," Edward said. "Hugh shot Zeppo? And you hit him? They didn't really explain why. What in God's name happened?"

"This is going to hurt."

"It already does."

"Come and sit down, Edward. It's a long story, but the important part is that Martin had the original handwritten manuscript of *Home to Greenwood*. Zeppo saw it. We found a sample of Hugh's handwriting and you sent us Esther's. Hugh didn't write it, Edward. Esther did."

He blinked at her. "You're saying she wrote it and let him take credit? Why? I don't understand."

"Probably because she loved him and he was having trouble with his own work."

"It's . . . it's unbelievable. He shot Zeppo because of that?"

She explained the chain of events that had brought them to the Presidio and to Zeppo's apartment. "Hugh admitted he pushed Martin off the boat because he'd only just discovered that his old buddy knew all about it." Jean was reluctant to tell him what else Hugh had confessed.

"It was in Esther's handwriting?" Edward said.

"Just like the sample you sent, according to Zeppo."

Edward sat perfectly still, staring across the room. Finally he turned to Jean. "He killed her, didn't he?" His voice was constricted with pain.

Jean put her hand on his arm. "He admitted that, too. Esther must have had second thoughts and asked him to come clean, and he couldn't do it."

"I wondered at the time whether he might have done it, but I thought he loved her and had no reason to hurt her. Now I find he had a good reason, but there's no way to prove it."

"I'm afraid you're right. Tell me, was he really at his apartment all night after the wedding?"

"Yes. Did you think I lied to protect him?"

"I wondered."

Edward shook his head. "No, I didn't. But I would have if he'd asked, and Laurel probably would have, too. He's been as close as a brother all these years." He pounded a fist into his open hand. "How could he look me in the eye after what he did? How could he cry for her, pretend to grieve for her?"

"If it means anything, he says he regrets killing her."

"It means nothing from a cold-blooded liar like him." Edward leaned forward, his elbows on his knees, and worked his hands together. "First he killed her, and then he spent the next thirty years lying to me. Well, the lying's over now." He sat back, his face hard and determined. "He won't get away with it any longer."

Jean scrutinized his expression with alarm. "Edward, don't go near him. He'll be convicted of attempted murder. He'll go to prison and lose the thing he values most—his precious reputation."

"He won't lose as much as she lost, as I lost."

"Don't even think about revenge. He's not worth it."

"But she is." He stood up. "I have to call Laurel. Let us know how Zeppo's doing."

"You're not driving home tonight, are you?"

"No, I'm staying at Hugh's apartment. He gave me a key, like a good brother. Goodbye, Jean, and thank you." He turned toward the door, his hands thrust into the pockets of his denim jacket, his resolve clear in his walk and the line of his shoulders.

CHAPTER 40

$\mathcal{A}$ taxi took Jean through the cold foggy night to Beau's. Roman opened the front door. "Anything new?" he asked as they joined Peter and Diane in the living room. Diane's eyes were red-rimmed and puffy, and she clutched a wad of tissues.

Jean flopped into the wing chair. "Zeppo looks like a corpse, but apparently he's doing OK. I ran into Edward Bongiorni and told him what happened. He's pretty upset."

"God, he must be devastated," Diane said. "I can't even imagine what's going through his mind."

Jean knew exactly what was going through his mind but kept it to herself. "I need a drink. Can I have a Cognac?"

"Of course," Roman said. "Always good in a crisis." He poured her a snifter.

Jean drank it quickly and it hit her hard. She realized she'd only had a couple of fried calamari since lunch. "Is there anything to eat?"

Roman brought her a plate of leftovers from their Jardinière dinner, duck breast with lentils and baby turnips, which she ate ravenously.

"I see even near-death experiences don't affect your appetite," Roman remarked.

"I have to keep my strength up in case Setrakian drops by," she said. The phone rang and Jean leaped up to answer it.

"Ms. Applequist?" Inspector Hallock said. "I know it's late, but at the ICU they said you'd just left. We would've contacted you earlier, but we've been tied up for several hours. Officer Snyder told me what happened this evening."

Jean was so relieved it wasn't the hospital calling with bad news that she was polite to him. "Yes, she was very helpful. Thank her for me."

"I'd like to ask you a few questions, but there's no reason we can't do it in the morning."

Jean stared at the phone. Hallock was being polite, too. What had gotten into him? "Uh, OK. But I want to be at the hospital as early as possible."

"How about if I come by around eight o'clock?"

"I'll expect you then." She hung up. "Will wonders never cease. Hallock is being considerate."

"Maybe he's starting to appreciate you, Jean," Roman said. "You did disarm a crazed gunman while naked using only a paperweight and a bottle of wine."

"Rivenbark was overmatched," Peter said. "Jean naked is a pretty disarming sight."

Jean glanced at the couch. Peter had his arm around Diane, who had fallen asleep against him.

"And on that note, I think we'll go to bed." He woke Diane and they went upstairs.

Jean kissed Roman on the cheek at the back door. "Good night, Roman. Thanks for everything."

"*De nada*. You've helped me through a crisis or two."

Jean locked up and went upstairs to Beau's room. She put fresh water into the red vase that held the tropical blooms Zeppo had given her. She took a shower to wash off the last of his blood, then dug through his suitcase for his Zorro T-shirt, which she wore to bed. His scent was on the sheets and she found a curly red hair on his pillow.

Jean was afraid she'd be wakeful, but Cognac and sheer exhaustion put her out in minutes. Once during the night, half asleep, she reached for Zeppo, wanting him, smiling in anticipation of his certain response. When he wasn't there and she came fully awake and remembered why, she went downstairs for another glass of Cognac.

✍

JEAN LAY in bed the next morning and considered what to say to Hallock. She'd have to tell him about the manuscript even though it would get Zeppo and her into trouble. She had no other option—the manuscript was the reason Hugh had attacked them. She'd have to mention the car attacks because they were why Zeppo had invented the thumb drive. Since she didn't know what Zeppo would say, she planned to stick pretty close to the truth.

She took out Zeppo's phone and scrolled through the numbers. Time to make the call she'd been dreading. A woman answered.

"Is this Hannah Greenwald?"

"Yes?"

"You don't know me. My name's Jean Applequist."

"Ah, the legendary Jean. I know you well. Michael's been talking about you for months." Her voice was low and warm, with more New England in it than Zeppo's. It was strange to hear him called by his real name.

"Hannah, I have bad news," Jean said in a rush. "Zeppo . . . Michael is in the hospital. He's been shot in the shoulder, but he's going to be fine."

Hannah gasped. "Shot? Who shot him?"

"Hugh Rivenbark."

"The writer? Why in the world?"

"It's a long story. We've been investigating Martin Wingo's murder."

"That wretched man! Even in death he's making problems for Michael. How bad is it?"

"He has a broken clavicle, but they say that should heal up fine. They've been pretty encouraging."

"Tell me what happened."

Jean gave Hannah a summary of recent events. When she'd finished, the woman sighed. "Well, I can't be too angry with you. Aside from getting him shot, you've made him happier than I've ever seen him."

"I'm so sorry, Hannah."

"The fault is Rivenbark's and Martin Wingo's, not yours." She was silent for a moment. "Of course the police will soon find out who Michael is."

Jean had been so worried about Zeppo's wound that she hadn't even thought of that. "My God, you're right. What should we do?"

"There's nothing we can do except damage control. Tell him I'll call him tomorrow."

Jean put on jeans and the Zorro T-shirt and went downstairs—Hallock was waiting for her in the living room.

"I got the outline of the attack last night from the patrol officers," he said, "but I'd like to hear the whole story. Why don't you start at the beginning?"

She explained how Martin had asked Zeppo to send the manuscript back.

"So you never saw the thing."

"No. Zeppo told me about it, but we couldn't figure out why Martin kept it. Then two weeks ago we went on a trip to Mendocino to see Hugh." Jean omitted all the blue box characters from her tale. "He said that he hadn't known Martin had the manuscript. The next day we took a bike ride and someone tried to run us down in a car."

"Why didn't you report it?"

"The guy missed, so we just blew it off," she said, knowing how idiotic it sounded.

"Could it have been Peter Brennan?"

"No way. We were still getting along then. I didn't start with Zeppo until later."

"Any other boyfriends who might be jealous?"

"I don't keep the jealous ones."

"I see. So what happened after you got home from Mendocino?"

She described the second attempt, and then told him about seeing the wedding card and how Zeppo had told Hugh he'd scanned the manuscript for protection. She even told him why they'd gone to the Presidio and the details of the final encounter with Hugh.

Hallock shook his head, his expression grim. "By rights you should both be dead. You're a couple of lucky bastards. What I want to know is why you and Zeppetello didn't tell me about this manuscript right away. Were you going to wait until the guy in the car killed one of you?"

"Come on, Inspector. You'd never have taken Zeppo's word against someone like Hugh Rivenbark. Even Diane didn't believe us. Anyway, we had no proof—there was none—and we assumed it'd be a waste of time trying to convince you."

"Your speculations on whether I'd believe you are immaterial. The fact is that you and Zeppetello withheld knowledge that bore directly on my investigation. I should have heard about the manuscript the first time I talked to him. And the minute he saw the wedding card, you two should have come to me." He was controlling himself, but Jean knew he was angry—his face was beet red.

"Remember your reaction when I told you Martin got out of the bay? I was expecting more of the same."

"Like I said, what you were expecting won't matter when you're charged with withholding evidence in a homicide." Hallock put away his notebook and stood. "The doctor says I'll be able to get a statement from Zeppetello today. We'll see if that changes anything."

After Hallock left, Jean joined Peter and Diane at the kitchen table. "Never talk to the police on an empty stomach," Jean advised. She put cream cheese on a garlic bagel and told them what Ivan had said.

"I knew about Flavia, of course," Diane said. "Martin still spoke to her occasionally."

"I knew her, too," Peter said. "Martin told me he was through with her."

"Any idea why he'd go to her place instead of home?" Jean asked.

Diane shook her head. "No, none. He told me their affair was long over." She sighed. "It seems the deeper you dig, the more his assurances turn out to be lies." Peter squeezed Diane's shoulders. "I'm going home today, in spite of the press," she told Jean. "I've decided not to let them keep me out of my own house."

"Good for you," Jean said. "What about you, Peter?"

"Diane's taking me to my apartment. I have to get ready for the arraignment."

After breakfast Roman dropped Jean at the hospital. She asked about Zeppo at the nurse's station and was told that he was awake, but the police were with him. Soon Hallock and a uniformed officer emerged from the ICU.

"His statement is consistent with yours," Hallock told her. "Rivenbark is still unconscious, and the doctor says that because of the severity of the concussion he probably won't remember what happened last night anyway. So unless the tech crew turns up something that doesn't jibe, you look to be in the clear as far as assault goes. The withholding evidence charge is another matter. I'll get back to you on that." He nodded brusquely and left.

The nurse beckoned to Jean. "He's just had his morphine, so he should be frisky for a little while. Don't overdo it."

Jean stepped into the glass-walled room and Zeppo turned toward her, looking frail and pallid, his blue-green eyes glazed and vulnerable behind his glasses. He smiled. "Hi, gorgeous."

She kissed him gently. There was a medicinal smell about him and he didn't taste right. A rough coppery stubble covered his cheeks and chin. "Hi, big boy. How're you feeling?"

"Pretty doped up, but not too bad, considering."

"Zeppo, please forgive me. That was such a stupid thing to do. I never should have insisted we go there. I never should have—"

"Jeannie, don't. You didn't force me into anything. In fact I wanted you so badly by the time we got off the bridge that the only way to discourage me would have been to shoot me sooner. My self-control has gotten as lousy as yours."

"You could have died, Zeppo. All because of that phone call to Hugh."

"Yeah, we really screwed up. But we'll never prove he killed Esther or tried to kill Martin. He'd have gotten away with everything. As it is, he's going down for kidnapping and attempted murder, but mine instead of Martin's. So as long as I'll be OK, I'd say it was worth it."

"Except now we'll never know whether that Marcassin is real—it'll spend the rest of eternity in a police evidence room. You know, the doctor said Hugh probably won't remember any of it. So in a weird way we got our privacy back."

Zeppo smiled. "I'm glad I can remember."

"Zeppo, what did you tell the police? All about Hugh, but nothing about the blue box?"

"Right. I told the truth, but I didn't mention that Hugh had nothing to do with the car attacks. I figured that way we'd have the best chance of keeping our stories straight."

"Good," Jean said. "That's what I thought, too. Hallock's threatening to charge us both with withholding evidence."

"Terrific."

"The next thing we have to do is talk to Flavia," Jean said. "Roman and I can do that. He speaks five languages, including Portuguese. We'll work on the rest of it when you're better. Oh, I told Edward about the manuscript. When he left he was talking payback."

"A nice mellow hippie like him?"

"Imagine how he feels. Hugh not only murdered his twin, he's had him buffaloed for thirty years, as my grandmother used to say. Keep this stuff about Edward between us, OK? I don't want him getting busted if he goes after Hugh."

They talked, Zeppo dozing occasionally, until the ICU nurse chased Jean away in the late afternoon. Roman picked her up and they stopped at her place; she had to go to work on Monday and needed clothes.

In Noe Valley, Roman insisted on entering her apartment first in case of unwanted visitors. "Why, it's actually neat," he said when she came in.

"It's easy to keep it clean. All I have to do is live somewhere else." She pulled clothes out of her closet and then checked her phone—her message light blinked frantically. She pushed the playback button. Most of the callers were reporters, whom she ignored. A few worried friends and relatives had phoned, and she made a note of each name.

"Jean, this is Simon," began one message. "Please give me a call. It's important." His voice held little warmth.

Jean hit pause. "He's seen the news. What should I do?"

"Call him," Roman said. "If he wants to see you, tell him you're busy."

Jean dialed Sputnik. It took a few minutes for a hostess to find Simon.

"Hello?" he said over background music.

"Simon, it's Jean."

"You're all over the news," he said. "Imagine my surprise when I learned that you were a friend of Martin Wingo's."

"Did you know him, too?" Jean asked innocently. "What a coincidence."

"I don't believe in coincidences. The man who got shot was Wingo's assistant. He was at the club with you. We're neither of us stupid, Jean, so drop the act."

"Look, we've been helping out his widow," Jean explained. "We were checking on anyone who'd had a run-in with Martin." Roman frowned at her and made a throat-slitting gesture with his hand. She ignored him. "I know he tried to blackmail you, and I also know it didn't work. We only care about who killed him."

"If you'd asked, I'd have told you that I was in Las Vegas that whole weekend with witnesses. You could have saved yourself the time and effort of coming on to me."

"Simon, I enjoyed our lunch. That wasn't an act."

"What does any of this have to do with Oksana?"

"We're not sure." Jean knew she'd already said too much. "Her name came up." She heard muffled voices as Simon spoke to someone at the club.

"I have to go," he said to Jean. "We'll talk later." He hung up abruptly.

"Why in hell did you tell him so much?" Roman demanded.

"I felt bad," Jean said. "He thought I was playing him. I actually find him attractive."

"You fool, don't you have enough on your plate right now?"

Jean didn't want another of Roman's lectures on promiscuity. She pushed the play button again. A familiar deep, resonant voice made her sit up straight. "Hello, Jean. This is Kay Wingo. I'd like to get together and discuss things. Please call me." She left a number.

Jean hit the pause button again and looked at Roman. "Whoa. Did you hear that?"

Roman smiled, excited. "Indeed I did. Call her. And make the meeting in a public place."

"How dumb do you think I am?" She dialed the number and Kay answered.

"Jean, we need to talk," Kay said. "Are you in the city? We could meet now."

Jean mouthed "now" to Roman, and he nodded. "That would be fine," she said to Kay.

"Why don't we meet for a drink?"

"How about the Fault Line near Union Square?" Jean asked.

"I'll be there in forty-five minutes."

"Excellent," Roman said. "This should prove most enlightening. Don't let her know we suspect her of anything."

"You're as bad as Zeppo. He always thinks I'll blurt things out."

"As you just did with Emory. You should change your clothes, by the way."

She glanced at Roman, who wore a blue and purple Jhane Barnes shirt and dark pleated slacks. He looked ready for just about any restaurant in town. Jean took off the Zorro T-shirt and jeans and put on her pencil skirt and a gray shantung blouse.

At the restaurant, Jean looked around the half-full bar. They'd arrived first. "OK," she said to Roman, "since you're the bodyguard, you sit at the bar."

"Oh really?" Roman said, raising an eyebrow. "I don't sit at the table with the players?"

"You'll intimidate Kay. Look at you. As long as she thinks you're just a big dumb yahoo like Donald, we'll be OK."

"And you're going to handle this with your usual tact and diplomacy?"

"Don't get sarcastic," Jean said. "She called *me*, remember? I promise no more blurting."

As they bickered, Kay and Donald came into the bar. Kay wore a beautifully cut chocolate brown dress and Donald had on an ill-fitting blue suit. He sat a few stools down from them while the maître d' showed Kay to a table. "What did I tell you?" Jean whispered to Roman. "Bodyguards at the bar."

"OK, we'll do it your way. But if you're going to be in charge you can pay the bill, and I'm having a very expensive drink."

"A triple Jack Daniels? Then I'll have to drive home."

"You'll never drive my car. I'll order their most costly wine." He sat on a stool and examined the list of wines by the glass.

"Hey, go crazy. Kay can pick up the tab." Jean walked toward Kay, smiling.

"Please sit down, Jean," Kay said. She glanced toward the bar. "Who's that man you were talking to?"

"Just a friend. I see you brought one, too." Donald poured Diet Pepsi over ice and Roman sipped a small glass of deep golden wine—it looked like Sauternes, a favorite of his. Apparently he'd made good on his threat. Jean watched with amusement as the two men eyed each other. Donald was taller than Roman and much heavier, but not nearly as fit. They both looked dangerous. "I'll bet my gorilla can whip your gorilla."

Kay looked at her uncertainly for a moment before deciding to laugh. "I hope we never find out," she said. Once the waiter had taken their orders, Kay's expression grew serious. "Jean, let me tell you how sorry I am about everything that's happened to you and Diane."

"Why don't you tell me what I'm doing here?" Jean said.

"I understand that you and Zeppo are looking into Martin's death at Diane's behest. I'm assuming that's how you got mixed up with Hugh. I'd like to know whether you intend to keep investigating now that Zeppo's in the hospital."

"Why do you want to know?"

"I'll be frank. I'm concerned that any revelations about Martin and his blue box will negatively affect my political fortunes."

"You knew about that?"

"Do you think there was anything about that man I didn't know?" Kay said sharply. "I was married to him for twenty-three years." The waiter appeared with Chardonnay for Kay and a Central Coast Syrah for Jean.

"Diane doesn't want anyone to find out about it either, but we have to clear Peter Brennan," Jean said when he was gone. "Things look pretty good, though, now that Hugh's under suspicion. Anyway, if it does go public you could always say it's news to you."

"If I did that I'd look stupid. And if I said I knew about it, I'd look as guilty as Martin." Kay toyed with her wine glass. "Are there any other angles you've been pursuing?"

"Not really. We've assumed all along that the motive was in the blue box, and Hugh was just an extension of that idea." Jean sipped her rich red wine, thinking how much Zeppo would like it.

"What will you and Zeppo do next?"

"Nothing until he's up and around. We'll see where things stand then."

Jean could tell Kay was dissatisfied with her answers; her expression was cross and impatient. Suddenly the woman gave her a piercing look. "Don't play games with me, Jean," she said softly. "People who do always lose."

"Why would I?" Jean said innocently. "We both want to find out who killed Martin, don't we?"

"Of course we do." Kay was back in character, civilized and sleek. "Well, this has been pleasant, but I must run." She signaled for the bill. "I'll get it."

"How about paying for my gorilla's drink, too? He just had a glass of wine."

"Very well."

"Thanks. See you around." Jean stood, eager to leave before Kay saw the check. She walked to the bar and told the bartender to put Roman's wine on Kay's tab. The man looked past Jean, and Kay nodded to him. "Let's go quickly," Jean said to Roman. They hurried out the door.

"Sauternes, right?" she said as they walked toward the car. "What kind?"

"Yquem, of course. It was ambrosial."

"What did it cost?"

"A hundred and twenty dollars for a two-ounce pour, but I thought it a bargain. How often do you find the '75 by the glass?"

Jean howled with laughter. "Serves her right. You know, I'm getting to be a good liar. It just takes practice."

"I doubt you'll ever be in Kay Wingo's league. Tell me what she said."

"She pretended it was all about the blue box. She knows about it, and she's afraid it'll hurt her politically. But she was really fishing around to see if we know anything about her. I told her I'm waiting for Zeppo to get well before I do any more investigating. She probably thinks I'm a bit dim."

"Come on, let's see if Flavia's home."

"Shouldn't we call first?"

"No," Roman said. "We'll take her by surprise."

Near South Beach, they parked near PacBell Stadium and walked to Martin's condominiums, part of a mixed-use redevelopment project that included offices, shops, and condos with views of the bay.

In the pale brick and glass lobby, a security guard took their names. He called Flavia, who didn't want to see them.

"May I please talk to her?" Roman asked.

The security guard handed Roman the phone and he spoke a few words in Portuguese. He listened briefly. "Obrigado." He gave the phone back to the guard, who talked to Flavia and then directed them through a door to an interior walkway flanked by handsome landscaping.

"What did you tell her?" Jean said as they searched for Flavia's number.

"That we're friends of Zeppo's and we want to talk about the last night of Martin's life."

Flavia waited for them in her doorway. She was all Zeppo had said: dark, petite, beautiful, and artificial. Her features were that uniquely Brazilian mix of Portuguese,

Indian, and African, with a nose that seemed too pert for the ethnic face. She wore coral-colored leggings and a cropped white T-shirt that showed off a washboard stomach. Her high, firm breasts were too big for her small frame, and her forehead was smooth and strangely immobile. Glossy dark brown ringlets spilled out of a white plastic clip on top of her head—she'd apparently stopped straightening her hair. She was slightly sweaty and barefoot, and her dainty toes sported coral polish. Jean thought the full lips and bedroom eyes were probably hers.

"Please come in," she said, wiping her neck with a white towel. She had a mellifluous voice and a pronounced accent. "Pardon my appearance—I've just finished my Pilates."

"Thank you for seeing us," Roman said, shaking her hand.

As Jean shook the offered hand, Flavia swept her with sharp, appraising eyes. Jean knew the look: checking out potential competition. Jean had met women like this before, for whom other women were little more than rivals in the struggle for high-powered men. She found the whole attitude rather sad, especially since Flavia, in spite of all the surgical intervention, looked to be over forty.

"I heard about Zeppo on the news," Flavia said. "How is he?"

"He'll be fine," Jean said.

"That's good. I've always been fond of him. Come, let's sit down."

The living room was decorated in bright, warm colors, with sisal mats on the pale hardwood floors. Jean chose a wicker and wood chair, and Roman sat next to Flavia on a sofa upholstered in a vivid tropical print.

Roman took the lead, apparently realizing that Flavia would rather talk to him. "I'll get right to the point," he said. "We know the boat that rescued Martin dropped him very near your house. Did he come here?"

"I knew someone would ask me that eventually. Yes, he came here."

"Will you tell us about it?"

Flavia looked at her long coral nails. "It was his wedding day, so I wanted to be alone. I watched *Black Orpheus*, ate a pint of Häagen-Dazs dulce de leche, and drank too much brandy. When his phone call woke me up, I didn't even know he was missing. He told me he'd fallen into the bay and wanted to change his clothes. About twenty minutes later I went down and let him in the side entrance. He was wearing nasty old gray sweats that were much too big for him and carrying his wet tux in a plastic grocery bag. He put on jeans and a sweater and shoes that he kept here."

"What happened to the sweats?" Roman asked.

Flavia wrinkled her store bought nose. "I threw them away."

"Then what?"

"He told me to go back to bed, that he had to meet someone. I watched him walk along the street and turn toward the parking structure."

"Did you see whom he met?"

"No. You can't see inside the structure from here."

"What time was this?"

"Around four thirty."

"Why haven't you gone to the police?" Jean asked.

"I'm engaged. My fiancé would hate it if he thought Martin was still in my life. I was hoping the killer would be found without my help."

"I'm sorry, but I think you'll have to talk to the police," Roman said. "An innocent man has been arrested."

"I know, Peter Brennan. I'm actually glad you came to see me. It saves me from having to make the decision myself." She crossed her shapely legs and leaned slightly toward Roman. "They'll be angry that I didn't come forward before."

"The investigating officers are Oscar Davila and George Hallock," Roman said. "Will you call them tomorrow?"

"Yes, of course."

"Who's your fiancé?" Jean asked.

Flavia smiled proudly. "Ralph Beasley. We're to be married in August."

Jean raised an eyebrow. Beasley was often mentioned in the same breath as Bill Gates when people discussed fabulously wealthy computer nerds.

Roman looked around the room. "Martin must really have loved you to give you this beautiful house."

"I believe he did love me. He wouldn't marry me, but he gave me this condo."

"Why wouldn't he marry you?" Jean asked.

Flavia shot her a haughty look. "Is that any of your business?"

"Excuse my friend," Roman said soothingly. "She's often too blunt. We're interested in Martin and Kay's marriage because we think she might have had something to do with his death. Otherwise we wouldn't be asking you painful questions. I'm sorry we've upset you."

"That's all right—*you* haven't upset me." Flavia favored Roman with a dazzling smile. Her teeth were as flawless as the rest of her. "I don't mind saying that I fell hard for Martin. He was everything I'd ever wanted in a man, and I told him so. He said he loved me, too, but that Kay didn't want a divorce and would cause trouble for him if he tried it. I confronted Kay and demanded that she divorce him. She said that nothing would make her happier, but it wasn't up to her."

"What did she mean, it wasn't up to her?" Jean asked.

Flavia gave a graceful shrug. "She had to do whatever Martin said. He knew something about her that could hurt her in politics. Of course I was furious with Martin for lying to me. That's when he told me that even though he loved me, he would never marry me. He said we were too much alike. That was his problem with Kay, too. You see, Kay and I knew what he was, and he didn't like that. He needed someone he could fool." Flavia's face took on an odd, unhappy expression; Jean realized the woman was frowning without wrinkling her forehead. "So after the heart attack he married his little innocent."

"Do you know what he had on Kay?" Roman asked.

"No," Flavia said. "All the things he knew about people, and he never told me a single secret, no matter what I did for him."

"Did he leave anything here, like papers or a DVD?" Jean asked.

"No, just clothes and toiletries. He was very careful never to leave business papers here."

"Tell me, Flavia, were you still seeing Martin?" Roman asked.

"You mean was I sleeping with him?" She gave a sly smile. "When he came by that night I hadn't seen him in at least a week."

"Thank you again," Roman said, standing up. "If you have any problems with the police, don't hesitate to call me." He took out his wallet and handed her a business card.

Flavia read the card. "You're an editor? You look more like a model." She stood, too, and gave him another high-voltage smile. She said something in Portuguese, a question judging from the inflection. Roman chuckled and they spoke back and forth. Finally he took her hand and kissed it. She showed them out with a friendly wave.

"What was all that?" Jean asked as they walked to the car.

"She wanted to know if you were my girlfriend. I told her I didn't have a girlfriend, but I used to have a boyfriend. She was very disappointed."

"So was I." Jean took his arm. "Isn't this great? Peter's off the hook now. He was at Diane's with witnesses while Martin was at Flavia's."

"Indeed," Roman said.

"Ivan saw Martin make a few calls: We know he called Diane, Flavia, Frank, and presumably whoever he met."

"Could it have been Emory?" Roman asked.

"He says he was in Las Vegas the whole weekend. What I don't get is why Martin would call whoever it was in the first place."

"He may have needed backup for whatever he had to do. Do you think Flavia was telling the truth about Martin cheating on Diane?"

"I wouldn't put anything past him," Jean said. "Sounds as if Flavia has really scored—she's marrying someone even richer than Martin."

"In the nick of time, too. Hers is a game for the young."

They got into Roman's car and he started the engine. "Where to?"

"I'm starving," Jean said. "I need comfort food. Let's get Thai."

CHAPTER 41

*T*he doorbell woke Jean the next morning. She looked into the guest room for Roman, who'd slept at Beau's with her last night, but he was already gone. She went downstairs warily as the bell rang again, alert to the possibility that the press had found her. She didn't think Setrakian would be dumb enough to come in by the front door.

Jean looked through the peephole to see Diane holding a newspaper and looking angry. Jean unlocked all the locks and let her in. "What's the matter?"

"Zeppo is all over the front page," Diane announced, handing her the paper and storming past her into the house.

Jean read the paper. The headline on the front page below the fold said "Shooting Victim Was Cheswick Ripper Suspect." She'd already seen the old photos Zeppo in handcuffs and one of a smiling Sarah.

"Well, fuck," Jean said, walking slowly to the kitchen as she read. "We were afraid this would happen." She looked at Diane. "Why the hell are you so pissed?"

"Are you telling me you knew about this?"

"Yeah, I knew. I also know it's a crock." Jean sat down at the kitchen table.

"How do you know?" Diane demanded, sitting across from her.

"It's simple: I know Zeppo."

"And based on that reasoning you got into bed with a man who may have raped a woman and stabbed her to death. One of these days you're going to misjudge the wrong man."

"Excuse me, but aren't you boffing the suspect in your husband's murder?"

"I've always known Peter was innocent. I've never trusted Zeppo."

"Martin knew all about it and he believed Zeppo."

"What? He never said anything to me."

"I thought you were getting used to the idea that he had a lot of secrets from you."

"Don't try to turn this into an indictment of Martin," Diane said.

"Get off my back, will you? I've got to worry about Zeppo now, not your paranoia." Jean took a breath. "Listen: I know you're behaving like this because you're worried about me. But I do know a few things about men, and Zeppo's innocent."

Roman came in the back door and looked at the paper. "I see you've discovered that Zeppo's deep dark secret is no longer secret. I must say, Jean, this goes beyond anything I suspected." He noticed their angry faces. "What are you two fighting about?"

"Diane's pissed because I'm sleeping with a killer."

"Zeppo's no more a killer than you are, Diane," Roman said. "I've been reading about the trial on the Net—it's an infamous case of sloppy small-town police work. By the time the pros from Boston homicide were called in, it was too late."

Jean told them what she knew about it. "The worst part came later—his family saw to it that he spent two years in a mental hospital."

"Does Zeppo know who the killer is?" Roman asked.

"He thinks it's his father."

Roman raised an eyebrow. "I'm beginning to understand his problem with authority figures."

The phone rang and Jean answered. "I just heard about Zeppo on the TV news," Peter told her. "Did you know all this?"

Jean braced herself for another lecture. "Yes, I knew. I found out the day before you and I broke up."

"That's why you slept with him, isn't it?" Peter said, but he wasn't angry. "The whole thing's in character for you—using sex to show you believed him."

"I'm sorry, Peter. I hope you see why I didn't tell you anything."

"Yes, I do see. In any case, that's behind us now. I'll do what I can to help him. And thank you for finding Flavia Soares. Pfeiffer expects the D.A. to drop the charges against me by the end of the day."

"That's great, Peter. Hey, will you talk to your girlfriend? She's over here pitching a fit. She thinks Zeppo's a deranged sex killer because it says so in the paper."

"I might have believed it myself a few days ago. But the paper also says I'm a greedy, cuckolding, backstabbing murderer. I've got a whole new perspective on the police and the media. Let me talk to her."

Jean handed the phone to Diane and joined Roman at the kitchen table for coffee.

"Flavia phoned me this morning and asked if I'd take her down to the Hall," Roman said. "I said I would—that way we'll be sure she goes."

Jean poked him. "She hasn't given up on you yet, huh?"

"I'm sure she has. But unlike you, she needs male support in difficult moments."

"I'd better get over to the hospital and tell Zeppo before someone else does," Jean said.

"Go get dressed. I'll drop you on my way to Flavia's."

Diane, contrite and apologetic, left to meet Peter. As she went out the door the phone rang again. It was Kyle calling from the magazine. "Hey, you OK?" he said. "I saw the news."

"I'm fine, thanks," Jean said.

"Your friend who was shot—did he really stab that woman?"

"Of course not. I draw the line at dating murderers."

"Why didn't you tell me you were using your vacation to investigate a murder?"

"I thought we were being discreet," Jean said. "Who knew we'd end up on the front page?"

"Look, I know I sound like an insensitive prick, but I need you to come by the office today and ID the Central Coast images."

Jean had forgotten all about them. "But it's Saturday. Can't I do it Monday?"

"Has to be today. The slides came in late and Carol's going to lay out the story this afternoon. We can't miss the press date."

"OK, OK. I'd drive myself down, but there are some safety issues."

"Why don't I drive you?"

"Great. Pick me up at S.F. General at noon. I'll be at the main entrance."

Jean got dressed and Roman dropped her at the hospital. Zeppo was sitting up in bed reading when she arrived. She kissed him softly. "How are you?"

"Much better. I'm moving to a regular ward today and I finally got a shave."

She sat next to him. "I've got good news and bad news. Last night we talked to Flavia." She gave him a summary of their conversation. "Roman's taking her to see Hallock now, so Peter should be a free man soon."

"So we got our money's worth from Ivan. What's the bad news?"

She laid her hand on his chest. "Your cover's blown. The police must have run your fingerprints and someone leaked it to the press."

He sighed and sank into the bed. "Ah, shit. It wouldn't have happened if I hadn't investigated Martin's death. Now my life is trashed and we still don't know who killed him."

"Once Martin was dead and they had your fingerprints, it could have happened any time. Anyway, your life is far from trashed. You have friends, money, even a car, which is more than I have. And we're not through yet—we'll find the killer. We found Hugh, didn't we?" She sat as close as she could, gently stroking him, wishing she could offer more physical comfort.

"Yeah, we found Hugh. One down and one to go. And so what if a lot of strangers think I'm a psycho? Of course, my family thinks so, too."

Jean took a walk outside to get some non-hospital air while Zeppo moved to his new room. As she turned to go back inside, she noticed George Hallock sitting on a nearby bench, smoking. "You'd think hanging around a hospital would discourage you from smoking," she commented, joining him.

"I have a high-stress job," he said. He blew a plume of smoke. "I just heard from Oscar—he's got one Flavia Soares down at the Hall. Says you and Villalobos found her."

Jean had discussed this line of questioning with Roman over Thai food the night before, and they'd agreed to leave Ivan out of it. "That's right," she said. "Zeppo mentioned that she and Martin were close, so we went to talk to her and got lucky."

"You have any idea how Wingo got to South Beach?"

"No. Does it matter?"

"It does to me. I don't like loose ends."

"Flavia told us that Martin had something on Kay Wingo," Jean said. "That he made her stay married when she didn't want to. Maybe Donald Grimes was the man Martin met."

"We'll see. I'm on my way to talk to Soares." He gave a dismissive wave of his cigarette. "Anyway, we looked at Kay

Wingo and Grimes a long time ago. Just to keep you from pestering her, I'll tell you that she was in Washington the night of the wedding. One of the wedding guests called her there to tell her about Wingo going into the bay, and she called Grimes and a few other people during the night to talk about it. We've got the phone records. No matter what you think of her politics, she still needs a motive."

"What do you think of her politics?" Jean asked.

"She has some good ideas, but that doesn't mean I wouldn't be on her if I had a reason."

Jean decided to take advantage of his cooperative mood. "Someone also mentioned Simon Emory, the nightclub owner. Have you talked to him?"

"Yeah. Leave him alone, too—he's got an alibi. Took all his bouncers to Vegas for the weekend. He was at a casino winning at craps when Wingo bought it."

"What about Zeppo and me? Are we still going to get busted for withholding evidence?"

Hallock blew out a cloud of smoke. "Probably not. I can't see bothering with it. Now I know why you didn't report the attempts to run you down. I thought you were a couple of real flakes. You were protecting Zeppetello's ass. Or should I say Van Vleck."

"Yeah," Jean said, her tone apologetic. "It didn't do much good, though, did it?"

"You can't keep a thing like that quiet once you're involved in a crime, even if you're the victim. I called a detective I know in Boston. The thinking in the BPD is that the kid got screwed. For different reasons, everybody hated the way it came out—the investigating officers, the D.A., the judge, the jury, the family, everybody but the defense attorney. A lot of police academies nowadays use Van Vleck as an example of how not to do things, right along with O.J. and JonBenet Ramsey." He shook his head. "It galls me to see a case like that, where the police work is so bad they'll never find the truth."

Jean was pleasantly surprised by Hallock's reaction. "Did you talk to Rivenbark today?"

He stood up and took a final pull on his cigarette, grinding it out on the pavement. "Don't push it too hard. I'm not going to tell you all the department's business. The D.A. has scheduled a press conference for Tuesday morning. Buy a paper on Wednesday."

"I'll do that," Jean said. "Thanks, Inspector." She went back into the hospital and used Zeppo's cell to call Roman. "Hey," she said, "I just talked to Hallock. He says we're not going to be charged with withholding evidence."

"You two are pals now?"

"He's being very reasonable about Zeppo." She told him what Hallock had said. "How did things go with Flavia?"

"When I left she was batting her eyelashes at Oscar Davila. Television has found you, by the way. The cretin on Channel 7 referred to you, Diane, Peter, and Zeppo as a 'four sided love triangle.' "

Jean laughed. "God, I'll be glad when this is over."

She hung up and mused about Zeppo for a while, then scrolled through his saved numbers, looking for Gwen Lansing, his Goth friend. Jean pushed dial.

"Hi, Gwen. This is Jean Applequist."

"Hey, I've been reading all about you. And Zeppo—what a shocker."

"Do you think he did it?"

"No way. I've met a few guys who got their kicks knocking women around, and Zeppo's nothing like them. Anyway, now I know why he made up all that crap about his family."

"Good, I'm glad you're with me on that," Jean said.

"Heavy about Peter Brennan."

"They're going to drop the charges. We found a witness who saw Martin alive after Peter supposedly killed him."

"If I were a guy, I'd stay as far away from you as I could. Look what happens to your boyfriends."

"This is a first, believe me. Listen, will you visit Zeppo? To show people trust him?"

"Sure. I can get over there this afternoon. How about five o'clock?"

"That would be great. He's at S.F. General." Jean gave his room number.

"See you then. I'll be the one in black."

⌒∾

ZEPPO'S NEW room looked like every other hospital room Jean had ever seen, except for the uniformed officer Hallock had stationed outside his door. She brought Zeppo up to date, explaining that they wouldn't be charged with withholding evidence and detailing Simon's airtight alibi and her conversation with Kay.

"Sounds like Kay's getting nervous," Zeppo said.

"By the way, I have to go to work for an hour or so today."

"You'll be back full time on Monday, won't you?" Zeppo said. "I guess life has to go back to normal sooner or later. Even my life. They'll never let me into U.C. Davis now— they'll find out I made up my high school records."

"You could always go to a community college and then transfer to a U.C. as a junior."

"Yeah, but I felt good about getting into a decent school without my family's help."

Jean glanced at the wall clock. "Shit, I have to go. I'll be back as soon as I can."

She kissed Zeppo goodbye and dashed down to the front entrance, where Kyle waited at the curb in his blue Mini Cooper. "Now tell me everything," he said without preamble.

Jean recounted the story as they drove across town to Opera Plaza. "So there you have it," she said. "We messed up, but it could have been a lot worse."

"It's what I've been telling you all these years—don't let your gonads rule your life. Although your sex life sounds a hell of a lot more exciting than mine."

"I can do without that kind of excitement."

They left the car with an attendant and took the elevator up to the second floor. The building seemed empty. Kyle unlocked the door to *Wine Digest*'s office and led the way to the conference room, where color slides were spread out near a light box.

"Here they are," he said. "They're good, just really fucking late. Next time I'm going digital no matter what."

"I'll find my notes," Jean said.

"You want some coffee from downstairs?" Kyle asked.

"Sure," she said. "The usual. And can you get me one of those cheese croissants?"

"No problemo." Jean heard the deadbolt turn behind Kyle.

Jean's cubicle was at the far end of the room. She booted up her computer. Might as well check her email. More than two hundred messages awaited her. As she scrolled through them to see if any were urgent, she sensed someone come into her cubicle. "Hey, that was fast." She turned her head. The man behind her was Armand Setrakian.

CHAPTER 42

$\mathcal{J}$ean jumped up from the chair and backed away from him. "Kyle!" she shouted. "Call 911!" No answer.

Armand took a step toward her, flexing his big hands, blocking the doorway so she couldn't get past him. "Now you'll get what you deserve, bitch," he said.

"That was you in the cars, wasn't it?"

"Yeah. But this time it'll be up close and personal."

"You think you can rape me?"

"I know I can, but I won't. A woman like you would get over that. I'm going to give you something to remember me by." He reached into his back pocket and brought out one of the sculpting tools Jean had seen in his barn— a wicked-looking short-bladed knife with a piece of cork stuck on its tip.

"You don't scare me, asshole."

Setrakian pulled off the cork and dropped it. "I'm really going to enjoy this."

"Kyle, help!" No answer. She steeled herself—she was on her own.

As he lunged for her she tried to go around him, but he caught her by the arm and forced her back until she lay half on the desk, scattering books and papers. He used his weight to hold her down, the edge of the desk hard against her lower back. He brought the knife up and moved it toward her face. She grabbed his right wrist with both hands, using all her strength to push him away, but it was no good—in a moment he'd cut her. The grin on his face was feral and malevolent. "Every time you look in the mirror, you'll think of me, bitch."

Suddenly Armand seemed to levitate off her. "What the fuck!" he exclaimed.

Jean righted herself and was astonished to see Ivan pull Armand out of the cubicle by his ponytail. Armand slashed at his attacker, but Ivan brought the edge of his hand down hard on Armand's wrist and the knife fell to the carpet. Ivan released the ponytail and Armand spun toward him, fists up. Ivan hit him in the stomach with a sharp right jab and kneed him in the chin when he bent double. Armand crumpled to the floor. Ivan grinned at Jean, rubbing his fist. "You OK?"

"Yes, thanks to you," she said gratefully. "What are you doing here, anyway?"

"Following you. I heard your boyfriend was out of action, so I thought you might want to go for a boat ride."

"Well, I'm flattered." She looked at Armand, who hadn't moved. "He's not dead, is he?"

"Nah. Do you want him to be?"

"No, that's OK," she said quickly. "Look, I need to sit down. Come tell me how you got here." She and Ivan went into her cube and sat.

"I followed you from the hospital. I wanted to talk to you alone." Ivan gestured at Armand. "This guy unlocked the office door and went in after the other guy left. When I heard you yelling I came in."

Armand groaned, and Ivan rose and knelt next to him. He rolled the semiconscious man onto his stomach, and tied his ankles and wrists together with a beige phone cord from Jean's office. "Who is he?" he asked Jean. "Why'd he want to cut you?"

"Armand Setrakian. He's pissed because I told a reporter that he keeps attacking women."

Ivan nodded. "Oh, right. The sculptor. Want me to break his fingers?"

Jean thought about it. Tempting, but she decided against overkill. "No, really, you've done enough. Thanks anyway."

Kyle arrived carrying a cardboard container that held two coffees and a small white bakery bag. He stopped short when he saw the tableau outside Jean's cubicle. "Whoa! What the hell?"

"We had a little attempted assault," Jean said.

"My God, Jean. You OK?"

"Fine."

"Who are these guys?"

"The man on the floor is Armand Setrakian," Jean said. "Ivan here pulled him off me. Ivan, this is Kyle."

"Jesus," Kyle said, putting his box on her desk. "I never should have left you alone."

Armand groaned again. "I'd better call the police," Jean said.

"Then I'm outta here," Ivan said.

"You're leaving?" Jean said. "What am I supposed to tell the cops? That *I* did this to Armand?"

Ivan shrugged. "Say Kyle did it."

"No fucking way," Kyle exclaimed.

"Kyle," Ivan said, "listen up. I don't want any trouble with the pigs for business reasons. So here's the deal: You brought coffee, you heard her yell, you pulled him off by the hair, you gut-punched him, you kneed him on the chin. He never tagged you. Got it?"

"Are you both on crack?" Kyle said. "He'll tell the police you did it."

"Sure, but if you and Jean stick to the same story, the fuzz will assume he's making me up so they won't think he got his ass kicked by a little faggot like you."

"Ivan, please," Jean said. She turned to Kyle. "Listen: I owe this man a lot, maybe my life, and he can't get involved with the cops. Please, Kyle—as a favor."

"OK," Kyle said reluctantly. "But you owe me big time."

Jean grabbed some tissues from a box on her desk and went over to Armand, who was stirring. She wiped the phone cord down as best she could. "Kyle, put your fingerprints on the cord," she said. "Grab it, especially the knot."

"Smart, too," Ivan said. "You've got it all."

"If we get away with this, it'll be a miracle," Kyle said.

Armand stirred and strained against his bonds. "Untie me, you motherfucker," he snarled when he saw Ivan. "My back is breaking."

Ivan leaned down and pulled Armand's head up by his hair. Armand glared at him, gritting his teeth in agony. "Every time you take it up the ass in prison," Ivan said, "you'll think of me, bitch." He stood up. "I gotta go."

"I'll see you out," Jean said.

As they walked down the corridor, Ivan leaned toward her. "So you want to go for a boat ride?" He wiggled his eyebrows. "Maybe a mustache ride? You owe me a little something."

Jean laughed. "I owe you a whole lot, Ivan, but you're not really my type. Maybe Zeppo and I can come for a cruise when he's better."

"It's like that, huh? I may be older and fatter than what you're used to, but I've still got a few moves left."

"I don't doubt it. How about this: I promise we won't mention you and Martin, no matter what happens. And if you ever need anything besides sex, let me know."

Ivan took the receipt from the Spindrift Restaurant from his pocket, wrote on the back, and handed it to her: "Ivan Gunnar" and a phone number. "If your boyfriend doesn't pull through, give me a call."

"I'll do that. Thanks again." She accepted his bear hug and didn't complain when he patted her ass.

"Peace," he said as he went out the door.

CHAPTER 43

$\mathcal{J}$ean called 911 from the conference room. Her next call was to Peter's cell. "Peter, where are you?"

"We're visiting Zeppo. You OK?"

"Armand Setrakian attacked me at my office, but Ivan intervened. Listen," she said over his exclamations, "let Zeppo and Diane know I'm going to tell the truth about why we went to see Armand, and admit that we sent those letters. There's no need to mention the blue box—we'll say Martin just wanted to force him to sell the land. And don't mention Ivan. Got that?"

"Yes, but what—"

"Tell Zeppo I'll be there as soon as I can." She hung up and dialed Roman's cell. "Roman," she said, "can you come to the office? I need moral support. Armand came after me and Ivan stopped him. He's lying here hogtied."

She heard a sharp intake of breath. "Are you OK?"

"I'm fine now, but it got pretty lively."

"Where was Kyle?"

"Getting coffee." She heard sirens. "I'll explain later. I have to let the police in."

Roman showed up shortly after the emergency response crew and managed to be polite to the police. Kyle gave a statement and slipped away as soon as the police would let him, visibly uncomfortable with the admiration of the investigating officers. One of the officers assured Jean that

Hallock and Davila would be notified. She remembered to phone Carol, the art director, to tell her not to come in.

When they were finally alone, Roman looked at Jean. "Now tell me why Ivan's name didn't come up in your statement to the police."

She gave him the unedited version of recent events as she ate the croissant Kyle had bought her.

"I never should have let you leave Beau's house," he said, scowling. "It's fortunate that our troglodyte friend Ivan is so smitten with you."

"It's all that muliebrity," Jean said. "Ivan's a bizarre creature. He reminds me of a big, dumb, cuddly attack dog. Like you with a lobotomy."

"In any case, he's made my bodyguard duties considerably lighter. I'd say he's earned his anonymity." Roman dropped her at the hospital, with instructions to call him when she was ready to come home.

Jean was glad to see that Diane and Peter had left; she wanted to be alone with Zeppo. He was upset when she told him what had happened but relieved she wasn't hurt.

"Sending those letters exposing Setrakian was pretty dumb," Zeppo said. "Sorry you had to deal with the fallout."

"Hey, I'm fine. Setrakian's the one who's dealing with fallout."

"Turns out Ivan's a pretty good guy after all."

"I wouldn't go that far," Jean said. "Let's just say he's complex."

Around five o'clock Gwen arrived, all in black as promised. "Hey, Zeppo," she said. "You look like a train wreck."

He grinned. "You should see the other guy."

The three of them visited until Zeppo started yawning.

"OK," Gwen said, standing up. "Time to let the patient rest. See you tomorrow, Zeppo."

Jean rose, too. "I'll be back in the morning," she said. "Call me if you think of anything you want."

"I want a shower. I want this sling off. I want a month with you on a desert island."

"I'll give you a rain check." She tousled his hair and realized he was nearly asleep. She took off his glasses, set them aside, and joined Gwen in the corridor.

"I'm really glad you came," Jean said.

"I wouldn't have missed it. Who knew he was such an interesting guy?"

Jean took out Zeppo's cell. "I have to call my ride." From the waiting area Jean tried Roman's cell but was sent straight to voicemail. Puzzled, she called his house and Beau's number, leaving messages.

"That's strange," she said to Gwen. "I can't find him. Now what?"

"Let's get a drink."

There were plenty of innocent explanations for Roman's absence, and now that Setrakian was out of the picture, Jean felt like celebrating a little. "OK. Where?"

"There's a fun place in my neighborhood, not too far from here."

Jean followed Gwen to an ancient black VW bus. They drove into the Mission, parked on Guerrero, and walked a block to a small neighborhood bar. The scruffy, cheerful place held about a dozen patrons. Loud rock played on the jukebox. After a quick appraisal, Jean ruled out wine. A bartender with biker tattoos gave them draft beers, which they carried to a booth. Jean tried Roman again.

"Still not home," Jean said.

"If you can't get hold of him, I'll give you a lift." Gwen sipped her beer. "So you and Zeppo, huh? No wonder he was so skittish before. Is Polly right?"

"Absolutely. That boy is seriously oversexed. But you won't hear me complaining." Jean lost her joking tone. "That's what got him shot. We couldn't wait."

Gwen patted Jean's hand. "Hey, he's going to be fine. Now that the secret's out, he doesn't have to lie to everyone he meets. He can make real friends."

"I hadn't thought of that. Maybe Hugh's bullet will have one good result."

"I hate it that Zeppo almost got killed because of that son of a bitch Martin."

"I don't know how you worked for him," Jean said. "I never could have."

"I never had to deal with him," Gwen said with a shrug. "He only spoke to me once."

"To complain about your clothes?"

"No, he always nagged my boss about that. Martin was cleaning out his office and he came back to the production department late, when everyone was gone but me, wanting to borrow an X-ACTO knife. He didn't know what they were called, and he got impatient when I couldn't figure out what he was talking about. He finally took one off a desk and left."

"What did he want with an X-ACTO knife?"

"He said he was working on a retirement project. He wasn't rude, exactly. But he made it clear he thought I was a moron."

Jean stared into space, thinking hard.

Gwen looked at her. "What?"

"Gwen, listen: Do you have keys to the office?"

"Yeah."

"Will you take me there now?"

"What for?"

Jean looked at the intelligent face under the makeup and decided to trust her. "Here's the short version. Martin had blackmail evidence about people. Since he died, someone has searched his office, boat, and house. You just gave me a great idea about where Martin might have hidden evidence."

"At the office somewhere?"

"Yeah."

Gwen downed her beer. "Let's go."

They went out to the VW. "OK," Gwen said over the engine as she drove toward Pier 3, "where are we going to look?"

"In the model of the Martin Wingo Building. Zeppo told me Martin was going to take it home with him. He probably didn't want to walk around carrying the evidence in case he had another heart attack. You said he needed an X-ACTO knife for a retirement project. I think his project was more blackmail."

"You could be right. I worked on that model—the thing is mostly foam core, but part of it is hollow. It'd be easy to make a slit and slide something in."

Gwen used a card to access the empty parking lot. They walked across the Embarcadero to Pier 3. Except for the foyer, the Wingo-Johansen offices were dark. Out the window, the lights on the Bay Bridge looked like strings of luminous pearls.

Jean examined the Martin Wingo Building while Gwen fetched an X-ACTO knife. The little plastic gargoyles leered at her. Looking closely, Jean noticed a strip of tape along the back of the model.

Gwen came up next to her. "We're cool. There's no one else here. See anything?"

"Yeah. Right here."

"Aha!" Gwen cut through the tape, exposing a six-inch slit in the cardboard. Pushing it open, she used two slender fingers to pull out a Ziploc sandwich bag that contained a mini-DVD in a plastic sleeve and a small beige envelope. The DVD was unmarked; the letter was addressed to Martin Wingo in New York City and the return address was Kay Bennett on 25th Avenue in San Francisco. The postmark was February 3, 1982.

"There might be fingerprints, so we have to be careful," Jean said. Gwen gently pulled out the two-page handwritten letter, touching it only with her long black nails, and laid it on the floor. The women sat close on the off-white carpeting, leaning against the model's Lucite base, and read it together. The sharp backhand writing was easy to make out.

Dear Martin,

Sorry to hear you're struggling with calculus. You should have gone to law school with me—no math required beyond adding up your fees.

Now for the bad news: The rabbit died, as they say. No wonder I've been feeling queasy all the time. I was afraid it was an ulcer. I cut up that fucking useless diaphragm and threw it away. I'm not going to let a goddamned baby ruin everything I've planned. I know you're ambivalent about this, but we have to focus on our goals. For a woman to make it in politics, really make it at the highest level, she can't be hauling a passel of brats around in a station wagon while her male contemporaries are getting things done. I don't want to start in my forties what my classmates will start in their twenties. You understand this better than most men—in spite of your male chauvinist tendencies, you do comprehend *real politik*. And if you wanted a brood mare I don't think you'd have stuck with me for so long.

I'll have the abortion next Thursday. I found a doctor who'll also perform a tubal ligation. Most of them think just because I'm young I don't know what I want. I should be fine in a few days, and Barbara will take care of me. I've got enough money to cover it, but will let you know if I need more. So there it is: If we get married, you're out of the gene pool. Sorry about that.

I really miss you and can't wait until spring break. Won't it be nice to fuck without getting spermicide all over everything?

XXXOOO, Kay

Jean and Gwen sat back and looked at each other.

"I'm beginning to have a grudging admiration for Martin," Jean said. "He kept this letter for thirty years. The guy was prescient. How'd he know she'd turn into Mrs. Rational Right?"

"Man, she's cold. I know women who've had abortions, and it's always an emotional workout even if they're really sure about it. She sounds like she's having her tonsils out."

"I know what you mean. It's not the abortion and the sterilization that'll finish her. That might have come out any time, because obviously there are other people who know about it—the doctor and nurses, whoever Barbara is. But Kay could say she got religion later, regrets it, wants to prevent others from making the same mistake, bullshit like that. What would finish her is the icy, calculating tone of the letter."

"She could say it's a fake," Gwen said.

"I bet it'd do its damage anyway. You know, Martin changed his mind about kids. Diane told me they were going to have a family. That's why most doctors won't sterilize people that young—hell, even I might change my mind someday."

"I'm going to have kids for sure—everyone says I'm really maternal." Gwen held up the DVD with her nails. "What about this?"

Jean wanted to see that particular bit of evidence alone—it almost certainly involved Simon and Oksana. "I'll take it back to my uncle's and watch it."

Gwen tapped the letter. "What should we do with it?"

"Give it to the police, of course." Jean thought for a minute. "I think I'll fax it to Roman first. I usually don't believe in violating a woman's privacy, but this letter will be public soon enough no matter what I do."

Gwen picked up the letter and envelope with her nails and led Jean into a small office behind the receptionist's desk, turned on the copier, and soon had copies. Jean faxed the whole thing to Roman. Gwen returned the letter to its envelope and handed it to Jean, and they put the copy back in the model. Jean slipped the original and the mini-DVD inside her bra.

Zeppo's phone was out of juice, so Jean borrowed Gwen's and tried Roman's cell again. It was still off, and no one was home at his house or Beau's. She looked at her watch. Almost eight o'clock. "Where is that man?" she muttered.

"Do you think something's really wrong?"

"I'm not sure. He has a lot of demands on him and lots of sick friends. It could be anything."

"Then don't sweat it," Gwen said. "I'll run you home." They piled into Gwen's bus and drove to the Castro.

Jean patted Gwen's knee as she pulled up to Beau's house. "Nice work, sister. See you tomorrow." Jean ran up to the front door. Gwen waited until she was inside before driving off.

CHAPTER 44

*T*he alarm was still set, so Jean felt safe once she was inside Beau's house with the front door relocked. She dropped her purse and jacket on a chair and checked the phone messages. None from Roman. She was getting worried.

Jean went out the back door and through the garden. Roman wasn't home, but his car was still in the garage. She was now confused as well as worried. Thinking he may have had a Bash Back emergency, she called Lou Kasden, Nick Rigatos, and a few more of his friends. No one had seen him.

Back in Beau's kitchen, Jean thought about calling Zeppo, but was reluctant to tie up the phone—Beau didn't have call waiting. She'd have to try and find Zeppo's phone charger. As she wondered what to do next, the phone rang and she raced to answer it.

"Jean, it's me."

"Oh Roman, thank God. Where are you?"

"At the Hall of Justice," he said angrily. "A couple of cops picked me up for questioning about those sailors who got stomped, and they confiscated my phone. I'll bet anything Davila put them up to it."

"Are you all right?"

"I'm fine, but it took Elaine, my lawyer, a while to get here, so they've been jerking me around for hours."

"You didn't do it, did you?"

"Not this time. I was teaching a class that night. I have nine witnesses."

"Do you want me to pick you up?"

"No thanks. Elaine will bring me along soon. How did you get home?"

"A friend of Zeppo's. Listen, Roman: I found the evidence against Kay—and the DVD. I have them here now."

"Say no more. This is a police line. I'll be there as fast as I can." He hung up.

Jean sighed with relief and a sense of accomplishment. She just had one more thing to do—watch the DVD. She poured herself a glass of Pinot Gris from the open bottle in the fridge and went into Beau's study, where she turned on his TV and DVD player, slipped the disk in, and took the remote to an overstuffed chair. She hit play.

The screen showed a skinny young woman with pale blond hair and bright blue eyes. She was beautiful and exuded a powerful sexuality. So this was Oksana. She sat in a desk chair in Martin's office—Jean recognized his view of the bridge over her right shoulder.

"What do you have to sell?" Martin's voice said offscreen.

"When I come to this country my English is terrible," she said, looking directly into the camera. She had a strong accent. "So I work in a sweatshop in Manhattan making purses and learn English."

"Go on."

"Later, when I am speaking better English, my boss made me be a prostitute. It was like hell." She glanced away from the camera for a moment. "Then a girl told me about a man in San Francisco named Simon Emory who will pay my boss, and then I can work for him as a waitress until I pay him back. I wouldn't be a prostitute. So that's what happened. I work in Simon's club.

"Then I meet Spider, a bartender there who is very sweet and funny and likes me a lot. He buys me pretty things and takes care of me. He is so different from the other men I know."

Martin made encouraging noises off-camera.

"Spider found a better job in San Jose, but he must go right away. He says I should come with him." Her smile was an odd mix of happiness and disbelief. "He wants to marry me. So I say I'll go with him."

"And why is this important?" Jean heard an impatient note in Martin's voice.

"That's what I'm telling you," Oksana said sharply. "Simon has papers . . . files on all of us, so if we run away he tells Immigration and they come get us. I want to find my file and burn it. I took a key and when he is gone I search his office. I don't find any files on people, but I find a big envelope full of articles from the newspaper. The articles are about a thing I remember in New York. A container came from Rotterdam. It sat on the dock and it started to smell bad. They open it and it is full of dead people. Illegals like me. I came in that way, by container."

"I read about that," Martin said. "They died from the heat, didn't they?"

"Yeah. It was summer. The man who should let them out never came. I saw pictures of him in the articles. He used a different name, his hair is longer and blond, with a beard, but I know him. Simon Emory."

"Simon Emory is the man who let those people die?" Martin's voice was almost gleeful.

"That's what I said."

"Well, well, well," Martin said. "You needed money and knew I'd pay for information about Emory. Does your boyfriend know about this?"

"No. He's very sweet, but not so smart. Only I know. And now you."

Martin was silent for a few moments while Oksana fidgeted in her chair and studied her short pink nails.

"So you're willing to sell out your savior just to leave town," Martin said.

"No one is my savior," Oksana said coldly. "I am on my own since I am ten years old. I see a chance, so I take it."

"A woman after my own heart," Martin said. Jean heard a rustling sound and the screen went blank.

Jean turned off the TV and stared at the screen. She'd seen the container story on TV a couple of years back, footage of police bringing the bodies out. She remembered being horrified by the incident. What a ghastly way to die— trapped in an oven with a hundred other people, waiting to be set free in the promised land.

Jean felt a deep surge of elemental female rage at what men had done to Oksana. Big dumb Spider had won her heart simply by being kind to her. And Simon—Jean had no doubts that he'd killed her. She popped the mini-DVD out and returned it to her bra. Time to call Hallock.

The doorbell and loud banging on the front door startled her. She crept to the door and looked through the peephole. It was Spider, weeping aloud, his face red and wet with tears.

"Spider!" she called. "What's wrong?"

"They found her. Oksana. She's dead!"

"Who found her?"

"The cops. They found her in the bay." He wiped at his nose with the back of a hand.

Jean felt a rush of sympathy and an equally strong rush of curiosity. Besides, Oksana had put to rest any fear or suspicion she might have had of Spider. "You'd better come in." She unlocked the locks and led him to the living room, where he collapsed onto the sofa and put his head in his hands, sobbing.

Jean sat next to him and laid an arm around his heaving shoulders. "Do you want a drink?" He nodded.

She went to the kitchen and poured a slug of Roman's Bourbon into a tumbler, adding a few ice cubes. On the way back she grabbed a box of tissues from the bathroom. She handed him the drink and sat down. He blew his nose loudly and took a gulp of Bourbon, which seemed to help.

"Tell me what happened," Jean said.

Spider let out a shaky breath. "I know this cop from the gym, and I told him she was missing. He called today and said they found a woman in the bay that might be her, but she was all messed up on account of being in the water so long. I asked did she have a spiderweb tattoo on her lower back." Spider started to sob again. "He said she did. It's her."

"I'm so sorry, Spider."

Spider wiped his face and finished his drink. "He said she was strangled. She had broken bones. Her nose and both wrists."

"My God." Jean felt sick to her stomach. "Spider, why did you come here?" Another important question occurred to her. "And how did you find me?"

"When I heard she was dead, I couldn't call Zeppo because he was in the hospital, so I went to your apartment. You weren't there, so my cop friend asked around and found out you were here. I need to find who killed her, but I'm not good at stuff like that. You and Zeppo have to help me." He took some deep, gasping breaths. "I loved her more than anything. Now my life is shit." His face twisted up and he began to cry again.

He was in such agony that Jean decided to offer him some comfort—the certainty that Emory would be punished. "Spider," she said. "Listen to me: I have a DVD that shows Oksana telling Martin Wingo that Emory caused the deaths of some illegals in New York. That's what she sold. When she went to pay Emory off, he must have suspected something. He must have hurt her to make her say where she got the money, and then killed her."

"Emory killed her?"

"I'm sure of it. He must have taken her things from her apartment so you'd think she left town. I'll call the police right now and give them the DVD. They'll arrest him tonight."

"She was so small, and he broke her bones." He stood abruptly.

Jean noted with dread that Spider had the same look on his face that Edward had that night in the ICU. "Spider," she said, getting up and moving between him and the door. "Stay with me. You have to tell the police what you know. Let them take care of it."

Spider pushed her aside and charged out the door. "I'm gonna tear him apart!"

"Spider, no!" Jean watched helplessly as he ran down the stairs and out toward Castro Street. With a sigh she closed the door and locked it, realizing that she'd neglected to lock up when she let Spider in.

She never should have told Spider all this. When would she learn to stop blurting things out? Roman was right—she had really shitty impulse control. As a detective she was still a hopeless amateur.

She had to call the police. As much as Simon deserved whatever Spider would do to him, she didn't want Spider hurt. She hurried down the hall to the phone, but a whiff of something in the air stopped her short—Simon's cologne.

Jean spun around, remembering Roman's advice: Get out of the house. The closest exit was the front door. As she ran for it, Simon stepped out of the dark dining room directly into her path. He held a slim silver automatic.

"Hello, Jean," he said softly. His expression was complicated—equal parts sadness, regret, and rage. His beige eyes were unnerving.

She backed up against the wall, her heart pounding and her breathing shallow. He must have let himself in the unlocked door while she was dealing with Spider. Why had she told Spider the truth? Why hadn't she invited Gwen in for a drink? And where the hell was Roman? "I'm not afraid of you," she said with a lot more conviction than she felt.

He came toward her. "Where is it?"

"Where's what?"

"The DVD. I heard what you said to Spider." Simon, inches from her, grabbed her arm. Jean struggled, but stopped when he shoved the gun barrel under her chin. "Where is it?" he demanded.

Jean concentrated hard on forcing down her rising panic. "It won't do you any good. Too many people know about it now."

"Only you and that moron Spider." Simon pulled her into the living room and pushed her into the straight-backed chair, training the gun on her. "Jean. No more games. Give me the DVD."

"Why should I? You'll kill me either way, just like Oksana. And Martin."

"For the last time, Wingo was already dead when I got back from Vegas," he said angrily. "Someone saved me the trouble."

"What about those people in the container?"

"A sin of omission. I charged one of my trusted employees with opening the container, but he went on a drunk. By the time he sobered up it was too late. He paid for that error with his life." He flipped the automatic's safety off. "That's why I no longer delegate anything important."

"That still leaves Oksana," Jean said. "Not only did you kill her, you hurt her first."

"Oksana was completely feral. After what I did for her, she endangered my entire operation, all the good I'm accomplishing, for money."

"You fucking hypocrite. Why in hell are you doing it if not for money?"

"Atonement," he said, the anger gone from his voice. "I help these illegals to atone for those hundred deaths."

Jean laughed at him. "I get it—you help the ones you don't strangle."

"This is such a shame, Jean. You and I could have had something." He shifted the gun to his left hand and hit her hard across the mouth with the back of his right. Jean nearly fell out of the chair. She tasted blood where her teeth had cut her cheek.

Jean knew he wouldn't kill her until he got the DVD. She had to stall until Roman got home. But stalling was going to mean pain—she couldn't get rid of the image of Oksana with a broken nose and two broken wrists. How much of that could she take? And how could she warn Roman so he didn't get shot coming in?

"Where is the DVD?" he said in a low voice.

"I hid it," she said as calmly as she could. "You'll have to search all these books."

"No. You'll show me, and soon. I doubt your pain threshold is as high as Oksana's." He hit her again, catching her on the cheekbone. "Which book?"

Jean pulled herself back into the chair, breathing deeply, remembering Roman's training: Don't panic, think clearly, look for an opportunity. "I'm too upset," she said. "I can't remember."

Simon put the gun on the end table and gently took her right hand in his. He bent over and kissed it, then twisted it hard until she screamed, the pain sharp and agonizing. She felt something snap.

Jean was as angry as she'd ever been in her life. With her left hand she grabbed his testicles through his loose slacks, twisted, and pulled hard. Simon pushed away from her, roaring with pain and fury, releasing her broken wrist as he folded over to protect his groin. She leaped out of the chair and ran toward the front of the house.

Jean looked back to see him scoop the gun off the end table, giving her precious seconds. Unlocking the front door was out of the question. She raced up the stairs, Simon behind her. He stumbled and groaned in pain with every step. She ran down the hall, expecting to be shot in the back.

Beau's room was dark, but light filtered in from outside. She grabbed the red vase off the dresser and threw it with all her strength as Simon came through the door. The thin glass shattered against his upraised arms, scattering water, tropical flowers, and red shards everywhere, slowing him just long enough for Jean to open the bedside drawer and pull out the Colt with her left hand. She turned to face him, and Simon raised the automatic. Jean emptied the gun into him, all six rounds. The noise was overpowering and the room filled with acrid smoke. He slammed back into the wall and slid to the floor.

CHAPTER 45

"**J**ean!" Roman called from below.

"Up here," she called. The gun felt heavy and ugly in her hand. She dropped it and sank onto the bed, breathing hard, her ears ringing, heart thudding against her ribs, wrist throbbing with pain.

Roman ran up the stairs and down the hall, barely pausing when he saw Simon in a bloody heap against the wall. He stepped over the broken glass and knelt down, taking Jean by the shoulders, anxiously looking her over. "Are you shot?"

"No, just banged up. Check him."

Roman stood and turned on the overhead light. "Who is he?" he asked as he kicked the silver automatic away from Simon's open hand.

"Simon Emory."

"Ah." He felt for a pulse on his neck, pulled his eyelids back. "He's dead."

"Dead," Jean repeated faintly.

Roman sat next to her and put his arm around her. "Where are you hurt?"

"He broke my wrist." She held out her right arm. "It hurts like hell."

Roman ran his fingers gently along her arm, making her flinch. Her wrist was already starting to color and swell. He touched her cheek. "And your face—he hit you. What happened?"

"I fucked up. Spider came here to tell me they found Oksana's body and then left. I forgot to lock the front door, and while we were talking Simon got in."

Roman went to the nearby phone and punched in 911. "A friend of mine has shot an intruder to death," he said after a few moments. "She has a broken wrist." He gave his name and Beau's address.

As her adrenaline receded, Jean felt shaky, exhausted, and dizzy. Roman hung up and looked at her. He sat on the bed again and placed his hand on her back, gently pushing her forward. "Put your head between your knees and take some deep breaths. You're about to faint."

Jean did as he said, and after a few moments felt her head clear. "I'm OK now," she told him. She sat up slowly.

"You're sure?"

"Yes. I've got blood in my brain again." She looked more closely at Roman. His lower lip was cut and swollen on one side. "What's wrong with your lip?" she asked.

"I had words with one of the arresting officers." He stood and leaned down to examine the dead man's wounds. "That's a nice tight pattern. Good shooting. And left-handed, too."

"He was only about three feet from me. I couldn't have missed if I tried."

"But you kept your nerve. I'm proud of you. Come downstairs and talk to me." He helped her up and walked her carefully down the stairs, supporting her as weak knees made her stumble. Jean sat at the kitchen table while he made ice packs for her wrist and face, and poured her a glass of Cognac.

She took a drink, trying to pull herself together and stop trembling. "I saw the DVD. Remember when they found those illegals baked alive in a container in New York? Simon was responsible and Oksana knew about it. She sold the information to Martin, so Simon killed her."

"Where's the DVD now?" Roman asked.

Jean patted her chest. "Right here. And I faxed you a copy of Kay's letter. Better go hide it before the police get here."

Roman dashed to his house and returned in a few moments looking righteously satisfied. "That letter exceeds my wildest dreams," he said. "Thank you. It's not often I can put such a definitive stop to a dangerous homophobe."

Jean explained everything: the drink with Gwen, their discovery in the Martin Wingo Building, Spider's visit, and the fatal encounter with Simon.

"The old grab, twist, and pull," Roman said. "A very effective technique."

"Men are so poorly designed." She tried to smile back, but the right side of her face had stiffened up. "Some bodyguard you are."

"You obviously don't need a bodyguard."

"Oh Roman, I didn't want to kill him."

"He was in your house uninvited, he'd hurt you, and he was chasing you with a gun. Self-defense doesn't get any more clear-cut than that." Roman squeezed her left hand. "You've had quite a day, haven't you?"

"I've never had a worse one. I wish I could talk to Zeppo."

"First stop is the ER. We'll see him after that."

They heard sirens, and soon the police had taken over the house.

∿

HALF AN hour later Jean sat on Roman's oak and leather Stickley sofa, her arm in a sling that a paramedic had given her, and faced Inspector Hallock across the coffee table. She wished she could have more Cognac. Roman was in the kitchen with another homicide inspector.

Hallock pulled out his notebook. "What was Emory doing here?"

Jean had given the inevitable questions a lot of thought as she waited, and had concocted a story that didn't stray far from the truth. "That woman they pulled out of the bay today worked for Emory. She found out he's wanted for murder in New York under a different name. Martin Wingo was pissed at Emory over a business deal and Oksana knew this. She told Martin about it and he recorded it. Emory found out and killed her. He sneaked in here and overheard me saying that I had the DVD."

"How'd you get hold of it?"

"I'm getting to that. Flavia Soares told us Martin had something on his ex-wife. Based on a couple of remarks people made, I figured he might have hidden it in an architectural model at his office, and I had a Wingo-Johansen employee take me there this evening. It was a long shot or I would have called you."

"Sure you would."

"We checked, and there it was. The DVD was in there, too, so I took it. Then I came back here and watched it."

She told him about Spider's visit. "You need to find him, Inspector. He's pretty crazed. He shouldn't be driving around."

"I'll send a car. Where's the DVD now?"

Jean pulled the letter and mini-DVD from her shirt and held them out to Hallock. He put on a pair of latex gloves and took the letter from Jean, raising his eyebrows as he read it. He pulled out two evidence bags and placed the letter and envelope in one and the DVD in the other.

When Jean was done with her tale, Hallock closed his notebook. "That's enough for now," he said. "I'll need to ask you more questions after you've seen a doctor."

Roman came in from the kitchen accompanied by a short, muscular black man in a tan sport coat who'd been introduced earlier as Inspector Belnap. "Roman Villalobos, who's the tenant here, claims the Colt is registered to him," he told Hallock. "Says he lent it to her for protection.

Villalobos was down at the Hall until just before the shooting. The officers who picked him up confirm that. We talked to a neighbor, and she says he was unlocking the front door when the shooting started."

"Thanks, Belnap," Hallock said. "Get Davila over here, will you?"

"Mind if I stay?" Roman asked.

"Suit yourself," Hallock replied. "We're just about finished." He smiled at Jean, and she realized she'd never seen him do that before. "Well, Ms. Applequist, you've saved the taxpayers in two states a lot of money."

"I know you don't think much of Bash Back, but their self-defense course is the reason I'm alive."

Roman leaned against the windowsill, his hairy arms crossed over his chest. "You can be our poster child," he told her.

Davila came into Roman's living room and looked at Jean. "Ms. Applequist, that was a remarkable, courageous thing you did. I'm glad you weren't seriously hurt." He and Roman glared at each other.

"Tell me, Inspector," Roman said to him, "did you suggest to some of your friends that they take me in for questioning this afternoon?"

Davila smirked. "Why would I do that?"

"Why indeed? Just remember this: If things had turned out differently, if Jean had been killed because I wasn't here, you'd be on the slab next to her."

Davila moved toward Roman, who pushed off the windowsill and stood ready. Hallock quickly inserted himself between the two men. He took Davila by the shoulders. "Hey, Oscar," Hallock said. "Go pick up Spider Brandt." Davila didn't like it, but he left.

When he was gone, Hallock turned to Roman. "I'm giving you a break because of her," he said in a harsh whisper, "but don't ever say that kind of shit to him again. You want to get dragged down to the Hall once a week for questioning? Now go ahead—take her down and get that arm seen to. We'll be in touch tomorrow, Ms. Applequist. You'll have to stay out of the house until the crime scene people are through."

"She'll be here with me," Roman said. Hallock went out across the garden.

At S.F. General, the X-rays of Jean's wrist showed a spiral fracture of the radial head. Her face was only bruised. An intern set her wrist, put on a cast that covered her hand and thumb and went up past her elbow, gave her a new sling and some painkillers, and told her to go home.

Instead, she and Roman detoured up to Zeppo's floor. Several hospital staffers they passed on the way looked disapprovingly at Roman. "What's the matter with them?" Jean asked.

Roman put his arm around her shoulder. "They think I beat you up. Little do they know I'd be risking my life if I tangled with you."

At the nurse's station, Roman used his persuasive powers on a young female nurse, who agreed to let them talk to Zeppo when she woke him for his next blood-pressure reading. Jean fell asleep leaning on Roman's shoulder as they waited. Finally the nurse told them Zeppo was awake. The policewoman guarding his door let them go in.

"Jeannie, my God!" he exclaimed, sitting up. "What happened to you?"

Her mouth was too painful and swollen to kiss him. "You should see the other guy."

"The other guy took six thirty-eight caliber slugs in the chest," Roman said.

Zeppo gripped Jean's good hand as she told him all about it.

"I can't believe this," Zeppo said. "You've been hurt and almost cut up and and had to shoot someone to death, and we still don't know who killed Martin. Man, investigating this mess is the dumbest fucking thing I ever did in my life, and that's saying a lot."

"But we got Rivenbark, Setrakian, and Simon Emory, and that letter will really mess Kay up." Her smile came out lopsided. "Anyway, if we hadn't been playing detective you'd never have gotten into my pants, and that would have been a real tragedy."

Zeppo pulled her down and gently touched her unbruised cheek. "That was really smart, figuring out where Martin hid everything," he said. "I should have thought of it myself."

"You didn't know about the x-acto knife. In fact, if I hadn't hung out with Gwen, we never would have found it."

The nurse finally insisted they leave. Back at Roman's, Jean put on a Bash Back T-shirt and spent the night in his big bed with him, comforted by his nearness, dopey with painkillers. She felt perfectly safe for the first time since she'd joined the investigation.

CHAPTER 46

$\mathcal{J}$ean woke alone in Roman's bed. She was simultaneously sickened and elated by what she'd done, and her wrist and face hurt. At least the scrapes and bruises from her fall were nearly healed. She sat up and took a pain pill, amazed to see it was after eleven o'clock. Voices drifted in from Roman's kitchen—Diane and Peter were here.

Jean got up, put on her sling, and faced the bathroom mirror. The entire right side of her face was swollen and multicolored. Her hair was longer on the left—no help there. She sighed and went out to the kitchen.

Diane jumped up from her seat at the kitchen table. "Jean, thank God you're alive," she said

"You look awful," Peter said, going to her side. "Are you in a lot of pain?"

"I'll be OK—I just took a pill." She waved them away and sat down at the table. "Can I have some coffee?" Her bruised mouth made her sound drunk.

"I phoned your office and told them not to expect you anytime soon," Roman said as he put the cup in front of her.

She tried to sip the coffee, which smelled wonderful, but stung her mouth. Roman dropped ice cubes into her cup. "I'll buy you some straws today," he told her. His own lip was still swollen where the cop had hit him.

"You must have been terrified," Diane said.

"Mostly I was angry. Meanwhile, we still don't know who murdered Martin."

"I've decided I can live without knowing," Diane said sadly, taking Jean's good hand. "I've had to accept that just about everything my dear husband told me was a lie. If he was still blackmailing Kay and Emory and still seeing Flavia, who knows what else he was up to? The last thing I want is for someone else to get hurt. So no more investigating, OK?"

"If you say so," Jean said, though she knew Zeppo would keep at it once he was out of the hospital.

Diane's butterscotch leather Hermès bag lay on the table. She pulled it toward her. "I have a gift for you, Jean. It's a token of my appreciation for all you've risked and all you've accomplished." She handed Jean a small box tied with white ribbon—a Tiffany box.

"Why, it's a blue box," Roman said. "How appropriate."

Jean felt better already—jewelry, and probably expensive. If she sold whatever it was, she'd have the money to go to Thailand. Maybe she'd take Zeppo with her.

Peter opened it for her. Inside lay a pair of keys on a plain silver ring. Jean gasped—they were the keys to Martin's Porsche Carrera. For a moment she was lost in a fantasy of high speed, an open road, and herself at the wheel of the bright red car.

She stared at Diane with her mouth open. "Oh, Diane! This is the most perfect gift I've ever gotten. Look, Roman. The keys to the Porsche."

Roman raised an eyebrow. "That's a dangerous gift for a woman who drives like a bat out of hell."

"She's earned it," Diane said. "You can pick it up any time."

"The sad part is, I won't be able to drive it for weeks," Jean said. "Even when the police release his Jag, Zeppo won't be able to drive it, either. I have to call him right away."

"I'd like to do something for him, too," Diane said. "Any suggestions?"

"Not unless you can get him into college. He was admitted to U.C. Davis based on forged high school records, so I doubt they'll let him in now. Let me think about it."

⁘

In the afternoon Roman helped Jean dress and took her to see Zeppo, but both were too tired to visit for long. Back at Roman's she lolled around, sleepy from pain pills, feeling alternately triumphant and sorry for herself, unable to eat much besides the smoothies Roman made for her.

George Hallock knocked on Roman's door around five o'clock. "I've got some news for you," he said. "They've taken down the crime scene tape. Can we sit outside? I need a smoke."

"I'll join you." Roman took a pack of Camels from a kitchen drawer and grabbed an ashtray off the counter.

Jean made a disgusted face as she followed them out to the garden and moved upwind of the smoke. "Can't you do your male bonding over a drink?"

"The inspector is still on duty," Roman said. He shook out a cigarette and lit it. Hallock, holding his Marlboro Lights, looked at Roman's pack. "I haven't had one of those in years," he said wistfully.

Roman offered him one. "Help yourself."

Hallock lit a Camel with a plastic lighter, inhaling deeply. "Ah, that tastes good." He blew out a big cloud of smoke. "So, Ms. Applequist. Simon Emory was definitely the man wanted for the container deaths. Closing that case made a lot of New York cops very happy."

"What about Oksana's murder?" Jean asked.

"I expect we'll close that case, too." Hallock wagged his cigarette at Roman. "I imagine we have you to thank that Kay Wingo's letter has been on the Internet since the middle of last night."

"Just trying to be a good citizen," Roman said.

"Hey, I'm not on your case," Hallock said. "Her aide, Donald Grimes, is a real upright Christian. The letter shook him up. He came straight down to the Hall this morning and admitted he broke into the Wingo house the night of the wedding, and also searched the office and yacht. When Kay Wingo heard her ex was in the bay, she called from Washington and ordered him to find the letter. She told him the security codes and where to find the keys. She denies it, of course. I told her the letter had her fingerprints on it, so she admitted writing it, but claims she didn't know Martin still had it, that he must have approached Grimes about it and he took matters into his own hands."

"*Did* the letter have her fingerprints on it?" Jean asked.

Hallock gave her a sly look. "The technicians are working hard on this one. But thirty years is a long time, forensically speaking."

Jean grinned at him. "Inspector, I'm shocked. And her a former state senator."

"A suspect's a suspect to me," he said with a shrug. "This one's just more slippery than most. But she's in for some rough times even if she dodges that bullet."

"What about the last break-in at the house?"

"I like Emory for that one. We'll see."

"What do you think happened that night after Martin came ashore?" she asked.

"Wingo arranged to meet someone outside the Soares woman's condo, but we don't know who or why. Later they must have fought, and Wingo lost. Once he was unconscious, the killer changed him back into the tuxedo and took him to Aquatic Park."

"Why do that?" Jean said. "It would have been really hard getting an unconscious man into wet clothes."

"Yeah, it would," Hallock said. "We think the perp wanted it to look like Wingo never came ashore."

"But he must have known that Flavia and whoever pulled Martin out of the bay would say different."

"Could have been to destroy evidence. When we find the guy, we'll ask him."

"Who's your main suspect now?" The breeze shifted, and Jean fanned away smoke with her good hand.

Hallock took a deep drag on his cigarette. "Well, we know Wingo had blackmail evidence on his ex-wife, Setrakian, Rivenbark, and Emory, but all of them have alibis. We've been talking to some of the people he did business with, and it looks like those four are just the tip of the iceberg. We're going to dig deeper into his business dealings, interview his employees, track his movements—find out who else he was squeezing."

Jean felt a wave of anxiety. That meant Hallock would start with the person who worked most closely with Martin—Zeppo.

"I'm also determined to find the boat that dropped Wingo at South Beach," Hallock said. "It's like a stone in my shoe." He took a last affectionate drag on his cigarette and ground it out. "I want you to come down to the Hall on Tuesday to answer some more questions on the Setrakian incident. He's telling a wild story about getting punched out by a fat guy named Ivan."

As he stood, he gave Jean one of his rare smiles. "Well, I'll be getting back to the Hall. You take care, Ms. Applequist. I'll keep you posted."

Roman let Hallock out and came back to sit with Jean. "It seems Inspector Hallock is a pretty good cop," he said.

"He'll go after Zeppo now, and Diane, too."

"I predict he'll have the blue box out of her within a week."

"You're right," Jean said. "She'll never be able to stand up to a serious police interrogation. Then they really will charge Zeppo with obstruction and withholding evidence. He might even do time."

"So might you and Diane, and Peter could be disbarred if they can prove he knew about it," Roman said. "In fact, the smartest thing you four could do is go to Hallock immediately and tell him everything."

"I suppose so." Jean yawned. Her wrist hurt again and she felt exhausted. "We'll deal with it tomorrow. Is it time for my pain pill yet?"

Roman stood and held a hand out. "Time for a nap, too. Come inside and I'll fix you up."

In a little while Jean lay in Roman's bed, the curtains drawn. Roman worked in his office at the end of the hall—she could hear the faint clicking of computer keys and low, soothing music, a cello playing Bach. Soon she was in a deep sleep.

Jean was having a lovely erotic dream about Zeppo, both of them uninjured, when she rolled over onto her cast and a stab of pain woke her. She reluctantly opened her eyes. It was dark outside and she could no longer hear music. Back to ugly reality.

Roman was right—they had to level with Hallock. Whatever punishment they were in for would be infinitely worse if they waited until he uncovered their deceptions. As she thought about what lay ahead, she felt a pang of dread for herself, but especially for Zeppo. He'd be the star witness and would have to tell everything he knew about Martin's operation. The whole process would be agonizing for him. Travis Treadway and Felix Ursini would go down, too, and who knew how many other people from the blue box. The police would scrutinize Frank and even Roman. Not to mention her biggest fan, Ivan.

Jean lay for a long time in the dark, rerunning the events of that night through her mind. What had Martin intended to do before coming home? Why would he deliberately meet someone who had a reason to kill him? He must have been confident he could control whoever it was.

She considered another possibility: What if the person Martin called had no reason to kill him until he got to Flavia's?

Jean tried to imagine what Martin could have said or done to set his killer off. She came up with only one scenario that worked, one she'd never taken seriously before. She looked at it this way and that, but could find no contradictions with the facts of the case, and it even explained things that had been bothering her. The more she examined it, the more sense it made.

She finally got out of bed and went in search of Roman, who stood at the kitchen sink trimming artichokes.

"Roman," she said. "I think I know who killed Martin."

CHAPTER 47

$\mathcal{R}$oman helped Jean fasten her seat belt and backed out of his garage. "If you're right, Diane will be crushed," he said.

"She'll also be crushed if we're all prosecuted for obstruction of justice in her husband's murder investigation—it was her idea to cover up everything," Jean said.

Roman drove the short distance to Bernal Heights and pulled into Frank's driveway. The patch of grass and annuals looked dry and neglected. Roman rang the bell, and in a few moments Frank answered, looking even more haggard and careworn than the last time Jean saw him. Now she knew why.

"Jean!" he said, embracing her. "Am I glad you're OK. I heard about what happened. You sure you should be out running around?"

"It looks worse than it feels. Frank, this is my friend Roman."

The two men shook hands. "Diane says you've been a big help," Frank said. "Thanks for that. Come in and have a seat." Trigger made his arthritic way over to them and Roman scratched his head.

They sat in overstuffed chairs near the television, which was tuned to a basketball game. Frank switched it off. "What brings you over here?" he asked.

"We've just spoken to Inspector Hallock," Jean said. "He's on the verge of figuring out about the blue box, and when he does Diane and Zeppo will be in big trouble. We all will. Peter could be disbarred, and some of us may go to prison."

Frank sat back, frowning. "That's terrible news. I don't know how much more of this Diane can take."

"We're worried about her, too, and scared on our own accounts," Jean said. She paused—she didn't want to blow this. "There is one way to spare her. To spare all of us. It's up to you."

"What's that?" Frank asked.

"You have to admit you killed him," she said gently.

He looked away and said nothing. After a moment he stood and went to the glass door, staring out over the city, arms crossed.

"I know how it must have been," Jean said. "He called you that night and told you to meet him at Flavia's. You went because you were used to doing what he said. You've been backing him up for years, and he was going to confront Hugh Rivenbark."

Frank sighed and rubbed his eyes.

Jean pushed ahead. "But when you got there you realized he hadn't changed at all, that he was still sleeping with Flavia and still blackmailing people. You couldn't stand it that Diane was married to a shit like him. Something happened—you confronted him, had an argument—and you hit him. Once he was unconscious, you decided to set Diane free. You changed his clothes because he'd been in your car. He must have had Trigger's hair all over him."

Frank was silent for several seconds. "Diane always told me you were smart," he said without turning around. "I did it for Diane. I thought one sharp pain would be easier on her than years of suffering at Martin's hands."

"Tell us what happened," Roman said in a soft, encouraging voice.

Frank turned from the window and dropped heavily into his chair. "It was pretty much like Jean said. Martin called my cell and I met him at Flavia's. He got in my car and said he wanted me to go with him to Hugh's apartment. The deal was that if Hugh agreed to give him The Eyrie, Martin would say he didn't see who pushed him into the bay and would keep quiet about something else he knew about Hugh. I told him I wanted no part of it, that I'd had enough of his blackmail games. He laughed at me. He said, 'You've been going along for ten years. Have you suddenly grown a backbone?'

"Then I accused him of seeing Flavia behind Diane's back. He said, 'Diane won't know about it unless you tell her. Why shatter her illusions?'"

"He was a wretched man," Jean said, quoting Hannah.

"I must have gone crazy for a moment—I pulled him out of the car and hit him. He was semiconscious. We were still in the parking structure near Flavia's condo. No one else was there. I put him back in the car and drove him to Aquatic Park, where I changed his clothes."

"Why did you take the trouble to put the tuxedo back on him?" Roman asked.

"I couldn't bring myself to throw him in the water naked. He was an evil man, but he was my daughter's husband."

"I'm so sorry to force your hand, Frank," Jean said. "You know how I felt about Martin. But right now we have to protect Diane and Zeppo."

Frank gave a half-hearted smile. "I got what I wanted, didn't I? Diane is free of him, and wealthy. She's found a good man In Peter. I've given her a better life."

"You need to talk to George Hallock," she said.

"I'd have called him soon anyway. My conscience is killing me. I can't eat or sleep and my ulcer's acting up." He stood. "I'll call him now. You still have his card?"

Jean took Hallock's card out of her purse and handed it to him. He walked to a phone on the kitchen counter, lifted the receiver, and dialed.

CHAPTER 48

On a foggy afternoon a week after Jean shot Simon Emory, Roman picked her up in his Prius and headed for San Francisco General to take Zeppo home. Jean had visited him every day and couldn't wait to get him alone. The plan was that he'd stay with her until the cast and sling came off so they could help each other with two-handed tasks like cooking and getting dressed.

Jean's face was healing fast but she'd have the cast on for five more weeks, which meant her Porsche would languish in Roman's garage beside Zeppo's Jag until then. She was back at work, and typing one-handed was driving her crazy. It had taken her an entire day to write up the tasting notes from a vertical of Penfolds Grange, the great Australian red.

With Frank's confession in hand, Hallock had closed the Martin Wingo case. Although Diane was devastated, Frank had spared all of them any further police attention.

The police had also discovered that Armand Setrakian stole a *Wine Digest* office key from the receptionist's purse the day before the fight with Jean. Several more women had accused Armand of assaulting them and he'd been denied bail. According to an Internet auction report Jean had read, the value of his work had tanked.

Kyle did his reluctant hero act as promised, looking daggers at Jean whenever he had to retell the story. She'd already bought him lunch three times as installments on her debt to him. Jean had decided to keep quiet about Treadway's wine scam after receiving a desperate phone call from Travis begging her not to expose him for his daughters' sake. Besides, he'd supplied the weapon she'd used on Hugh, the bottle of Marcassin Chardonnay, which he claimed was the real thing. Jean was working on getting it back from the police. With any luck, storage conditions in the evidence room wouldn't ruin it.

Spider had given her a tearful thank you for dispatching Oksana's killer. Ivan had called several times; he might be a sexist, racist, homophobic brute, but he was growing on her. She'd sent him a case of good wine as thanks.

The police had been unable to build a case against Kay Wingo for ordering Donald Grimes to search the house, office, and boat, but the letter did its work anyway—she'd been forced to withdraw from her various political affiliations. Jean had followed Hugh Rivenbark's activities closely—he'd been granted bail and was back at The Eyrie in the company of a male nurse-bodyguard, awaiting trial. She hoped he still had a headache.

Zeppo, in jeans and a Celtics T-shirt, waited on a bench in front of the hospital. He hurried to the car as they pulled up, opened the door, and helped Jean out, giving her a one-armed hug and a deep kiss, knocking their slings together. His bony frame felt so good against her that she didn't want to let go, but Roman had the car doors open and Zeppo's suitcase stowed, so they reluctantly ended their embrace.

Roman and Zeppo embraced as well. "We're buying you lunch," Roman said. "What have you been craving?"

"Besides Jean, you mean?" Zeppo said, grinning at her. "You know what I'd really like? A *carne asada* burrito from La Cumbre."

"Done," Roman said. They drove through the Mission to the taqueria, where they ordered three burritos, rice, and beans to go. Soon they were seated around Jean's kitchen table. Eating the overstuffed burritos was challenging with one hand, and Jean ended up with guacamole on her shelf, but it was deliciously worth it.

When they were done eating, Roman cleared the table and Jean produced a lumpy white envelope. "I've got a welcome home present for you, Zeppo," she said, handing him the envelope. "Here's a little something from Diane."

He pulled out a familiar platinum watch with a new black leather band. "Wow," he said. "Martin's watch. She doesn't want it?"

"Not anymore, and she knows how much he meant to you. Hey, keep going. The best gift is still in there."

Zeppo took out a one-page letter, read it, and whooped loudly. "It says I'm admitted to U.C. Davis. Awesome. How'd she do that, Jeannie?"

"She's been thinking about endowing a chair at the Haas Business School at Cal in Martin's name, so she finally did it, gave them $2 million. Only she made a condition: They have to let you into Davis."

"I'm amazed," Roman said. "It's almost Martinesque—if he'd been a philanthropist."

"Diane learned a few things from him," Jean said.

"I bet it was your idea, Jeannie. Thanks so much. This is really great."

Roman stood. "That's my cue to depart," he said. "I'm sure the two of you would like to get reacquainted in the Biblical sense." He hugged them both and left.

Zeppo turned to Jean. "I thought he'd never leave," he said. He gently pulled her close and gave her a long, slow kiss. They undressed awkwardly, helping each other, struggling with buttons and slings, and got into bed.

Jean ran her hand over him. "You're even skinnier than before. It's a good thing I'm padded."

"You've lost weight, too," he said as he touched her. "God, I've missed this."

"So have I."

They were careful at first, trying not to jostle their arms, but soon they'd forgotten their injuries. After some trial and error, Zeppo lay back on the bed and Jean straddled him. They both came quickly, and Jean collapsed on the bed next to him as he pulled her close with his right arm.

"Whew," she breathed. "I think we just set a new record for the fastest fuck."

"The first time was quicker," he said, nuzzling her short hair. "I almost came when you touched me."

"You always were easy."

"Not you. You were very hard to get, for a tramp."

"Watch your mouth, you weasel." Jean lay happily in the crook of his arm, thinking about the prospect of having him in her apartment for the next few weeks. She'd lived with lovers a few times before, but never for very long; men tended to assume that cohabitation meant monogamy. Usually the prospect of having someone around 24/7 made her apprehensive, but she thought the arrangement with Zeppo might just work out. It was only for a few weeks, and anyway, she couldn't see starting something new with her arm in a full cast.

◦✍◦

In the evening Jean and Zeppo curled up on the red sofa and ate leftover rice and beans while they watched a movie on television—*Out of the Past*, a favorite of Jean's.

After a commercial there was a news break, and Zeppo turned up the sound when they saw Hugh Rivenbark's photo.

"This morning, Rivenbark's nurse discovered his body at the bottom of a cliff behind his Mendocino County home, the same cliff where his wife fell to her death thirty years ago," the announcer said. "A spokesman for the sheriff's office said there is no evidence of foul play and that investigators have not ruled out suicide. More at eleven." Zeppo turned off the sound and they looked at each other, eyes wide open.

"It was Edward," she said. "Had to be."

"It's just as likely that he jumped. Think about what was going to happen to him—disgrace, a trial, prison. His life was pretty much over."

"I hope that's what the sheriff decides. I'd hate to see Edward suffer any more whether he killed Hugh or not." She took Zeppo's hand. "It really is over now, and we're the last ones standing. It's hard to believe that a couple of nobodies like us could make so much trouble."

"Hey, who's a nobody?" Zeppo said indignantly. "I just have to say the word and I can be on any daytime talk show in the country."

"Now that's something to aspire to."

"Shacking up is making you nervous, isn't it?" he said.

"Just a little."

"Look at it this way: The place will be a lot cleaner with me here. Plus you now have your own personal one-armed sex slave."

They settled in to watch the end of the movie, and Jean felt the familiar warm, rosy anticipation for the night ahead. Maybe, just maybe, she could stand this.